THE POLITICS OF MAGIC

SERIES IN FAIRY-TALE STUDIES

A complete listing of the books in this series can be found online at wsupress.wayne.edu

THE POLITICS OF MAGIC

DEFA FAIRY-TALE FILMS

QINNA SHEN

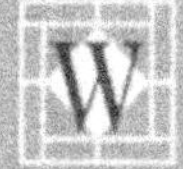

Wayne State University Press
Detroit

19 18 17 16 15 5 4 3 2 1

ISBN 978-0-8143-3903-9 (paperback)
ISBN 978-0-8143-3904-6 (e-book)

Library of Congress Control Number: 2014953446

Published with the assistance of a fund established by Thelma Gray James
of Wayne State University for the publication of folklore and English studies.

Designed and typeset by Bryce Schimanski
Composed in Chaparral Pro

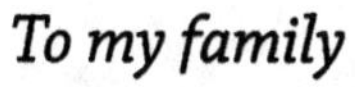

To my family

CONTENTS

ILLUSTRATIONS

ACKNOWLEDGMENTS

Many people and institutions have assisted me in writing this book. The task of acknowledging them should be easy. Yet I am feeling a lack of originality in finding language that can sufficiently express my sincere gratitude to all of them. This book did not develop from my doctoral thesis but is related to it. Therefore, I would like to thank my wonderful thesis advisor, Katie Trumpener, for the guidance she gave me throughout the years. My dissertation on reconfiguring the witch in East German women's writing begins with a survey of the witch image in German literature and culture. The Grimms' fairy-tale collection provides stereotypical depictions of the witch that are then countered in feminist writings as well as in East German literary revisions of the witch. That work combined with my interest in East German cinema led me to discover the wonderful collection of DEFA *Märchenfilme*. The editors at Wayne State University Press, especially Donald Haase and Annie Martin, have been most wonderful in their continuous support.

It is safe to say that I would not have completed this book without the opportunity to teach fairy-tale courses at Miami University in Ohio, where I worked from 2008 to 2011 and am now working again. That teaching experience and the inspiring discussions with students allowed me to become very well acquainted with the original print tales and to see the changes DEFA had made. Thus, I want to thank the Department of German, Russian, Asian, and Middle Eastern Languages and Cultures at Miami University for the wonderful courses I was given to teach. Margaret Ziolkowski, the department chair, graciously arranged my teaching in such a way that I was able to conduct archival research in Germany in spring 2011. A short-term research grant from the German Academic Exchange Service (DAAD) enabled me to travel to Berlin and Potsdam to collect material as well as watch fairy-tale films that were not yet commercially available. The project has further received generous funding from the DEFA-Foundation in Berlin and the Center for the Humanities at Loyola University Maryland, where I worked between 2011 and 2014.

Several archives in Germany allowed me to watch films onsite and supplied important materials about them: Bundesarchiv-Filmarchiv in Berlin, Deutsches Rundfunkarchiv in Potsdam-Babelsberg, Pressedokumentation at Die Hochschule für Film und Fernsehen (HFF) "Konrad Wolf" in Potsdam-Babelsberg, and Filmmuseum Potsdam. The staff at the DEFA-Stiftung, Manja Meister, Sabine Söhner, Konstanze Schiller, and Laurence Wegener, as well as Susanne Reiser at HFF, Jörg-Uwe Fischer at the Deutsches Rundfunkarchiv, and Heidrun Schmutzer at Filmmuseum Potsdam helped me enormously. I want to thank the DEFA-Stiftung in Berlin and Filmmuseum Potsdam for providing images and giving me permission to use them.

The project has also benefited from the advice of researchers and former DEFA employees in Germany—Beate Hanspach, Willi Höfig, Christa Kozik, and Dieter Wolf—and from pleasant conversations with colleagues at Loyola, Miami, and elsewhere, especially Benita Blessing, Benjamin Sutcliffe, and Nicole Thesz. Mentors and colleagues read my chapters and gave me great suggestions for revisions: Seán Allan, Mila Ganeva, Thomas Maulucci, Katie Trumpener, Valerie Weinstein, and Jack Zipes. Evan Torner proofread the entire manuscript and generously shared his own expertise on DEFA films. The two external peer reviewers that the publisher secured were most insightful with their comments and suggestions. My co-editor Martin Rosenstock also graciously read my work with a red pen. The editorial, design, and production team at Wayne State University Press helped significantly to bring the book to print.

The library staff at Miami and Loyola, especially Nicholas Triggs, supplied me with countless books, articles, and films through the interlibrary loan system, which makes American universities truly the best place to do research. Manfred Flügge and Mila Ganeva took time out of their schedules to retrieve materials for me in Berlin. Daniel Meyers at Miami is one of the best language lab directors one can find. The wonderful faculty technology center lab manager at Loyola, Marion Wielgosz, helped me with technical aspects of the book manuscript and saw the project through to its conclusion. Working on DEFA films introduced me to the wonderful network of DEFA enthusiasts associated with the DEFA Film Library at the University of Massachusetts Amherst. I would like to thank Barton Byg and Skyler Arndt-Briggs for all the work they do to promote scholarship on and interest in DEFA films. Last but not least, I want to thank my family and friends for their love, friendship, and patience that has sustained me through this and many other projects. My two children, Charles and Cindy, had to get used to their mom sneaking away on weekends to work.

Related essays have been published in *Focus on German Studies* (2008), *The Brecht Yearbook* (2010), *Marvels & Tales: Journal of Fairy-Tale Studies* (2011), and *Directory of World Cinema—Germany* (2012). I take full responsibility for errors that might have crept into this book and welcome constructive criticism and further conversations about these films that I have so come to cherish.

INTRODUCTION

Tales of the Time: An Overview of DEFA Fairy-Tale Films

The Importance of DEFA Fairy-Tale Films

"Winter is a time for fairy tales" (Winterzeit ist Märchenzeit).[1] Fairy-tale adaptations by former East Germany's state-sponsored film company, DEFA (Deutsche Film-Aktiengesellschaft), were often prepared as Christmas presents for the country's old and young.[2] Even after the German Democratic Republic (GDR) became a state that existed only "once upon a time" after Germany reunified in 1990, fairy-tale films continued to be shown frequently on German television, especially at Christmastime. When NDR (Norddeutscher Rundfunk) aired the DEFA-made television film *Rapunzel oder der Zauber der Tränen* (Rapunzel or the Magic of Tears, Ursula Schmenger, 1988)[3] on the first day of Christmas in 1990, a reviewer wrote, "Ideologically entrenched GDR film productions are vanishing into the archives now. The fairy-tale films, which belong to the best in the world, constitute an exception."[4] The reviewer foregrounded the world-class quality of these films as well as their presumed immunity to GDR ideology and consequent longevity. Such a eulogy to DEFA fairy-tale films differed from the accusation made by some West German critics that the GDR cultivated children's films only as "a vehicle for transmitting ideology."[5] The truth, however, may lie somewhere in between. DEFA fairy-tale films were not entirely resistant to the ideology and politics that pervaded the structures of GDR cultural production. Yet the films, especially of the 1970s and 1980s, actively employed slave language (*Sklavensprache*, coded criticism that would otherwise be censored, see chapter 4) to criticize the regime and society in ways that contemporary films could not do with impunity.

This book ventures a cultural history of DEFA's fairy-tale films from the immediate postwar period to reunification. Between Paul Verhoeven's *Das kalte Herz* (The Cold Heart) in 1950 and Konrad Petzold's *Geschichte von der Gänseprinzessin und ihrem treuen Pferd Falada* (The Story of the Goose Princess and Her Loyal Horse Falada) in 1989, DEFA produced over forty feature-length, live-action fairy-tale films based on nineteenth-century folk and literary tales, for example, by Wilhelm Hauff, the Brothers Grimm, Hans Christian Andersen, Ludwig Bechstein, Bettina and Gisela von Arnim, E. T. A. Hoffmann, and Theodor Storm, and on folklore from other (socialist) countries (see Appendix).[6] The fairy-tale films played an important role in the GDR's claim to the realist–humanist tradition and allowed the country to promote the values of a socialist state. Half of the adaptations were based on the tales of the Brothers Grimm, because not only did the Grimms' collection occupy a significant position in the GDR, but they also enabled DEFA to respond to the National Socialist, West German, and Disney fairy-tale adaptations, which all drew heavily on the Grimms.

The more than forty classic fairy-tale films (*Märchenfilme*) include films commissioned by the GDR television (Fernsehen der DDR). These films, however, do not include feature films based on modern literary tales (*Filmmärchen*) set in the contemporary world that interweave reality with fantastic elements, such as *Susanne und der Zauberring* (Susanne and the Magic Ring, Erwin Stranka, 1973), *Philipp, der Kleine* (Philipp the Small, Herrmann Zschoche, 1975), and *Ein Schneemann für Afrika* (A Snowman for Africa, Rolf Losansky, 1977). Nor do they include the animation, puppet, and silhouette films made by DEFA's animation studio, which was established in Dresden in 1955. In contrast to the public and private interest devoted to fairy tales in general, this large body of DEFA fairy-tale films has so far received disproportionally little critical attention, leading Joachim Giera, once a DEFA dramaturge, to plead that scholars should "finally study DEFA fairy-tale films, especially in light of the current heated debate about the cartoon series *Simsala Grimm*" and "revive an interrupted tradition that is worth continuing."[7] This book responds to that appeal by focusing on DEFA adaptations of traditional folk and literary tales.[8]

DEFA fairy-tale films claimed the largest viewership in the GDR until DEFA Westerns (*Indianerfilm*) surpassed them in the late 1960s.[9] The fairy-tale films also paved the way for the studio's other films to enter the global market. It is thus surprising that a scholarly monograph has yet to treat this corpus. Based on the number of viewers, *Die Geschichte vom kleinen Muck* (The Story of Little Mook, Wolfgang Staudte, 1953) was the most successful DEFA film.[10] Yet it has not made its way into the German cinema canon.[11] The absence of canonical fairy-tale films, even commercially successful ones, indicates a broader dilemma surrounding these films. Because they were generally considered to be for the entertainment and education of children, they are regarded as intellectually and aesthetically uninteresting for serious scholarship. In addition, although the films were popular successes, they evince a suspicious didacticism and present an ideal version of reality and a happy ending that conflict with historical reality. This may also partly explain why a comprehensive book on DEFA fairy-tale films has not been written until this one. Because people assume these films are not intellectually robust and the plotlines are too tedious to remember, a seemingly "easy" genre ironically becomes either unworthy or too daunting to tackle.

This book is the first comprehensive, critical, book-length treatment of DEFA fairy-tale films; it closes a gap in DEFA studies as well as in scholarship on fairy-tale film adaptations. The book interprets the films on thematic and formal levels, examining their embedded agendas in relation to GDR cultural politics. It compares the films with earlier print versions of the tales and analyzes the revisions that DEFA made in the film versions. The volume also distinguishes DEFA fairy-tale films from National Socialist, West German, and American/Disney adaptations of the same tales. DEFA fairy-tale film production was closely tied to DEFA's other productions, using the same personnel and resources. This study points out thematic and aesthetic features in the fairy-tale films that are similar to those in DEFA's contemporary features, thus incorporating the films into the larger discourse of the state's founding narrative as well as the history of DEFA cinema. It also reveals difficulties some of these films ran into with censorship. The archival documents and published reviews help reconstitute the cultural and historical context in which these films were produced and received. Such a project intersects with the studies of literature, folklore, film, media, culture, politics, and history. It is significant for not only folklore studies but also German, Eastern European, cultural, film, media, and gender studies.

The book's title, *The Politics of Magic*, is not intended to suggest that DEFA fairy-tale films were merely mouthpieces of official ideology and propaganda. On the contrary, these films run the gamut from politically dogmatic to implicitly subversive, from kitschy to experimental. Their fairy-tale cloak permitted them to convey ideology in a subtle, indirect manner, which makes the films appear to be primarily in the service of humanist education and the socialization of the young. They are not easily identifiable as products of a socialist culture. This ambiguity allowed viewers to forget Cold War politics for a while and to delve into a world of magic where politics took on an allegorical form. The fact that DEFA fairy-tale films developed an international audience starting with the production of *The Cold Heart* and *Little Mook* attests not only to these fairy-tale films' universal appeal but, more importantly, to the surprising marketability of this branch of GDR cinema and its impact beyond the GDR's own narrow temporal and geographic boundaries.

DEFA fairy-tale films helped establish the studio's domestic and international reputation and also grossed much needed hard currency for the GDR. About one-fifth of the most watched DEFA films in the GDR were the fairy-tale films. At the top of the chart was *Little Mook*, with thirteen million viewers.[12] They were also exported to numerous countries outside the Eastern bloc, including Western Europe, North America, and Asia.[13] A number of films could boast of worldwide popularity, such as *Little Mook*, *Das singende, klingende Bäumchen* (The Singing Ringing Tree, Francesco Stefani, 1957), *Das Feuerzeug* (The Tinderbox, Siegfried Hartmann, 1959), *Schneewittchen* (Snow White, Gottfried Kolditz, 1961), *Die goldene Gans*

(The Golden Goose, Siegfried Hartmann, 1964), and *Drei Haselnüsse für Aschenbrödel* (Three Hazelnuts for Cinderella, Václav Vorlíček, 1974). Some won prestigious awards at international film festivals.

With few exceptions, the West German government did not pay much attention to DEFA (children's) films until the late 1970s. This deliberate negligence in the Cold War era led Thomas Schmidt, who played Little Mook in the most successful DEFA fairy-tale film, to state erroneously, "DEFA films were not allowed to be screened in the Federal Republic of Germany. Not until the end of the eighties did my stepfather [Peter Podehl] manage to bring this wonderful film to West German television."[14] In fact, *Little Mook* was distributed in West Germany in 1955, albeit with few copies, in contravention of the general ban in West Germany of DEFA films in the early 1950s notwithstanding.[15] In addition to *Little Mook, The Cold Heart, Der Teufel vom Mühlenberg* (The Devil of Mill Mountain, Herbert Ballmann, 1955), *The Singing Ringing Tree*, and *The Tinderbox* were shown in the Federal Republic of Germany (FRG) before the Berlin Wall went up.[16] The fairy-tale pedigree allowed them to penetrate the Iron Curtain, which still permitted the circulation of well-made adaptations drawn from the shared cultural past. With these few exceptions, however, DEFA (fairy-tale) films were indeed largely absent from West German screens before the late 1970s.

This slowly began to change after Willy Brandt's New Eastern Policy (*neue Ostpolitik*) and the "normalization" of the relationship between the two German states in 1972. Studying the distribution of DEFA children's films in West Germany between 1979 and 1990, Klaus-Dieter Felsmann and Bernd Sahling emphasize the increasing prestige DEFA children's films enjoyed in West Germany and their welcome presence at local cinemas, film festivals, and children's and youth's film weeks.[17] A significant number of the exported films were fairy tales, including *The Cold Heart* (1950), *Little Mook* (1953), *Wie heiratet man einen König: Ein Märchen von Klugheit und Liebe* (How to Marry a King: A Tale of Cleverness and Love, Rainer Simon, 1969), *Wer reißt denn gleich vor'm Teufel aus* (The Devil's Three Golden Hairs, Egon Schlegel, 1977), *Der Meisterdieb* (The Master Thief, Wolfgang Hübner, 1978), *Schneeweißchen und Rosenrot* (Snow White and Rose Red, Siegfried Hartmann, 1979), *Der Prinz hinter den sieben Meeren* (The Prince behind the Seven Seas, Walter Beck, 1982), *Gritta vom Rattenschloß* (Gritta of Rat Castle,

Jürgen Brauer, 1985), *Die Geschichte vom goldenen Taler* (The Story of the Golden Coin, Bodo Fürneisen, 1985), and *Der Bärenhäuter* (Bearskin, Walter Beck, 1986). Among them, *Little Mook* and *Gritta of Rat Castle* consistently made the "hit list" of BAG-Filme in the late 1980s.[18] Increased exposure to DEFA children's films also helped West German viewers and critics form a more objective and differentiated view of films from the other side.[19]

At the 1982 Berlinale, the West German filmmaker Haro Senft argued that the international recognition that many DEFA children's films received was because of the generous budget that the GDR government allotted to these films, and he deplored the lack of funding for films in the FRG: "Every year four children's films can be made there with a budget of up to 2.5 million East German marks for each of them. That means a total of 10 million East German marks are made available. This sum alone exceeds the entire cultural funding that our Interior Ministry gives to West German filmmaking, let alone better modes of distribution and screening."[20] Likewise, a West German reviewer of DEFA's *The Prince behind the Seven Seas* (1982) urged his own country's culture industry to emulate its East German counterpart: "If such a fairy-tale film receives frenetic applause—and it does not have a reactionary message or an orgy of violence—then allow me to ask this question: why not make more fairy-tale films in this country?"[21] This petition for the fragmented West German film industry to follow DEFA's commitment to fairy-tale films was made in the early 1980s, at a time when the FRG finally opened up more to DEFA films. The belated reception of the fairy-tale films due to West Germany's earlier, deliberate boycott of most DEFA films indicated a missed opportunity for the eventually victorious West Germans to appreciate how their East German neighbors dealt with their shared cultural heritage. Because West Germany neglected fairy-tale films, the DEFA fairy-tale films became the only lasting body of *German* fairy-tale films shot in the twentieth century.

Controversies and Rehabilitation of Fairy Tales

Although fairy-tale films helped establish DEFA's international reputation, they were preceded by intense debates over the suitability of fairy tales for socialism. These debates extended back to the early Soviet era, when folk and fairy tales were censured as reiterating aristocratic and bourgeois values. In "The Political Uses and Themes of Folklore in the Soviet Union," Felix J. Oinas explains the reasons for the initial condemnation of folklore:

> The belief that folklore reflected the ideology of the ruling classes gave rise to a strongly negative attitude toward it in literary circles in the 1920s. The so-called Proletcul't (Proletarian Cultural and Educational Organizations) declared that folklore was hostile to Soviet people, because it reflected the *kulak* ("rich farmers'") ideology. Numerous Proletcul't leaders called for the annihilation of folklore. A special Children's Proletcul't sought to eradicate folktales on the basis that they glorified tsars and tsareviches, corrupted and instigated sickly fantasies in children, developed the kulak attitude, and strengthened bourgeois ideals.[22]

However, the popularity and folksiness of fairy tales in the end trumped their bourgeois editorial imprint and redeemed them to socialist advantage.

At the First All-Union Congress of Soviet Writers in August 1934, Maxim Gorky gave a keynote speech that defended fairy tales' proletarian origin. He stressed "the close connection of folklore with the concrete life and working conditions of the people," "the life optimism of folklore," and "the high artistic value of folklore."[23] At the same congress, Andrei Zhdanov, the secretary of the Central Committee, declared the doctrine of socialist realism to be the guideline for artistic productions in the USSR, with which writers as "engineers of human souls" should ideologically educate and transform the masses. This aesthetic mandate of socialist realism consequently served as an instrument to further the goal of centralization and bureaucratization of cultural life in the Stalinist period.[24] Hence, Gorky's vindication of fairy tales and the institutionalization of socialist realism occurred around the same time. After this, folk and fairy tales were restored to socialist culture and art. Together with the rehabilitation of fairy tales and mythology, Gorky promoted revolutionary romanticism as a significant component of socialist realism.[25] As Oinas points out, fairy tales have been "used consciously for propagating the cultural construction and political education of the masses for one goal—the realization of socialism and communism."[26] Politicizing fairy tales was the only way they could be reintegrated into socialist cultural production.

Gorky's endorsement of folklore asserted the compatibility of fairy tales and socialist realism. One of the central categories of socialist–realist aesthetics was *narodnost'*, which can mean, among other things, "accessibility and comprehensibility, simplicity, antielitism."[27] Art that was "foreign to the people" and "of labored perception" was rejected, and the objective of this political–aesthetic doctrine was to remove "the borders between high and low culture and the classics and folklore."[28] Hans Günther writes that, in contrast to nineteenth-century realism, "now images were primarily sought in the preliterate tradition—myth, folklore, heroic epics, and the like. Paradoxically, a society with an officially declared orientation toward the future, in which the art of the avant-garde left indelible marks and that widely used modern means of communication in propaganda, directs its gaze toward the remote past, the result of which was a quaint folklorization of modernity."[29] This paradox can be explained by an indisputable affinity between folktales and Marxist philosophy. The heroism and optimism inherent in folktales parallel the Marxist projection of historical progress and radical change.

In the postwar years, fairy tales became a contentious issue because of the most recent Nazi crimes against humanity. The printing and circulation of the Grimms' tales were restricted or banned outright in the Allied occupation zones. As early as September 1946, Berlin's school boards received a memorandum titled "German Fairy Tales as Cause for the Degeneration of German Youth" from the British military government, which insisted on a significant reduction of fairy tales, myths, and legends in teaching curricula. In 1947, British Major T. J. Leonard justified the decision by calling German fairy tales "first steps in cruelty" that would dispose the youths' unconscious minds toward cruelty and perversity.[30] The tendency toward violence in the Grimms' tales led critics to infer that the German *Volk* was capable of committing the atrocious acts that had occurred in concentration camps such as Belsen and Auschwitz.[31] The famous German tale "Hansel and Gretel" was seen as having anticipated the crematoria of Auschwitz,[32] and "Snow White" allegedly foreshadowed the torture chambers of the extermination camps.[33] Yet the ban was lifted not too long after, apparently invalidating prior accusations against the Grimms' tales regarding their association with Nazi brutality.

In the Soviet Occupation Zone, the matter looked quite different. As early as 1945, a small selection of seven of the most famous tales had been published in their original text in the Altberliner Verlag Lucie Groszer, and "Hansel and Gretel," remarkably, made the short list.[34] The East German émigrés returning from the Soviet Union appreciated fairy tales even more because the debate over fairy tales had been settled for the most part in the 1940s in the Soviet Union, permitting tales from the Grimms' collection to appear there in large numbers after the war.[35] Nonetheless this did not prevent a similar debate over the value of fairy tales from continuing into the 1950s in East Germany.[36] Richter-de Vroe, an East German dramaturge, attributes the initial resistance to fairy tales to the GDR's official aesthetic of socialist realism and the violence contained in the tales: "A narrow understanding of realism made fairy tales appear idealistic, illusorily romantic, and mystic. Bloody, gruesome details seemed to lead to disastrous, negative thoughts and behaviors; to fight and overcome potential impact as such belonged to the main ideological tasks of the time period after the liberation from fascism."[37] At the time, fairy tales were obviously seen as at odds with, if not in opposition to, the pressing issues of denazification and democracy. Early DEFA children's films such as *Irgendwo in Berlin* (Somewhere in Berlin, Gerhard Lamprecht, 1946) and *Die Kuckucks* (The Cuckoos, Hans Deppe, 1949) focused on contemporary issues in answering the call from above to make socially relevant films that addressed the postwar present.

However, contemporary significance was soon discovered for fairy tales as well. In addition to the Soviet rehabilitation of fairy tales, the Socialist Unity Party of Germany (SED) recognized the importance of folk and fairy tales for the GDR's claim to the German cultural heritage (*Erbeaneignung*). Since its founding, the GDR saw the need to legitimize its regime in competition with West Germany. The fairy-tale tradition became instrumental for the GDR to reconnect with the German classical–humanist heritage. As proposed by Georg Lukács, the famous Hungarian Marxist philosopher and literary critic, the GDR's selective reception of the German literary heritage favored the Enlightenment and classical, revolutionary, and realist traditions but rejected Romanticism, Biedermeier ideas, naturalism, the avant-garde, and modernism.[38] The classical–humanist heritage was more palatable to East Germans than Marxism–Leninism in the early postwar years. The general secretary of the SED Central Committee, Walter Ulbricht, was quoted as saying, "Do not begin with Marx and Engels. They will not understand that."[39] Instead, the SED began with Goethe and initiated a cult of Classicism.[40] However, it is to be noted that fairy-tale writers and collectors such as Wilhelm Hauff and the Grimm brothers belonged to the period of Romanticism. Patricia Herminghouse explains this contradiction between the GDR's rejection of Romanticism and acceptance of certain Romantics as follows:

> Admittedly, there were a few timid admissions of single writers, such as E. T. A. Hoffmann, Eichendorff, and Hölderlin, who were often legitimized by emphasizing their affinities to Classicism or Realism, thus as exceptions to the decadence and formalism which were considered characteristic of the period as a whole. Likewise, Achim von Arnim and Clemens Brentano, as well as the Grimm brothers, were praised for the social quality (*Volksverbundenheit*) of their various anthologies of folk literature.[41]

It was the perceived connection to the people that made the folk and fairy tales acceptable to the cultural functionaries.

The affinity between traditional folktales and the GDR ideology rendered folk and fairy tales applicable centuries later. Originating in the peasant and working-class milieus, many tales represent utopian wishes to obtain wealth, power, and love. David Bathrick observes, "Contrary to previous assessments, the fairy tales were now seen as important documents of class struggle, 'a fantastic revolution of the suffering people against the suppression of their feudal masters and bourgeois property relations.'"[42] Despite its bourgeois, Protestant revisions, the Grimm folktale collection's purported solidarity with the common people transformed it into sacred cultural heritage. Yet the GDR also edited the Grimms' folktales to comply with its historically specific cultural politics of socialist humanism. An early selection of Grimm tales edited by Walther Pollatschek and Hans Siebert and published by the Kinderbuch Verlag in Berlin in 1952 was a sanitized version with "a number of revisions and deletions to make the stories conform to prevailing socialist sensibilities."[43] This edition was criticized as "narrow-minded" and as reflecting the then unsatisfactory state of Marxist–Leninist fairy-tale studies.[44] Anneliese Kocialek's editions were more widely accepted for her cautious editing "without grossly tendentious distortion of the texts."[45] Three strictly held taboos in her selections and revisions were violence, anti-Semitism, and the Christian religion. Tales such as "The Jew in the Thornbush" (*Kinder- und Hausmärchen* [KHM] 110), "Mother Trudy" (KHM 43), and "The Juniper Tree" (KHM 47) were not included in Kocialek's selections.[46] A complete edition of KHM did not appear in the GDR until the 1989 volume published by the Aufbau Verlag.[47]

Similar to the print versions, DEFA film adaptations maintained these taboos. An obvious change that DEFA made to original print tales was to stave off violent imagery and unforgiving retaliation, partly due to lessons learned from the official critique of its first fairy-tale adventure, *The Cold Heart*. Subsequently, DEFA removed elements of bloodthirsty revenge on and extreme punishment of the villain that were typical of nineteenth-century tales. Any residual violent episodes such as those in Götz Friedrich's *Rotkäppchen* (Little Red Riding Hood, 1962) and Wolfgang Hübner's *Jorinda und Joringel* (Jorinda and Joringel, 1986) were pointed out and criticized. The films also abided by the GDR's atheist state philosophy. Christian references in the original versions were glossed over, for example, in *The Cold Heart* and *Bearskin*. The presence of religion as the opiate of the masses (to paraphrase Karl Marx) was implied in such films as *Die Geschichte vom armen Hassen* (The Story of Poor Hassan, Gerhard Klein, 1958), *Das hölzerne Kälbchen* (The Wooden Calf, Bernhard Thieme, 1959/1961),[48] and *The Master Thief*. Ironically, *The Wooden Calf* had a hard time receiving official approval for public release because of the negative image of the priest. For realpolitik reasons, the officials tried to avoid provoking the church establishment around 1960 (see chapter 2). *The Golden Goose* (1964) strategically spared religious figures from mockery (see chapter 2). But in 1978, it was a nonissue for *The Master Thief* to maintain the original plot of stealing the parson from the church.

Magic and Socialist Realism: Establishing a Fairy-Tale Tradition at DEFA

Making films based on these supposedly uncontroversial classic fairy tales did not come without controversy, however. The questions arose of whether DEFA should adapt fairy tales into films and, if yes, how and in what format. The fact that Nazi Germany had made twenty or so live-action fairy-tale adaptations between 1933 and 1945 did not make DEFA's decision any easier. It was more due to Soviet influence and the films' welcome distinction from Disney's renowned but reactionary animations that the live-action format finally won the approval of the administrators. The emphatic statement by the famed Soviet director of live-action fairy-tale films Alexander Rou that "film and fairy tale are made for each other" attests to the unique capacity of film to turn verbal magic into virtual reality.[49] With the technical possibilities of the moving image, magic can become reality before the viewers' eyes.[50] In the 1930s and 1940s, Rou succeeded with live-action fairy-tale feature films such as *Po shchuchemu veleniyu* (Der Zauberfisch/Wish upon a Pike, 1938) and *Vasilisa prekrasnaya* (Die schöne Wassilissa/Vasilisa the Beautiful, 1939). Eugene Schwartz,[51] the Soviet playwright of many literary tales, served as another role model for DEFA fairy-tale filmmakers.[52] Another Russian live-action fairy-tale film director, Alexander Ptushko, directed *Kamenny zwetok* (Die steinerne Blume/The Stone Flower, 1946), which premiered two years later in the Soviet Occupation Zone with far-reaching impact (see chapter 1).

In 1955, Werner Hortzschansky too, as director of the German Central Institute for Teaching Materials (*Deutsches Zentralinstitut für Lehrmittel*), wrote of the advantages of fairy-tale film adaptations.[53] He praised the achievements of Soviet filmmakers in fairy-tale films such as *The Stone Flower*, which proved that film not only was a suitable medium for appropriating fairy tales but could also provide models for DEFA. However, Hortzschansky self-contradictorily endorsed only puppet and animation adaptations, arguing that live-action films destroy fairy-tale illusion.[54] This was in spite of the fact that the Soviet models he had just complimented were shot with real actors (*Realfilme*). He had shared a long-existing and prevalent reservation about live-action fairy tales, because the presence of real people allegedly suffocated the kind of imagination that a more abstract form of representation allowed.[55] This argument was, however, neither new nor particularly East German, as

I will discuss below. Hortzschansky's self-contradiction unconsciously gave away his halfhearted promotion of Soviet films. This indicates that the Soviet model was not freely selected but very much adopted out of political, ideological, and aesthetic necessity. Given all the former UFA (Universum Film AG) employees and West Germans working at DEFA at the time, the studio desperately needed an idea that would seem "ideologically correct" to the Soviet occupiers. Confusion and contradiction as a result of tumultuous encounters between Soviet and German cultures was inevitable. But live-action fairy-tale films were soon accepted at DEFA.

Because of the difficult production conditions in the postwar years as well as the Soviet military administration's ambivalent attitude toward fairy tales,[56] the first fairy-tale adaptation, *The Cold Heart*, was not made until 1950, four years after DEFA was founded on 17 May 1946.[57] But the popular success of the first two live-action fairy tales—*The Cold Heart* and *Little Mook*—laid the cornerstone for this genre. Fairy-tale films were considered an especially useful tool for advancing the socialist–humanist education of children and youth in the GDR. Reporter Klaus Schulze published a piece called "Our Children Watch Fairy-Tale Movies: An Encouragement for DEFA" in 1951 in *Die Neue Filmwelt* that urged DEFA to emulate the Soviet model, while at the same time taking a swipe at West Germany:

> Anyone who passes one of our movie theaters on a Sunday morning will see the cinema filled with children's cheers and laughter. Excited little ones crowd the entrance in anticipation. Then there is again a film for children and youth, like every Sunday.
>
> The popularity these films enjoy is clear to those who are there one hour before the show. Those who cowatch such a fairy-tale film and see the children's faces glowing with enthusiasm and excitement after the show will witness what a deep impression these films make on the young audience. I especially remember the recently shown Soviet fairy-tale films *Wish upon a Pike* (Alexander Rou, 1938), *Vasilissa the Beautiful* (Alexander Rou, 1939), and *The Adventures of Nasreddin* (Nabi Ganiyev, 1947).
>
> At the same time in the western half of our home country (*Heimat*), young people are shown films that arouse the basest instincts in

> them. Very consciously, in that part of Germany the youth are being ideologically prepared for a new world conflagration (*Weltbrand*). In the Soviet Union, by contrast, all the love and care go to children. The best films are also made for them. Especially in the field of films for children and youth, DEFA has a great role model in the Soviet productions, which should be the guide for DEFA.[58]

The didactic nature of folk and fairy tales with their universal moral lessons could help carry out the mission assigned to DEFA to assist in building a democratic and peaceful Germany. At the ceremony where the Soviet military administration handed over the official license to DEFA, Colonel S. Tulpanov, an official from the Soviet occupation government, stated:

> The film company DEFA has important tasks to undertake. The greatest of all is the struggle for a democratic Germany and the education of the German people, especially the youth, to strengthen their sense of true democracy and humanity so that they gain respect for other people and nations. Film as popular art must become a sharp and powerful weapon against counterrevolution and in favor of the growing democracy, against war and militarism and in favor of peace and friendship among all people in the whole world.[59]

According to Barton Byg, "antifascism" and the "socialist–realist film" emerged as the two most significant genres in the DEFA "canon,"[60] and these two themes feature in the fairy-tale films as well. In the clichéd formula of fairy tales, as is well known, good will always triumph over evil. In the early decades of the GDR, evil was inevitably associated with National Socialism, capitalism, colonialism, and imperialism, ideologies that state socialism rhetorically condemned. Thus these DEFA fairy tales were consistent with the GDR's antifascist founding myth, albeit indirectly. The persecution of the disfigured Mook, for example, took on a contemporaneous layer of meaning in the postfascist GDR. He could, Jack Zipes writes, represent the Jews or anyone who would have been murdered in Nazi Germany; he could even stand in for the persecuted Communists during National Socialism, who needed to tell their stories to the younger generations in the GDR to gain the sympathy, respect, and legitimacy that was their due.[61] Götz Friedrich's *Little Red Riding Hood* (1962) shows the most direct influence from the Soviet Union by adapting Eugene Schwartz's play via Hans Rodenberg. The film suggests that only within a movement standing in solidarity (of Little Red Riding Hood and her animal friends) might the weak overcome the strong and good conquer evil. In parabolic fashion, these productions were tied in with the GDR's antifascist agenda and foundational narrative.

Socialist realism appears, at first glance, diametrically opposed to fairy-tale films, in which magical occurrences are the order of the day. And in fact, reviews of these films did not discuss them in terms of socialist realism. However, Hellmuth Häntzsche, who was the chief pedagogue at DEFA, explicitly pointed out that the aesthetic contribution DEFA fairy tales made was their *socialist–realist* appropriations of the progressive humanist heritage. He labeled a number of DEFA fairy-tale films "socialist–realist," including *The Cold Heart*, *Little Mook*, *The Tinderbox*, *Little Red Riding Hood*, *Dornröschen* (Briar Rose, Walter Beck, 1971), and *Three Hazelnuts for Cinderella*.[62] Häntzsche could describe these films as socialist–realist because this aesthetic concept was always more about content than form. Socialist realism set very specific ideological imperatives. In addition to the aforementioned *narodnost'*, or closeness to people, some basic concepts of socialist realism included "ideological commitment," "party-mindedness," and "national/popular spirit."[63]

It was also imperative for GDR cultural productions of the time to seek viable methods of applying socialist realism. In 1947, the Second Party Congress of the SED made it a fundamental goal to build a socialist society and made socialist realism the sole and only aesthetic form to attain that goal.[64] In 1952, the Politburo issued a resolution titled "Für den Aufschwung der fortschrittlichen deutschen Filmkunst" (For the Revival of Progressive German Cinema), in which socialist realism was designated as the only valid art form. Then in 1954, right after Stalin's death and the 17 June 1953 revolts but before the Thaw (*das Tauwetter*), the Fourth Party Congress reiterated that the task for filmmakers was to master the methods of socialist realism.[65] Socialist realism thus became an important artistic criterion for the early DEFA fairy-tale films as well.

It is clear that as long as the film *narratively* fostered socialist–humanist tenets, magic (through *Trickeffekte*, or special effects) was perfectly acceptable in the GDR. It was more important for the fairy tales to use magic and enchantment as a means of demonstrating class conflict and the moral integrity of the working class than it was to superficially ban magic as antithetical to socialist realism. As a result, fantasy in fairy tales combined with socialist realism to form an aesthetic hybrid, which made these films artistically and ideologically distinct from others of the genre made in the West in terms of their conceptualization of power, class, gender, and spectatorship. Yet in the GDR at the time, cultural functionaries repeatedly measured DEFA fairy-tale films by a socialist–realist yardstick and found them wanting.

Production and Reception of DEFA Children's and Fairy-Tale Films

In July 1952, an SED Politburo's resolution recommended that DEFA establish a production group for children's films. In December 1953, an independent department for children's films (*Kinderfilmabteilung*) was established within DEFA, thereby institutionalizing and regularizing the production of children's films. The year 1953 is generally considered the start of a continuous production of children's films at DEFA.[66] Unprecedentedly, children's films constituted a separate production category alongside feature films, newsreels, documentaries, and scientific films. Subsequently, a dramaturge group dedicated to developing scripts for children's films came into existence in summer 1954. Their first project was to adapt the Grimms' "The Brave Little Tailor" (KHM 20), which came out in 1956 to unfavorable reviews (see chapter 2).[67] Herbert Ballmann, then head of the children's film production group, took charge of a fairy-tale adaptation of a Harz mountain legend. *The Devil of Mill Mountain* (1955), in comparison to *The Cold Heart* and *Little Mook*, adhered more to socialist realism, with elements of revolutionary romanticism (see chapter 2). The original production group for children's films existed only briefly and was dissolved in 1957.

A series of regulations and decrees pressured children's films to align with socialist ideology. At the 1958 film conference, Alexander Abusch, then secretary of state and the first deputy minister of culture, demanded that children's films take their "themes from the brand new socialist lives of our children" and claimed that "the adaptation of fairy-tale material should not spread mysticism, but educate children in the spirit of social justice and to love the working people."[68] *The Singing Ringing Tree* (1957) was vehemently attacked in 1958 by the official print media (see chapter 3). From 1958 onward it was necessary for children's films to carry out a fundamental reorientation in the socialist direction.[69] In 1958, the GDR inaugurated the National Center for Children's Film and Television (Nationales Zentrum für Kinderfilm und -fernsehen der DDR), which became a member of the UNESCO (United Nations Educational, Scientific and Cultural Organization) Centre International du Film pour l'Enfance et la Jeunesse (International Center of Films for Children and Youth) in 1960 and began to represent the interests of German children's films at the international level.[70]

In 1963, a film group—Arbeitsgruppe "Kinder- und Jugendfilm"—was founded within DEFA's feature film studio and existed until 1970.[71] Walter Beck's *König Drosselbart* (King Thrushbeard, 1965) was its first collaborative project (see chapter 3).[72] In the 1960s, the production of children's films reached a certain stability. But in the second half of the 1960s, except for *How to Marry a King*, there were hardly any noteworthy adaptations of traditional fairy tales, because this period saw DEFA's big push for contemporary films, 70-mm films, adventure films with Manfred Krug, and especially Westerns (*Indianerfilm*). The Hauptverwaltung Film (HV-Film), which was the film department in the Ministry of Culture, discussed problems surrounding children's films to guarantee future production of three children's films per year. As a result of this discussion, the Ständige Kommission Kinderfilm (Standing Commission of Children's Film) was established shortly before 1970.[73]

According to Benita Blessing, the fairy-tale films, many of which are children's films, had it relatively easy with censorship because censors did not allot children's films sufficient attention to discover critical double entendres.[74] This may be true in many cases. This book, however, also reveals that tensions between politics and art also overshadowed fairy-tale films, conspicuously in the cases of *The Singing Ringing Tree*, *The Wooden Calf*, *Das Kleid* (The Robe, Konrad Petzold, 1961/1991), and *How to Marry a King*. The process of censorship in the GDR varied a little with institutional changes over the years, but typically censors intervened at two stages during a film's production: at the beginning, when HV-Film had to approve DEFA's annual production plan, and toward the end, when the film was completed and HV-Film was expected to issue a certification for the film. The dramaturges who were the "artistic consultant and ideological midwife"[75] also exerted control over the political and ideological content of the films. With respect to critical fairy-tale films that passed scrutiny, the censors either did not identify (with certainty) subversive elements or they identified them but found them too opaque to justify the economic waste of shelving a film that had been heavily invested in.

Film directors were divided in what they considered appropriate for children. Since the SED did not view *The Cold Heart* and *Little Mook* as ideal films for promoting a socialist–humanist education, there were repeated efforts within the DEFA studio to make *unbedingte Kinderfilme* (i.e., films incontrovertibly geared toward children). The seasoned children's film director Walter Beck was a staunch supporter of making children's films that did not lose sight of children in the audience. He attempted to create fairy-tale worlds in a studio through a sober, theatrical, and Brechtian setting befitting the reception level of young audiences. As found in my discussion of Gerhard Klein's *The Story of Poor Hassan* in chapter 2, some critics questioned the suitability of the Brechtian style for children's films. As Dirk Jungnickel writes, "[Beck] increases his stylization in films such as *The Prince behind the Seven Seas* and *Bearskin* to, in my opinion, nearly unbearable sterility."[76]

By contrast, proponents of the theory of "an undivided audience" sought to connect all generations and avoid treating children as viewers with limited cognitive abilities.[77] Egon Schlegel, the director of *The Devil's Three Golden Hairs*, was an energetic advocate of this theory: "The children themselves do not want to be treated as children, but as partners."[78] Rainer Simon, too, consciously distanced himself from the then-dominant aesthetic style in DEFA fairy-tale filmmaking with stylized backdrops and pedagogical finger-pointing and saw young audience as "equal partners."[79] Their films, the so-called *bedingte Kinderfilme* (films conditionally suitable for children), did not cater to a young audience alone. When Simon made *How to Marry a King* and *Sechse kommen durch die Welt* (How Six Made Their Way in the World, 1972), Beck criticized him for reverting back to the "contingent children's film" and thus breaking the aesthetic line Beck himself had tried to establish for DEFA fairy-tale films.[80] Due to this two-pronged approach aiming at both child and adult audiences, different levels of reception arose. Whereas a child would perceive a fairy-tale film as universal, an adult might see things specifically East German in it. For example, in reference to Klein's Brechtian tale *Poor Hassan*, Christoph Funke in *Der Morgen* observed that children hardly understood the parable and focused on the obvious plot.[81] Adult members of the audience, on the other hand, should have been able to recognize the film's ideological intention (see chapter 2).

The overall consistency in making fairy-tale films owed much to the institutional importance accorded to children's films and the accompanying financial and personnel resources that the state made available. Children's and fairy-tale films had the same resources at their disposal, followed the same production and review procedures, and enjoyed fair shares of screening spaces as other feature films.[82] Personnel commitment was also significant to the distinction of these films. A great number of artists steadily contributed to making fairy-tale films.[83] Heinz Kersten, a rarity among West German critics as he devoted himself to DEFA films, repeatedly mentioned that high-profile theater actors and actresses and famous DEFA directors did not consider themselves too good for children's films and that this made a significant difference in offering good quality films for children. In his review of *How to Marry a King*, Kersten wrote, "[Children's films from the GDR] are made according to this principle: only the best is good enough for children. This was a new discovery for many West Germans."[84]

The participation of popular actors and actresses made a huge difference; these included Erwin Geschonneck, Eva Kotthaus, Hans-Peter Minetti, Willy A. Kleinau, Werner Peters, Christel Bodenstein, Ekkehard Schall, Rolf Ludwig, Günther Simon, Manfred Krug, Arno Wyzniewski, Eberhard Esche, Jaecki Schwarz, Rolf Hoppe, Katharina Thalbach, Lore Frisch, Dieter Franke, Ernst-Goerg Schwill, Renate Blume, Helmut Schreiber, Fred Delmare, Peter Dommisch, Hannes Fischer, Gerd E. Schäfer, Wolf Kaiser, Eva-Maria Hagen, Käthe Reichel, Gerry Wolff, Bruno Carstens, Dieter Wien, Christine Schorn, Jutta Wachowiak, and more. Many of these actors and actresses were simultaneously engaged in theater productions, and theater was routinely given priority.[85] A number of notable figures appeared in minor roles, for example, Hans Klering, one of DEFA's founders, in *The Devil of Mill Mountain*, *The Robe*, and *The Devil's Three Golden Hairs*; Rolf Losansky in *The Wooden Calf*; Harry Hindemith in *Snow White*; Martin Hellberg in *Briar Rose*; Egon Schlegel and Winfried Glatzeder in *How to Marry a King*; and Heidemarie Wenzel in *Bearskin*. Very different from DEFA's *Indianerfilme*, which consistently cast the Serbian actor Gojko Mitic as the Indian chief, DEFA fairy-tale films used many different actors and actresses in their leading roles. Many later famous actors debuted in fairy-tale films. The little attention these films have received from DEFA film scholars seems incommensurate with the significant participation of famous DEFA directors, scriptwriters, and actors in them.

Although children's films officially enjoyed importance and distribution equal to DEFA feature films for adults, in reality, they were not treated exactly the same. They were considered "a kind of experimental field" (*eine Art Experimentierfeld*) for young and novice directors.[86] The junior directors (*Nachwuchsregisseure*) were often given child- or youth-related material to make their first feature-length film before being permitted to work on more high-profile features. Even experienced, famous directors, such as Rainer Simon and Iris Gusner, debuted with a fairy-tale film. Cinematographer Wolfgang Braumann pointed out the dilemma DEFA children's films faced: "Children's films have an advantage: They almost always have a full house. And often the audience even applauds at scenes, which rarely happens otherwise. The disadvantage is, however, that the adults ignore them, and the public takes too little notice of them."[87] Braumann's comment reveals that children's films had a certain stigma of naïveté and simplicity attached to them.

In addition to the challenge of attracting broader attention was the dilemma of the apparent contradiction between portraying stories of royalty and the GDR's antifeudal ideology. The use of fairy tales meant that DEFA had to deal with stories about kings and queens, princes and princesses, which, if not ideologically reactionary, appeared anachronistic at the least. As an actually existing socialist regime, the GDR had presumably done away with social relations typical of feudal or capitalist societies. Nevertheless, royal personages populate the majority of DEFA fairy-tale films. The enduring presence of royalty can be explained by the fact that they are adaptations of traditional fairy tales and the elimination of royalty would somehow weaken their connection to genre conventions. The anachronism of traditional tales, according to a reviewer in *Bauernecho*, could be explained away by the fact that the tales were an integral part of German cultural heritage, and, upon revisions, the humanist values immanent in these tales should outweigh the obsoleteness of social relations represented in them:

> It is often asked whether such old tales of castles and kings are still useful in our time. Of course one cannot answer this question simply with an all-inclusive "yes" or "no," because one has to remember that the tales collected by the Brothers Grimm were old folktales and most of them had a deeply humanist meaning. However, it is often necessary to correct the old versions according to our life experiences, our knowledge, to recover their original meaning.[88]

This comment made in 1960 in association with *Das Zaubermännchen* (Rumpelstiltskin, Christoph Engel and Erwin Anders, 1960) acknowledged the gap between old tales and the GDR present. But the critic also contended that, after necessary revisions, the inherent humanist values could bridge that gap and justify the old tales. Beate Hanspach, dramaturge of a few DEFA-produced television fairy tales, stressed the obligation—both professional and personal—that many filmmakers felt toward the fairy-tale tradition so that "old tales about princesses, kings, and sorceresses belong absolutely to a new, i.e., socialist cultural policy."[89] This made clear that fairy tales enjoyed the favor of DEFA filmmakers, but it was inevitable that DEFA would revise the traditional tales to suit the realpolitik of the GDR.

In its earlier decades, DEFA fairy-tale production was marked by a negotiation between inheriting tradition and updating it to fit the current sociohistorical reality. In the 1950s, the dominant view still deemed traditional tales inviolable, especially those by the Grimm brothers. This was evident in the reception of *Das tapfere Schneiderlein* (The Brave Little Tailor, Helmut Spieß, 1956), the first DEFA adaptation of a Grimm tale, which was attacked by official and popular print media because of its radical departure from the Grimmian original: in the new ending, the tailor no longer marries the princess but a gardener's daughter. Such a working-class victory was criticized for anachronistically establishing a GDR-style government during the period of the Grimms' writing. So as not to repeat the mistakes of *Little Tailor* but nonetheless to align the film with antifeudal and antibourgeois politics, the animation studio in Dresden did not simply adapt the Grimms' "The Farmer's Clever Daughter" (KHM 94) or revise it but rummaged folktale collections to find alternative versions in which the farmer's daughter does not end up marrying the king. The effort led to the discovery of fifteen such versions. Hence in the 1961 hand puppet version, the peasant girl humiliates the king as a stupid despot and marries a peasant boy instead (see chapter 4). Ultimately, *Little Tailor* and the puppet-animated *The Farmer's Clever Daughter* (1961) reject royalty as marriage partners for lower-class citizens. Only *Little Tailor* violated the taboo of "tampering with" the Grimm canon, whereas *The Farmer's Clever Daughter* (1961) simply avoided the Grimms altogether.

In the 1960s, fidelity to the commonly known version (*Werktreue*) still received due praise, but revisions became considered less and less blasphemous. In his article series on "Märchenfilme und ihre Zeit," Walter Beck advocates making necessary changes to print tales because of the tales' own dynamic nature and the different historical contexts in which a print tale and a film adaptation are situated. On another occasion, Beck writes, "Making fairy-tale films based on literary sources is 'not the business of a copier.'"[90] In his 1971 *Briar Rose*, the evil thirteenth fairy is changed into a Fairy of Diligence. Reviewers overall welcomed the positive changes. Likewise they spoke favorably of revisions made in films such as *Rumpelstiltskin*, *King Thrushbeard*, and *Froschkönig* (The Frog King, Walter Beck, 1988). A critic wrote in *Brandenburgische Neueste Nachrichten*, "It was and still is every generation's legitimate right to tell old stories in a new form, expand the scope, find more exact motivations for actions and characters, and bring the tale's inner truth closer to [contemporary] social reality."[91] Films like Gottfried Kolditz's *Snow White* (1961) and *Frau Holle* (Mother Hulda, 1963), however, were criticized for being not much more than superficial book illustrations.[92] Thus starting in the 1960s, although loyalty to the print tales was still appreciated, revisions were expected and even deemed necessary. In the course of the four decades of DEFA fairy-tale filmmaking, one can observe increasing latitude with cultural heritage in terms of its inviolability, and the adaptations of the 1980s saw more labels like "freely adapted." Reviews also gradually pointed to the edited nature of the Grimms' tales and endorsed the necessity of revisions to speak to the here and now.

This book focuses on the domestic, not the international, reception of DEFA fairy-tale films. Through examining press reviews, it demonstrates that, over the course of the GDR's existence, they showed a clear slackening of energy. Those of the early films were original, sharp, and divided. But they gradually became monotonous, less original, and less critical, with some exceptions—as in the case of Rainer Simon's films. Sometimes the same review was reprinted in multiple news outlets. With regard to critical fairy-tale films, newspaper reviews of the time did not speculate on possible subversive elements; usually, they summarized the plotline, moral lessons, information about the crew, and so on. In the worst scenario, Bettina Hindemith suggests, reviews in the GDR were commissioned business[93]; instead of helping distill the relevance of the films, film critique in the GDR "avoids controversial subjects and stays silent. It implies that if one wants to write about film critique in the GDR, one reads between the lines at all cost to infer what was never written."[94] The silence in the reviews should be read dialectically. For one thing, the reviews avoided eliciting political references from the films because the political subtext was often hard to pinpoint. More importantly, reviewers may have deliberately not said what they were thinking if that insight was likely to alert censors and put the film and the filmmakers in a precarious situation.

Dagmar Schittly argues that the GDR audiences, old and young, were not naïve viewers, and usually understood well the small, ironic, hidden insinuations that a film had to offer; there existed a complicity (*Komplizenschaft*) between the artists and the GDR audiences.[95] For example, none of the contemporary reviews of Simon's *How Six Made Their Way in the World* (1972) drew a parallel between the kingdom of Malabunt and the GDR. Not until the GDR disappeared did Dieter Wiedemann and F. B. Habel, among others, articulate the film's clear allusion to the "trapped" GDR.[96] Probably, reviewers of the time chose not to divulge the film's critique of the regime out of consideration for the film and the filmmakers. In some other cases, critics retrospectively saw prophetic potency that foreshadowed the demise of the GDR. Thirty years after the making of the film, Ralf Schenk viewed the abandoned throne and scattering crowd in *The Robe* as portending the implosion of the GDR.[97] Jack Zipes finds *Der Eisenhans* (Iron Hans, Karl Heinz Lotz, 1988) "fascinating because it is an unusual anticipation of the collapse of the totalitarian regime in East Germany and was filled with all sorts of contradictions."[98] Such hindsight could naturally only come a posteriori. Yet the possibility that such potentially subversive projection was encoded in the films and could survive censorship is attributable to the fairy-tale cloak, except, of course, in the case of *The Robe*, the only banned DEFA fairy-tale adaptation.

Thematic Analysis of DEFA Fairy-Tale Films

DEFA fairy-tale films show some degree of ideological and political consistency. To demonstrate that films share common themes and similar agendas, the chapters of this book at times juxtapose tales from different decades. However, in spanning forty years, characteristics and certain emphases developed against specific historical and political backgrounds in each decade. The structure of the chapters follows a roughly chronological order. Chapter 1 centers on the first two DEFA fairy-tale films, for which DEFA discovered in Hauff's "bourgeois" stories class struggles that presented opportunities to critique social injustice and capitalistic greed. The two films demonstrated affinity and compatibility between East German and nineteenth-century values, reflecting the GDR's effort to process and inherit the German cultural tradition. Although Hauff's 1827 novel *Jud Süß* also provided the template for Veit Harlan's notorious anti-Semitic film *Jud Süß* (Jew Süss, 1940), broad humanist values are present in Hauff's tales, a compelling reason for them to have been chosen in the first place. These values are, in turn, in keeping with Marxist and anti-capitalist elaborations in the DEFA studios. With the popular success of these films, a new genre was launched in DEFA film history that is based on Soviet models but also harkens back to Germany's own humanistic and cinematic traditions. In this context, the Soviet film *The Stone Flower* is examined to see how it shaped and framed the East German cinema scene. Chapters 2 through 5 are dedicated, respectively, to the four decades (1950s–1980s) of the GDR's existence, although the temporal boundaries are more fluid than fixed.

The films of the 1950s and 1960s (chapter 2) often concern themselves with class struggle and proletarian rule. The affinity between nineteenth-century folksiness and GDR proletarian politics provided the East German government much needed opportunities for self-promotion that did not appear too aggressive. The fairy tales offered the GDR a retrospective, critical look at bygone societal forms to reaffirm the state's own socialist structures as a historical necessity. At least rhetorically, the DEFA adaptations kept up the folksy spirit and the championing for the masses found in traditional tales. Under the veneer of magic and fantasy, DEFA adaptations, especially of the 1950s, offered indirect legitimization of the transfer of political power to the exploited and oppressed. While the ending in traditional tales often suggests a limited revolutionary potential and a reconstitution of the social and economic status quo, the DEFA ending expands on the genre's revolutionary potential and evinces a new and radical force—but cloaks it in an allegorical fairy tale. To that end, the generic descriptions of the hardworking and virtuous lower-class protagonists and of the foppish, greedy, and exploitative members of the upper class follow a proven formula of good and evil. The "happily ever after" for lower-class heroes ineluctably resembles a Marxist utopia. The fate of "never happily after" befalls aristocratic members of society, who are routinely ridiculed as stupid, immoral, and obsessed with power and wealth, thereby justifying regime change and societal renewal.

It is not the evil, stupid aristocrats but the good monarchs and princesses who require closer examination, given their implicit disharmony with the GDR's antifeudal, antiaristocratic ideology and the need for reinterpretation. Chapter 3 focuses on tales that play out primarily within the aristocratic circle, commencing with *The Singing Ringing Tree*. However, the politically motivated attack on *The Singing Ringing Tree* warned of the precariousness of adaptations of "bourgeois" tales, by a West German director to boot. To avoid further accusations of "revisionism," filmmakers thereafter carefully selected tales from which a "politically correct" lesson could be distilled. These stories often involve a "demotion" in class status for the royal protagonist, as in *Snow White* and *King Thrushbeard*, in which princesses are made to work and King Thrushbeard is disguised as a minstrel. Young monarchs symbolically differ from old kings who represent decaying social systems. In a way, these noble protagonists, often down-to-earth and not elitist, have stepped down from their thrones and walked into a mundane life that the audience could relate to.

Similar to arrival novels (*Ankunftsromane*) and contemporary films (*Gegenwartsfilme*), fairy-tale films feature a typical trajectory through which the hero arrives in socialist reality. They stress the role work plays in creating a "socialist personality" and prioritize love over the pursuit of physical wealth. In the Cold War climate, these films, many of which date from the 1960s, convey a socialist–puritanical contempt for gold and associate the capitalist West with greed and the socialist East with hard work and generosity. Lower-class heroes as well as members of the upper class with lower-class qualities are entitled to a "happily ever after," which is often brought about not through class struggle but through a generational conflict between old and young monarchs. Whereas generational conflict in contemporary youth films such as *Berlin—Ecke Schönhauser* (Berlin—Schönhauser Corner, Gerhard Klein, 1957) and *Berlin um die Ecke* (Berlin around the Corner, Gerhard Klein, 1965/1990) often unfolds between the old Communists and the rebellious youth (*Halbstarken*),[99] in fairy-tale films the generational gap can be found between the old king and the future king. Thematically, chapter 3 focuses on the portrayal of royalty in GDR fairy-tale cinema; therefore, not class struggles and revolution, themes dealt with in chapter 2, but love and work, themes of equal importance in West Germany and elsewhere, constitute the focus. This chapter compares DEFA and West German/Disney adaptations of the same tales in terms of their different conceptions of gender and power relations.

DEFA films of the 1950s and 1960s speak the "master language" of the newly established antifascist and anticapitalist state. In Dieter Wiedemann's phrase, these tales function as "mediation of politics" (*Politikvermittlung*).[100] The fairy-tale films of the 1970s and 1980s, however, show the tension between "conformity and protest" that Wiedemann observes of

DEFA films of that period in general.[101] In comparison to earlier adaptations that reiterated and reinforced GDR founding narratives, revolutionary ethos obviously waned over the decades. The book's last two chapters construe fairy tales as ambitious sociocritical projects, although conformity and subversiveness often coexist in the same film and in the same period. Inspired by Jack Zipes's analysis of the slave language in Central and Eastern European fairy-tale films, the last two chapters analyze some DEFA fairy tales as covert satires that use slave language. Chapter 4 focuses on the only banned DEFA fairy-tale film, *The Robe* (1961/1991) as well as on films of the 1970s that insert regime critique into seemingly harmless fairy tales.

These films were politically ambitious because they moved from the grand narratives of the founding myth to internal critiques of GDR society and of the regime, using slave language disguised in fairy-tale films that pretended to be innocuous. Fables and tales, as Kristin Wardetzky points out in "Sklavensprache: Märchen und Fabeln in repressiven Gesellschaftssystemen," are historically the genre of encryption that can make surreptitious allusions to social taboos. The kingdom in *The Robe*, for example, is surrounded by a thick, solid wall. In the wake of the construction of the Berlin Wall in 1961, the film suggested an image of the GDR as a walled-in dictatorship. Rainer Simon's *How to Marry a King* (1969) presents a king close to his people and capable of reform, a political utopia that put the contemporary regime to shame. Simon's *How Six Made Their Way in the World* (1972) satirizes the GDR as a claustrophobic space where lack of artistic freedom results in the stultification of talents. Egon Schlegel's *The Devil's Three Golden Hairs* (1977) portrays a sociopolitical dystopia through a subterraneous palace that is cut off from its people.

Chapter 5 is devoted to the much understudied final decade of DEFA films in the 1980s. These films rehashed themes similar to those of earlier chapters, but new topics also emerged that undoubtedly captured the zeitgeist of that decade, including themes of young love, Romanticism, women's emancipation, peace, and ecology. Novels by Romantic authors such as E. T. A. Hoffmann and Bettina von Arnim were also adapted for the first time, with the exception of the early DEFA/Swedish coproduction of Hoffmann's *Das Fräulein von Scudéri* (Mademoiselle de Scudéri, 1819).[102]

Celino Bleiweiß's daring adaptation of Hoffmann's anti-Enlightenment tale, *Zauber um Zinnober* (Magic around Cinnabar, 1983), illustrates the kind of massive distortion of reality that would permit a talentless man to wield the greatest power. The film implicitly critiques the GDR's one-sided promotion of the intellectual history of the Enlightenment, echoing the critique from the 1970s and the 1980s about how instrumentalist and positivist thinking led to environmental and nuclear disasters. A number of the 1980s films, including *Jorinda and Joringel* (1986) and *Iron Hans* (1988), advocate pacifist and ecological causes. The compelling links to the feminist, environmental, and pacifist movements demonstrate the potential of fairy tales to be harnessed by dissident movements in the GDR. The Grimms' tale "The Goose Girl" (KHM 89), which was deemed ineligible for adaptation in the 1960s due to the heroine's resignation, was filmed on the eve of the *Wende* (the 1989 revolutionary events) to present a wise ruler and his dedication to the truth, a potentially reformist message for the then ossified GDR government. Like the majority of DEFA fairy tales, these films were made for both children and adults. The serious topics and political ambitions did not help them at the box office but distinguished them as conveyers of popular concerns and as advocates of a social conscience.

Formal Analysis of DEFA Fairy-Tale Films

Narrative analysis is the focus of this book, with some attention to the aesthetic and formal characteristics of the films. Generally speaking, DEFA fairy-tale films were conservative in their aesthetic. Because of both the binding political contract of socialist realism and the expectations of young viewers in the audience, extensive formal experimentations would have appeared out of place. Yet socialist realism has always lacked clear contours in terms of formal requirements. Therefore, despite the administration's repeated emphasis on socialist realism, DEFA fairy tales also exhibited a wide variety of formal traits: Hollywood, UFA, *Bilderbuch* (picture book), theatrical, Brechtian, and cinema verité. They showed strong influence from the theater not least because after DEFA started cutting its proportion of "bourgeois specialists" from West Germany owing to ideological and political reasons, it had to make up for that loss with massive recruitment from its theater personnel. The employment of Brechtian aesthetics, most conspicuously in Gerhard Klein's *Poor Hassan* and Konrad Petzold's *The Robe*, was a conscious departure—and a modernist one, at that—from both the UFA tradition and socialist realism. Rainer Simon experimented with the documentary style (cinema verité) in his two fairy-tale films—*How to Marry a King* (1969) and *How Six Made Their Way in the World* (1972). From the late 1960s onward, especially after Erich Honecker's 1971 declaration that there should be no taboos in art—provided all works display a firm socialist position—socialist realism's hold on DEFA films subsided. Despite the regime's later desperate retraction of its own liberal policies and reemphasis on socialist realism,[103] the state aesthetic had lost the clout it once had.

The most conspicuous, genre-specific, formal characteristic of fairy-tale films is the presence of special effects. At the DEFA studios, these were created first by Ernst Kunstmann and his daughter Vera Kunstmann and, after their departure, by Kunstmann's students Kurt Marks and Erich Günther. The Kunstmanns conjured up unforgettable magic in many DEFA fairy tales, including *The Cold Heart*, *Little Mook*, *The Devil of Mill Mountain*, *The Tinderbox*, *The Singing Ringing Tree*, *The Robe*, and *Die goldene Jurte* (The Golden Yurt, Gottfried Kolditz and Rabschaa Dordschpalam, 1961). Ernst Kunstmann was known for guarding his trade skills carefully and was reluctant to let his students in on his "secrets." When Kunstmann reached retirement age in 1963, he left the studio for good. In addition, film directors of cinema verité increasingly rejected artificial sets, special effects, and rear projection techniques. Therefore Kunstmann was not even employed as a consultant after he left.[104] DEFA's department responsible for special effects declined, and projects such as Walter Beck's *The Frog Prince* were delayed partly due to the lack of adequate technical support.[105]

Among the variety of visual styles, two main strands stand out: the suggestively timeless tales represented by Walter Beck and Ursula Schmenger's[106] studio films and the historicized films by Rainer Simon and Wolfgang Hübner, whose stories play out in a specific historical period. Simon set *How to Marry a King* in the Renaissance era of the fifteenth and sixteenth centuries through an aesthetic stylization that imitated

Renaissance art. Hübner's *The Master Thief* (1978) takes place toward the end of the eighteenth century in Brandenburg, Prussia, and is thus faithful to the Grimms' tale (KHM 192), which references potato dumplings and by doing so indicates a specific historical and geographical context.[107] A rather unusual fairy-tale film, Hübner's *Gevatter Tod* (Godfather Death, 1980) sets the story during the time of the plague in the early sixteenth century in Görlitz. Hübner's *Jorinda and Joringel* (1986) takes place during the Thirty Years' War to imbue the simple love story with a message about war and peace.[108]

Many historical castles in the GDR contributed significantly to the visuals of DEFA fairy-tale films, especially the later ones: Schloss Hartenfels in Saxony in *Briar Rose* (1971), Moritzburg near Dresden in both *How Six Made Their Way in the World* (1972) and *Three Hazelnuts for Cinderella* (1974), Burg Kriebstein in Saxony in *Iron Hans* (1988), Schloss Reinhardtsbrunn in *Rapunzel or the Magic of Tears* (1988), and Burg Falkenstein in Sachsen-Anhalt and Burg Schönfels near Zwickau in *The Story of the Goose Princess and Her Loyal Horse Falada* (1989). The fairy-tale films were able to take advantage of the culture and history, the sceneries and landscape that the East German *Heimat* offered and turned the GDR into, to use Benita Blessing's term, a "fairy-tale land."[109] According to the discussions of filmmakers at international conferences and symposia, "The fairy tale is absolutely national. To preserve this national character, artists should turn to historical sources and national paintings and use nationally unique costumes, everyday details, and indigenous landscape."[110] DEFA fairy-tale filmmakers certainly blended in German history, art, music, customs, architecture, and landscape and made the films very German indeed.

Except for a couple—*The Wooden Calf*, *Der kleine und der große Klaus* (Little Claus and Big Claus, Celino Bleiweiß, 1971)—the majority of the fairy-tale films were shot in color. Color stock was expensive, but it proved necessary for attracting young audiences to these films. Various techniques in image composition also distinguish these films as well-made artifacts. Walter Beck's *Briar Rose* is primarily composed of symmetrical images. When the prince comes to kiss Briar Rose awake, he sees three scenes from a hundred years ago frozen. The moving images are intercut with still photographs to create the impression that he is seeing the freeze actions as they happened a century ago. When Briar Rose awakens, the three scenes come alive again. The medium of film vividly rendered these dramatic events by combining still images and motion pictures. Dissolve was also a frequently used technique in DEFA fairy-tale films. In *The Singing Ringing Tree*, for example, the image dissolves each of the three times the princess refuses to adapt to the plebian life and again three times when she helps animals. Dissolve is a useful device that helps structure the film narrative, as *The Singing Ringing Tree* uses the magic number three to trace the princess's loss of beauty and then its recovery. In another example, *Die Gänsehirtin am Brunnen* (The Goose Girl at the Spring, Ursula Schmenger, 1979), dissolve is used each time there is a transition from the main narrative to the three flashbacks that are presented as the protagonist's dreams. This book does not focus on the cinematography, film editing, music, architecture, sets, costumes, masks, and so on but nevertheless considers them worthy objects of study.

National Socialist and West German Fairy-Tale Films

DEFA fairy-tale films undoubtedly surpass their West German counterparts. To discuss West German fairy-tale films, however, it is necessary to briefly mention Nazi fairy-tale films, because it was largely the same filmmakers—Alf Zengerling, Hubert Schonger, the Diehl brothers, and Fritz Genschow—who made fairy-tale films after the war. Most of these National Socialist films are only available in archives and are not easily accessible, except maybe *Der kleine Muck: Ein Märchen für große und kleine Leute* (Little Mook: A Fairy Tale for Big and Small People, Franz Fiedler, 1944).[111] In *Es war einmal . . . im Dritten Reich: Die Märchenfilmproduktion für den nationalsozialistischen Unterricht*, Cornelia Endler points out that the German fairy tales, especially the Grimms' collection, were indispensable components in National Socialist education because of their great potential for ideological interpretations that supported National Socialism's supposed "roots" in teutonism (*Volks- d.h. Germanentum*).[112] She examines the importance of fairy tales for the Nazi ideology and the integration of animated puppet films (*Puppentrickfilm*) into the school curriculum. Popular, folksy material, especially the Grimm collection, received ideological, racist, and sexist interpretations along the National Socialist alignment. Educators strictly rejected *Realfilme* with real actors.[113] Therefore the twenty or so live-action fairy-tale films made during 1933–1945 were not part of the curriculum but were briefly discussed in "Außerschulische Märchenfilmproduktion bis 1945" (Extracurricular fairy-tale film production until 1945).

Ron Schlesinger, author of *Rotkäppchen im Dritten Reich: Die deutsche Märchenfilmproduktion zwischen 1933 und 1945*, surveys nineteen live-action fairy-tale films made between 1935 and 1941 and 1943/1944, each film with filmographic data, a synopsis, his critique, and often a still photo. He also observes that Nazi fairy-tale films were systematically instrumentalized to serve Nazi ideology and propaganda.[114] For example, at the end of *Der gestiefelte Kater* (Puss in Boots, Alf Zengerling, 1935), Puss is praised with "Hail to the Tomcat Murr! He is our savior! We live again!" (Heil dem Kater Murr!—Er ist unser Erretter!—Wir leben wieder!).[115] In Zengerling's *Dornröschen* (Briar Rose, 1936) and *Rumpelstilzchen* (Rumpelstiltskin, 1940), he changed the king to absolutely positive authority.[116] In *Dornröschen*, although confiscation of spindles would deprive poor people of their means to make a living, the king promises to provide for them.[117] In *Rumpelstiltskin*, the vices are heaped on the treasurer instead of the king, and Rumpelstiltskin in the end turns the treasurer into a donkey.[118] In *Tischlein deck dich, Esel streck dich, Knüppel aus dem Sack!* (The Magic Table, the Golden Donkey, and the Club in the Sack!, Alfred Stöger, 1938), the filmmaker added a scene in which a chatty peasant is threatened to be punished with an obviously anti-Semitic "yellow mark" (*einen gelben Fleck*) on his blue pants.[119] In *Schneewittchen und die sieben Zwerge* (Snow White and the Seven Dwarfs, Carl Heinz Wolff, 1939), Snow White's father leads his army to war and is thus absent for the rest of the film. Hubert Schonger's *Der standhafte Zinnsoldat* (The Steadfast Tin Soldier, 1940), instead of a focus on love, presents a war story between tin soldiers and a troll, suggesting that Germany was fighting only a defensive war (*Verteidigungskrieg*), not an aggressive one (*Angriffskrieg*). The film received the commendation "educational for the people" (*volksbildend*) and was on the propaganda film list of the Wehrmacht.[120] The Nazi adaptation *Rotkäppchen und der Wolf* (Little Red Riding Hood and the Wolf, Fritz Genschow and

Renée Stobrawa, 1937) is set in the Third Reich and frames the fairy tale in color in the middle of the black-and-white film. "Uncle Hunter," played by the director/scriptwriter Fritz Genschow, wears the insignia of the Nazi eagle and swastika on his hat.[121] The film pleased the regime leaders and received the commendation "educational for the people" (*volksbildend*).[122]

After the war, the Nazi fairy-tale films were trashed for their ideological manipulation.[123] West German educators continued to reject fairy-tale adaptations with real actors.[124] The most decisive objection against live-action fairy-tale films, according to the West German critic Steffen Wolf, was that they necessarily concretize the originally indistinct fairy-tale images, create stereotypical clichés, and no longer allow any differentiation. Therefore the so-called realistic fairy-tale film leaves no room for children's imagination and destroys any sense of timelessness in the fairy tale.[125] Like many West German educators before him, Professor Martin Keilhacker from the Pädagogische Universität Mannheim also opposed transposing fairy tales onto the screen: "Precisely the thing that is precious in fairy tales, the thing that gives them eternal youth and awakens in us an unquenchable desire, is unimaginable, is something entirely fictive, and no filmmaker will ever succeed in capturing and reproducing it in images."[126] Live-action fairy-tale films were criticized as "worthless kitsch."[127] Paul Heimann made an even more sweeping rejection of fairy-tale films: "Fairy tales have no place in film at all. The word is the adequate expression for fairy tales."[128]

All these rejections of live-action fairy-tale films contributed to the fact that the West German government implemented a Youth Protection Act that forbade all children under six to attend public film screenings from 1957 onward. This legislation was not revoked until 1985. Since in West Germany children's film was effectively synonymous with fairy-tale films before 1989, this ban basically stymied filmic adaptations of fairy tales on the other side of the Iron Curtain.[129] Thus the abovementioned plea by a West German critic that the FRG should step up its efforts in producing its own fairy-tale films was made in 1982 because of and despite the domestic adversity this genre was experiencing.

The 1957 Youth Protection Act had a crippling effect on the production of fairy-tale films in West Germany. Earlier, from 1949 to 1961, about forty fairy-tale films, not a small number, were produced in West Germany—mostly by Zengerling, Schonger, and Genschow. Especially between 1953 and 1956, this genre experienced a short-lived boom in the FRG.[130] Indicative of the free market economy, different producers often adapted the same tales, because they worked with different distributors and competed with each other,[131] whereas isomorphism and duplication were not common in DEFA, given the studio's structures of central planning. West German producers likewise drew on the Grimms' well-known tales. One practical reason was that the easy recognition of these titles saved producers the trouble of much advertising effort, as the title alone would bring a crowd.[132] Since the *Heimatfilm* was de facto the dominant genre in West Germany in the 1950s, its fairy-tale films evince traces of the *Heimatfilm* as well.[133] As Katie Trumpener observes, the West German fairy-tale films of the 1950s "move between Heimat film folk-costumed traditionalism and kitschy cuteness (particularly in films featuring talking animals)."[134]

In comparison with East German fairy-tale films, their West German counterparts are rather banal, both aesthetically and politically. They show a lack of technical, human, and financial investment. The plots are replete with trivial subplots to fulfill the length requirement. Neuschwanstein appears merely as an add-on, nondiegetic backdrop in quite a few of these films but otherwise is not integrated into the action of the film, unlike in DEFA fairy tales, in which real castles serve as actual shooting locations.[135] Multiple reasons account for the low quality of the West German fairy-tale films. In addition to limited technical and personnel availability, there were simply no financial subsidies from the government for fairy-tale film productions. The "payoff time" (*Amortisationszeit*) for a children's film took four (black-and-white) to six (color) years, whereas it took only one to two years for a regular feature film. Thus the financial risk was too big for a producer to take at a time when television's impact was rapidly expanding.[136] The poor quality of these films also reflected the fact that West German film producers did not take the youth audience seriously enough.[137]

As a result, these low-budget fairy-tale films almost ruined the reputation of the genre, as attested by Steffen Wolf's much quoted critique of these films: "They disqualify themselves due to inadequate design, outdated technology, unsatisfactory acting, and lack of imagination on the part of their makers."[138] Since the implementation of the Youth Protection Act in 1957, the children's film production lay paralyzed in West Germany during the 1960s. Not until the early 1970s did public interest revive in children's film, owing in part to debates about preschool education, new ideas developed in children's television, and international recognition for the New German Cinema.[139] Going into the 1980s, West Germany started to import children's films from Scandinavian and the socialist countries such as Czechoslovakia, the GDR, and the Soviet Union.[140] Daniela Berghahn notes that the West German reception of DEFA fairy-tale films even outdid that of other feature films from DEFA: "Even East German box office hits like *Die Legende von Paul und Paula* (The Legend of Paul and Paula, Heiner Carow, 1973) and *Solo Sunny* (Konrad Wolf, 1980) were quickly taken off the cinema programs in West Germany because they were culturally too specific to appeal to audiences not familiar with contemporary GDR society. The only type of DEFA film of interest to West Germans were DEFA's fairy-tale films, which were regularly broadcast on West German television."[141]

West German critics accused DEFA fairy-tale films of instrumentalizing their source material, which, in DEFA's defense, was not a uniquely East German practice. West German fairy-tale films of the 1950s were also entrenched in ideology, didactics, and, even worse, what Wolfgang Schneider calls "pseudochildlike farce" (*Kindertümelei*).[142] In the East, the king together with the feudal system he represents necessitates condemnation and ridicule. In the West, very much as in Nazi pictures, the king comes off as an authoritative, likable father figure that aligned with West German conservative and paternalistic politics. For example, in *Rumpelstilzchen* (Rumpelstiltskin, Herbert B. Fredersdorf, FRG, 1955), a greedy king in the Grimms' tale is changed to a lover of horticulture who is rather benign and kind and is only misled by his two greedy counselors. The miller is not portrayed as a detestable braggart who claims that his daughter can spin straw into gold, which nearly results in his daughter's death. Instead the miller, extremely proud of his daughter, seems to be speaking in a metaphorical language that only exaggerates his daughter's ability a little. Likewise in Hans F. Wilhelm's *Der Teufel mit den drei goldenen Haaren* (The Devil with the Three Golden Hairs, FRG, 1955), the evil king is made respectable, leaving his counselor to be the villain figure.[143] Another difference is that West German fairy-tale films reflect middle-class affluence, whereas DEFA often shows plain, humble workers' milieus, as my comparison of the "Snow White" and "Little Red Riding Hood" adaptations demonstrates. The attitude toward power and wealth in the West German fairy-tale films stands in stark contrast to that of DEFA, mirroring the different ideological and political underpinnings of these films.

This book does not intend to deliver a comprehensive study of Nazi and West German fairy-tale films, nor does it make a thorough comparison between DEFA and Western or DEFA and other Eastern European productions. However, I would venture to say that—while fairy-tale appropriations were politicized on both sides of the Iron Curtain—the East Germans proved more consistent in and serious about their fairy-tale film adaptations than the West Germans. In West Germany, the Youth Protection Act caused the production of fairy-tale films to atrophy and the country had to rely on imports to satisfy its domestic need for fairy tales.

DEFA versus Disney Fairy Tales

Not only did DEFA fairy-tale films distinguish themselves from Nazi and West German fairy-tale films, but they also constituted an alternative model to Disney films.[144] The contrast between Disney and DEFA could not be clearer. Disney is a capitalist, private mass media and entertainment corporation; DEFA was the state-run studio of the bygone socialist GDR. Whereas Disney boasts a long list of world-famous fairy-tale films and cartoon characters, only a few DEFA fairy-tale films are still shown today.

Rosemary Stott's study of the Western feature films imported into East Germany shows that Hollywood films were eagerly consumed by GDR viewers.[145] Yet Disney's animation features were notably missing from the films imported from the United States. In fact, the GDR officially blocked Disney's animated cartoons from reaching its viewers. As a result, there was not a single animated Disney film shown on the GDR's official cinema circuit.[146] DEFA-Stiftung's database shows that only one Disney documentary—*Wilde Katze* (Jungle Cat, James Algar, 1959), which chronicles the life of a female jaguar in the South American jungle—premiered in East Germany on 26 September 1969, ten years after the film was released in the United States. On East

German state television, only two animated Walt Disney films were broadcast—*Dumbo the Flying Elephant* (1941, broadcast on 7 October 1989) and *Alice in Wonderland* (1951, broadcast on 26 December 1989). Notably, these two animation features were not broadcast until, respectively, about a month before and about a month and a half after the Berlin Wall fell.

The iconic Mickey, Donald, and Pluto were nowhere to be found on East German television. Other than the two animated features, the Deutsches Rundfunkarchiv database lists fourteen different Disney feature and nature films (not counting the rebroadcasts) that were shown on East German television, but only between 1986 and 1991, with four films broadcast before the Berlin Wall fell and the other ten after.[147] These exotic nature and feature films expanded GDR television's offerings in scientific, educational, and entertainment films. These Disney films appeared apolitical and ideologically harmless enough that they were allowed into the official program in the late 1980s. Given the GDR's anti-Disney position, one may assume that East German viewers were not very familiar with Disney cartoons unless they watched them while tuning into West German television. And some viewers were old enough to have watched them before the Second World War disrupted the distribution of Disney films in Europe.[148]

The GDR's anti-Disney stance imbued Mickey Mouse with a different symbolic meaning: although Mickey is the most recognizable cartoon character the world over, for the GDR, Mickey Mouse was the embodiment of American cultural imperialism and thus an illicit consumption taboo just like Coca-Cola. Disney's animated features were banned to prevent the reactionary, capitalist, and imperialist ideology in the Disney pictures from corrupting the East German youth. Only children's films made by socialist countries could, it was thought, instill the right values. Film reviews of DEFA fairy-tale films seldom mentioned Disney, and when they did it was in a negative tone. For instance, while criticizing the gruesome details in *The Cold Heart*, G. H. deplored the apparent delight Disney's *Snow White and the Seven Dwarfs* (1937) took in depicting terror.[149] It was important for the East German state to monitor foreign imports so as to offer sufficient entertainment to its children but not lose them to foreign media excitement. By monopolizing what East German youth and children could consume, the state guided and manipulated the aesthetic taste of its young audience. Thus in practice, the deliberate boycotting of Disney films protected domestic and Eastern European children's films.

DEFA could not compare with Disney in terms of visual extravaganza, technological innovation, or commercial success. However, DEFA treated fairy-tale adaptations very seriously and with a lesser focus on entertainment and technical aspects than on the artistic and political significance of the narratives for the state and its people. The Disney classics, as many critics have pointed out, consist of typical light entertainment filled with music and humor, often physical gags and slapstick. The narratives likewise undergo a process of Disneyfication characterized by a predictable plot and formulaic characters, infused with traditional American values and a conservative ideology.[150]

DEFA and Disney show different ideological positions on class, gender, and spectatorship. Following Donald Crafton's notion of "self-figuration," Jack Zipes observes Walt Disney's autobiographical imprint on his films. In "Puss in Boots" (1922), one of Disney's early silent animation short films, Walt Disney changed the protagonist from a cat to a young man who outsmarts the king and runs away with his beloved princess. Zipes asks, "But who is this commoner? Was Disney making a statement on behalf of the masses? Was Disney celebrating 'everyone' or 'everyman'? Did Disney believe in revolution and socialism? The answer to all these questions is simple: no."[151] Zipes interprets this change of protagonist as reflecting Disney's personal ambition to "break into the industry of animated films (the king) with the help of Ub Iwerks (Puss)."[152] If the early Walt Disney incorporated "revolutionary" ideas in his cartoons, once he was established in the animated film industry, his goal was to build his own empire. Zipes writes, "[Walt Disney's] close adaptation of fairy tales with patriarchal codes indicate[s] that all the technical experiments would not be used to foster social change in America but to keep power in the hands of individuals like himself, who felt empowered to design and create new worlds."[153] Walt Disney was notoriously unwilling to give credit to his animators in his early films, which, together with compensation issues, led to an embittered labor strike at the company in 1941. Walt Disney "accused the union leaders of being Communists and 'bad seeds.'" At the House Un-American Activities Committee (HUAC) hearings, he testified against the strike organizers as Communists and said "throughout the world all of the Commie groups began smear campaigns against me and my pictures."[154] Walt Disney's political involvement in the HUAC's anticommunist persecutions in the United States might have played a role in the GDR's rejection of Disney cartoons.

Disney tales are designed to promote the status quo of a capitalist society. Class bias is sugarcoated, downplayed, and glossed over amid anthropomorphic cuteness, gags, slapstick, and sentimentality. Conservative views continued even after Walt Disney's death in 1966. For instance, the willing servitude promoted in Disney's *Beauty and the Beast* (1991) would never have been possible in a DEFA fairy-tale film. In "Be Our Guest," Lumière the candlestick sings:

> Why, we only live to serve
> . . .
> Life is so unnerving
> For a servant who's not serving
> He's not whole without a soul to wait upon
> Ah, those good old days when we were useful . . .
> Suddenly those good old days are gone
> Ten years we've been rusting
> Needing so much more than dusting
> Needing exercise, a chance to use our skills!
> Most days we just lay around the castle
> Flabby, fat and lazy
> You walk in and oops-a-daisy!

This subservient mentality warrants a Marxist critique of the Disney ideology, which upholds patriarchal hierarchy and upper-class privilege. Disney's *Beauty and the Beast* negatively codes the revolution as mob violence and has Gaston dressed in red and the beast prince in blue.

In terms of spectatorship, DEFA explicitly advertised its fairy-tale films as targeting both children and adults,[155] whereas Disney animated features appeal primarily to a young audience with adults in tow. A commercial product, Disney films make little effort to cultivate a young audience's critical thinking. As Zipes points out, "The diversion of the Disney fairy tale is geared toward nonreflective viewing. Everything is on the surface, one-dimensional, and we are to delight in one-dimensional portrayal and thinking, for it is adorable, easy, and comforting in its simplicity."[156] With entertainment as his primary goal, Disney constantly reminded his animators to create good gags.[157] In contrast to the nonreflective viewing of Disney pictures, it was common for DEFA filmmakers to discuss their films with schoolchildren and to get their feedback. The serious mission with which DEFA children's films were vested often made them intellectually and psychologically more challenging than those made by Disney. Criticism of DEFA fairy-tale films often resulted from the studio's attempt to address both old and young audiences at the same time.

The two studios show different ideological positions on class, spectatorship, and gender, which this book touches on; they are also positioned differently on themes such as magic, romance, sexuality, and violence. (1) Whereas Disney sells its films with an excess of magic and fantasy, DEFA applies only a moderate dose of magic. In fact, DEFA deemphasizes the role of magic to foreground human agency. (2) Both Disney and DEFA fairy tales are primarily love stories. However, romance dominates every Disney narrative and marriage is often the only goal of the protagonists. DEFA, by contrast, often embeds love stories in larger moral and historical themes such as hard work, women's emancipation, or the peace movement. (3) Although Disney sanitizes traditional fairy tales and provides what is considered safe entertainment for children, the studio's animators do not shy away from making sexual innuendos or doling out violence to the villains. DEFA, by contrast, censors sexuality and violence to an extreme.

In conclusion, DEFA consciously constructed an alternative to Disney. Admittedly, the Disney formula proved commercially successful, but a comparison between DEFA and Disney could reveal what Disney did right and what went awry. The films Disney made are very diverse, and it would therefore be precarious to make broad generalizations here. Disney's films have received much critical attention and are not the subject of this book. This book concentrates on DEFA films and their comparison to original literary versions, with the distinction from Disney becoming implicitly clear.

Overview of Secondary Sources on DEFA Fairy-Tale Films

Books on fairy tales or DEFA films abound, but interdisciplinary scholarship on the intersection of the two is scarce. More research has been carried out by enthusiasts for DEFA children's films in Germany including Joachim Giera, Manfred Hobsch, Christel and Hans Strobel, Klaus Richter-de Vroe, Klaus-Dieter Felsmann, and Dieter Wiedemann. Yet the fairy-tale films are often put in the same category as other children's films. Relatively little research has been attempted at DEFA fairy tales as a unique set in and of itself. In *Zur Stilistik der DEFA-Märchen*, Patricia Kümpel tries to tease out a distinctive aesthetic style of DEFA's fairy-tale films by conducting a formal analysis of the three best-known DEFA classics: *The Cold Heart* (1950), *Little Mook* (1953), and *Three Hazelnuts for Cinderella* (1974). She applies the theories of Vladimir Propp and Max Lüthi and comes to the conclusion that these films fit the narrow definition of fairy tales.[158] Then she does a compelling, detailed look at the three films' *mise en scène*, camera work, editing, sound, special effects, and so on. Kümpel is right to point out the artistic achievements of the films and treat them as aesthetic products. Nevertheless, her approach does not convincingly distinguish DEFA fairy-tale films as unique in any capacity. In addition, her method suffers the same deficiency that any formalist approach to a print tale suffers: it is insufficient to analyze a fairy tale merely by looking at its formal aspects, the mere skeleton of a story.

Hellmuth Häntzsche, the chief pedagogue at DEFA, wrote a few books that provide a useful overview of the feature and television films for children in the GDR (see Works Cited). Ingelore König, Dieter Wiedemann, and Lothar Wolf have published two survey works with critical commentary on DEFA fairy-tale films: *Zwischen Marx und Muck: DEFA-Filme für Kinder* (1996) and *Märchen: Arbeiten mit DEFA-Kinderfilmen* (1998). Frank-Burkhard Habel's *Das große Lexikon der DEFA-Spielfilme* (2000) also provided me with a reliable source for identifying the fairy-tale films. Eberhard Berger and Joachim Giera's *77 Märchenfilme: Ein Filmführer für Jung und Alt* (1990) contains summaries and analyses of fairy-tale films from the GDR, the Soviet Union, the former Czechoslovakia, and Rumania, with important introductory essays to these national fairy-tale film traditions. The DEFA-Foundation recently published a picture-filled survey of these films: *Die DEFA Märchenfilme* (2010).

Critical scholarship in the English language is still very sparse and exists mainly in essay format. In "The First DEFA Fairy Tales: Cold War Fantasies of the 1950s," Marc Silberman investigates the first two, also the most famous, DEFA fairy tales against the historical background of social collapse after World War II and then studies these films as part of the GDR's attempts to mold its youngest citizens in its project of social(ist) renewal. His essay sets a good precedent for discussing these films as imbued with signs of the time. In *The Enchanted Screen*, Jack Zipes briefly discusses DEFA fairy tales within the broad context of fairy-tale films in general and makes an important observation about slave language in these films (see chapter 4). From a historian's perspective, Benita Blessing also works with these films as part of the DEFA children's film corpus by tying them to the GDR cultural politics and socialist–humanist education.[159] Recently Sonja Fritzsche read *The Cold Heart* and *The Devil of Mill Mountain* as mixing the fairy-tale and *Heimat* genres with socialist realism.[160] Daniela Berghahn's essay in *DEFA International* analyzes the British reception of *The Singing Ringing Tree* and its rise to cult status among viewers in the 1960s who watched this "exotic" film on a BBC children's television program.[161] In his introductory book on DEFA cinema, *East German Cinema: DEFA and Film History*, Sebastian Heiduschke includes *Little Mook* as one of his twelve selected films in order to discuss discrete aspects of East German children's films. DEFA fairy-tale films have also been promoted as teaching material in German-language classrooms by Peter Ecke and the DEFA Film Library at the University of Massachusetts Amherst with its teaching guides for three fairy-tale films.[162]

The Marketing of DEFA Fairy-Tale Films

Studying DEFA fairy-tale films, one certainly cannot ignore the political difficulties some films endured to make it to the movie theater. For *The Wooden Calf* (1959/1961), *The Robe* (1961/1991), and *How to Marry a King* (1969), censorship proved obnoxious or even fatal. Being products of collective efforts with additional restraints imposed by the state bureaucracy,

DEFA films are not auteur films in the sense of the New German Cinema.[163] However, film teams had a certain degree of autonomy over their aesthetic choices. Their films were ultimately commercial products and were made with an eye to a global audience. To take Rainer Simon's *How to Marry a King* as an example, in the application from DEFA Außenhandel, the studio's foreign export office, to the HV-Film, one can read the standard questions for distributing the films abroad, including (1) "which countries this film can be sold to" (2) "economic goals in foreign countries" and (3) "suggestions for participation in film festivals." For *How to Marry a King*, the answers were, respectively (1) socialist and capitalist countries, (2) 100,000 East German marks, and (3) Moscow/Gottwaldov and all appropriate youth film festivals.[164]

In the files kept in the federal archives (Bundesarchiv) in Berlin, even the number of viewers in major cities was recorded.[165] Thus the marketing of the films functioned as a commercial leverage to offset political pressures. The cultural functionaries were fully aware that domestic propaganda pieces lacked international appeal. This gave the fairy-tale genre an edge over many other films. The films also profited from a large degree of autonomy for DEFA's filmmakers and artists. What concerned filmmakers were less the ideological issues than the artistic, ethical, and social issues as well as the success of the films with audiences. Therefore, cultural officials had to compromise on certain films such as *How to Marry a King* (see chapter 4) as long as the ideological premise did not noticeably veer away from the party line. They had to admit to the fact that good entertainment would in turn help achieve attendant political goals more effectively than plain propaganda. For the sake of their domestic attendance rates as well as export revenues, the fairy-tale films had to be first and foremost aesthetically attractive, entertaining, and commercially viable. Consequently their fairy-tale character predominated.

All in all, DEFA succeeded in creating a film genre with its own characteristics that was and is universal enough to transcend the GDR. According to Barton Byg, DEFA's "greatest success story has been the distribution of DEFA fairy tales, which in 2000 exceeded the one million mark in total copies sold."[166] Almost all of these films are now available on DVD or at least in VHS format by DEFA's former distributor, the Progress-Film-Verleih, and the commercial home video distributor, Icestorm Entertainment GmbH. It was the catalog of fairy-tale films that motivated the founder of Icestorm, West German businessman Gerhard Sieber, to start a company marketing the vast DEFA film stock. These films were also among the first to be made available, along with the banned films of 1965 and the *Indianerfilme*.[167] This collection of films continues to attract an international audience, despite their leftist tendencies. When West Germans watched DEFA fairy-tale films, they also enjoyed them without noticing anything particularly "socialist." The universal appeal of fairy tales increased the drawing power of these films. Most remarkably, the lasting popularity of these DEFA films in Germany after the *Wende* distinguishes them from other studio films made at the time. Thus both the pre-*Wende* and post-*Wende* reception of the GDR fairy-tale films strongly suggests that these films indeed deserve more attention than they have been given so far.

1

INHERITING THE HUMANIST TRADITION

Subversion of Magic in Early Fairy-Tale Models

For the creators of DEFA fairy-tale films, a fundamental contradiction between the fantastic and the realistic elements of a given tale did not exist. A realist aesthetic was incorporated into their films, despite also containing magic and supernatural powers. This penchant for realism distinguished these films from their nineteenth-century iterations as well as contemporary ones in the West. Magic, that deus ex machina that typically rescues fairy-tale heroes and heroines from adversity, was given less importance than human agency. The first two DEFA fairy-tale films—Paul Verhoeven's *The Cold Heart* (1950) and Wolfgang Staudte's *The Story of Little Mook* (1953)—contain heavy doses of disenchantment. They reject fantastic solutions to the protagonists' real problems, instead emphasizing hard work and virtue as means to achieving a fairy-tale ending. Although a magical world projected on the silver screen is an essential ingredient in DEFA fairy-tale films, the function of magic is cut back to foreground the significance of human action. These films inherit the classical–humanist tradition but do not extricate themselves from the correlated bourgeois trappings, creating tensions between the contemporary need in the GDR to rescind what they labeled the "bourgeois mindset" and the films' ultimate inability to do so. The resultant difference between popular and official reception of these films revealed that merely inheriting the humanist tradition would not be enough for GDR standards. Humanism is not socialism on its own.

The Cold Heart and *Little Mook* are adaptations of Wilhelm Hauff's nineteenth-century literary tales (*Kunstmärchen*). Hauff's tales are, to be sure, very bourgeois in nature and not particularly Marxist, because the working classes should, in the Marxian sense, desire revolution and political agency, rather than simply ascend within (pre)capitalist structures as Hauff's protagonists do.[1] The dual agenda of satisfying contemporary ideological and political needs in the GDR in addition to inheriting a classical heritage resulted in some unique compromises within the adaptations: an admixture of socialist and bourgeois characteristics. For example, the bourgeois desire for material prosperity and the religious subtext in *The Cold Heart* were maintained, but both *The Cold Heart* and *Little Mook* made revisions that introduced socialist characteristics to the bourgeois tales. These included the prerequisite of work for prosperity and the rejection of unlabored wealth. Fairy-tale films, with their purported simplicity, reveal the ideological contradictions and the inherent symbiosis of bourgeois and socialist elements in GDR society.

Although these tales were adapted as an important part of the German cultural heritage, the authorities were nevertheless dismayed that these two films did not sufficiently contribute to the socialist education of children. In retrospect, this is unsurprising because, for its first two fairy-tale films, DEFA hired two directors, Paul Verhoeven and Wolfgang Staudte, who had their primary residence in the West. They were considered in the studio's own taxonomy to be quintessentially "bourgeois artists" (*bürgerliche Künstler*) as opposed to "communist artists" (*Parteikünstler*). Despite being one of the "progressive" artists from the West, even Staudte was mentioned together with other "bourgeois artists."[2] The popularity of DEFA's *The Cold Heart* and *Little Mook*, however, could be explained by the fact that they were made by "bourgeois artists" and hence were not at the mercy of Stalinization in the 1950s the way so many other DEFA films were. It is to be noted that both directors were engaged by UFA during the Nazi era. Hence their films inevitably demonstrated continuities and discontinuities with Nazi cinema.

When Verhoeven was to make *The Cold Heart*, he wanted to absolutely dissociate himself from the "disastrous German children's films of the 1940s with their childish farce (*Kindertümelei*) and their dusty, cheap curtained background."[3] However, aesthetically, his film still remained UFA to the core. Staudte's *Little Mook* contains resemblances to *Münchhausen* (Josef von Báky, 1943), a film that "represents the Third Reich's consummate cinematic achievement."[4] The similarities include the masquerade of blackface, a frame story of first-person tale-telling, oriental exoticism, and miraculous happenings (the speedy messenger in particular). The special effects likewise came from Ernst Kunstmann. Yet, Staudte's film differs from the Nazi adaptation of the same tale—*Little Mook: A Fairy Tale for Big and Small People* (Franz Fiedler, 1944), in which Little Mook is no longer a hunch-backed protagonist but instead an Aryan boy with a flawless appearance.[5]

The Cold Heart was one of only eight films produced by the studio in 1950 and *Little Mook* was one of the only five films DEFA made in 1953.[6] Given the low total number of feature films, DEFA could be said to have accorded the two Hauff adaptations significant attention and resources indeed. Both films did not, however, convince the East German cultural functionaries in the end and were criticized for lacking ideological thrust. My analysis of the films shows the similarities and differences between the films and their literary precedents (*Vorlagen*) to discern what "bourgeois" elements the films inherit and what "prosocialist" revisions they make. The differences are premised on the divergent sociohistorical contexts in which these works were produced. This comparison reveals key characteristics that distinguish DEFA fairy tales from those made in the West.

The two DEFA adaptations have drawn more scholarly attention than the earlier versions of the same tales.[7] In fact, scholarship on DEFA fairy-tale films usually treats only these first two films, since they arguably paved the way for later DEFA fairy-tale filmmaking. They are also repeatedly invoked as "classics" and role models for later DEFA films of this genre, as they garnered international fame for the studio. *The Cold Heart* was watched by almost ten million viewers in cinema and won the award for the best color film in the Sixth International Film Festival Karlovy Vary in Prague in 1951. *Little Mook* claimed a viewership of thirteen million and won recognitions at film festivals in Edinburgh and Montevideo.[8] These films affirmed the value of the fairy-tale tradition to the GDR using a film language accessible to a global audience. They helped remove suspicions of traditional folklore and made it possible for more DEFA fairy-tale films to come. Yet at the same time, the official criticism these films received showed the jarring difference between official and popular opinions at the time. I discuss these films as standing at the beginning of a long DEFA fairy-tale tradition. A look at their production and reception history also reveals the historical and contemporary models to which these films aspired and the societal boundaries they confronted.

But one question arises, namely, why did DEFA initially choose Hauff's tales over those by the Brothers Grimm? After all, the Grimms' tales dominated all later fairy-tale adaptations. Although both Hauff and Grimm collections constituted important parts of the German cultural heritage, the reasons to prefer Hauff in the early postwar years may have been manifold. First of all, the Allies briefly banned the Grimms' tales after the war, because they suspected a causal link between Nazi atrocities and the violence, irrationalism, and nationalism associated with the Grimm collection.[9] Thus DEFA might have been cautious and reluctant about using the Grimms' tales in the immediate postwar years. In addition, Hauff (1802–1827), who died at the early age of twenty-five, lived through the turbulent Napoleonic Wars and their aftermath. He idealistically equated the rich with evil and the poor with good, making his stories the most suitable for overtly Marxist and anticapitalist interpretations.[10]

Another reason could be that, due to the marked social basis for Hauff's tales, they proved more palatable to a socialist–realist reception of the German cultural heritage. According to a reviewer in *Deutsche Filmkunst*, Hauff's fantastic tales "show a strong inclination toward realism, demonstrate in his literary tales likewise his empathy for the simple truth of folk poetry; he knows to combine fantastic happenings organically. Many of his literary tales have taken a permanent place with our *Volk*, entered shared possessions and have actually become folktales."[11] The DEFA veteran fairy-tale film director Walter Beck also points out that the choice of Hauff's tales could be related to the virulent reservations about

Romanticism in the GDR: Hauff's narratives were generally perceived to be more *realistic* than classic romantic fairy tales.[12]

Finally, in a collection of Hauff's stories published a year after Staudte's *Little Mook*, Leopold Magon, a literary scholar, spelled out why DEFA chose to adapt Hauff's tales: "In Hauff's tales, the human definitely stands at the center of the events. This brings Hauff's tales closer to those of the pre-Romantics" that "describe moral behavior and its opposite in an exemplary manner."[13] The centrality of humanity and emancipatory endeavors therefore make these stories representative of the humanist legacy. These reasons perhaps justify why Hauff's tales became the first of their kind to be adapted to the East German screen, despite the fact that his 1827 novel *Jud Süß* (Jew Süss) also provided the template for Veit Harlan's notorious anti-Semitic film *Jud Süß* (1940). This further provokes the questions of whether and how East Germany came to terms with the Holocaust, something that is beyond the scope of the discussion here but has been addressed by scholars such as Thomas C. Fox and Anke Pinkert.

Besides deliberating about which German traditions to keep, DEFA also looked around the world for inspiration. Soviet films were a natural resource in this respect. Films from the Soviet Union were regularly promoted in the GDR both to dismantle "anti-Soviet sentiment" and "nationalistic arrogance" among the German population and to acquaint Germans with "the achievements in Soviet art."[14] According to Thomas Heimann, GDR viewers actually tended to reject propagandistic films from the USSR, especially those made during the war. But they did find acceptable genre films without overt political statements: comedies, fairy tales, and adventure films.[15] Reviewing *The Cold Heart* for *Junge Welt*, János Veiczi commented that DEFA fairy-tale filmmakers should learn technical innovations from the Soviets and emulate their artistic views to capture the humanistic, folksy, and naïve aspects of a fairy tale.[16] Another reviewer remarked that "love of people" and "respect for life" were essential values to take away from Soviet fairy-tale films.[17] Discussing the first two DEFA fairy-tale films, Marc Silberman writes, "As in many other cultural domains, the Soviet model quickly dominated."[18]

Alexander Ptushko's *The Stone Flower* (1946), the first feature-length color film made in the Soviet Union and winner of the prize for best color at Cannes in 1946, was the most enthusiastically received Soviet fairy-tale film in Germany. It was shown in all four occupation zones in Berlin from 11 April 1947 to September 1952 and was seen by over six million people.[19] Thereafter, a great number of Soviet fairy-tale films became popular in the Soviet Occupation Zone and were frequently shown in GDR cinemas.[20] They were also carefully studied, since the DEFA studio desperately needed an idea of what would seem "ideologically correct" to their Soviet friends and superiors, especially given the many West German artists and former UFA employees still working for DEFA. It would be a reassuring strategy to use Soviet films as role models.

Because of the formative influence *The Stone Flower* exerted on the East German cinematic scene, it deserves some attention before discussing its successors *The Cold Heart* and *Little Mook*. What strikes me about *The Stone Flower* is the latent, almost schizophrenic tension found in the film. On the one hand, it complies with the Soviet aesthetic requirement of rejecting formalism (associated with the Mistress of Copper Mountain figure in the film) and endorsing socialist realism through the male protagonist's receptivity to propositions on that particular worldview. On the other hand, the film rehabilitates the Mistress of the Copper Mountain in the end from being a seductive, coercive "witch" figure to a just, mythical goddess, one who has only been testing the protagonist. The film's endorsement of socialist realism thus turns out to be ambiguous in the end. In the form of a fairy tale with its presumed fantasy, Ptushko chose a genre that gave him leeway in observing the mandated state aesthetic. This film genre thus pleased many sides: the filmmakers were gratified with the ability to incorporate their own negotiated values and concerns into the final product, the state was reassured of its symbolic authority, and the populace's need for entertainment and distraction was addressed.

An Ambiguous Model of Socialist Realism: *The Stone Flower* (1946)

At the beginning of *The Stone Flower*, a group of kids from a factory town in the Urals come to Grandpa Slyshko at a late hour and beg him for a fairy tale. Initially, the elderly man scoffs at the idea, since fairy tales are only told by elderly women, and these kids are too old for that anyway. He nevertheless relents to the kids' insistence and is willing to tell them the story of a young malachite stone carver named Danila. Danila's story, he clarifies, is not a fairy tale but belongs to Russian folklore. This somewhat wordy and contrived beginning makes the distinction between fairy tales and folk narratives, reflecting the debate over folklore and literary fairy tales in the Soviet Union at the time.[21] Ptushko's *The Stone Flower* is based primarily on Pavel Petrovich Bazhov's "The Stone Flower" and "The Master Craftsman" in *Malakhitovaia shkatulka* (Malachite Casket: Tales from the Urals, 1944), which merges the realistic depiction of workers' hard lives with the fantastic mythological world of the prerevolutionary Urals. *Malachite Casket* was awarded the Stalin Prize. According to Marina Balina, Bazhov insisted that his collected tales belonged to the genre of the tale (*skaz*), not the fairy tale (*skazka*), and *skaz* puts its emphasis on history and its closeness to the historical song or *bylina*—an epic form of Russian oral folklore.[22] As Jack Zipes notes, *The Stone Flower* makes it clear that "if fairy tales were to be adapted and produced in the Soviet Union, they would have to be *new* kinds of fairy tales based on folklore of the people and the works of progressive writers. . . . [Children] were to listen to the deeply rooted folk tales told by wise men and to follow the examples of the protagonists that these wise men presented."[23]

At the end of his story, Granddad Slyshko says that the story is not that simple—indeed deceptively simple—and the children should use their little brains to figure out what it means: "The most powerful thing is your skill and human thought." The frame narrative recreates a storytelling setting and highlights the didactic purpose of folklore. The emphasis on "skill and human thought" reflects the socialist–humanist ideal of fully developed human beings who are in command of both their physical and intellectual capacities. Its stark divisions between the corporeal and the intellectual could be seen in capitalism as well, as Fritz Lang's *Metropolis* (1927) famously illustrates: the capitalist is allegorized as the Head, the workers as the Hand. Anchored in the capitalist ideology, Lang's film articulates a belief in capitalism's potential for a liberal reform in which, through a mediator figure, the Hand and the Head would eventually reconcile. Yet the Hand in this model still remains the Hand. Whereas Lang's anticommunist film pleads the case of a humane capitalism, the Soviet film implicitly proposes a contrasting solution that would emancipate the Hand: the Head and the Hand should become one and exist as dual qualities in each and every worker.

Within the framed narrative of Grandpa's story, the male protagonist Danila's perfectionist attempt to make "living" art (mis)leads him to enter into a Faustian bargain with the Mistress of the Copper Mountain. The Mistress first appears in the shape of a lizard and promises him the stone flower, at the sight of which he would be able to realize his dream of making "living" art; he would understand what real beauty is. Unsatisfied with his "lifeless" work, Danila abandons his bride-to-be Katya in the midst of their betrothal celebrations for the seductive Mistress. Katya remains faithful to Danila and comes to the mountain in search of him. Their love for each other withstands the test given by the Mistress—as is revealed in the end. The two lovers return from the mountain, and the film ends symbolically with them walking toward a bright future in the form of a rising sun.

In featuring an exemplary artist, the film provokes a discussion about art and what is meant by "living" art. In the film, when the landowner's wife commissions Danila to carve a floral vase, his teacher, the elderly malachite craftsman Prokopyich, says, "Who will see it in the master's mansion? Only the masters themselves and their servants, that's all." Danila counters, "The stone lives a long time. If those who live now don't see, those who come later will." This perhaps explains what Danila means by "living" art. Contemporary times, in his view, are of secondary importance to art. On the contrary, great art is self-sustaining, apolitical, and reaches posterity. For him, the reception of art can be postponed, as it can outlive the moment of its creation. This shows that Danila is initially a believer in *l'art pour l'art*, or art for art's sake,[24] an idea originating in the nineteenth century and making very different use of art than socialist realism does.

In addition to *l'art pour l'art*, the film implicitly engages with the formalism debate of the day. During Stalin's campaign to purge other literary and artistic currents and to instrumentalize culture for political ends, formalism—with its attention to ornamental form, techniques of composition, and constructivist approach—was condemned as "the departure of art from the people," "the degeneration of art," and "a deadly enemy of *narodnost'* in art."[25] The term "*narodnost*'" "has an exceptionally wide semantic range: it could mean accessibility and comprehensibility, simplicity, antielitism, but also organic development, traditionalism, folklore-based principles of creativity, and so forth."[26] Art in the Soviet Union acquired meaning only when it was available to the public and enjoyed by the common people. Formalism with its "devices of labored form in language and in composition" was censured to "arrive at senseless, 'subjectless,' formless, imprecise language or at language window-dressing, cheap beauty that lacquers reality."[27] It was said to prioritize artistic creativity over content and ideological tasks and was thus to be repudiated during the Stalinization of Soviet culture in the 1930s. In the GDR, formalism was likewise accused of being out of touch with the common people, as seen in the formalism debate that reached its apex in January 1951.[28]

Danila's individualistic striving and his initial focus on the aesthetic, formal, and atemporal aspects of a work of art make him precisely a formalist, bourgeois artist. In the film, formalism is associated with the Mistress of Copper Mountain and symbolized by the stone flower that, with special effect, seems to come alive with a dazzling beaming aura. In a strictly utilitarian sense, the stone flower as art in its secluded space in the mountains does not yield any use value to the people. It "makes one forget about earthly things" and has Danila betray his fiancée and abandon his ailing teacher, thus depriving him of humanity.

Yet during the tale, Danila's artistic views undergo a transformation. While working on his huge stone vase in the mountain, Danila realizes that he can derive "no joy from this work" because "people will never see it" (see Figure 1.1). Producing art that is sheltered away in a vault contradicts his newly gained belief in the necessary social relevance of his work. He now rejects private and elitist ownership of art and embraces the idea of its democratization. Symbolizing this repudiation of formalism, he rejects the sexual advances of the Mistress of Copper Mountain and becomes desperate to return to the outside world. The film suggests the conversion of Danila into a socialist artist who believes that art should be functional, be politicized, and above all appeal to and serve its own time and the common good. The end of the film implicitly signifies the people

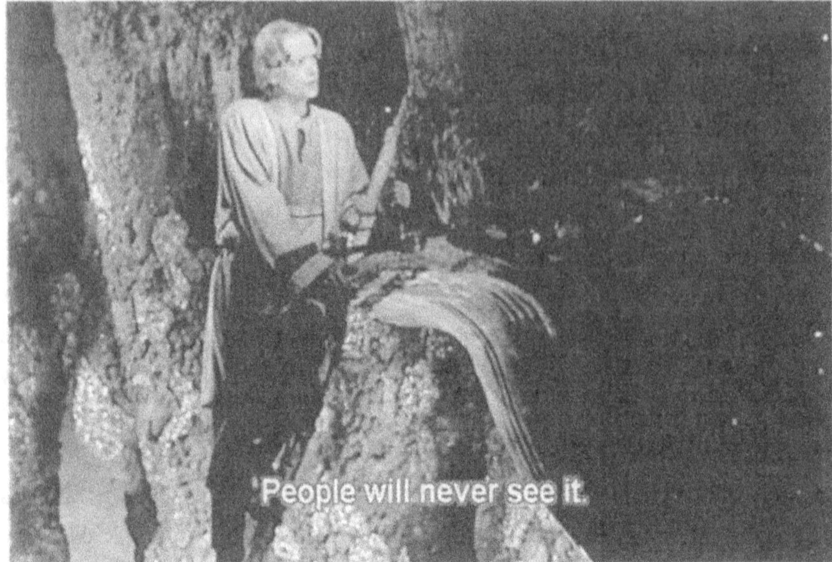

FIGURE 1.1. *The Stone Flower* screenshot: Danila loses interest in working on the stone vase, realizing that "people will never see it."

welcoming the artist back into their midst as he returns from his self-chosen exile during his pursuit of artistic perfection.

In another twist, the film leaves open whether or not Danila actually does embrace socialist realism after he emerges from the depth of the mountain. To the viewers' presumed surprise, the Mistress of Copper Mountain reveals in the very end that she has only been testing Danila.[29] Although the tales seemed to conform to socialist realism and Bazhov's *Malachite Casket* even won the Stalin Prize, a subversive layer of the tales hid behind a safe façade in this genre. According to Mark Lipovetsky, Bazhov wrote the majority of the tales from January 1937 to early 1938, the peak of the Great Terror, when Bazhov lived in seclusion to escape arrest. Bazhov was once an active member of the Socialist–Revolutionary Party—a former ally of the Bolsheviks, but he was forced into opposition and outlawed in 1918—and for this he had been expelled once from the Bolshevik Party in 1933 (his membership was later restored).[30] Bazhov's enormously popular tales were actually written as a mechanism of physical and mental escape from the Soviet Union of the 1930s into the prerevolutionary Urals mining area. The Mistress of Copper Mountain consistently assaults the authorities in Bazhov's written tales.[31] Hence, the mythological world of the Mistress of Copper Mountain became a defiant countermodel to the mundane Soviet authorities.

Analyzing Bazhov's *Skazy*, Lipovetsky interprets the Mistress of Copper Mountain as "a powerful alternative to the grand narrative of Soviet nationalism."[32] Ptushko's *The Stone Flower* supports Lipovetsky's observation of the Mistress being an antiauthoritarian figure. At the beginning of the film, an elderly woman who prepares herbal medicine for the elderly malachite craftsman has a brief altercation with the cruel foreman of the factory.

> **Elderly woman:** What a cruel man you are!
>
> **Foreman:** Stop, you old witch.
>
> **Elderly woman:** We will find a way to stop you.
> The Mistress of Copper Mountain has long had
> her eye on you.
>
> **Foreman:** I will have you banished to Siberia
> for your witchery.
>
> **Elderly woman:** Siberia is far away, and death is near.
> It won't overlook anybody. She will get you too.

Because the elderly woman knows herbal medicine, the foreman calls her a witch. She believes in the Mistress of Copper Mountain as a deity that metes out justice and reminds the foreman that he cannot outdo death even if he seems powerful. From this dialogue, the viewer can see that Ptushko—as well as Bazhov, who was involved in the film script—used the Mistress as a mystic authority whom ordinary Soviet citizens could invoke to defy authorities. Such antiauthoritarianism was not seen as subversive by cultural bureaucrats, apparently owing to the prerevolutionary period the tales are set in and the fairy-tale language.

The world of the Mistress of Copper Mountain exists in direct opposition to the real world and realism itself. Danila's choice of the real world over the mystic world could be read as rejecting the fantastic in favor of socialist–realist values. This complies with dominant Soviet cultural politics. However, the final revelation of the Mistress as only testing the young couple redeems the Mistress as a benevolent goddess. As a departing gift, she gives Katya a box for her loyalty and lets Danila keep the skills he has acquired: "And you, Danilushka, for your firmness, you will never lose your knowledge that you have learned here." Danila still needs to keep where he has been a secret and cannot tell others about her treasures. The ultimate authority conferred on the Mistress results in the film's ambivalent stance toward both formalism and socialist realism. The knowledge Danila secretly brings from the Mistress does not seem to conform to the demands of the real world. It is doubtful that Danila is going to become a bona fide socialist–realist artist. *The Stone Flower* is deceptively simple. The inherent contradictions demanded of art at the time and the lack of a clear contour of socialist realism might account for the ambiguity in the film.

On the surface, the film pays its dues to socialist realism. It depicts a hero from the people—in this case, Danila—who stands out as an exemplary worker. With Danila's apparent transformation, it emphasizes the didactic, moral, and utilitarian functions of art. Socialist realism also shows through the film's ideologically motivated portrayals of the factory owners and serfs, anticipating similar class-specific images in DEFA fairy-tale films. Although *The Stone Flower* does not focus on class struggle, the film indicates the need for it by depicting social injustice and oppression. The lower class is portrayed as hard working, virtuous, and talented—Prokopyich and Danila are the examples—while the upper class is merciless, parasitic, greedy, and stingy. Represented by the factory owner and his family, they are dependent on the lower class's talents but do not properly reward them. The owner receives half a million francs for the malachite box that Danila has carved but pays him only a few coins. Yet only superficially does the film give credence to socialist realism. By reversing the image of the Mistress and reinstating her authority over Danila, director Ptushko inserts a subversive note about contemporary times, thanks to the fairy-tale façade. Due to the prerogative that Soviet films enjoyed in the GDR, *The Stone Flower* and other films like it were not heavily scrutinized by either Soviet or East German functionaries, and thus they were spared critique and official derision.

Another contradiction lies in the film's portrayal of gender. The depiction of Katya combines patriarchal family values with the socialist image of the strong female worker.[33] At first, she is a demure heroine who patiently but vainly waits for her lover to come to their rendezvous. She bears no grudge and is even delighted when Danila reveals that the reason for his nonappearances is that he is carving a vase modeled on the flower she gave him. She remains faithful to Danila and brushes aside rumors that he is dead after his unannounced disappearance into Serpent Hill to see the stone flower. While Danila is gone, she dutifully nurses Danila's teacher, who is dying. In the process, however, she also acquires confidence and independence. Against convention, she learns the traditionally male craft from the elderly master carver and lives self-sufficiently as the new "master" of stone craft. The film contains an interesting role reversal in that Danila becomes, so to speak, a "damsel in distress" and cannot escape the sexually ensnaring Mistress of the Copper Mountain. Unlike most fairy tales, in which it is the man who comes to rescue the helpless maiden, in this case it is Katya who saves Danila from his entrapment. The ambiguous portrayal of Katya reflects the contradictions of the Stalinist Soviet Union: the socialist advocacy for women's emancipation on the one hand and the persistence of patriarchal practices in society on the other.

The Stone Flower was repeatedly evoked as a yardstick for measuring the quality of DEFA fairy-tale films. It was a highly revered masterpiece, and its influence was multifaceted and far-reaching. Jack Zipes mentions folkloric sources, class antagonism, lower-class protagonists, antielitist views of art, and a storytelling frame narrative as setting the political parameters for filmmakers in Stalinist postwar years.[34] Sonja Fritzsche observes the influence *The Stone Flower* exerts on *The Cold Heart* from the *Heimat* perspective. She points out that *The Stone Flower* places great visual emphasis on the Ural Mountains as *Heimat* and features the local identity and customs such as folksongs, folk dance, a traditional wedding ceremony, and traditional handicrafts.

In addition, I note a few more influences of *The Stone Flower* on DEFA. First, the live-action format paved the way for DEFA to make a serious case for *Realfilme* as a convincing format for fairy tales. Second, *The Stone Flower* does not depict a heroic and selfless working-class protagonist but, instead, a fallible one who undergoes a transformation during the course of the film. Third and also most important, the film posits its attitude toward magic as subordinate to human and real solutions. At the start of these early Eastern bloc fairy-tale films—*The Stone Flower* as well as *The Cold Heart* and *Little Mook*—magical interventions seem to provide answers to the problems the protagonists face: the Mistress of Copper Mountain initially offers what appears the only solution to Danila's dilemma, as the stone heart is to Peter's, and the magic slippers and the magic stick are to Little Mook's. Yet fantastic solutions are revealed to be temporary and even destructive. All these narratives ultimately reject fantastic solutions to real issues, making the films *countertales*. They offer a different interpretation of success and wealth than what the protagonists initially understood them to be, revealing the false consciousness of the protagonists and generating a moral that would prove ideologically sound in the GDR of the early 1950s. In this way, the fairy-tale film moves from enchantment to disenchantment or estrangement, an important strategy in socialist–humanist adaptations.

Jack Zipes points out that Grimms' fairy tales contain subversion of magic: "The *magic* fairy tales of the Grimms were designed by them as literary products to put an end to magic (*deus ex machina*, good fairies, supernatural luck, spells)—perhaps first even told by others with this end in mind—and to establish the significance of cunning and rational enlightenment."[35] I argue that DEFA fairy tales continued to prioritize "cunning and rational enlightenment" over magic as a plausible solution to conflict. This is not to say that all the films end with disenchantment. Rather, to further use Max Weber's terminology: some films conclude with "reenchantment," an enchantment that does not merely repeat the enchantedness at the beginning of the film but rather occurs after trials and tribulations, maturation, and transformation.[36] In *The Stone Flower*, the moment of reenchantment appears when the Mistress of Copper Mountain reveals her true intention and in *The Cold Heart* when the Little Glass Man revives Peter's wife.

The Stone Flower implicitly addressed contemporary issues—here formalism vis-à-vis socialist realism. *The Cold Heart* and *Little Mook* also incorporated their filmmakers' deep concerns about the present. Yet *The Cold Heart* and *Little Mook* had to face issues that *The Stone Flower* did not. Hauff's tales are, in essence, very *bourgeois*. They entail the typical folk and fairy-tale trajectory, which starts with a lower-class protagonist wishing for good fortune and concludes with him attaining riches and higher social standing through magical intervention. The prior bourgeois character of the tales proved to be hard to reconcile with the aesthetic demands of socialist realism, resulting in official dissatisfaction with these pictures. *The Cold Heart* and *Little Mook* also directly inherited the UFA tradition. *The Cold Heart* is a transitional piece between UFA and DEFA. Aesthetically, it continued more of the UFA tradition, but ideologically it subscribed to the Soviet and prosocialist views of work, wealth, and magic. Similarly, *Little Mook* also contains a lot of elements known from *Münchhausen*. Whereas Soviet influence on DEFA fairy-tale filmmaking is definitely palpable, the DEFA pictures still appear very *German*.

Wealth Is Incompatible with Humanity: *The Cold Heart* (1950)

The Cold Heart was the first noteworthy German fairy-tale film adaptation of a classic tale.[37] The film was also significant because of its introduction of color, its violence, its West–East crossovers, and its inherited tropes from *The Stone Flower*. Wolff von Gordon, then DEFA's chief dramaturge before he lost the position due to his political impartiality, suggested adapting Hauff's tale. He sought an adaptation "for our time . . . as a story about the blessing of work and the curse of money . . . in romantic pictures of the German fairy-tale world."[38] After the originally selected director, Erich Engel, left DEFA due to the studio's default on payment for his prior work,[39] the studio invited Paul Verhoeven from Munich to direct the milestone film in his stead. Verhoeven had been originally slated to film "Aschenbrödel" (Cinderella) as a ballet, a project that fell through due to it being too similar to Michael Powell and Emeric Pressburger's lauded British film *The Red Shoes* (1948). Verhoeven was valued for his experience directing the Agfacolor film *Das kleine Hofkonzert* (The Little Court Concert, 1945). Based on his as well as cinematographer Bruno Mondi's prior experience with color, DEFA entrusted them with the GDR's first color film in the postwar period, right on the heels of the first West German color film *Schwarzwaldmädel* (The Black Forest Girl, Hans Deppe, 1950).[40]

The DEFA-Kommission, which was then tasked to oversee all film productions for their ideological utility, came to the following evaluation of the original script: "The present script has been approved, but its 'petit-bourgeois character' is to be criticized. Changes must be made so that 'the ideas about solidarity of the workers and hope for a better world come to the fore.'"[41] This recommendation for the yet to be made film captured the political parlance of the day and highlighted the dilemma of film adaptations of still fundamentally bourgeois tales. Both *The Cold Heart* and *Little Mook* did not exactly depict the exemplary, positive heroes that the party had in mind in the early 1950s, and the films were criticized despite their overall popularity with audiences.

The Cold Heart is set in the Black Forest, where the dominant trades have traditionally been glassblowing and woodcutting. Each trade is associated with a supernatural guardian: the benevolent, angelic, leprechaun-like Little Glass Man (Paul Bildt) for the honest and hardworking glassblowers and the devilish Dutch Michael (Erwin Geschonneck) for the greedy, capitalistic lumberjacks. Peter Munk (Lutz Moik), the protagonist, resents his lowly status as a charcoal burner and aspires to the status and wealth of the merchant class. As a child born under a lucky star on Sunday, he manages to conjure up the Little Glass Man who grants him three wishes, two of which can be immediately fulfilled. Instead of wishing for wit, he wishes for a glassblowing hut that he knows nothing about and the same amount of money as the richest man in town, Ezekiel (Paul Esser). But Peter's gambling addiction and his ignorance about glasswork quickly put him in debt. Although he has magical pockets that always replenish themselves with the same amount of money as Ezekiel's, he lacks the foresight to see that he would end up with not a cent as soon as Ezekiel's pockets became empty. When he is suddenly penniless, Peter is believed to have cheated at gambling and is therefore at the threat of being arrested as a wizard and burned at the stake. This drives him to abandon his bride Lisbeth (Hanna Rucker) on their wedding day and strike a pact with the villainous Dutch Michael. Dutch Michael implants in Peter a stone heart in exchange for his human heart (see Figure 1.2). Peter then marries Lisbeth and enters the woodcutting business like Ezekiel. His stone heart enables him to accumulate wealth quickly and ruthlessly. His wake-up call comes when he strikes his wife dead for helping a beggar, who is really the Little Glass Man in disguise. Seeing his true remorse, the leprechaun fulfills his third wish: to revive his dead

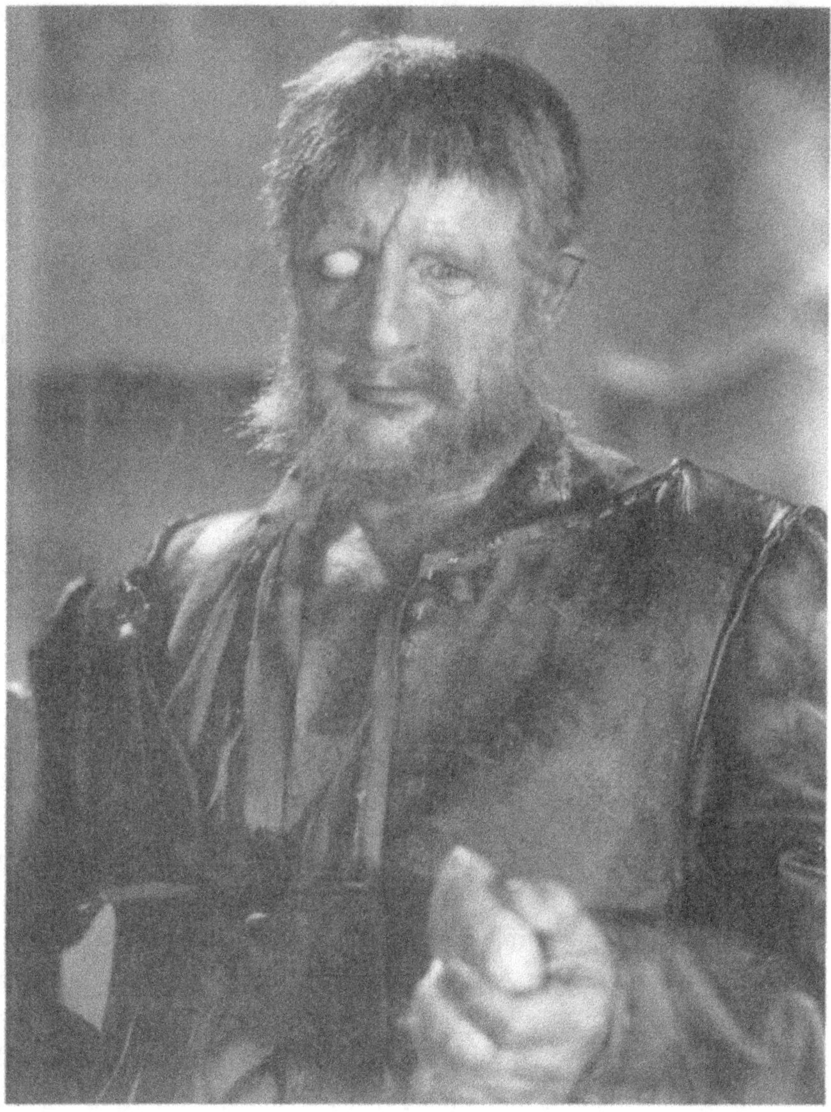

FIGURE 1.2. *Das kalte Herz*: Dutch Michael (Erwin Geschonneck) holding a stone heart. © DEFA-Stiftung, Erich Kilian.

wife. But before that, Peter has to regain his heart back from Dutch Michael, which he does with the Little Glass Man's help. Like Danila, Peter remains loyal to his working-class roots in the end and happily rejoins the workforce from which he has temporarily alienated himself.

In *Wilhelm Hauff: Mit Selbstzeugnissen und Bilddokumenten*, Ottmar Hinz argues that the severe economic crisis of 1825–1826 in southern and central Germany provided the social background for Hauff's portrayal of Peter Munk. Germany's petit bourgeoisie and educated middle class increasingly feared the unfettered onslaught of industrialization (represented by Dutch Michael) and thus sought refuge in restorative economic concepts (represented by the Little Glass Man).[42] The tale criticizes wealthy members of the upper class as possessing hearts of stone. Their real, organic hearts are in Dutch Michael's vault. As part of the nouveau riche, Peter relentlessly accumulates money. In icy winter, he evicts families who cannot pay rent. He forbids his wife to show kindness to the poor, and he counts his wealth every night. He even abandons his mother (Lotte Loebinger) to the point of starvation.

The film portrays a more hardened Peter by actually grafting the original story of Dutch Michael onto that of Peter. Hauff's version contains a tale about Dutch Michael, which Peter hears from an elderly woodcutter. In this tale within the tale, the physically robust Michael was once in the service of a rich timber merchant of the Black Forest, maneuvering rafts skillfully down the Rhine. But he deceives his master by selling the logs at a higher price in Amsterdam, instead of in Cologne. He makes himself and his men rich and sees to it that the honest man who disagreed with them is sold to the owner of a rotten ship as a slave.[43] The film attributes these crimes to Peter to give him a fuller story. In Hauff's version, Peter finds out the undesirable effects of a stone heart very soon, in that despite his wealth, he is unable to enjoy life. He asks Dutch Michael for his old heart back, a request that is declined. Hauff's Peter still remembers the past and nostalgically longs for his own heart, which makes his eventual repentance more convincing than in the film, in which he never shows any regret regarding his deal with Dutch Michael. Thus, by stripping the capitalistic Peter of all humanity, the final turnaround in the film appears unconvincing, for how could the stone heart even feel remorse after its owner kills his wife?

In many traditional folktales, as well as literary tales such as Hauff's, the preoccupation with wealth is a trait not only of the upper class but also of the lower class. The distinction is often made that the upper class's wealth is unjustified and the lower class's desire for wealth is legitimate due to obvious disparities between labor and compensation. While these tales generally depict wish fulfillment for the lower class, the desire of the members of the lower class for wealth is fulfilled only temporarily in *The Cold Heart*, because how that wish is fulfilled is both undesirable and unethical. Peter learns firsthand how wealth excludes compassion. After his experiences as an "insider" in the rich men's camp, he affirms his original way of living and happily resumes where he left off. At the end of Hauff's story, Peter "was an honest, industrious man. He was content with what he had, worked hard at his trade, and so it came about by his own efforts he became prosperous and was respected and loved all over the Black Forest."[44]

Hauff asserts, perhaps not very convincingly, that Peter *remains a charcoal burner* and manages to work his way up to *prosperity* anyway. His lower-class dream of becoming rich and admired is realized by hard labor alone. His rather bourgeois aspirations are fulfilled neither by magical means nor by a change of heart but by his own hands. In other words, the solution to poverty is self-reliance, and this is the moralistic message of the tale: "It's better to be content with a little than to have great riches and a cold heart."[45] This comforts the lower class by suggesting that the poor are happier and live more fulfilling lives than the rich. A real-life Peter would probably not experience upward social mobility. He would end where he started, only with higher moral convictions: he would rather remain a good-hearted and hard-working person than become upper class and lose his moral compass. This could be seen as the inherent conservatism of Hauff's story, which encourages people like Peter to set limits on their wishes and know their place in society. In this light, the tale aims to pacify the lower class and appears moralistic at best—reactionary and fatalistic at worst. Such a message explains why some critics "rejected [the tales] as the flawed reflection of Hauff's petty bourgeois and philistine spirit."[46]

In addition, Hauff's tale has a strong Christian message that, despite the removal of Christian vocabulary, is still present in the largely faithful DEFA adaptation.[47] The Christian moral of Hauff's story is that one should primarily concern oneself with not earthly wealth but one's soul and afterlife. When Peter expresses his initial discontent to the Little Glass Man, the latter answers, "What good does it do them to seem fortunate for a few years, and be all the unhappier for it afterwards?"[48] When the godless Peter strikes his wife dead, the Little Glass Man rebukes him instead of punishing him with death: "What good would it do me to bring the mortal part of you to the gallows? It's not earthly justice that you need fear, but other and sterner powers, for you have sold your soul to the Evil One!"[49] In Hauff's version, Peter should also "pray as hard as ever he could" to overcome Dutch Michael's evil powers in the end. In line with communist atheism, the film eliminates all these references to religion. Nonetheless, the Christian message is preserved with the constellation of the angelic Little Glass Man and the devilish Dutch Michael, who compete over Peter's heart and soul.

The film also implicitly evokes the religious notion of Heaven and Hell, when Ezekiel tells Peter what would happen to their hearts: "I once asked my school teacher. He said that dead people's hearts are weighed. The light ones rise, the heavy ones sink. I think our stones will be pretty heavy. But we've got lots of time 'till then."[50] The fact that DEFA, in this case through Verhoeven, quite faithfully adapted "The Cold Heart" suggests that the GDR not only carried on the humanist tradition but also inherited, consciously or subconsciously, the very bourgeois and religious elements that it intended to criticize. When DEFA recruited a West German director from Munich, it ended up dealing with a more religious and, aesthetically, UFA-style film. West German influences were increasingly abhorred in the course of the 1950s, as shown in the cases of state censorship of West German–directed DEFA productions: *The Singing Ringing Tree* (Francesco Stefani, 1957), *Spielbank-Affäre* (Murder in the Casino, Arthur Pohl, 1957), *Meine Frau macht Musik* (My Wife Makes Music, Hans Heinrich, 1958), and *Die Schönste* (The Most Beautiful, Ernesto Remani, 1957/2002).[51]

Apparently it was neither the bourgeois nor religious character of Hauff's tales that appealed to DEFA. On the contrary, it was the anticapitalist critique of greed and inhumanity that made the tales attractive. Analogous to the incompatibility of humanity with Danila's heightened aesthetic sensibility in *The Stone Flower*, *The Cold Heart* demonstrates that capitalistic pursuit of wealth is equally incompatible. In the East German context, the message that a person can only better his economic situation with his own hands appeared as "politically correct." The film teaches East

Germans to work hard and improve their lives through honest means. It implies the right way for a citizen, as well as for the new country, to earn respect from others is to adhere to socialist ideals. As long as "Peters" in the GDR maintained their humanity, their bourgeois dream of achieving wealth served the GDR's national interests.

In a way, *The Cold Heart* answered the SED's demand for cultural production to assist the fulfillment of the Two-Year Plan. In October 1948 in a meeting on the topic of "The Two-Year Plan and the Artists," Alexander Abusch, the vice-president of the Cultural Alliance (Kulturbund) and a key figure in the SED's Central Committee, postulated that cultural workers should become propagandists of the Plan and make the "revolutionary role of work" clear to GDR workers at large.[52] As mentioned earlier, the DEFA-Kommission approved the script of *The Cold Heart* on the condition that the film team make changes that foreground what work would bring for the future. The film's new ending, in which Peter is no longer a charcoal burner as in Hauff but joins the collective of loggers, apparently responds to that request. Peter and Lisbeth then run into an open field, similar to the final scene in *The Stone Flower*, in which Danila and Katya walk toward the rising sun. Personal happiness is shown as tied in with one's honest work and contributions to society.

The film version gives Lisbeth a larger role than the original story does, in which she "was said to be an excellent housekeeper, and she never stepped on to the dance floor, not even at Easter." Hauff considers such a traditional woman the "paragon of the Black Forest."[53] In the film, by contrast, Lisbeth is a veritable queen of dance. Obviously religious condemnation of dance as sinful no longer held true in East Germany. Foregrounding dance also helped distinguish its socialist nature and prefigured the presence of dance in later DEFA fairy-tale and other feature films. The image of Lisbeth is a mixed one of independence and obedience: on the one hand, she defies her uncle, rejects the well-to-do king of dance and prefers the good-natured charcoal burner; on the other hand, after her public humiliation by Peter's absence from the wedding, she, like Katya in *The Stone Flower*, patiently and loyally waits for her lover. Later, she quietly suffers from her husband's coldheartedness. Despite the domestic violence that kills her, she forgives him without a word after she is revived and is just glad that her "lost" husband has returned. Whereas Lisbeth appears only very late in Hauff's story, she is introduced at the very beginning of the film. In this way, the DEFA adaptation revises the tale into a love story between Peter and Lisbeth. It is out of love for Lisbeth that Peter is ashamed of his social status and resorts to magic. Likewise, it is out of love for Peter that Lisbeth quietly endures the cruelty of the new capitalistic Peter. In the end, it is the power of love that wrests Peter from the deadly temptations of fame, wealth, and power—things that, according to the film, do not bring real happiness. The film ultimately celebrates love and family, hard work, and true wealth.

The GDR audience had high expectations for *The Cold Heart*, especially in light of Soviet fairy-tale successes in the GDR such as *The Stone Flower*.[54] *The Cold Heart* was also well received among general viewers. Reviews praised its aesthetic quality, film technique, acting, costume design, special effects, and so forth. Ernst Kunstmann created the special effects in this film, including using the Schüfftan process to change the size of the two supernatural beings. The mask of Dutch Michael was often mentioned for its creativeness.[55] The combination of location and studio shooting in *The Cold Heart* prefigured the common method used to make films of this genre. This is significant in terms of audience reception because location shooting allowed DEFA fairy-tale films to showcase many natural or cultural sites of the *Heimat*, conceived in a broader sense beyond just a socialist *Heimat*. A number of historical castles and fortresses in the GDR, as well as the Thuringian hills and forest, offered authentic fairy-tale–like backdrops for live-action fairy-tale films. *The Cold Heart* bears many signs of state-approved cultural filmmaking.

Yet *The Cold Heart* met with strong criticism because of gory visuals that seemed to undermine the goal of socialist–humanist education. For example, *Neues Deutschland*, the official organ of the SED, published a review criticizing horror scenes in Dutch Michael's bloody torture chamber, where the pounding and twitching hearts of the rich people are hanging on the wall and the pool is boiling blood with horrible gurgling noises.[56] Co-workers in the studio also spoke of the film's "visual cruelty" as well as the "bloodthirsty torture chamber."[57] Whereas the heart transplant remains allegorical in Hauff, the film actually visualizes it. The "naturalistic" depiction of Peter's murder of his wife with blood streaming down her forehead was another example of what the reviewers cited as gratuitous violence.[58] Reviewers often made a point of praising films that did not fall for naturalistic depictions, criticizing them if they did. In *Kinderfilm in Europa*, Steffen Wolf explained why the GDR abhorred naturalism in cultural productions by contrasting the concept with socialist realism: "Naturalism only shows the negative side and the decay of the bourgeois society, yet through its hopelessness it actually propagates submission to the rule of capitalism. In contrast, socialist realism directs its focus on the new, the growing, the positive side of life: positive in the sense of struggling for peace, unity, democracy, national sovereignty, and socialism."[59] The GDR's rejection of naturalism also had a Soviet origin because a campaign against formalism and naturalism was waged in the Soviet Union in 1936.[60] Starting in 1948, "naturalistic exaggeration" was repudiated in favor of realism in the GDR.[61]

Some reviewers considered this film superior to fairy-tale films produced in the West. The color technique was praised as surpassing that of the American film industry, and the special effects were considered worthy of a classic.[62] At the same time, reviewers observed characteristics similar to those found in Western films. Reviewing for *National-Zeitung*, G. H. compared the similarly excessive representation of cruelty in *The Cold Heart* and Walt Disney's *Snow White and the Seven Dwarfs* and how it marred the joy one could have otherwise derived from the latter.[63] Jean Cocteau's *La Belle et la Bête* (Beauty and the Beast, 1946) was repeatedly mentioned as a counterexample to Soviet fairy-tale models, and unfortunately *The Cold Heart* ostensibly showed the same "veiled attraction to the neurotic"[64] and "demoralized," "decadent" traits.[65] The critique of Cocteau's film in the GDR differed from the critical acclaim it received in the West.[66] The surrealist, black-and-white cinematography of *Beauty and the Beast*, with bodiless arms holding candelabra or pouring wine and smoke-breathing caryatids following the passersby with rolling eyes, appeared too uncanny for socialist cinema.

The symbolic plotline offers itself up to Freudian or Jungian interpretations, but such readings were unbefitting GDR viewers. DEFA responded to official and media criticism of *The Cold Heart* by removing the most criticized scenes, such as the spring bubbling with blood in Dutch Michael's cave.[67] Since Verhoeven was West German, reviewers probably felt more justified in explaining the film's undesirable traits as of Western imprint. Scholars have also pointed out that *The Cold Heart* employed cinematography and acting similar to those of UFA films of the 1940s, especially the revue and the *Heimat* films.[68] The director was also criticized for refusing to sign the Stockholm Peace Appeal because all artists working for DEFA were expected to commit themselves to the cause of peace and progress without reservation.[69] The film thus remained Verhoeven's only collaboration with DEFA. In addition, the high production cost of 3.2 million East German marks exacerbated the acute financial difficulties DEFA was facing, and the production director, Fritz Klotzsch, lost his job as a result. This inherited UFA extravaganza was not permitted to continue, and *The Cold Heart*, although often evoked as a model to be emulated by later DEFA fairy-tale filmmakers, would remain unique and unparalleled in terms of its grand-scale sets, festive crowd scenes, and exquisite costumes.

Although in retrospect *The Cold Heart* was a rare cinematic gem, it attracted as much—if not more—criticism as praise at the time of its release. Critics pointed out that the film should have modeled itself after Soviet fairy-tale films such as *The Stone Flower*, which created "a simple folk-song atmosphere."[70] One reviewer commented that DEFA fairy-tale filmmakers should not only learn technical innovations from the Soviets but also emulate their artistic views to capture the humanistic, folksy, and naïve aspects of a fairy tale.[71] Another reviewer remarked that "love of people" and "respect for life" were essential values to take away from Soviet fairy-tale films.[72] Marc Silberman also obeserves that the Soviet model soon dominated the GDR's cultural production.[73] *The Cold Heart* was in any case held up to Soviet ideological and aesthetic precedents and was apparently found wanting.

Despite the limitations of the genre, a fairy-tale film like *The Cold Heart* still addressed contemporary audiences and their concerns. The popular success of the film attests to the resonance it achieved with postwar yearnings for recovery, prosperity, and happiness. The viewers could identify with poor Peter Munk and his dream of becoming wealthy like the West Germans, who seemed to be on their way to better living standards. Sonja Fritzsche reads *The Cold Heart* as infused with and evocative of postwar experience: war guilt, returning soldiers, refugees, social reintegration, reconstruction efforts, and a happy ending in the new socialist *Heimat*. For Katie Trumpener, *The Cold Heart* also "implicitly allegorized capitalist greed, Nazi war guilt and the problem of post-facto expiation."[74] Yet the authorities were disappointed with the film for its dark images and presumed that the film did not cater to socialist–realist principles. Peter Munk is himself not exactly a positive hero and goes astray during much of the film. My analysis here centers on the revisions the film made, partly requested by GDR cultural functionaries, and shows the film as having a compromised mixture of socialist–realist and conventional characteristics. The film deemphasizes a bourgeois overtone that it cannot fully suppress. The discrepancy between official critique of the film and its overall popularity and acceptance among the audiences points to precisely the difference between the agenda of the party and the popular zeitgeist.

The Humanizing Power of Magic: *The Story of Little Mook* (1953)

Three years later, workers constructed a small oriental city at the Babelsberg Studio and trucked in tons of sand to build an artificial desert. A second fairy-tale film was being prepared as a Christmas present to children. This time, Wolfgang Staudte was at the helm. This project served as indirect compensation for an irreconcilable disagreement Staudte had with Bertolt Brecht and his wife Helene Weigel about the filming of Brecht's play *Mutter Courage und ihre Kinder* (Mother Courage and Her Children, 1939).[75] Staudte was the director of the very first DEFA film *Die Mörder sind unter uns* (The Murderers Are among Us, 1946) and subsequently *Der Untertan* (The Kaiser's Lackey, 1951), which was based on Heinrich Mann's novel. DEFA did not want to lose this renowned filmmaker and thus offered him the same budget for a fairy-tale film as he had for *Mother Courage*.[76] *Little Mook* turned out to be another milestone film and helped DEFA establish its international reputation for fairy-tale films. The film lived up to, if not exceeded, the audience's expectations, and its success eclipsed even

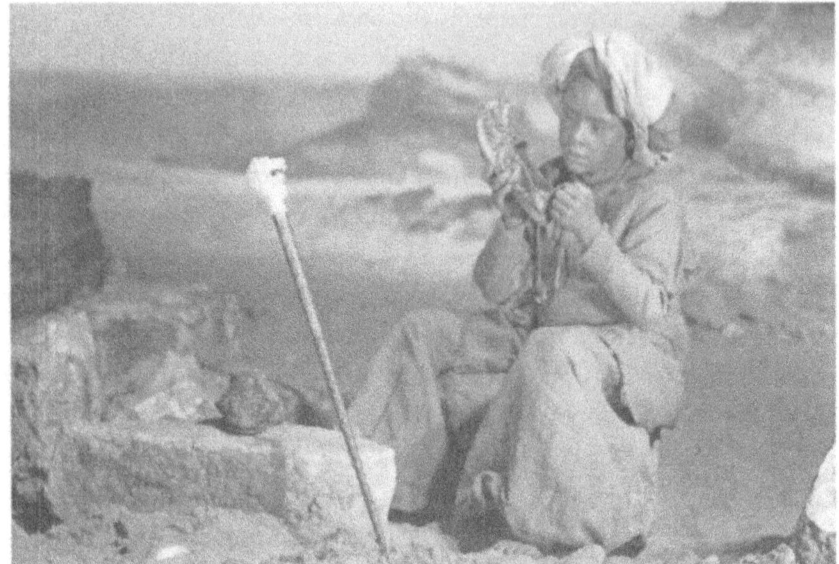

FIGURE 1.3. *Die Geschichte vom kleinen Muck*: Little Mook, realizing that his slippers are magical. © DEFA-Stiftung, Eduard Neufeld. (Filmmuseum Potsdam)

that of the Soviet films. It was celebrated at film festivals and became an all-time classic, getting distribution in seventy-one countries; *Little Mook* remained DEFA's best-selling export film until the end of the GDR.[77] In the FRG, however, only a few copies of the film were distributed in 1955. Not until the end of the 1980s would the film be screened again in West Germany; this time it consistently appeared in the "hit list" of BAG-Filme in West Germany.[78]

The success of *Little Mook* is partly attributable to the fortuitous discovery of Thomas Schmidt, then eleven years old (see Figure 1.3). Schmidt went along with his mother, Charlotte Ulbrich, when she auditioned for the role of Little Mook. Doubting the adequacy of an adult for the role, Ulbrich put a big turban on Schmidt's head during a break that got the attention of assistant director Siegfried Hartmann. It was also Schmidt's stepfather Peter Podehl who had cowritten the script for this film with Staudte. Schmidt witnessed the instant success of the film, was invited to interviews, and stood with the film team on stage. But then Podehl had a falling out with the DEFA management after he was asked to revise his script for an adaptation of Grimms' "The Brave Little Tailor" (see chapter

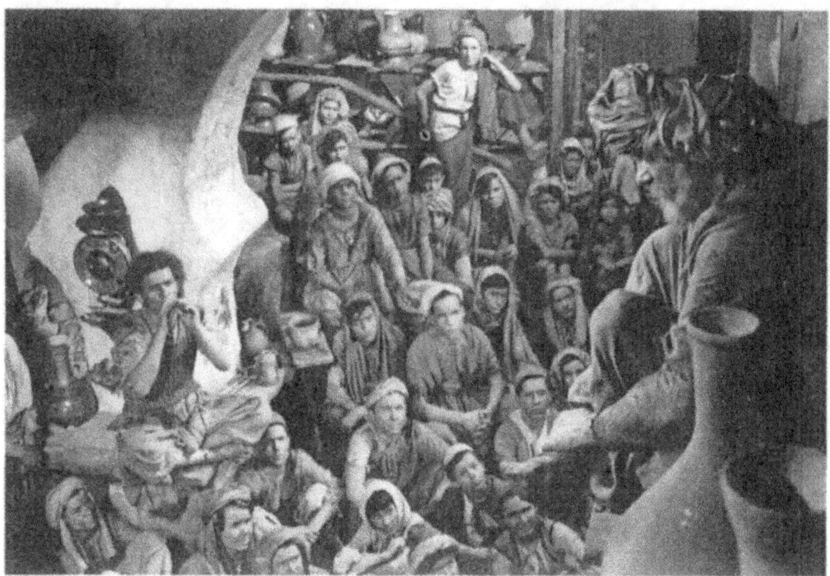

FIGURE 1.4. *Die Geschichte vom kleinen Muck*: Old Mook tells "The Story of Little Mook" to an enraptured audience. © DEFA-Stiftung, Eduard Neufeld.

2). As a result, Schmidt left for Munich in December 1955 with his family and was thus unable to enjoy the rise of the film to cult status in East Germany.[79]

Podehl believed *Little Mook* was so popular because "it is a wonderful story told in an unpretentious and unintentional manner, which is Staudte's signature. . . . because one could entertain himself without having the feeling that now I am again being indoctrinated with socialism. There is nothing like that in this film."[80] Podehl's remarks suggest that the filmmakers did not set out to adapt the tale with a socialist agenda. Staudte, for one, never toed the socialist party line.[81] Yet, his film is contrary neither to Marxist nor anticapitalist ideology.[82] In fact, Marxist themes of class struggle and the critique of capitalism are presented in a subtle manner that does not jeopardize the film's aesthetic and pedagogical values. This makes *Little Mook* entertaining and politically accurate, yet not propagandistic.

At the beginning of the film, children as well as adults yell "little man, evil man" (*kleiner Mann, böser Mann*) at Old Mook (Johannes Maus) for no apparent reason except that he has a hunchback. Old Mook then locks up these children and obliges them to listen to "his" story—the "Story of Little Mook," now told from a first-person perspective, not by a third-person narrator as in Hauff's original version (see Figure 1.4). In the tale within the tale, Little Mook's search for the merchant who sells good fortune takes him to an evil witch who inadvertently gives him magical slippers and a magical walking stick. With these, he becomes the chief messenger and treasurer at the sultan's palace. Framed by the evil prince Bajazid and the *ramudschins* (the sultan's advisors, played by Werner Peters and others), Little Mook leaves the palace only to return with magic figs to punish the evildoers with donkey ears.

In the original ending by Hauff, Little Mook lives "very rich but lonely, for he despises other human beings."[83] Such a misanthropic attitude would have been neither politically nor socially acceptable in the GDR. In the film, Little Mook voluntarily abandons the magic objects in the sand and enters the life of a working-class man; viewers meet Old Mook in a pottery shop at the beginning of the film. Staudte's new ending shows Little Mook ready to create his good fortune with his own hands without any supernatural help. This realistic solution to poverty better addressed the daily reality of the (East German) viewers, in which no magic was available and hard work was expected. One reviewer precisely reminded East Germans not to expect miracles, as they strove to fulfill their production quotas.[84]

A nineteenth-century tale usually ends with a redistribution of power and wealth, as the dreams of the lower class would have it. The social ascent of Little Mook gives expression to lower-class aspirations. With his magic gold-finding stick, he could have had abundant wealth. However, wealth and power do not amount to happiness for Mook. As Old Mook tells his audience, Little Mook still has not found the good fortune that he seeks. The new ending is more consistent with Little Mook's lack of interest in wealth and power shown throughout the film. In contrast to Peter in *The Cold Heart*, Mook is not corruptible, even when given the means to obtain wealth and power. He is, in fact, generally oblivious to their potential in satisfying his needs. Through Mook's actions, the film shows the correct ways to wield power and use wealth: Mook makes up to the former runner chief, Murad (Harry Riebauer), whose position he took, by saving Murad's sister; he pays the price-gouging Bajazid and greedy *ramudschins* ten gold pieces to set free a female slave and is even willing to give 300 gold coins to the malicious Bajazid, the ex-treasurer, whose job he took. In doing so, Mook belies what the previous runner chief said: "The good fortune of one is the misfortune of another" (English-dubbed version of the film). Mook replaces capitalist competition with a universal humanist spirit. He works to ensure that his good fortune redounds to the good of others.

In this adaptation of Hauff's tale set in an Arabian town, Staudte engaged German actors to put on blackface. Employing white Germanophone actors to pose as Muslims created a Brechtian estrangement effect. Katrin Sieg terms such performances "ethnic drag" in her study of ethnic impersonations in West German cultural representations after 1945.[85] Using Peggy Piesche's work on the films *Little Mook* (1953), *Hatifa* (Siegfried Hartmann, 1960), *Hamida* (Jean Michaud Mailland, 1966), *The Story of Poor Hassan* (1958), and *Die Söhne der großen Bärin* (The Sons of Great Bear, Josef Mach, 1966) as a foundation, Evan Torner notes that fairy-tale films and Westerns (*Indianerfilme*) specifically employ face-painted white bodies to signify nonwhiteness. Torner problematizes this "perilous" art form that "allows the white body to assume the somatic space of the racialized body under the white gaze without having to assume the permanent sociopolitical burdens of being racialized."[86] Both the blackface and after 1963 the "redface" represent race in proxy and assert white privilege. Hence, although Staudte at the time might have meant well in promoting racial equality and ethnic diversity, Torner's work shows overall superficial treatment of racial issues in the GDR. He writes, "The blackface was an expression of the fact that the GDR both did not actively persecute non-white subjects, nor could it accommodate them either, such that a supposedly post-racist society still barred non-white actors from participation in a story that—given the postcolonial wars of the 1950s and 60s—perhaps should not have been white-washed."[87] Logistically, blackface offered a practical solution to the problem of filming a foreign story without engaging foreign actors or shooting at foreign locations. As a result, the exotic remained the product of makeup artistry. Siegfried Schröder wrote in *Junge Welt* that the ethical content of this fairy tale would help youth as well as adults develop the sense of right and wrong and respect for people, regardless their color or race.[88]

Similar to *The Cold Heart*, *Little Mook* struck a chord with audiences and fed their dreams and needs through Little Mook's search for good fortune. The viewers who were watching the film had just experienced the failure of the 17 June 1953 uprising, which took place as the film was being shot. Staudte even requested to have someone stop the "tractor noise" (*Traktorenlärm*) from the street that was disrupting his shooting. Since this noise originated not from tractors but Soviet tanks, there was little he could do.[89] The workers' revolt was brutally suppressed. Their dissatisfaction with working conditions, shortages of raw material, and low pay was now exacerbated with the frustration at having lost to a militarily superior occupying power. Thus Little Mook's search for a good fortune might also have signified East Germans' collective desire for prosperity and social justice. The film offered the spectators diversions from the grim realities they faced. Dieter Wiedemann once postulated that the film's huge success might have even helped East Germans forget the drama of 17 June 1953.[90]

A closer look reveals that *Little Mook* resembled contemporary feature films of the time in aligning with the antifascist agenda, which was the most important political narrative of the GDR in the early decades. Little Mook is at first so poor that he owns nothing but broken shards of glass. He obviously also suffers abuse from the bullying kids, the schoolmaster, his greedy relatives, the gypsy woman, and from the fraudulent and avaricious Bajazid, who frames him and has him ousted from the palace. The persecution of the physically deformed Mook evokes persecutions against such persons during the Nazi era, although the press never explicitly read it as such. The National Socialist adaptation of the same tale changed the physically impaired protagonist to an Aryan boy without any infirmities; otherwise he could not have been a hero on the Nazi screen. Staudte's film, however, champions the disabled, presenting a protagonist who is deformed, but good-natured, smart, humble, helpful, and generous. The film's rehabilitation of a person with a disability could also suggest its condemnation of Nazi eugenic policies, to which someone like Mook would have been subjected. Jack Zipes suggests that Old Mook might have represented the persecuted Jews or Communists during National Socialism, the latter of whom were now "the poor leaders of the new German Democratic Republic" and needed to tell their stories to the younger generations to gain recognition, trust, and legitimization.[91]

In Staudte's version, Mook's story is not told just to one boy, as is the case in Hauff, but to a group of children, alluding to public education in the twentieth century. In the beginning, the children blindly follow their leader Mustafa to harass Mook. As the film progresses, however, Mustafa's authority diminishes as Old Mook's increases. The children develop a strong desire for Mook's story and stand their ground against Mustafa, who ends up tagging along to hear the story and, like the others, is changed by it. The film educates its audience about group behavior and socialization. Through the impact Mook's narrative makes on that social milieu, Staudte shows that a good story of resistance has a stronger appeal than a fascist-style leader who incites his peers to gang up on a person with a disability. The transformation of the group and of Mustafa himself, from tyrannizing street boys to well-behaved small citizens, demonstrates the enlightening effect of narrative and the humanizing power of magic. In so doing, the film implicitly contributed to the Soviet/East German agenda of denazification and reeducation in the immediate postwar years.

For a similar reason, Staudte significantly revised Mook's father, Mookrah. In Hauff's version, Mook's father is "ashamed of Little Mook's dwarfish figure and could not bear to see him, he neglected him and let him grow up in ignorance."[92] In the film, Mook's father, himself a learned man and a respected scholar, has taught Mook how to read and write. This change reveals the importance Staudte placed on education and on a strong father–son relationship. After the death of his father, Mook's extended family forces him to give away his little inheritance. In Hauff's original version, his father owes his relations more money than he could ever repay, which explains the callousness of the relatives toward Mook. In the film, however, the relatives are portrayed simply as heartless to show the dehumanizing power of greed. When Mook's relatives chase after him, an elderly man comments that "greed makes for quick feet."

Out of antifascist and pacifist convictions, Staudte invented an entire sequence in which a war is averted. This added episode conjures up memories of the recent past and is infused with postwar sentiment with which audience members could relate. The sultan, shown as usual sprawling on his throne, fusses over the fact that he has counted only thirty-one slaves in his bath that morning and wonders whether he will have to start drying himself. He blames the sultan of the neighboring country, who has been buying up his slaves. Therefore, he declares war on his neighbor with the absurd excuse that the sun rises earlier in that country than in his. Only through the intervention of Little Mook, Princess Amarza, and the ex–runner chief is the war avoided. The film shows that war is waged to satisfy the ruling class's greed, whims, and follies, with little or no regard for the destruction of people and land. In the film, the ex–head runner tears up the declaration of war that Mook the messenger is carrying. This war episode does not just echo the recent past[93] but also shows a counterscenario to it: people do not carry out the government's decision, and as a result war is stopped. In a utopian fashion, the people interfere in the political decision-making process, and the outcome is strikingly different than it was in the Third Reich. Reviews praised Staudte for adding this episode about thwarting an imminent but unjustified war.[94] The antiwar theme agreed with the world's advocacy of peace in the postwar period. The Potsdam Agreement, among others, had made it clear that the youth should be educated for antimilitarism and peaceful coexistence.[95] In his career, Staudte was deeply influenced by Lewis Milestone's antiwar film *All Quiet on the Western Front* (1930).[96] Even when making a fairy-tale film, he was still able to insert his personal convictions and contemporary concerns.

The film agrees with the GDR's anticapitalist ideology. Like the sultan, his courtiers resemble Little Mook's treasure-finding cane that is drawn to gold like iron to a magnet. The sultan rewards the winner of the foot race with six gold coins, but when the money reaches Mook, who won by wearing magical slippers, it has dwindled to one coin, the rest having been embezzled along the chain of the courtiers. These also siphon money from the treasury into their own pockets. They are resentful of Mook's quick rise within the palace, typical of members of the upper class intent on excluding the lower class from their midst. Their ploys result first in Mook's imprisonment and then his banishment from the palace. Mook's later discovery of magic figs enables him to get revenge on the conniving and corrupt court. He punishes the evil courtiers with donkey ears, making them—as jackasses—appear as foolish as they behave. When they have the donkey ears cut off, they grow instantly back, indicating their bearers have not changed at heart. This episode also conveys the dependence of the upper class on the lower class because they need Mook to cure them. A peasant's knowledge about crops, in this case fruit, makes him victorious, just like the farmer in the Grimms' tale "The Peasant and the Devil" (KHM 189), who uses his knowledge about the harvest to outsmart the Devil.

In Hauff's version, Princess Amarza plays a marginal role and also grows donkey ears. The film, on the contrary, portrays Amarza as a strong and independent woman. She is kindly disposed to Little Mook from their first chance encounter onward. She refuses to toss the handkerchief to start a race as is the custom. She gives Mook the ring received from the evil treasurer. She rebels against her father's disapproval of her paramour, Prince Hassan, from the enemy kingdom, secretly meeting and ultimately marrying her lover instead. Out of love for Hassan, she bribes the magician and fortuneteller to forecast the failure of the war, which makes the sultan call it off. Similar to *The Cold Heart*, this film anticipates female protagonists of future DEFA fairy-tale films who reject arranged marriages and pursue their freedom in choosing a marriage partner. Staudte invented this love story, adding a romantic subplot that has become a genre convention in fairy-tale films.

After Mook finishes his story, the children who scorned and ridiculed Old Mook at the start of the film all want to give him small gifts and help him. They make a "human elephant" to carry him through the town, shouting, "Make way for the Mook." This replicates the opening scene, in which the soldiers shout, "Make way for the sultan's elephant." Mook's story of triumph, of success in spite of lowly origins, has generated immense respect for him, and the children strongly identify with him. They feel that they should not mistreat Little Mook as the villains in the story did. He has made a fool out of the sultan and his evil staff and helped the princess marry her true love. Believing that Mook comes from a world of magic, they may think that he is fortune's favorite, and they do not want to end up growing donkey ears. They rejoice in Mook's final victory over the corrupt court and are deeply moved by his integrity and strength of character, which allowed him to abandon the magic objects and start a working life. The rags-to-riches story of Little Mook has an anticlimactic but "politically correct" ending: Mook chooses to become one of "us," a blameless proletarian like his listeners, although he could have lived in affluence. For that decision, the working-class children embrace Mook as their hero. Although social structure remains intact at the end, the audience would leave the cinema with the sense that the poor have prevailed.

Hauff's original story is one of six that a narrator named Muley tells during a caravan. The narrator is the boy who teased and tormented the three- or four-foot–tall Mook. Old Mook complains to Muley's father and tells him the "Story of Little Mook." The young Muley is then beaten by his father and told the story, so that the son will never laugh at Mook again. Hauff manipulates narrative position that highlights the pedagogical function of Mook's tale. Staudte did away with the caravan setting and has Old Mook narrate himself. By changing the third-person narrative to a first-person narrative, the authenticity of the tale increases. The children also take what Old Mook says at face value: the "Story of Little Mook" is his autobiography. The claim to veracity allows Old Mook to obtain mythical and awe-inspiring authority over the children, not only as storyteller but also as someone with an extraordinary life (story) to celebrate.

The press reviews of *Little Mook* were overwhelmingly positive. Reviewing for *Neues Deutschland*, Susanne König praised the film as "a true Christmas joy," affirming the revisions Podehl and Staudte undertook and expressing disapproval only at the somewhat caricatured portrayal of the members of the sultan's court.[97] Reviews repeatedly pointed to the film's accomplishments in preserving the qualities of a good fairy tale. For example, H. U. E. remarked in *Berliner Zeitung*: "The fairy tale comes to life in a new way; it breathes the spirit of the spirit of our times, and it remains nonetheless an intact and genuine fairy tale. This is precisely how one should adapt literary materials for films, if it is at all necessary to rework them, so that no violence is done to them."[98] The DEFA board, however, did not cite *Little Mook* as a good socialist children's film and faulted its "coolness" (*Kühle*), suggesting that the film did not show political partisanship increasingly required of DEFA films.[99] In a *Tribüne* review, C. Z. L. also used "cool"—in the sense of reserved, distant, and aloof—to describe the stereotypes portrayed in the film.[100] Official disapproval, however slight, appears to be a way of inserting a paternalistic political agenda into the critique of even one of the best artistic works the GDR had to offer.

As done with the frame narrative of *The Stone Flower*, Staudte framed his film with a storytelling setting. In the midst of narration, Old Mook stops twice at cliffhanger moments, once for a day and once for a few minutes. The discreet narration resembles that of Scheherazade, who tells the Persian king half of a story every night and ends it and begins another half the next day, thus saving her own life by making the king curious about the ending of each and every story.[101] The narrative setting suggests that Staudte had confidence in the life-changing effect of storytelling and in the educational capacity of film and literature. The director himself perhaps believed that, just like Old Mook, he himself would work magic and captivate the children of his time through his film. This self-reflective level of the film allowed the audience to see how Old Mook's own child audience is hooked and mesmerized. As a result, the behavior of all the children toward Old Mook changes, but an adult in the street still yells "the wicked man" toward Old Mook, who comments, "I'm sure he doesn't know 'the Story of Little Mook.'"

Like contemporary DEFA feature films (*Gegenwartsfilme*), fairy-tale films of the early postwar years addressed issues of importance to their audience. In the film, Little Mook shows the survival skills that were very much in demand during the postwar period. For example, he figures out the functions of the magic objects himself, instead of them being revealed to him in a dream, as in Hauff. Due to limitations posed by the genre, fairy-tale films could not deal with current subject matters as directly as Staudte's earlier DEFA films, such as *The Murderers Are among Us* (1946), *Rotation* (1949), and *The Kaiser's Lackey* (1951). These films addressed the recent past directly, whereas *Little Mook* implicitly did so. Thanks to its fairy-tale language, the latter appeared apolitical and timeless, thus enjoying the largest number of viewers; it topped the chart of all DEFA films in terms of statistics. Yet the fact that even such a successful film from one of the greatest German directors did not make it to the list of German canonical films is telling about the lack of critical acknowledgment ascribed to the fairy-tale films, of which *Little Mook* is exemplary.

Conclusion: Humanism Alone Is Not Socialism

All three films—*The Stone Flower*, *The Cold Heart*, and *Little Mook*—negate fantastic solutions in favor of realistic ones. In so doing, the films affirm the potential of the human, who, after all, "is enthroned at the heart of all the discourses of humanism."[102] They value human ingenuity, freedom, and dignity, and they emphasize humanity and community over materialistic possessions. It is no longer wealth but love, family, and friendship that are used to measure success. In fact, wealth, or rather obsession with wealth, becomes contemptible, corruptive, and dehumanizing. It takes on devilish features in *The Cold Heart* and is voluntarily abandoned in *Little Mook*. The incompatibility of greed and humanity constituted the essential message, thus dramatizing Marx's accusation of inhumane capitalism. Like many contemporary films that DEFA produced in this period, the narrative trajectory of *The Cold Heart* and *Little Mook* was built around what Seán Allan observes as the antithesis between two modes of order in GDR fiction: beginning with the disorder of capitalism and ending with the order of socialism.[103] Under socialism, only honest, hard work will yield wealth; and wealth does not come primarily in the form of capital but in the form of love and family.

Humanist considerations guided DEFA fairy-tale adaptations and motivated many of the revisions. Humanism is to be understood in the broadest sense possible, including universal humanist values such as love, family, friendship, solidarity with the common people, personal virtues, social responsibility, and so on. While clearly departing from Hauff, the GDR filmmakers also attempted to reach global audiences with an emphasis on the abandonment of the individual in favor of the collective. Yet the SED's official view of the first two DEFA fairy-tale films was not at all that favorable. *The Cold Heart* was attacked for its violence, naturalism, and mysticism, which exceeded a child's capacity to understand and were thus incompatible with the ideals of a progressive art.[104] *Little Mook* was criticized for its apathy (*Kühle*), which could be construed as lacking socialist zeal or revolutionary fervor.[105] Peter Podehl once attributed the film's popular success to its freedom from indoctrination and dogmatism. He implied that this film did not show, to use the political jargon, partiality (*Parteilichkeit*). Although both films were well received by the public, the official response ranged from lukewarm to harshly negative. Press reviews of *The Cold Heart* channeled the official judgment of the film. *Little Mook* fared better in press reviews. The official stance was later elaborated at the two film conferences taking place, respectively, in 1952 and in 1958, where it was made clear that inheriting the humanist tradition was not enough without making a direct contribution to the socialist education of future generations.

Leading party officials and filmmakers convened at the first conference of filmmakers on 17 and 18 September 1952, where the intention of the party was made clear, namely, "from now on the film is absolutely subordinate to the political line of the SED and should function as an excellent, effective instrument of propaganda, agitation, persuasion, and education."[106] This conference reinforced the role of ideology in film productions and examined how socialist realism could be realized in films.[107] At the 1958 film conference, children's films were again put under critical scrutiny. Steffen Wolf summarized the main criticisms of DEFA children's films as follows: (1) the films did not reflect the GDR reality (*Wirklichkeitsferne*), (2) there was indistinct "partisanship" (*Parteilichkeit*) and inadequate attention to the needs and demands of a really "socialist children's film," and (3) the filmmakers were guilty of "ideological ambiguity" that could allow "bourgeois ideology" to make inroads.[108] In terms of "partisanship," Anton Ackermann, director of the film division, offered the following explanation, thus making a clear distinction between humanism and socialism:

> Quite a few people restrict partisanship in art to partiality for general humanist endeavors and goals. . . . This is especially the case for almost all the children's films by DEFA, which therefore have not made a noteworthy contribution to the socialist education of our children. . . . Socialist morals and ethics should never be limited to general humanist ideals, which are passed down from the early bourgeois and even the prebourgeois era. . . . Only those who expand partiality in art to include combative partisanship against imperialism and in favor of socialism and communism are taking a Marxist position.[109]

What Ackermann was proposing was clearly socialist humanism, a humanism that first and foremost serves the GDR's state ideology. *The Cold Heart* and *Little Mook* apparently fell short of this political and ideological cross-examination. Nonetheless, this does not diminish their popular status and their significance in DEFA film history.

Although the two Western directors might not have consciously used the Soviet predecessor as a role model, this chapter has observed tangible similarities between the first two DEFA fairy-tale films and *The Stone*

Flower. The reasons might lie with the fame *The Stone Flower* enjoyed at the time, the universality of fairy tales, and the fact that DEFA films were products of teamwork rather than auteur films as in the West. *The Stone Flower* was repeatedly evoked as a role model by the GDR film critics of the time, and *The Cold Heart*, but not so much *Little Mook*, was harshly criticized for not following the Soviet forerunner. The two DEFA films also remained distinctively *German* in having recourse to German literary and cinematic traditions.

Whereas the film conferences in 1952 and 1958 reflected the intensification of the Cold War, the production and reception of the first DEFA fairy-tale films revealed that in the early years after the founding of the two separate German states, filmmakers and artists still entertained the vision of a united Germany that was, after all, also the SED's official policy at the time. Joachim Giera writes about *The Cold Heart*, "It was adapted in the hope of a pan-German future and in the illusion to change the world."[110] Although *The Cold Heart* was shot in Thuringia and in the Babelsberg studios, the story takes place in the Black Forest, now located in West Germany, which was also the site of numerous contemporary West German *Heimat* films. *Little Mook* echoed German aspirations for reunification. Commenting on the immediate political impact this film made, one reviewer wrote:

> East as well as West Berliners watched the premiere of the new color film *The Story of Little Mook* in the Babylon movie theater. Director Bernstein of Progress film distribution noted in his introduction that this rendezvous, as he called the meeting of East and West Berliners, is conducive to the upcoming Geneva Summit [of 1955] and again responds to the demand of all patriotic Germans that, after eight years of division, Germany be united and its capital city be restored.[111]

Such a sociopolitical impact was exactly what Staudte had expressed hope for a year earlier in an interview with *Neues Deutschland*: "The filmmakers cannot simply be divided by a border. Any child who knows a little history knows that no country can succeed with division in the long run. I don't know an East or West German film. I only know a good German film."[112] *Little Mook* became such a good *German* film.

2

ENTANGLED IN THE COLD WAR

Tales of Class Struggle and Political Allegories

The protagonists of the first two DEFA fairy-tale films—Peter Munk and Little Mook—come from the lower class, yet they neither initiate revolutions nor become kings. They are motivated by wealth and personal happiness, objectives both humanistic and bourgeois. Neither *The Cold Heart* nor *Little Mook* lived up to the expectations of the Stalinist cultural functionaries, despite the two films' entrenchment within the stated discursive positions of the time. Official criticisms of these films explicitly demanded unambiguous politicization of (children's) film and the use of socialist–realist aesthetics to glorify positive heroes from the working class (see conclusion in chapter 1). This mandate became reified in the third fairy-tale film: *The Devil of Mill Mountain* (1955). Subsequently, more DEFA fairy-tale films were adapted in which a working-class protagonist uses his intelligence and perseverance to become victorious over the upper class or even to become king. Thematizing ordinary people's struggles against the powerful is common practice. What distinguished East German fairy-tale films was that they shouldered a dual task of promoting the GDR both as a socialist republic and as heir to German cultural traditions and humanist Enlightenment. Made for both children and adults, the "politically correct" fairy-tale films presented class warfare in ways that a child would read merely as a moral tale, notably in *Little Red Riding Hood* (1962), but an adult would sense more ideological subtext. It is precisely this dual perspective that allows these films to be interpreted in terms of a combative Cold War environment. Whereas chapter 1 focuses on the films' connections to heritage, this chapter will highlight their conformism with state ideology and their nonetheless controversial receptions by the state.

The select films in this chapter explain both the source of—and solution to—class conflict: oppression provokes and leads to rebellion. Such ideological indoctrination seemed unnecessary since theoretically a socialist GDR had put an end to oppression and class struggle. Yet, lessons about class struggle with its antibourgeois, anticapitalist themes could reeducate those citizens who were not savvy about Marxist principles as well as ritualistically re-rehearse Marxism for true believers. Fairy-tale films dramatizing feudalistic and capitalistic oppression that necessitated class struggle in the first place could assist in touting GDR citizens' support for the country's ideological superstructure. Hence the GDR often felt the need to revisit the reasons for socialist revolution to ideologically position its state culture vis-à-vis that of the West. The antagonism between weak and strong, poor and rich and the reversal of power relations at the end of a fairy tale were utilized to represent the triumph of German Communists over the fascists, the bourgeoisie, and—eventually—the capitalists. Especially in the 1950s, the fairy tales adapted by the DEFA feature film studio and by the animation studio in Dresden were tales that primarily thematized struggles of folk heroes against feudal oppressors, of the poor against the rich, evoking the SED's communist, antifascist narratives of liberation. The formulaic happy ending of fairy tales coincided with the GDR's millennial optimism that was an imperative of East German cultural production.

Since traditional tales often revolve around the social ascent of a member of the lower class, the revolutionary and utopian impulses of folk and fairy tales make the tales ideal candidates for embodying Marxist–Leninist ideas about class struggles and proletarian rule. Many, including Ernst Bloch, August Nitschke, Dieter Richter, Johannes Merkel, and Jack Zipes, have observed this salient feature of folk and fairy tales. They argue that folk and fairy tales originated among the oppressed classes in precapitalist societies and incorporated the disappointments, fantasies, and utopian dreams of their creators, offering necessary psychological compensation for those to whom the comforts of the upper classes were unattainable and could only be lived vicariously in the imagination. Although fairy tales are marked by their specific sociohistorical context, the themes of class struggle and power shifts presented them as ready-made material for East German reappropriations. Ernst Bloch notes how seemingly anachronistic fairy tales embody signs of the time and reflect present circumstances:

> How can the fairy tale mirror our wish projections, other than in a totally obsolete way? Real kings no longer even exist. The atavistic and simultaneously feudal–transcendental world from which the fairy tale stems, and to which it seems to be tied, has most certainly vanished. However, the mirror of the fairy tale has not become opaque, and the manner of wish-fulfilment which peers forth from it is not entirely without a home. It all adds up to this: the fairy tale narrates a wish-fulfilment which is not bound by its own time and the apparel of its content.[1]

According to Zipes, "What Bloch admired most about the best of folk and fairy tales was their antiauthoritarian quality—the disregard for hierarchy, the ceaseless impulse to break out and realize the surging dreams of the imagination."[2]

In addition to being entertaining, DEFA fairy tales were appropriated to transmit state ideology to young viewers, as Steffen Wolf explained, "because to these films were ascribed a very specific didactic function from the first day of its existence onward: they should 'participate in the formation of the young and indeed socialist generation in Germany.'"[3] In December 1953, a separate department for children's films was established and greatly expanded in 1955 under the leadership of Hellmuth Häntzsche, the chief pedagogue at DEFA, who championed socialist–realist principles in children's films.[4] Werner Hortzschansky, director of the German Central Institute for Teaching Materials, suggested in *Deutsche Filmkunst* that it was necessary to make fairy-tale films to redress the problematic German fairy-tale films from earlier periods, that is, the Weimar Republic and the Third

Reich, in which kings and princes were glorified and attributed only positive traits, whereas workers were often depicted as servile and not so smart. East German fairy-tale films should, according to Hortzschansky, reflect current societal conditions. They were to highlight social conflict contained in the tales, especially the resistance of the masses against the ruling system and the yearning of the oppressed for a better and brighter future.[5]

In the East German context, the antiauthoritarianism of the 1950s and 1960s targeted the "enemy classes" and societal forms that the GDR superseded. These toppled "enemy classes" or societal forms were usually personified by the king and his cohorts, rich farmers (*Großbauern*), and the like. Similar to the negative portrayal of kings and princes (*Fürsten*) in Soviet fairy-tale films,[6] the antagonists were equated with evil in DEFA films. By doing so, the seemingly outdated tales could be retrofitted for East German circumstances. The resultant DEFA image of the king verged on outright cliché, as Steffen Wolf observed, "Because the king—ideologically speaking—is the personification of feudalism, exploitation, decadence, and an overthrown social system, he could be nothing but evil. If the original version does not allow for such a characterization, then the kings are demoted to being stupid and silly, naïve and absurd, ugly or at least unsightly figures, who are not infrequently misrepresented to the point of becoming an ugly caricature."[7]

The title of "king" appeared both feudal and anachronistic at the time. Yet in DEFA fairy tales, workers were symbolically crowned as kings, reflecting the rhetoric put forth by the party. The new king of humble origins could be construed as a political allegory of the East German government, which understood itself as a democratic political entity representing the peasants, workers, and soldiers. These films were intended to mirror the political reality of the newly established state and to help construct a new identity for the fledgling socialist country as an antifascist and proletarian state. Against this political backdrop, the romantic concept of the *Volk* was adapted for the East German context and gradually acquired political and ideological contemporaneity.

The new understanding of *Volk* seemed to redeem the term from its racialized connotation during National Socialism. The *Volk*, now presumably consisting of peasants, workers, and soldiers, formed the basis of the proletarian rule of the SED, at least in theory. In "Der Märchenstreit," Kristin Wardetzky points out that the unreflective use of the term *Volk*, although problematic due to Nazi ideology, was not uncommon in the GDR, where the term was no longer defined in white supremacist terms nor used as a means of discriminating against the lower class as plebeians (*vulgus*).[8] Recent studies examining racism in the GDR indicate that the redefined concept of the German *Volk* was still racially charged.[9] Yet changes in political and social realities instilled a new sense in the identity of the East German *Volk* as collectively belonging to the new socialist *Heimat*. And, given the folk origin of many of the tales, the fairy-tale films were significant in winning the hearts and minds of the East German populace during the Cold War.

This chapter shows DEFA's predilection for tales that contain class conflict and symbolic power reversal in the end. These films presumably catered to the official call for "politically partisan" films. Nonetheless, despite their socialist–realist bent, many DEFA fairy-tale films were considered controversial, so much so that these films received increasingly serious attention by state agencies—from production to reception—often to the detriment of the films themselves. The "politically partisan" fairy-tale films were preceded by *The Devil of Mill Mountain* (1955), which was the first fairy-tale film to receive official praise for avoiding the shortcomings of *The Cold Heart* and *Little Mook*. With its socialist–realist style and reference to the present, this film finally met the official demand for absolute subordination of film productions to political purposes expressed at the first film conference in 1952.

Political correctness did not necessarily spare a film from negative press attacks, as happened to *Little Tailor* (1956) for its contemporization (*Aktualisierung*). After both *Little Tailor* and *The Singing Ringing Tree* (1957, see chapter 3) received harsh criticism from the official press on issues of the princess, Gerhard Klein's *The Story of Poor Hassan* (1958) used a parable to reify Marxism. Yet Klein's film stylistically distinguished itself from conventional or Disney pictures by applying Brechtian techniques of the epic theater. Klein's aesthetical resistance alongside ideological conformism proves, as historians Dolores Augustine and Jeannette Madarász point out, that East Germans generally could be subversive and conformist at the same time. The use of the epic theater tropes in Klein's "political partisan" film was criticized, however, as inappropriate for children's cognitive level.

The year 1959 saw two fairy-tale adaptations: Siegfried Hartmann's *The Tinderbox* (1959) and Bernhard Thieme's *The Wooden Calf* (produced in 1959, premiered in 1961). Whereas *The Tinderbox* was praised as a successful adaptation, *The Wooden Calf* encountered tremendous difficulty with censorship, and its public screening was delayed until 1961. Although both films focused on representative class conflict and lower-class rebellion, the negative reaction toward *The Wooden Calf* demonstrated that, in this case, the realpolitik concerning church–state relations took precedence over socialist ideology. Hartmann's *The Golden Goose* (1964), discussed next, is one of the best-known DEFA fairy-tale films, although it is necessary to explain why exactly this particular film made a name for itself internationally. Whereas some other films possess similar cinematic qualities, this film successfully combined a simple narrative with songs, humor, and action to create a work of lighthearted entertainment.

The chapter closes with Götz Friedrich's *Little Red Riding Hood* (1962), which adults might have seen as allegorical class warfare under the veneer of a simple, familiar story, whereas young audiences understood the film as a plucky heroine's victory over two evil animals. The 1962 version used a script by Hans Rodenberg, who in fact had directed a fairy-tale play based on a piece by Russian playwright Eugene Schwartz in 1951.[10] Therefore, thematically the DEFA version more closely adhered to fairy-tale films of the 1950s.

A Socialist–Realist Legend: *The Devil of Mill Mountain* (1955)

After *The Cold Heart* and *Little Mook* failed in the eyes of the SED to set an example for children's films, the third fairy-tale film catered to the party's directive that filmmakers go beyond a mere humanist stance by adopting a militant partisanship in support of Stalinist ideology. In 1952, the Politburo issued a resolution called "For the Revival of Progressive German Cinema," in which socialist realism was designated to be the only valid art form. The Fourth Party Congress in 1954 reiterated that the task for filmmakers was to master the methods of socialist realism.[11] As discussed in the Introduction, socialist realism concerns content over form, politics over aesthetics. Herbert Ballmann, then head of the children's film production group, took charge of a third fairy-tale film, the first adaptation of a legend from the Harz mountain region. Ballmann's previous children's film, *Das geheimnisvolle Wrack* (The Mysterious Wreck, with a script by Kurt Bortfeldt, 1954), alludes to the East–West conflict and calls for vigilance against saboteurs and agents.[12] Given his track record, Ballmann would be an ideologically reliable director to bring out the Harz legend's revolutionary pathos and desired agitational qualities.

Mill Mountain was announced under the working title *Der steinerne Mühlmann* (The Stone Miller).[13] The story takes place in the thirteenth century, a time when farmers were attempting to rebel against feudal lords and their accomplices. Yet, at the beginning of the film, the farmers are held back by fear of reprisals and deep-rooted superstition.[14] Criminal members of the upper class—the evil miller (Willy A. Kleinau), the chatelaine (Werner Peters), and the bailiff (Gerhard Frei)—put on devil masks and set fire to the rival mill, where two lovers—the poor but beautiful and brave Anne (Eva Kotthaus) and the good miller Jörg (Hans-Peter Minetti) work. Overcoming their superstitions, the exploited peasants finally wake up and unite behind the lovers in their fight for freedom and to rebuild the mill. Their plight wins sympathy and the timely intervention of three friendly forest spirits—supernatural charcoal burners, who give the peasants coals that change to gold, a trope that plays on the double meaning of *Kohle* as both coal and money in German. The coal-turned-gold is a typical gift from these spirits as can also be seen in Anneliese Probst's *Sagen und Märchen aus dem Harz* (1954). The evil miller is then turned into a rock on Harz mountain as punishment. Thus the legend behind the boulder known as "The Stone Miller" also "testifies to this day to the victory of the good cause of the people."[15] Although set in the medieval period, the film illustrates an important ideological point about the power of the collective in the GDR. Anne and Jörg act in the interests of the ordinary people, rely on the collective to finally win the battle against evil, and achieve their personal happiness in doing so. Even the supernatural power in this case does not appear in the singular but is represented as a group of three charcoal burners. The three evil allies, however, pursue egotistical, individualistic, and immoral goals and thus succumb to internal strife as well as the power of the people.

In December 1954, when the film was evaluated for its official release, it was praised precisely because it had avoided the "brutality in *The Cold Heart* and the detachedness in *Little Mook*."[16] The film's dramaturge Walter Schmitt not only saw "elements of revolutionary romanticism" in the film but also emphasized the power of the people, thus making implicit references to current ideology: the three good spirits "are not supernatural powers at all, but no more than supernatural representations or incarnations of the ancient wisdom of the people."[17] In the same vein, a review in *Neues Deutschland* said that these supernatural beings embody the best qualities and forces of the *Volk* and that the fantastic merely serves as simple reification of abstract ideas.[18]

With a prominent cast, including national prize winners Willy A. Kleinau in the role of the evil miller and Werner Peters in the role of the chatelaine, the film proved "a big success," with a viewership of over 4.3 million.[19] It was exported to West Germany in 1955.[20] Although newspaper reviews of the time echoed the official judgment, later critics pointed out the film's dramaturgical flaws and its inability to arouse interest in children of later generations, indicating that the reviews of the time overrated the film and prioritized politics over aesthetics.[21] Sonja Fritzsche sees *Mill Mountain* as a cross-pollination between the fairy-tale and *Heimat* genres with socialist–realist trappings. She further contends that the film reflects the East German social realities of postwar years, for example, refugee problems (since Anne is an adopted orphan) and women's function as catalysts for the coming revolution and in the construction of a socialist state.

Herbert Ballmann's subsequent films such as *Das Traumschiff* (The Dream Ship, 1956) and *Tinko* (1957) were criticized by GDR cultural officials as being increasingly narrow-minded; the director gradually fell out of favor with the party and left the GDR in 1959, causing quite a stir in the West German press.[22] What eventually led to Ballmann's departure from the GDR (*Republikflucht*) was his outspoken criticism of the SED's cultural policies during the short-lived Thaw. In the wake of Stalin's death in 1953 and especially following Khrushchev's denunciation of Stalin in February 1956, East German intellectuals entertained a vision of social and political reforms in the GDR. Filmmakers and artists demanded the democratization of culture and the limiting of SED interference in film productions.

Famous filmmakers such as Martin Hellberg, Kurt Maetzig, Slatan Dudow, and Konrad Wolf pleaded for more freedom for artists, greater autonomy in film productions, and the expedition of the film approval process. Ballmann did not mince words at a special board meeting at the studio in May 1956, protesting both the state's oppressive bureaucratic control over filmmaking and the lack of vibrant, critical interaction with audiences.[23] Although his films *The Mysterious Wreck* and *Mill Mountain* toed the party line, Ballmann let it be known that he did not stand by such earlier works: "One thing is for sure, I cannot say that the films I have made so far represent the good conscience of our people."[24] With this, he implied that these films reflected the party's will, rather than his own or that of the people. For such comments, he was attacked by the SED leadership. When the political rein tightened after the Thaw ended in 1957, Ballmann struck a reconciliatory tone: "I have made grave and huge mistakes both in my work as well as in my relationship with the party. I'll keep looking for the right path and I am thankful when the comrades help me with it."[25]

Even though he showed a humble attitude in his self-criticism, he was obviously never forgiven for his earlier criticisms. Eventually, he fled west.[26] The Ballmann case supports Dolores Augustine and Jeannette Madarász's recent conclusions that power in the GDR was always contested and negotiated and that power was simultaneously exerted from above and below. Ballmann at first defied the GDR power structure but then had to retract his outspoken criticism. His defiance prevailed when he fled the country. In view of this, his fairy-tale adaptation of *Mill Mountain* is to be seen as socialist art by a not so socialist artist.

"Vulgarizing Marxism": *The Brave Little Tailor* (1956)

After DEFA produced three fairy-tale films without exclusively targeting children, Helmut Spieß directed the first DEFA fairy-tale film explicitly conceived of as a children's film—*Little Tailor* (1956). Spieß worked as dramaturge for *Little Mook* and became a director by chance: he filled in for Wolfgang Schleif to direct *Hexen* (Witches, 1954) after Schleif became noncommittal about working for DEFA after the 17 June 1953 uprising.[27] Robert Baberske, a prominent cinematographer from the Weimar era—with films such as *Berlin: Die Sinfonie der Großstadt* (Berlin: Symphony of a Metropolis, Walter Ruttmann, 1927) under his belt—shot *Little Mook* and later *Little Tailor*. Peter Podehl, who cowrote *Little Mook*, was slated to be its screenwriter. Yet in the eyes of the DEFA management, Podehl's script stayed too close to the Grimms' version, in which the tailor also possesses negative traits and appears boastful and vain; in the studio's opinion, the tailor would need to embody more positive characteristics and stand out through his bravery.[28] The DEFA board of directors merely attempted to ensure that socialist–realist imperatives be followed. This authoritarian instruction about the protagonist echoes Joshua Feinstein's observations about DEFA films: that the GDR cultural officials rejected the aims of a realistic cinema in favor of flawlessly heroic protagonists.[29] Podehl refused to keep writing under such circumstances and left the GDR with his family in tow, including his stepson—the child star of *Little Mook*. His successor was Kurt Bortfeldt, who came to DEFA in 1951 from Real-Film in Hamburg. Bortfeldt had cowritten the script with Anneliese Probst for the revolutionary romantic and socialist–realist fairy-tale film *Mill Mountain* and appeared willing to abide by the studio's requirements.[30]

Reactions to *Little Tailor* from critics and educators were overwhelmingly critical. The revisions made in Bortfeldt's screen adaptation stood at the heart of the controversy. In the Grimms' tale, a little tailor, emboldened by killing seven flies with one stroke, leaves his tailor shop and goes on a journey to seek his luck. His wits enable him to overpower giants and overcome a series of challenges that win him the princess's hand in marriage. After discovering her new husband's humble origin, however, the princess tries to get rid of him. The tailor–king foils her plot but keeps his marriage vows. Although the ending of the Grimm tale indicates that the tailor will make a better king, it is left open whether he will assimilate himself into the existing political structure or if his rise is symbolic of a large-scale change in the social structure. The fact that the little tailor stays married to such a princess suggests that he does not intend any radical social change. As Jack Zipes points out, the revolutionary potential of many European folktales is clear, yet limited by ideological constraints:

"The change in the tale does not involve a change in social conditions and relations. The protagonist simply improves his position in regard to material wealth and power."[31]

Since the GDR's class structure was substantially different from that of nineteenth-century Germany, Bortfeldt expanded and revised the Grimms' tale to signal overt class conflict and the liberation of the proletariat. The film adds a number of characters and portrays them along the lines of stereotypical class depiction. The beginning sequence adds an exploitative tailor master and his wife, from whose oppression the little tailor (Kurt Schmidtchen) frees himself. A cowardly and vain Prince Eitel (whose name means "vanity," played by Horst Drinda) is added; he helps the king plot against the little tailor in an attempt to cheat the latter out of his reward. To that same end, the film depicts aristocratic society as utterly ridiculous. The whiny and cruel King Griesgram (whose name means "grouch") seems consumed by his sorrow, but he is actually hiding an onion in his hand to produce tears. Princess Liebreiz (whose name means "loving charm") is not loving but rather conniving and vicious. The film also adds a princess's maid (Christel Bodenstein), the daughter of a gardener, who constantly suffers the princess's tyranny. This addition prepares the viewer for the most radical change in the film: the tailor no longer marries the princess as in the Grimms' version but marries the maid (see Figure 2.1). This new ending conveys the sense that even when the protagonist rises to the upper class, to remain lower class at heart is of extreme importance; a pretty, helpful, and hardworking girl from the lower class has immanently desirable qualities, and marrying her proves to be nothing but a logical decision.

Whether or not the tailor should have married the princess later became the focus of the debate. One reviewer insisted on the genre-specific marriage of a member of the lower class with the princess, *simply because she is a princess*: "Regardless of all human weaknesses, the princess in fairy tales is, after all, the ideal, the dream, the goal of all endeavors of the heroes."[32] It goes without saying that the marriage of a member of the working class to a princess is fantastical and lacks social reality in the first place. Such an outcome projects the sexual and social ambitions of lower-class males into a fictional realm and becomes a staple genre convention.

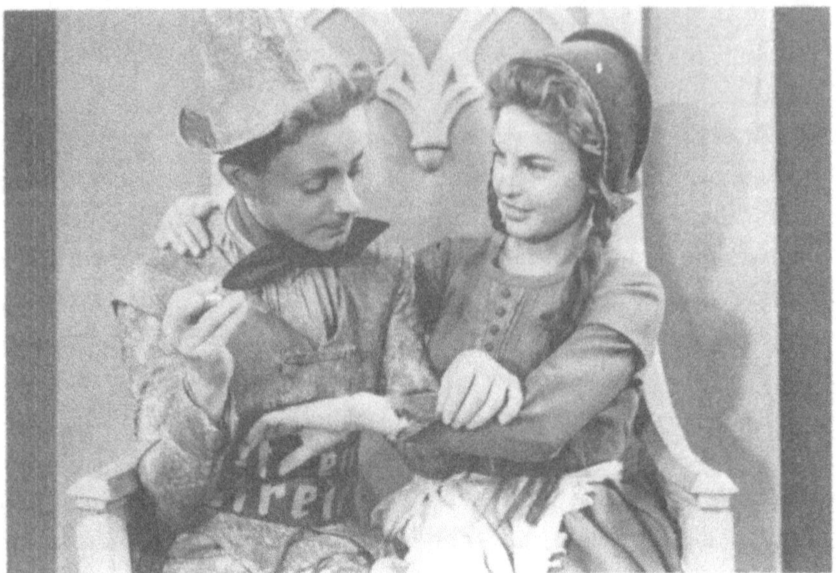

FIGURE 2.1. *Das tapfere Schneiderlein*: The tailor-cum-king mends the maid's sleeve. © DEFA-Stiftung, Waltraud Pathenheimer. (Filmmuseum Potsdam)

Yet, reviewers of the film were very concerned about the confusion such changes would cause in young children regarding which version to believe. Werner Hortzschansky writes, "The content of a fairy-tale film must remain the same as that of the fairy-tale text familiar to children. Contradictions to the read or orally presented tales or doubt about the correct rendition must not arise in children" (19). For these critics, a largely faithful adaptation of "The Brave Little Tailor" might have achieved the same pedagogical result. A princess in classic tales as well as in Disney pictures is typically the identification figure for young girls. But in DEFA films, she belongs to nobility, and by default she is not entitled to the audience's affection. The negative image of the princess is a *countertale* element in many DEFA fairy tales.

Another significant change is the addition of peasants. In the film, a group of peasants come to the palace to demand that the king send "the warrior—Seven with One Blow" to subdue the wild boar that has been destroying their land. In so doing, the little tailor does not kill the wild boar just on behalf of the royal palace but in the interest of the people and the country. Therefore, after the little tailor outmaneuvers the beast, the peasants carry the tailor on their shoulders as a hero. In the final scene, not only do the king's guards flee as in the Grimms' tale but all the aristocrats hasten away, afraid that the almighty tailor will kill them all. The *Volk* cheers at that sight. The country has a new king from the lower classes and an entirely new government composed of people from the social class to which he belongs. The film suggests the integrity and incorruptibility of working-class rule. As the scriptwriter Bortfeldt envisioned it, "the film should give a clear impression that, in the end, the tailor will be a fairer and better king than the one he dethroned."[33] Hence the film heralds an absolute overhaul of the political system.

Progress, DEFA's distributor, advertised the film as a complex, antifeudal film that mixes an old beloved tale with satire on hereditary aristocracy.[34] The defiance toward and contempt for nobility is in agreement with the proletarian, antifeudal, and antibourgeois ideology of the GDR. Hence, it is rather unexpected that the tendentious yet politically up-to-date reworking of the tale did not sit well with (re)viewers who were obviously dismayed by the revisions, criticizing the film's lack of "respect for a literary work."[35] The debate touched on whether such proletarianization of a well-known tale would damage the fairy-tale character and ruin the fairy-tale atmosphere. *Neues Deutschland*, the official organ of the SED, published Horst Knietzsch's critique of the film, which cited the 1952 resolution of the Politburo of the SED Central Committee that "in matters of film art, the Politburo warns against all tendencies in vulgarizing Marxism while reworking and adapting the German cultural heritage, German legends, and fairy tales."[36] Knietzsch wrote, "The creators of this film have abrasively categorized all fairy-tale characters along class lines."[37] In an ironic tone, he then gasped at his own lack of knowledge that "the Brothers Grimm were trained Marxists."[38]

Thus the criticism of "inappropriate contemporization" from the film critic for *Junge Welt*, Günter Stahnke, later a DEFA director himself, was a typical review skeptical of the necessity of establishing a "people's rule (*Volksmacht*) . . . once upon a time."[39] Hellmuth Häntzsche, the chief pedagogue at DEFA, called *Little Tailor* one of the two failed fairy-tale films, the other being *The Singing Ringing Tree* (see chapter 3).[40] However, these critics did not offer constructive suggestions for what a refined, yet convincing and partisan application of Marxism would look like on film, which meant there was a certain confusion about what form a "politically partisan" film should take in the mid-1950s. After the construction of the Berlin Wall in 1961, Kurt Schmidtchen, the leading actor who played the little tailor, left for West Germany. *Little Tailor* was then removed from circulation.[41] DEFA's animated film studio in Dresden later created *Das tapfere Schneiderlein* (The Brave Little Tailor, Kurt Weiler, 1964). In the end, the tailor marries the princess and becomes king. The Dresden studio believed that this ending did not constitute "feudal apologetics" but rather expressed "the great wishes of our forefathers who wanted to see one of their own rule." With that, the film workers thought that the revision in the earlier DEFA version appeared "narrow-minded."[42]

Little Tailor was, in fact, the first GDR adaptation of a Brothers Grimm tale. Given the importance of the Grimms' collection to the GDR's discourse on the humanist heritage, this film triggered an intense discussion between experimental filmmakers and conservative traditionalists regarding cultural heritage.[43] Traditionalists repeatedly evoked the SED's 1952 resolution against all tendencies toward vulgarizing Marxism to support their point of view that Grimms' tales and other German folktales were enshrined as sacred and not to be tinkered with.[44] This rather unexpected reaction to the film proved ironic, given that DEFA's board of directors initially disapproved of Podehl's more faithful adaptation. Apparently, it was problematic to represent the tailor's flaws as in the Grimms, yet it was overkill to give a Grimm tale a radical socialist ending. Scriptwriter Kurt Bortfeldt explained his conceptualization of the little tailor and defended to some degree the revisions he made, saying that he sought "a development in consciousness" (*eine Bewußtseinsentwicklung*) of the protagonist over the course of the story. While clever, playful, and naïve in his early encounters with the giants (played by Wolf Kaiser and Gerhard Frei), the tailor is made wise through experiences, and in later adventures, he makes *conscious* decisions not in favor of the royal court but for the benefit of the disadvantaged peasants. Thus logically, he does not want to marry the deceitful, arrogant, and vain princess who even schemes to have him killed.[45]

In retrospect, DEFA's *Little Tailor* was judged too harshly. As a matter of fact, the revisions it made anticipated many more similar changes in later DEFA films that continued to question the desirability of a spoiled princess. Under the humanist and egalitarian rubrics, personality, not social status, was the preferred yardstick for marriage partners. If the princess was seen to be unruly and hopelessly malign, the lower-class protagonist could only reject her. In such cases, the films routinely create a female character from the lower class who serves as a contrast to the princess and wins the heart of the protagonist. Revisions of this kind are undertaken, for example, in Iris Gusner's *Das blaue Licht* (The Blue Light, 1976) and Ursula Schmenger's *Der Hasenhüter* (The Rabbit Catcher, 1977). In the Grimms' "The Blue Light" (KHM 116) and Ludwig Bechstein's "The Rabbit Catcher," the protagonist ends up marrying the princess and becoming the king, even though the princess has proven nothing but unworthy. The contradictions and inconsequence that a marriage with such a princess entails are obvious. Hence, despite the strong criticism *Little Tailor* received for its ending, the solution DEFA continued to adopt was to have the protagonist reject the princess and instead happily unite with a common girl. And interestingly enough, in the mid-1970s, reviewers no longer took issue with replacing the princess with a peasant girl or blamed the films with "vulgarizing Marxism." The reviews of the 1970s films were in general not as vociferous or critical as those of 1956, when *Little Tailor* came out. Partisan films along the proletarian line had at that point become part of the norm.

Being DEFA's first avowed children's fairy-tale film, *Little Tailor* adopted a *Bilderbuch* style, in that the images resembled an illustrated book. Whereas earlier DEFA fairy-tale films still followed more of a realist cinema—despite special effects—*Little Tailor* embarked on a new path that experimented with ways to target a young audience. It used a bright color scheme and artificial, simple, but imaginative production designs. Subsequently, numerous fairy-tale films used the *Bilderbuch* aesthetic, including *The Singing Ringing Tree* (1957), *Snow White* (1961), *Mother Hulda* (1963), and *The Golden Goose* (1964). With an animated silhouette sequence foreshadowing at the very beginning, *Little Tailor* strived to create a linear, episodic, and comic narrative that would both educate and entertain young viewers. Between episodes, the transitions are induced with wipes or dissolves instead of simple cuts. The sprightly music created with harpsichord and various wind instruments is also crucial for creating a children's film atmosphere. The young audience was enthusiastic about the film[46]; they noticed the different ending without accusing the film of being politically overstated.

A Brechtian Parable: *The Story of Poor Hassan* (1958)

The criticism of *Little Tailor* resulted from the critics' insistence on remaining loyal to the known classic version as well as the permissiveness of the period of political Thaw during which such criticism could be uttered. Any aspirations for social reforms or greater freedom in cultural practices arising from the Thaw, however, were soon crushed. The Hungarian uprising in October 1956 and similar tendencies in Poland alarmed the East German leadership and stirred fear of revisionism on its own soil. The SED took a series of measures to stymie oppositional thinking: the arrest of Wolfgang Harich, Walter Janka, and others on charges of counterrevolutionary conspiracy signaled the SED's hardline politics.[47] The Thirtieth Plenary of the SED Central Committee in early 1957 sounded the alarm: "The revisionists are among us." The cultural conference in October 1957 created a document, "For a Socialist German Culture," and a separate meeting for DEFA was planned, the second film conference in 1958, which intensified a dogmatic cultural atmosphere.[48] The first film conference of socialist countries, which took place in Prague in September 1957, also laid its emphasis on the fight against revisionism.[49] Another meeting on children's films in 1959 stressed that children's films ought to follow the ideological and pedagogical guidelines more closely.[50] The tightened cultural politics influenced the choice of fairy tales, the types of revisions, and the reception of the films.

It was in this cultural–historical context that Gerhard Klein directed *Poor Hassan* (1958), which was based on a folktale of the Uighurs who live in the southeast of the former Kazakh Soviet Socialist Republic, today the Republic of Kazakhstan.[51] The oral tradition of other socialist countries was also considered part of the heritage in the GDR discourse of *Erbeaneignung*, or the appropriation of cultural heritage.[52] Another case in point was the 1961 DEFA–Mongolian coproduction, *The Golden Yurt*, which was created to celebrate the fortieth anniversary of socialist Mongolia. *The Golden Yurt* adapted a traditional Mongolian tale about a youngest son's journey to save his hometown from drought. To reward his virtue, the family's old and torn yurt is turned into a golden yurt, which symbolizes the happiness that socialist Mongolia brings to its people. This DEFA–Mongolian coproduction reflected the friendly bilateral relations between the GDR and the Mongolian People's Republic.[53]

Similar to *The Golden Yurt*, *Poor Hassan* tells a story about poor people's existential struggle for water. For *Poor Hassan*, Klein consciously deployed the form of Brecht's didactic plays (*Lehrstücke*).[54] The Brechtian aesthetics verged on modernism and was deemed to be contravening the socialist–realist mandate in the GDR. As Joshua Feinstein has pointed out, "[socialist realism] existed as a monolithic orthodoxy by focusing attention on the official ostracizing of radical modernist aesthetics, such as the epic theater of Bertolt Brecht."[55] In the GDR, Georg Lukács's advocacy of classical humanism and socialist realism and his censure of Romanticism and modernism dominated official cultural politics (see chapter 5). Brecht and Lukács disagreed on the concept of alienation. For Lukács, alienation was something that socialism had overcome.[56] Brecht was criticized by Lukàcs for being "formalistic." Eugene Lunn comments:

> As early as 1932, in one of his rare direct comments on the dramatist, Lukàcs had attacked Brecht's plays, in particular the didactic *Lehrstücke* of the period, arguing that Brechtian method prevented the development of a true socialist realism because it lacked the treatment of representative, yet individualized, characters in psychological conflict. Instead Brecht's characters represented merely abstract functions in the class struggle, speaking in disembodied arguments and agitational dialogues. Lukács regarded the "estrangement" effect as a merely formalistic device artificially imposed on the material. This critique was similar to Lukács' general assault upon the modernist avant-garde.[57]

Although Brecht opposed Lukács's judgment of him,[58] Lukács's deprecation of Brecht's aesthetics predestined Brecht's vacillating reception in the GDR, which Marc Silberman succinctly summarizes as follows:

> Brecht's return to East Berlin in 1948 and the establishment of the Berlin Ensemble were celebrated by the East German government as a major public relations coup, since he represented a strong ideological line of continuity with left intellectuals of the Weimar Republic; nonetheless, in the course of the fifties until he died

> in 1956, Brecht's politics and aesthetics were treated by the government's cultural functionaries with great suspicion because his "formalism" did not fit the dogmatic image of Socialist Realism. After his death, however, the work at the Berlin Ensemble quickly became acceptable as a model of political theatre motivated by critical, interventionary thinking (Brecht's *eingreifendes Denken*) when applied to the fascist past and to western capitalism, but not to the domestic socialist development.[59]

Thus according to Silberman, after Brecht died in 1956, the formal difference of epic theater was brushed off to the advantage of its content and political intervention. Hence, Klein's deliberate formal choice for *Poor Hassan* honored the late GDR playwright and poet whose renown had only increased since his recent death. The innovative use of Brechtian techniques resulted in a partisan parable. Brecht often used parables as "historically distant parallels to contemporary issues and events" to illustrate his Marxist, antifascist politics and ethics.[60] Aligned with the characteristics of the epic theater, the parabolic storytelling is emblematic, anti-illusionistic, and antinaturalistic.[61]

Poor Hassan opens with a camera rolling toward the main actor, Ekkehard Schall, who plays Hassan, a laborer. Schall turns to face the camera and introduces himself, his parrot, and the other characters of the film by leafing through a huge book.[62] The refreshing and sobering preamble clearly employs Brecht's dramatic theory and practice, making the audience aware that the film is a parable. Set in a desiccated Middle Eastern desert, *Poor Hassan* revolves around the laborer Hassan's oppression and final rebellion against his suppressors, who are represented by the rich merchant Machmud (Erwin Geschonneck) and the pallid and sickly magistrate Kadi. Social division of the wealthy and the poor is symbolically established by way of Hassan's humble hut standing next to Machmud's opulent residence. The class division appears to be exacerbated by Machmud's monopoly of the water supply in the dried-out region. When Hassan accidentally kills Machmud's dog during an attempt to defend himself, the corrupt judge sentences him to be the replacement watchdog for Machmud. Following a montage sequence of serene images taken in Machmud's yard, which is accompanied by the slave Fatima's beautiful song, the camera abruptly takes the spectator's focus along an iron chain to Hassan and shows him shackled to a leash. Instead of being outraged at his animalization, Hassan says, "It is beautiful here." The sharp contrast between Hassan's abject existence and the serene images and sounds found in Machmud's yard and Fatima's song is a moment of Brechtian *Gestus* and alienation (*Verfremdung*) in the film.[63]

After failing to bark like a good watchdog to prevent the theft of Machmud's horse, Hassan is forced to perform all of the duties of the stolen horse. Believing that his fate is Allah's will, Hassan puts up with all the humiliation dealt him by the members of the upper class. His resignation is symptomatic of the lack of consciousness among the lower class, which is impeded by religious thinking. "Hassan the horse" rebels against his unjust punishments at the end of the film. When the two members of the upper class sacrilegiously negotiate the price of the slave Fatima during prayer time, Hassan loudly protests against their actions and literally casts aside his yoke, a device he wears around his neck to draw water from underground. Shortly afterward, Hassan is hitched to a carriage and forced to pull Machmud and Kadi through the desert. After Machmud whips Hassan until he faints, Hassan secretly frees himself upon regaining consciousness. He runs the horse wagon into a boulder lying ahead of them, breaking up the wagon and unseating its passengers. He orders them to bark, as Machmud once ordered him, and then leaves them in the desert to be devoured by lions (see Figure 2.2).

Ekkehard Schall was one of the most prominent actors of Brecht's works. He was a member of the Berliner Ensemble from 1952 till 1995 and was married to Brecht's daughter, Barbara Brecht-Schall.[64] In the film he narrates, acts, and sings, so that distance is maintained between the actor and his character. Erwin Geschonneck, who plays the merchant, also came from the Berliner Ensemble and, against Brecht's will, left the Ensemble for DEFA.[65] Due to the prominence of the Berliner Ensemble, the carry-overs of Brechtian epic theater practices and actors "trained in gestic acting"[66] enriched DEFA films, as they did *Poor Hassan*.

Brecht's own relationship with DEFA was brief (partly due to his untimely death in 1956) and rather strained. Although they shared didactic and entertainment goals for the media, Brecht cringed at DEFA's

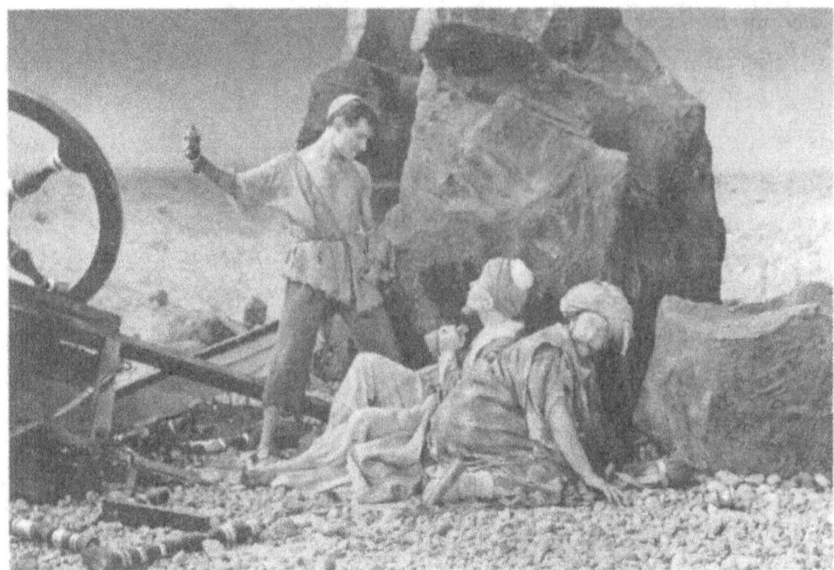

FIGURE 2.2. *Die Geschichte vom armen Hassan*: Hassan (Ekkehard Schall) takes revenge on the magistrate Kadi and merchant Machmud (Erwin Geschonneck). © DEFA-Stiftung, Eberhard Daßdorf. (Filmmuseum Potsdam)

ideological dogmatism just as he did at Hollywood's commercialism. His loyalist yet critical attitude toward Marxism accounted for his reservation toward the East German Stalinist regime and his fraught relationship with DEFA. DEFA made a few attempts to film Brecht's plays; all failed, however, with the most cited example being the botched collaboration between Brecht and DEFA on *Mother Courage and Her Children* (see chapter 1). Nevertheless, Brecht's influence on the cultural life in the GDR was enormous. After all, he was East Germany's most famous artist during its early years; many made pilgrimages from the West to see his productions. Barton Byg also points out that Brecht's collaborators Slatan Dudow and Hanns Eisler remained influential in the GDR. Dudow was the mentor of young filmmakers, including Gerhard Klein.[67]

Klein's *Poor Hassan* is reminiscent of Brecht's early learning play, *Die Ausnahme und die Regel* (The Exception and the Rule, 1930), which centers on a rich merchant's killing of a laborer in the Mongolian desert and his later acquittal. The ending of Klein's parable resembles, yet reverses, Brecht's play by having Hassan kill his master—a more revolutionary ending. Klein's dramatic structure also suited the GDR's foundational narrative better than Brecht's prerevolutionary play. The film reflects Marxist–Leninist state ideology by directly critiquing inhuman capitalism, in which the exploited are deprived of human dignity. However, by making Hassan's character the physically stronger one, this film suggests that the working class has the muscle to topple capitalist rule. In the end, the poor people repossess the fruit of their own labor. After Hassan chases away the guards at Machmud's gate, he leaves the door wide open. This suggests that wealth or property, symbolized in this case by water, is made accessible to the common people. One review found it unconvincing that Hassan can send the armed guards fleeing by simply shouting, "Go away!"[68] In defense of the film, one can contrast Hassan's seemingly supernatural power with the decadence of the ruling class. After the ruling class is overthrown, it will not be long before that power system's infrastructure begins to crumble and its cronies start to scatter in all directions. The ending could even be read as an allegory of 1945 and the collapse of the Third Reich.

Brechtian techniques are employed to activate the audience and make the film a political lesson instead of a purely aesthetic one. To Brecht, art is charged with a political mission. Lunn writes, "By accentuating contradictions between everyday appearance and what is historically realizable, Brecht hoped to galvanize his audience into action outside the theater."[69] Fairy-tale films such as *Poor Hassan* also bridged the gap between traditional tales and DEFA ideals in formulating a coherent sociopolitical agenda beyond mere entertainment and education. The Brechtian alienation effect reduces the cinematic illusion that the silver screen creates. For example, while Hassan is resigned to the cruelty of the merchant and his accomplice, his degradation to an animalistic existence provokes anger from the audience, who are alienated from the character's initial inaction.[70] Hassan's suffering drives home the oppression of the lower class and the necessity for revolution. Echoing Brecht, Klein believed the way to effectively convey a film's message was to get the audience out of a passive state while watching. He asked during the Party Activists' Convention in 1958, "What is more important? Depicting hate toward the enemy or encouraging [it] in the viewer?"[71] In *Poor Hassan*, he did both.

The fact that the parable takes place in a Middle Eastern town with German actors in exotic attire playing Arabs further conjures up Brechtian alienation as well as "ethnic drag" (discussed in chapter 1). By employing German-speaking "Muslims," the film conveniently achieves the desired distinction between the actor and the character. Following Staudte's *Little Mook* (1953), *Poor Hassan* was the second film set in the Middle East. This dislocation created a distance between the story and its German audience, who would be less likely to take the celluloid world as their own. The empathy for other people's suffering achieved through "ethnic drag" indicated that the oppressiveness and greed of the ruling class were universal and that socialist consciousness should be promoted globally. The making of this film supported the cause of international socialism.

The minimalist and indexical cinematography of *Poor Hassan*, however, led commentators to doubt the film's overall appeal to younger audiences. Christoph Funke in *Der Morgen* observed that the young audience most likely missed the parabolic message: "The children could hardly understand such a parable, and the official premiere with the presence of many children also showed that they only focused on the obvious plot."[72] Rosemarie Rehan expressed the same doubt in *Wochenpost*: "I believe folks at DEFA should discuss in this context whether one can transpose Brecht's dramaturgy onto a film just like that."[73] Steffen Wolf also commented that Klein's Brechtian didactic film "distanced itself from young viewers' intelligence."[74] Hellmuth Häntzsche, however, defended *Poor Hassan*: "This adaptation should in fact have set an example in terms of how such an artistic form could be made effective for children. Unfortunately this experiment stands rather unrepeated in fairy-tale filmmaking in the GDR."[75] As I discuss in chapter 4, *The Robe* (1961/1991), not a children's film per se, also applies Brechtian style through the script written by Egon Günther; however, due to its ban in the GDR, *The Robe* was a taboo topic.

As a committed socialist filmmaker, Klein made films that ideologically aligned with the GDR's interests in the Cold War. Although his *Berlin—Ecke Schönhauser* (Berlin—Schönhauser Corner, 1957), also with Ekkehard Schall in the leading role, reveals social problems in East Germany, it celebrates the East overall as the preferable *Heimat* with a better future and presents the West as a breeding ground for crimes and sins. At a time when East

Germans were leaving the "better" Germany en masse and crossing the border unhindered, the film warns of the corrupting influences from the West for East German youth and precludes the West as a better choice. Whereas in a contemporary film such as *Berlin—Schönhauser Corner* Klein could openly demonstrate Cold War allegiance, *Poor Hassan* indirectly yet also effectively juxtaposes inhuman capitalism—characteristic of the West—and socialist promises after Hassan's revolutionary victory at the end of the film. The ideological preference is to be inferred through the typical equation of rich and evil, poor and good. Whether a contemporary feature or a fairy tale, the conventional story of oppression and exploitation undoubtedly applied to the situation of divided Germany. Stylistically, Klein's *Berlin—Schönhauser Corner* did not toe the official line and therefore fueled a debate over neorealism. In *Poor Hassan*, although quite a visual contrast to *Berlin—Schönhauser Corner*, his borrowing of the modernist epic theater form nonetheless encountered skepticism that questioned the suitability of the Brechtian mode for children.

A Low-Born King and a Valiant Paramour: *The Tinderbox* (1959) and *The Golden Goose* (1964)

In comparison to the films discussed above, Siegfried Hartmann's *The Tinderbox* (1959) had greater success with the public with 5.5 million viewers.[76] This popularity and the positive reviews were partly due to the film's loyalty to the original literary version, in which the lower-class protagonist happily marries the princess—after the apparent faux pas of *Little Tailor*. DEFA was able to keep the class-oblivious marriage because this princess is herself a victim of absolutist rule and thus an eligible marriage partner for the hero. *The Tinderbox* and Hartmann's internationally more prominent fairy-tale film *The Golden Goose* (1964) illustrate the rise of a member of the working class to power and a princess's liberation from her authoritarian father. The male protagonists are valiant paramours and need not reject the good princesses. Thus these films obviously would not stir up such controversy as *Little Tailor* did in terms of "vulgarizing Marxism." *The Tinderbox* was the first DEFA fairy-tale film that ends with a marriage between a commoner and a princess as in its original version. After the debacles of *Little Tailor*

(1956) and *The Singing Ringing Tree* (1957), *The Tinderbox* returned to the royal palace but engaged a different, rather weakened depiction of the princess, preempting any "ideological errors" that its unfortunate predecessors were accused of. And the gender relations are characterized by the typical fairy-tale plot of saving a damsel in distress.

Hartmann's *The Tinderbox* redressed the flaw of his earlier film *Fiete im Netz* (Fiete in a Net, 1957), which came out two years earlier. *Fiete in a Net* was specifically reprimanded for insufficient portrayal of socialist everyday life and for being "neo-Biedermeier,"[77] "morally and socially indifferent,"[78] and "a flight into atemporal and asocial rural idyll."[79] Like *The Singing Ringing Tree*, *Fiete in a Net* came out at a time of disciplinary scrutiny of children's films in the GDR. Hartmann's adaptation of Hans Christian Andersen's "The Tinderbox," however, won wide approval for its experimentation with a *realistic* rendition of a fairy tale containing fantastic occurrences, reinforcing again the idea that (socialist) realism and fantasy are not necessarily diametric to each other. The film adaptation foregrounded the value of true friendship in the soldier's final triumph over the king. In so doing, the film remedied the ideological deficiency found in *Fiete in a Net*. The performance by the well-known actor Rolf Ludwig in the leading role also helped increase the film's appeal. Ludwig's engagement in this fairy-tale film was often referred to as an example of top actors willing to play for children. Johannes Maus, who played Old Mook, appeared in the role of the shoemaker Meister Schaft.

The film begins with a revolutionary song innocently clad in fairy-tale language. The soldier sings about his unpaid service in the royal army; he is on his way to the city to dethrone the king: "Left, right, my patience is now running out/Step down from the golden throne!/'Get your payment from the Devil!'/Wait and see!"[80] The song foretells the ending of the story and shows the soldier as more aware of his mission than his prototype in Andersen. He then meets a witch who asks him to retrieve a tinderbox from the bottom of a hollow oak tree in exchange for lodging and a meal. Down in the tree, he comes on three treasure boxes filled, respectively, with bronze, silver, and gold coins guarded by three ferocious looking watchdogs, each one bigger than the last, thanks to the special effects by Ernst Kunstmann and his daughter. The soldier reemerges from

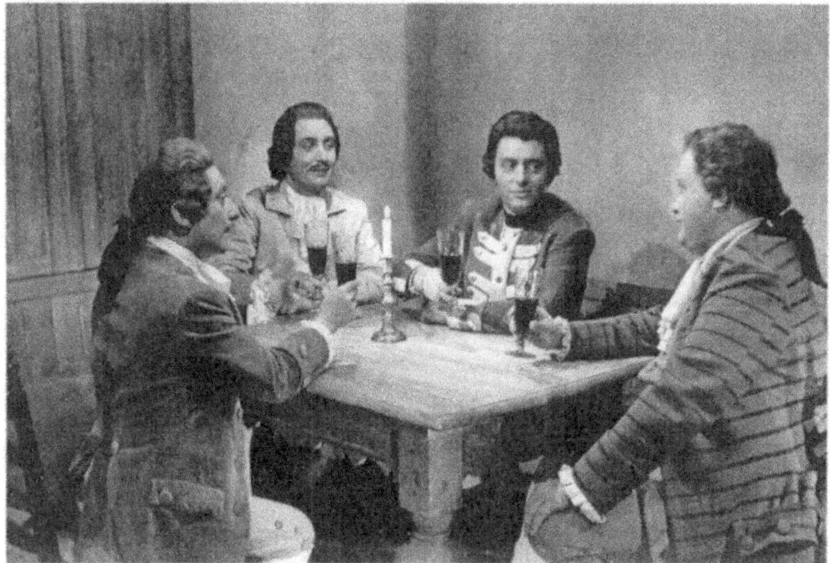

FIGURE 2.3. *Das Feuerzeug*: Three dandies enjoy life at the expense of the soldier (Rolf Ludwig). © DEFA-Stiftung, Hannes Schneider.

the oak fully loaded with gold, kills the treacherous witch-turned-snake, and keeps the tinderbox for himself.

Once in town, the rich soldier kindly pays the dues for a shoemaker apprentice, gets himself a nice outfit, buys presents for children in the marketplace, and pays for an elderly woman's purchase. But he also pays for his new "friends" from the well-to-do circles, represented by three upper-class dandies: the Vain (Rolf Defrank), the Miser (Heinz Schubert), and the Fatty (Hannes Fischer) (see Figure 2.3). As soon as he is penniless again, however, these "friends" treat him with contempt and only his lower-class friends remain true to him. This experience allows him to see through the hypocrisy and greed of the upper class. In this dire situation, he discovers the magic of the tinderbox: when he strikes it, the supernatural dogs appear to do his biddings. The dogs fetch him gold coins in an instant. When the foppish dandies realize their mistake and try to further enjoy life at his expense, the soldier retorts, "Friends like you are not even good for good times." In Andersen's tale, the soldier does not learn a lesson about friendship: despite the fact that his "friends" abandoned him when he ran out of money, he resumes friendship with the same "fine friends."[81] Not the soldier in Andersen but the one in the film undergoes this personal growth. He now spends his money wisely, showing the young audience the right way to dispense wealth.

It is the talk of the town that the king has imprisoned the princess in a copper castle because it is prophesied that his daughter will marry a soldier. The king tries everything in his power to prevent the oracle from coming true. The film invents an arranged marriage for the princess, a recurrent theme in DEFA fairy-tale films. The soldier orders the supernatural dogs to carry the princess to him at night, which the princess thinks was a dream and about which she tells her parents the next morning. The king finally succeeds in capturing the soldier and sentences him to death. The shoemaker apprentice saves the day by managing to retrieve the tinderbox. The giant dogs chase away all the nobility and their cronies, who, however, do not all die violent deaths as in Andersen. But the blood in the dogs' jaws indicates, echoing Marx's theory, that violence wielded by the oppressors can only be countered with violence from the oppressed. At the end, the people joyfully celebrate the soldier and the princess's wedding.

Andersen's tale was inspired by Grimms' "The Blue Light," which Iris Gusner later adapted in 1976. Both stories involve a soldier climbing down to the underground to retrieve an item for a disingenuous witch. The recovered item—certainly magical—helps bring the princess to his room at night. Only in the Grimms' tale, the soldier humiliates the princess by making her do a maid's work, whereas in Andersen, the soldier is moved by the sleeping princess's beauty, kisses her, and is determined to marry her. In both stories, the soldier is imprisoned, but, with help from a loyal friend and the magical item, he vanquishes his opponents anyway and realizes a marriage that transcends the classes.

To the delight of (re)viewers, Hartmann adapts the story faithfully, with an eye to highlighting the moral of true friendship. To that end, the film enlarges the role of the apprentice, who appears in Andersen only as deus ex machina to save the soldier from being hanged. The apprentice boy is introduced at the beginning of the film as a beneficiary of the soldier's generosity. When the soldier is deserted by all his upper-class friends, the boy brings him food, and his loyal friendship sets up the final turn of events. As the commentary in *Zwischen Marx und Muck* points out, "The realistic value of a friendship is more clearly emphasized as the pillar moment of the tale than the tinderbox's irrational magic power."[82] The director explained why he chose to make this film: "In a poetic way, *The Tinderbox* is a fable with a clear and unambiguous message: good friends always help and are worth more than money. He who only flatters and leaves you in the ditch when you are in need is not your friend. So be careful with whom you make friends."[83] *The Tinderbox* can be seen as a good example of the emphasis on socialist humanism in DEFA fairy-tale films. As fantastic as it still is, it makes an attempt at disenchantment to highlight humanistic values such as personal strength and collective power.

After his *Fiete in a Net* was criticized for lacking reference to the GDR reality, Hartmann took a demonstrative ideological and political stance in *The Tinderbox*. The wealthy and the poor are clearly divided in the film in both their appearance and morality: the poor look forward to the soldier saving the princess, whereas the wealthy and powerful mock him and obstruct his efforts. The innkeeper (Fritz Schlegel) is a typical example of people who worship money. The end of the film portrays the opposing reaction of the crowd who come to witness the soldier's execution: the bourgeois and upper-class people gloat over the soldier's misfortune, and the working-class people are solemn and saddened. But this film's political maneuvering was not criticized in 1959, as *Little Tailor* was back in 1956, which proves that a successful adaptation in the 1950s required loyalty to the classic tale with a distilled message that was politically and socially meaningful.

The divide between the rich and the poor in *The Tinderbox* is inevitably taken to reflect the difference between the two German states in economic terms. Economic standing is, in this context, indicative of moral character. The equation of the well-off class with wanting morality led the distributors, among others, to conclude that this film was not suitable for distribution in the FRG: "This dichotomy is all too characteristic of the current situation in the FRG, where people are sensitive to Andersen's tendency to show the rich as hardhearted in hopes of moving them to act charitably to the poor."[84] Nonetheless, the film ran successfully in West Germany starting in 1961.[85] Although it aligned with GDR ideology, *The Tinderbox* did not come across as exclusively socialist or propagandistic.

The theme of friendship possessed a universal appeal, allowing it to cross GDR borders and survive the country that made it.

In 1964, a second fairy-tale film by Siegfried Hartmann came out, this time based on a Grimm tale—"The Golden Goose" (KHM 64). It was a bigger international success than *The Tinderbox* and was shown at the international children's film festival in Gijón, Spain; it was also played at the Broadway in New York and in Cuba, Canada, England, Albania, Italy, and Japan.[86] In the United States, the film was dubbed and distributed by K. Gordon Murray and was shown in American theaters at "kiddie matinees." According to Jim Morton, all of the fairy-tale films that Murray purchased hailed from West Germany except *The Golden Goose*. Had Murray not run afoul of the IRS, which confiscated all his films, he might have been able to import more DEFA fairy tales. He was intent on reclaiming his films, when he died of a heart attack. Owing to Murray, *The Golden Goose* was brought to the United States earlier than *The Tinderbox* and *Little Tailor*, which were purchased by a New York distributor, Barry B. Yellen, who followed Murray's lead.[87]

A typical male Cinderella story, the film tells of a cobbler named Klaus who marries the princess and inherits half of the kingdom by making the solemn princess laugh. Mistreated at home as a simpleton by two older, lazy brothers (Uwe Detlef Jessen and Peter Dommisch), Klaus is kind and shares his meal with an elderly woman, who gives Klaus a goose with feathers of gold. A chain of curious and greedy people are then stuck to the magnetic feathers, including the greedy innkeeper, played by the same actor (Fritz Schlegel) who plays the innkeeper in *The Tinderbox*. In the Grimms' version, a parson and a sexton also get glued to the magic goose. After the difficulty *The Wooden Calf* (1959/1961) had with censorship (see below), it is not surprising that religious personnel were left out and spared ridicule in *The Golden Goose*. This train of attached people helps create a comic scenario that finally brings the princess to laugh and wins the bridal contest for Klaus. The Grimm tale progresses linearly, as is typical of fairy tales, but the DEFA adaptation introduces most characters early on and uses montage to depict parallel events in and outside of the palace.

The film's script and dramaturgy were rather uninspired. The few press reviews that could be found were positive but banal. DEFA had numerous other great fairy-tale films that received more enthusiastic and critical attention than *The Golden Goose*. Yet, it was *The Golden Goose* that was exported to many countries and translated into English. American viewers' familiarity with this film owed much to Murray's fortuitous import of this particular film to the United States. The light entertainment the film offers, with colorful costumes, joyous music, cheerful acting, and many clever ideas may have played a role in Murray's choice. For example, the film starts with an animated golden goose introducing the opening credits. At the end, the real "golden" goose touches a book page that announces "The End" of the film. Kaspar Eichel plays the jaunty, happy-go-lucky Klaus. The film was so popular that Eichel and Karin Ugowski became identified with their characters, something that the actors themselves felt very ambivalent about.[88] The success of the film demonstrates that light entertainment, not political infiltration, is the recipe for both domestic and international success.

Nonetheless, the antifeudal and anticapitalist rhetoric is still subtly embedded in the film. It explains why the princess cannot laugh as resulting from the boredom of courtly life. (Karin Ugowski said in an interview that it was hard not to laugh on command, just as hard as to have to cry on demand.[89] It is obvious that she could barely suppress her laughter when she teases the courtly scholar Weisenstein played by Gerd E. Schäfer on the seesaw.) To show the fatuous king's obsession with wealth, the film places a giant treasure chest within a guarded fence with seven locks on; moreover, the king's staff has to count the treasure thrice a day. The film creates a Prince Störenfried (Troublemaker) who brings his gang to kidnap the princess and usurp the kingdom. Although the king does not keep his promises and despises a son-in-law of humble origin, Klaus defends the palace against intruders. Applying physics theory and thus adding a modern touch to the traditional tale, Klaus uses a pulley to haul the treasure chest to a safe place upstairs. He relies on his own intelligence and bravery to accomplish all these tasks, whereas, in the Grimms' tale, a magic dwarf has to complete the tasks for the protagonist. Similar to *The Tinderbox*, *The*

Golden Goose reduces the function of magic and increases that of self-help and solidarity among members of the lower class.

Both *The Tinderbox* and *The Golden Goose* end with a member of the lower class taking over power. However, these films lack a concrete vision regarding how this new regime is going to work. They do not offer realistic, feasible blueprints for what is to come after the (temporarily) happy endings. The happy yet limited projection into the future is symptomatic of the myopia in the nineteenth-century tales, which in turn resembles Marxist utopia. Pitted against the GDR reality, the happily ever after again remains merely a fairy-tale notion.

Tales of Little Farmers: *The Wooden Calf* (1959/1961) and *Little Claus and Big Claus* (1971)

If everything went as planned, Bernhard Thieme's *The Wooden Calf* would have seen the light of day in the same year as *The Tinderbox*. However, it experienced great difficulty with authorities and did not premiere until May 1961. Even after drastic revisions, a critic, Charlotte Czygan, lambasted the film as "one of the weakest of its kind" and in the same breath praised Hartmann's *The Tinderbox* as an exception that lived up to the expectations of artistic adaptation:

> This journal [*Deutsche Filmkunst*] on many occasions has indicated the difficulties with cinematic adaptations of traditional folktales. Except for Siegfried Hartmann's *The Tinderbox*, which did justice to the genre-appropriate demands for an artistic transformation, such undertakings have usually failed due to violent contemporization, idealistic conceptualization, or an uninspired and inartistic creation. DEFA's *The Wooden Calf* . . . has to be considered one of the weakest films of its kind.[90]

This devastating critique was rather curious for a film that closely followed the socialist–realist imperatives and depicted the clear-cut struggle of poor farmers against the rich and powerful. This section analyzes the film's socialist–realist revisions by way of a comparison with its original version—the Grimms' "Little Farmer" (KHM 61). Then it explains why the film was almost banned. At the end I will also briefly discuss Celino Bleiweiß's *Little Claus and Big Claus* (1971), because Andersen's "Little Claus and Big Claus" is precisely a rewriting of the Grimms' "Little Farmer."

In a number of DEFA tales, class struggles do not unfold between ordinary people and aristocrats but between poor and rich farmers, portraying the proletarians' collective and successful fight against their rural oppressors. *The Wooden Calf* abided by socialist-realist tenets and made a number of necessary revisions to the original tale. In the Grimms' story, a little farmer who does not own a cow tricks a cowherd into herding a wooden calf and then takes him to the mayor after it is stolen. The mayor rules that the cowherd should recompense the farmer for the loss with a cow—real of course. Then the little farmer kills the cow and plans to sell the cowhide in town. On his way, he witnesses how the miller's wife secretly treats the priest with a delicious meal during her husband's absence, and when the miller comes back, she hides the priest and food away. By revealing the truth as a "fortuneteller," Little Farmer extracts 300 talers from the miller. He tricks the rich farmers into believing that a cowhide is worth 300 talers on the market, which causes them to kill all their cows. In the end, the little farmer has wiped out the entire village and becomes a rich farmer himself. Although he outwits his class enemies, he likewise victimizes the "little people"—a cowherd, a miller, and a shepherd—who are all members of his own class. His motivations are economic and egotistical. He clearly lacks the potential to be the leader for a proletarian revolution, and so his rags-to-riches story is a questionable model for the masses.

The DEFA adaptation brings out the revolutionary thrust of the tale and recasts the little farmer (Günther Haack) as an absolutely socialist hero. Under his leadership, the poor farmers stand their ground and expose the scheme of the rich farmers, who steal their calves to remove them from the meadows. Little Farmer carves a wooden calf, no longer because, as in the Grimms' tale, he believes that the wooden calf would magically grow into a real cow but because he wants to fool and catch the thief. Unlike in the Grimms' tale, he now sides with the cowherd (Hans-Peter Reinecke) against the court's decision and demands that the court discover the thief's identity. This request is rather tongue in cheek, since it is clear to everyone that the village mayor (*Schultheiß*) himself is the thief. Little Farmer does not deceive the smith but shows camaraderie with him throughout the film. Likewise, the episode about tricking the shepherd is revised. In the end the rich farmers are chased away from the village instead of being "wiped out" as in the Grimms. This more humanistic ending is consistent with the apparent DEFA norm of removing villains from power rather than eliminating them, a practice that began with *The Murderers Are among Us* (1946), for which Wolfgang Staudte had to revise his ending so that Mertens no longer kills his former captain but delivers him into the hands of justice.[91] The village mayor's last words "I'm innocent!" (*Ich bin unschuldig!*) also recall those of Brückner, the captain-turned-capitalist in *The Murderers Are among Us*.

Rather unexpected for a realistically depicted tale about class struggle, the State Film Approval Board declared *The Wooden Calf* "failed" (*mißlungen*) after an intense discussion on 1 April 1960. The contention revolved around the sarcastic depiction of the Catholic priest (Walter Jupé). It was argued that such a figure would potentially stir up trouble, especially in the countryside, and could have damaging political ramifications. A second viewing had to be scheduled for 13 April 1960, this time chaired by State Secretary Erich Wendt and attended by representatives from the State Secretary for Church Questions, the Ministry for Education, and the Pioneer Organization. Hans Seidowsky from the Ministry for Culture declared that the GDR at the moment could not use any film that had an anticlerical character, especially not an anti-Catholic one, because the state had an even better relationship with the Catholic than with the Protestant Church. Everyone else agreed with him. The film was again denied a public release and had to be modified. Not until 21 December 1960 was a revised version begrudgingly approved. Censors acknowledged its relative improvement: the erstwhile depiction of the priest was now without a definitive character and his influence on the plot no longer decisive, but the picture was nonetheless somewhat problematic because he was still recognizable as a priest (see Figure 2.4).[92]

The film enlarges the role of the priest, who in the Grimms' tale only appears briefly at the miller's house. Due to the many cuts and reshoots, viewers would not know how the priest was originally portrayed. In the

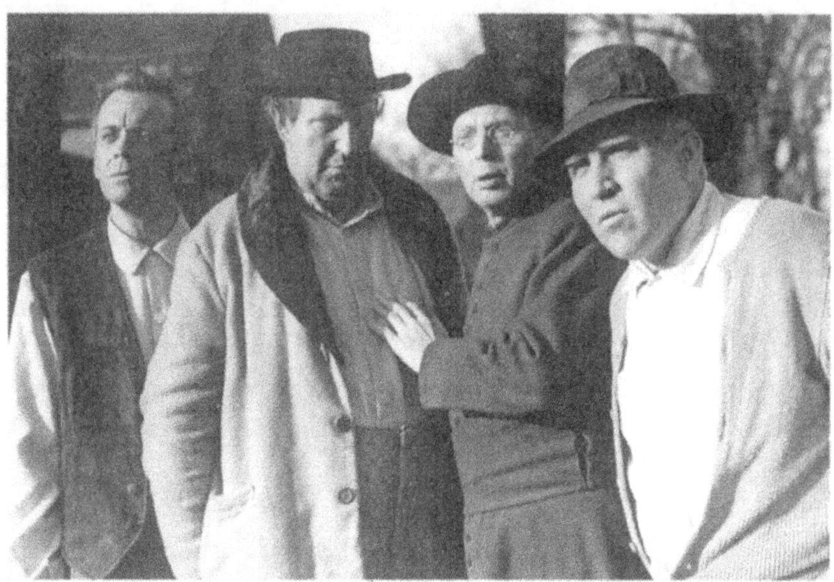

FIGURE 2.4. *Das hölzerne Kälbchen*: The priest (Walter Jupé) with three rich farmers. © DEFA-Stiftung, Hans Bernd Baxmann.

released version, the uptight priest tries to maintain a somewhat neutral position between the rich and poor farmers, but he is bribed by the mayor and thus exposes his own corruptibility. Little Farmer and the smith discover him in a chest where the smith's wife (Lore Frisch) has hidden him. The priest then gives them as hush money the 100 talers he received from the mayor. Later when the little farmer falls into the mayor's trap and is about to be drowned in a sack, the priest needs to hear his last confession, thereby releasing him from the sack and saving him involuntarily. Despite the forced revisions, the film clearly portrays the priest as a weakened, compromised religious figure and an instrument of the political powers that be. The authorities feared that this problematic image of the priest might have unwanted repercussions in the GDR. Although the essentially negative quality of the priest was not changed despite cuts and reshoots, the difficulty the censors gave the film team was demonstrative of their good will toward the church establishment in the GDR.

The censors' fear of political consequence for the sarcastic depiction of a priest had to do with the pragmatic and complex relationship between the churches and the state around the 1960s. On the one hand, the state philosophy of scientific atheism and programmatic sidelining of church presence resulted in the gradual secularization of society. Churches in the GDR slowly came to acknowledge the power of the state and the party, and in return, the government ensured religious toleration. On the other hand, the state tried to use the churches' all-German ties to hinder the rearmament of the FRG and welcomed the considerable hard currency subsidies from the Western church to the East German church. When *The Wooden Calf* was made and evaluated, the SED at least rhetorically sought to mobilize Christian support for its "socialist human community," arguing that "Christianity and Marxism do not represent a contradiction."[93] Thus the image of the dubious and manipulated priest was unwelcome. The film would be Bernhard Thieme's only feature film.

"The real causes for *The Wooden Calf*'s failure," wrote Charlotte Czygan in *Deutsche Filmkunst*, lay in "the vulgar, naturalistic adaptation of the literary work and the superficially didactic production."[94] Her criticism resembled the accusation of "vulgarizing Marxism" that *Little Tailor* received. She further pointed out that, although the rich farmers are outwitted, the film is not done in a way that is fairy-tale–like or fantastic, but is naturalistic. The film is, not explicitly but implicitly, criticized for being "schematic," which, as Joshua Feinstein defines it, means using "simplistic plots in order to convey an ideological message."[95] Resembling a trickster figure, Little Farmer uses his wit and repeatedly dupes his adversaries. The rich farmers are, furthermore, depicted as overly stupid: the mayor cannot tell a wooden calf from a real one; three rich farmers believe a cowhide could sell for 300 talers and thus slaughter all their cattle; they believe they are carrying Little Farmer in a sack to be drowned, but they in fact are carrying a sack of rocks. These dramaturgical flaws stem partly from the Grimms' template. But in staying true to partisan principles, the film makes tendentious revisions along class lines, revisions that nevertheless arouse suspicions of schematism.

A decade later, the black-and-white television film *Little Claus and Big Claus* told a tale that is similar to *The Wooden Calf* and received positive reviews. The fact that two affiliated stories were adapted, ten years apart, demonstrates the importance of class struggle in the countryside and the triumph of "little farmers" for DEFA. Celino Bleiweiß's *Little Claus* was also DEFA's first fairy-tale film commissioned by Fernsehen der DDR, the television broadcaster of the GDR. *Little Claus* has a plot similar to that of *The Wooden Calf*. It likewise has a shady sexton (Arno Wyzniewski) disgracefully hiding in a chest at the miller's (Hannes Fischer) house, but the film was approved without much hassle. After its premiere on television in 1971, the film came to the movie theater a year later.[96] This again attests to the fact that the reception of DEFA films had as much to do with the historical period the film was made in as with the film itself.

DEFA highlights the socialist–humanist qualities of Little Farmer and Little Claus (Fred Düren). Whereas traditional fairy-tale heroes act in isolation, these protagonists have wives and children. Compared to earlier children's films such as *Somewhere in Berlin* (1946), in which the father, traumatized by war and despondent, has to reintegrate into the new reality, the fathers in these fairy-tale films have arrived in (proto-)socialist reality. The addition of child characters also brings the film closer to the young audience and eases them into lessons about class struggles. The innocence and sense of justice of child characters fortify the legitimacy of the revolutionary cause.

Both films critique capitalism: the rich farmers, driven by their insatiable greed, succumb to the wit and cunning of the little farmers. However in the course of ten years, revolutionary pathos in fact waned. *The Wooden Calf* follows socialist realism more closely than *Little Claus*. Whereas *The Wooden Calf* features crowd scenes that show the villagers collectively building a house or beating up the rich farmers and sending them packing, *Little Claus* lacks such an agitprop (agitational propaganda) depiction of collective struggles. The later film focuses mainly on Little Claus's single-handed confrontation with Big Claus. Whereas Little Farmer is a distinctive socialist–realist hero, Little Claus remains somewhat ambiguous. For example, after Big Claus slaughters Little Claus's only horse, Little Claus's wife (Monika Woytowicz) urges him to take Big Claus to court. But Little Claus is resigned to his situation: "What should I complain about? Me, Little Claus, against Big Claus? . . . It makes no sense and would only end badly for us. . . . One kind of justice for Big Claus and a different kind for Little Claus. What could you do about it?"[97]

The ending of the film is also devoid of any agitational effect. Whereas ten years earlier Little Farmer had tricked the rich farmers into believing that cows grazed at the bottom of the lake, it is obvious that ten years later Little Claus is merely teasing Big Claus. Hence whereas *The Wooden Calf* portrays farmers united and in the end violently fighting against local dignitaries, *Little Claus* retreats from earlier propagandistic narratives. When *The Wooden Calf* was too communistic and thus not acceptable in West Germany, *Little Claus* was shown there. It struck a West German reviewer as resembling a *Heimat* film (*heimatfilmisch*).[98] The idyllic countryside with Little Claus's field, hut, wife, and seven children indeed evokes images of West German *Heimat* films. Since none of the East German reviews brought up *Heimat* films in this context, it suggests that reviewers in the East and West drew on cinematic registers familiar to them.

A Moderate Version of Eugene Schwartz's Antifascist Agitprop: *Little Red Riding Hood* (1962)

The famous tale of Little Red Riding Hood has been interpreted from various standpoints, especially by feminists and psychoanalysts.[99] It has also been instrumentalized by different regimes to serve their own political and ideological purposes. The National Socialist adaptation *Rotkäppchen und der Wolf* (Little Red Riding Hood and the Wolf, Fritz Genschow and Renée Stobrawa, 1937) is set in the contemporary Nazi period in black-and-white and frames the actual tale in the middle of the film in color. Uncle Hunter, played by the director/scriptwriter Fritz Genschow, wears the insignia of the Nazi eagle and swastika on his hat and arrives in time to rescue Little Red Riding Hood and her grandmother from the wolf.[100] In the Soviet Union and in the GDR, the tale was appropriated mainly from a Marxist perspective as a struggle of the presumably weak against the strong and was thus enacted as an allegorical battle between different classes and ideologies. The well-known DEFA adaptation of *Little Red Riding Hood* (1962) directed by Götz Friedrich features a more active heroine who uses snuff (pepper in Schwartz) to defeat the wolf (see Figure 2.5). In an article for *Deutsche Filmkunst*, Friedrich explicitly stated that resistance forces—represented by the heroine and her animal friends—"must be mobilized so that good can win out, and this is the message from *Little Red Riding Hood*."[101]

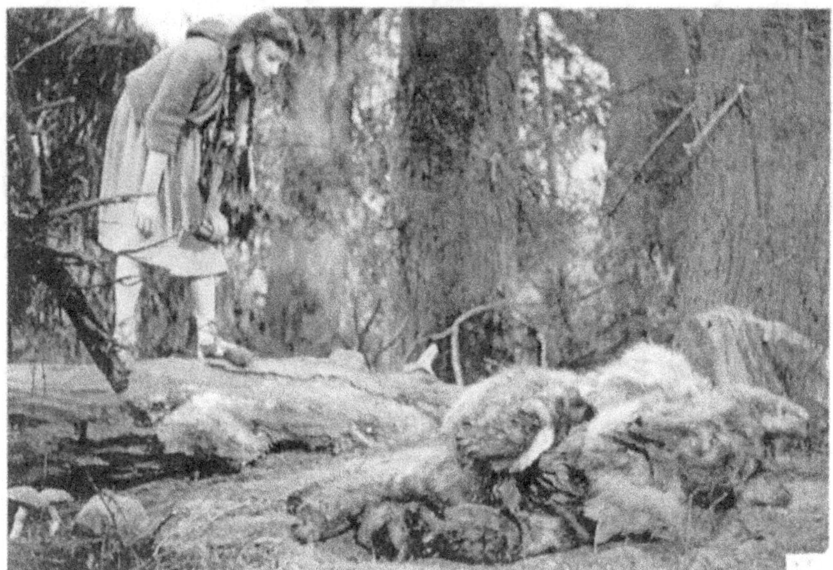

FIGURE 2.5. *Rotkäppchen*: Little Red Riding Hood (Blanche Kommerell) defeats the wolf. © DEFA-Stiftung, Karin Blasig.

However, it is little known that this film was adapted from Eugene Schwartz's play *Little Red Riding Hood* (1936) by Hans Rodenberg, who lived in Soviet exile until 1948.[102] The famous Jewish Russian playwright adapted the Grimms' tale in the mid-1930s and incorporated an antifascist message about solidarity. Only with a solidarity movement could the weak overcome the strong and restore peace in the forest/world. This DEFA film shows more direct Soviet influence than *The Cold Heart* and *Little Mook* because, through Rodenberg, it is based on Schwartz's play. But the DEFA film is only a moderate version of Schwartz's loaded agitprop.

Schwartz's allegorical play takes place "today in Russia."[103] Little Red Riding Hood is fully aware that the wolf is on the lookout to attack her by surprise, but she bravely schemes a plan to trap the wolf. She declares, "In a word, I'm going to war with The Wolf."[104] According to the English translation of the play, the heroine "gives new meaning to the word 'red' in the title," because "Schwartz here creates the ideal young pioneer."[105] Red not only refers to the red cap she wears but also assumes the symbolic meaning associated with communism. Although she is still eaten by the wolf, she does not passively wait to be saved, as in the Grimms. Instead, calling out from inside the wolf, she sends her "airborne reconnaissance"—her avian friends—to fetch Comrade Forester. The publisher notes that "the addition of Comrade Forester as a kind of guardian angel of the forest reflects that aspect of Soviet propaganda that is a part of Russian children's theatre."[106] The politically charged play ends with a victory proclamation and precaution against enemies:

> All:
> We have finished with the war.
> One, two! One, two! (This refrain is repeated every other line)
> The Wolf is caught, The Fox is caught!
> Victory is attained.
> Because we are friends,
> We rushed boldly into battle.
> And now we're going home!
> But keep your eyes open, friends.
> Endless is the evil of The Wolf.
> Never forget your enemy!
> Farewell, my friends.[107]

Schwartz's revolutionary play instills socialist–realist style and revolutionary pathos in the famous fairy tale. The political overtone of the play is strident, and the villains could represent any enemies of communism. The play became a staple of the Soviet repertoire since 1937, when it was first performed at the New Theater for Young Spectators in Leningrad. In the prewar and war years, the themes of bravery, friendship, solidarity, and battle with evil allies inevitably evoked association with the antifascist struggles around the world. Because of the Hitler–Stalin pact in effect between 1939 and 1941, the antifascist overtone of the play had to be suppressed at least for the duration of the pact.

In adopting Schwartz's version, both Rodenberg's 1951 play as well as Friedrich's 1962 film were implicitly tied in with the GDR's antifascist agenda and founding myth, albeit in parabolic language. As a stage director and scriptwriter, Hans Rodenberg stood out with his unusual political stature because he became a member of the SED's Central Committee after returning from his Soviet exile in 1948. In the Soviet Union, he was put in charge of envisioning a future film industry in Germany as soon as the war ended.[108] In the GDR, he founded Theater der Freundschaft in Berlin-Lichtenberg and was its first director. According to Kristin Wardetzky, due to the controversy over fairy tales Rodenberg hesitated for a long time to finally stage the well-known tale of Little Red Riding Hood based on Schwartz's one-act play. Since Schwartz adapted the Grimms' tale, Rodenberg's theater production at once paid respect to the German heritage and nurtured the Soviet–East German cultural ties. His Marxist, didactic play in 1951 gained a "programmatic significance" for his theater and laid the foundation for a Marxist conception of fairy-tale plays. The play was highly praised in the East German press as having "such a current reference" that it "activates children to do something for peace."[109] But Rodenberg's leftist adaptation attracted criticism from the West. Wardetzky mentions a review in the *New York Herald Tribune* that compared the wolf to Wall Street and imperialism and equated the hunter with Stalin.[110] In 1952, the Politburo appointed Rodenberg to become DEFA's primary director, a position he held until 1956.[111]

The plotline of Friedrich's film greatly resembles that of Schwartz's play. The DEFA film also adds a fox, a bear (Ernst-Georg Schwill), and a rabbit, all played by real actors. Although Friedrich's film was based on Schwartz's play via Rodenberg, the Soviet predecessor was, surprisingly, not discussed in interviews or Hellmuth Häntzsche's discussion with younger viewers, which was published in *Sozialistischer Kinderfilm*, a special edition of *Film: Filmwissenschaftliche Mitteilungen* (*fwm*) in 1962. It is clear that the children compared the film with only the Grimm version.[112] The reason might lie in the strikingly propagandistic Soviet play that indeed resembled a tribute to Stalin through the figure of Comrade Forester. After Stalin's death in 1953 and Khrushchev's denunciation of him in 1956, the Soviet model would have been better left unmentioned. Also due to the different artistic form of theater and film, scriptwriter Rodenberg and director Friedrich followed the plot but radically rewrote the narrative and changed style. Actually none of the DEFA fairy-tale films can compare with Schwartz's play in terms of belligerent language and straightforward propaganda.

The DEFA adaptation is, in contrast, primarily didactic and entertaining. It divests itself of the majority of the agitational language present in Schwartz's play. There is no more Comrade Forester who comes to the rescue, just Little Red Riding Hood's parents. DEFA's rabbit is brave, loyal, and alert but far more moderate than Schwartz's rabbit, which, for example, delivers the following dramatic speech after it is trapped:

> What can I do? How can I save the girl now? Help! (Crying loudly.) Help! No one hears me. (To the audience.) Should I let her perish? No! I have to call out, to shout. Maybe someone in the forest will hear me. (He yells louder.) Help! I'm not afraid of anything any more. Help! (Pause.) No one. But I won't give up. I'll keep calling until all my brother rabbits come to my aid. We'll win yet. (He starts drumming on the trap with his front paws and calls.) Brother rabbits! Brother rabbits! Let's join together. Faithful rabbit hearts will endure to the last.[113]

As in Schwartz, the wolf does not die at the end of Friedrich's film. Instead the grandmother stitches its belly back together. In Schwartz's version, the wolf chews through the rope and escapes, only to be caught again. Little Red Riding Hood's friends "drag him to the people for trial and punishment!"[114] In the DEFA version, Little Red Riding Hood's father and the bear tie the wolf's paws with rope and carry it away, although it is not clear where to. This humanistic ending, as one reviewer put it, "appears absolutely ridiculous."[115]

As with many other DEFA fairy-tale films, *Little Red Riding Hood* was advertised as "for big and little people." The requirement to appeal to different age groups posed a challenge to the dramaturgy. The film team catered to the youngest audience with camera work and montage editing befitting a children's film; they used neither modernist techniques nor special effects.[116] Yet critics noted the increased level of violence in the film; in particular, there are two scenes in which the grandmother and Little Red Riding Hood are devoured. Expressionistic shadow play is used here to depict the violent struggle between the wolf and its victims. Therefore, the film unleashed at the time an(other) intense discussion among educators surrounding violence in old fairy tales.[117] According to the abovementioned special edition of *Film: Filmwissenschaftliche Mitteilungen*, educators expressed serious concerns about the film's portrayal of evil. The portrayal scared the younger audience, who were riveted on the wolf's appearance, their eyes showing only "fear and terror."[118] The filmmakers defended their conception of evil in that they "identify evil with morbid social forces in the world, which could maintain their power only through collusion of brutal violence with underhanded trickery."[119] They insisted that they should not mitigate the impression of cruelty; otherwise, the danger of evil could be minimized or made unrecognizable.[120] For the young audience, this deep message went unnoticed; older viewers could better comprehend the filmmakers' dialectic conception of evil.

In reaction to this controversy, Hellmuth Häntzsche explicitly spelled out how good and evil in fairy tales could be interpreted in socialist–realist art. According to him, the GDR could not insulate their children from the social reality as it was. The antagonistic contradictions between socialist and capitalist camps made it necessary to familiarize children as early as possible with the battle between good and evil and expose evil in its various disguises and effects. He wrote, "The relation between good and evil, as long as the subject allows, should be concretized in the aesthetic, that is, to let collision be primarily recognized as that between antagonistic classes. Therefore in representing a fairy tale it is not enough merely to let evil be conquered by good, but the nature of evil has to be made clearly visible and understandable to children in their aesthetic experience. Only then are they enabled to recognize and assess evil."[121] Häntzsche's comments indicate that he agreed with the filmmakers.

In the film, the wolf and the fox represent evil, powerful allies with selfish, ulterior motives and thus their alliance falls apart in a critical moment. The film team deliberately designed costumes and makeup in a way that would distinguish good from evil animals. Only the eyes could be seen of the evil animals; the bear shows more human features; and the child actor who plays the brave rabbit shows his entire face.[122] The film conveys a dialectical and complex view of evil: The wolf is strong, fierce, and brutal in appearance, but he is cowardly on the inside, afraid of the hunter's traps and rifles and depends on the sly fox to get him prey to attack *from behind*. To deceive Little Red Riding Hood and her grandma, the fox pours white flour on the wolf for it to disguise itself as a dog; the wolf has to learn to wag its tail. For the child audience, the film conveys a typical fairy-tale message of good overcoming evil. But for Häntzsche, the filmmakers, and adult viewers, the film can be read as an allegory of class struggles and a contest between socialism and its enemies.

Although disappointing and too theatrical for many,[123] the director asserted, "No one made it easy with the film, and no one had it easy."[124] He believed that he was hired for this film because he had worked as an assistant for Walter Felsenstein and since 1953 had been an assistant and dramaturge at the Komische Oper Berlin. Although Friedrich did not assist Felsenstein in staging the musical play *Das schlaue Füchslein* (The Cunning Little Fox, 1956) per se, his familiarity with it was desirable. Its influence on the costumes, makeup, pantomimic acting, lighting, and color of his *Little Red Riding Hood* is obvious.[125] Friedrich mentioned the Russian composer Sergei Prokofiev's symphonic fairy tale *Petya i volk* (Peter and the Wolf, 1936) as another model. *Little Red Riding Hood* is Götz Friedrich's only feature film. In 1973, he became yet another director to defect to the West.[126]

Friedrich's *Little Red Riding Hood* outshines its counterpart in West Germany. The West German *Rotkäppchen* (Walter Janssen, 1954, FRG) is a close, but padded out adaptation of the Grimms' version. It reinforces traditional gender roles by having Little Red Riding Hood cook, bake (cupcakes and a Gugelhupf cake), wash, and mend, and her five brothers chop wood, fell trees, and go fishing. Little Red Riding Hood is naïve, perhaps not even recognizing the undisguised wolf–grandmother. The wolf dies as in the Grimms, since West German adaptations attempted to be as close to the original as they could. The colorful, well-appointed house reflects the typical West German bourgeois household and stands in contrast to DEFA's modest, proletarian farmhouse. The two German states left their indelible marks on the films they made.

Conclusion

The films elaborated on in this chapter are diverse as regards topic and aesthetics, but all dramatize class struggles and a triumph over evil, represented by the feudal class, merchants, rich farmers, and the wolf. They can be read as political allegories of the GDR's successful establishment of governance and its superiority over other societal forms. They interpret East

Germany as a Workers' and Peasants' State and its position within the Cold War. The worker-cum-king image did not precisely reflect the GDR political reality, however. It was not the working class per se, but the party as the vanguard of the working class that ruled the country. The SED accepted Stalinism from its inception and formed a new elitist power circle. Over the years, it adopted many regulations to cement the hegemony of the party, which merely needed the populace to legitimate their elite status.[127] The 17 June 1953 revolt provided the most damning evidence against the GDR's claim to be the first Workers' and Peasants' State on German land, when it turned to the Soviet military to suppress its own workers.[128] Hence the rule of the worker in DEFA fairy tales remained just that: a fairy-tale notion.

These "politically partisan" films did not lack defenders or detractors, and the history of their reception often makes interesting stories. Political loyalty did not spare them from censorship or harsh criticism, attesting to a lack of a clearly defined policy in the 1950s. It was hard for filmmakers to know the whims of the party, and they needed to figure things out as they went along. In the case of *Little Tailor*, although Peter Podehl's script was more faithful to the Grimms' tale, the portrayal of a flawed lower-class protagonist seemed to contravene socialist–realist precepts. Podehl's successor, Kurt Bortfeldt, then presented the tailor as maturing from a naïve, clever adventurer into a conscious ally of the peasants. Understandably, Bortfeldt made a radical revision by having the little tailor reject the princess and marry the maid. These politically motivated revisions were, however, criticized as debasing Marxism. The forced cuts and reshootings that *The Wooden Calf* endured show that "political partisanship" was no safeguard against censorship or criticism. This time, it was because the officials tried to forestall any potential damage this film could cause to public relations. In the case of *Poor Hassan*, despite its prestigious director Gerhard Klein, the print media criticized it for its use of Brechtian dramaturgy in a children's fairy tale. In a similar vein, *The Singing Ringing Tree* (1957) from the same period was notoriously reprimanded for failing the partisan politics and was attacked (see chapter 3). *The Robe* (1961/1991), also from this period, was banned for the duration of the GDR (see chapter 4). It is obvious that the crisis the GDR faced, especially from the 17 June 1953 revolt to the building of the Berlin Wall, intensified the scrutiny of its cultural productions. The controversies these fairy-tale films provoked certainly were in excess of what would be expected for children's tales, whose filming was supposedly an easy task. The less eventful reception of *The Tinderbox* and *The Golden Goose* showed that correct morals combined with light entertainment were still the safe recipe for the creations of fairy-tale cinema.

In addition to the films discussed here, the list of DEFA fairy-tale films that represent class struggles and ridicule evil rulers includes *Hatifa* (Siegfried Hartmann, 1960), *Die schwarze Mühle* (The Black Mill, Celino Bleiweiß, 1975), *The Master Thief* (1978), *Der Spiegel des großen Magus* (The Mirror of the Great Magus, Dieter Scharfenberg, 1981), and *Die vertauschte Königin* (The Swapped Queen, Dieter Scharfenberg, 1984). These films have a similar structure typical of fairy-tale narratives. They also reinforce Marxist ethics that sympathize with and empower the working class. They span four decades, attesting to thematic consistency or, to use rather unflattering terms, monotony and anachronism. The preference to adapt class-conscious and leftist tales constitutes one of the hallmarks of DEFA fairy tales in comparison to those of the West.

3

LOVE IS REAL WEALTH

Money, Work, and the Cold War

Many East German fairy-tale films no longer ended as their nineteenth-century forebears did: with members of the lower class achieving wealth and power through the unfailing help of magical benefactors. In accordance with Cold War rhetoric, the pursuit of wealth was relegated in DEFA films to being merely capitalistic in nature. Friendship, love, and diligence are values that were encouraged in their stead. The primacy of work and the corruptive power of wealth were the guiding principles in the DEFA studio's selection and revision of tales, especially the seemingly anachronistic tales about kings and princesses. In contrast to the films analyzed in the second chapter, in which the protagonists originate from the working class, most films discussed in this chapter feature protagonists of noble birth: benign monarchs, loving princes, and adorable or redeemable princesses. Since the aristocratic class—in the Marxian sense—does not work but rather robs the fruit of labor from the working classes, DEFA filmmakers had to make necessary revisions to modernize traditional tales about kings and princesses, so they would both address the sociohistorical circumstances in the GDR and yet still remain meaningful stories.

Aligned with GDR cultural politics, which heroicize the working class, DEFA attributed qualities typical of the working class to positive characters of the upper class, while associating negative characters from all class backgrounds with greed and laziness. A haughty princess, for example, undergoes a semisocialist education to become a quasisocialist personality and acclimate to the new GDR reality. Thus Princess Tausendschön in *The Singing Ringing Tree* (1957) and Princess Roswitha in *King Thrushbeard* (1965) have to revoke their princess attitudes and learn to work like a good socialist woman worker. Good-natured princesses such as Snow White and Briar Rose likewise share qualities of the working class. The same virtue of diligence elevates a common girl to the status of a princess or queen, such as the miller's daughter in *Rumpelstiltskin* (1960) and Cinderella in *Three Hazelnuts for Cinderella* (1974). In the case of *Mother Hulda* (1963), the diligent Goldmarie is rewarded by the titular character. Whereas the princess in the Grimms' "The Frog King, or Iron Heinrich" (KHM 1) is rewarded with the frog-turned-prince without even keeping her promises, she has to work as a kitchen helper in DEFA's *The Frog King* (1988) while awaiting an opportunity to belatedly act on her three promises and win true love. Siegfried Hartmann, the scriptwriter for *Rapunzel and the Magic of Tears* (1988), combines "Rapunzel" (KHM 12) and "Maid Maleen" (KHM 198) so that Rapunzel, now a princess, has to work as a kitchen maid to reunite with her blind prince, eventually restoring his eyesight with her magic tears. Although degradation of princesses is common in traditional tales, DEFA made sure that these were also working princesses.

Good kings were often young monarchs like King Thrushbeard. They differentiate themselves from old kings, symbolizing the generational conflict with an affirmation of the new generation. The new regime under the rule of the young monarch and the princess promises to be more virtuous and also enjoy the approval of the people. In so doing, these old stories centering on the feudal class are made acceptable for educating and entertaining the GDR viewers, thereby also reconciling the fairy-tale tradition with the antifeudal and antibourgeois state ideology.

From the very beginning, GDR fairy tales adapted the originals to heighten the merit and importance of hard work. Positive characters who are rewarded with love are hardworking and serve as identification figures or role models for the young audience. Although traditional tales such as those by the Brothers Grimm commend industriousness as a virtue, work or industrial labor acquired significant economic and political connotations in the context of postwar reconstruction and the building of a socialist state. Discussing the 1952 GDR edition of *Kinder- und Hausmärchen* edited by Walther Pollatschek, Rüdiger Steinlein observes the striking emphasis on the value of work and the collective efforts of people to improve their lives, instead of relying on magical help. Pollatschek changed, for example, the ending of the tale "The Magic Table, the Golden Donkey, and the Club in the Sack" (KHM 36). In the original ending, the tailor and his three sons no longer lift a finger for the rest of their lives, thanks to the possession of magical items. In Pollatschek, however, the sons could not stand idleness and happily go back to plying their trades. Only the father locks up his sewing gear due to old age; he nonetheless keeps himself occupied by tending a goat.[1]

The rejection of laziness and exaltation of diligence—although shared by most societies—reflected the sociopolitical and economic reality of the GDR. While West Germany, buttressed by the Marshall Plan, boasted an "economic miracle" and attracted thousands of East Germans before the building of the Wall in 1961, the socialist state stagnated economically.[2] Hence, the GDR government preached against the corrupting power of gold, attempting to gain some moral ground by contrasting socialism and capitalism in terms of the fairy-tale dualism of good and evil. It was implied that if East Germans worked hard enough, their country would not only be morally superior to their Western counterparts but also be able to economically catch up with West Germany. The GDR's claim to working-class diligence showed its preference for "soft power" over militaristic and financial "hard power," of which it accused West Germany.[3] Although the GDR used "hard power" itself (and the West "soft power" to great effect), it nevertheless painted an ascetic and morally unimpeachable self-image to win the hearts and minds of its citizens and allies in the Cold War. The values and ideals that it conveys through its fairy-tale films helped assert the image of the GDR as anticapitalist and anti-imperialist.

The first three DEFA fairy-tale films—*The Cold Heart*, *Little Mook*, and *Mill Mountain*—praise work over wealth as the primary means to achieve happiness. *The Brave Little Tailor* even ends with the tailor–king mending the sleeve for his new bride—a gardener's daughter. According to the veteran fairy-tale film director Walter Beck, the inclusion of work in fairy-tale films shows the films' reference to GDR society, a society in which work had a critical and formative importance.[4] In a subtle manner, DEFA fairy-tale films exalted work as the contemporary production novels (*Produktionsromane*) and reconstruction films (*Aufbaufilme*) of the 1950s. They shared the principles of the Bitterfeld Way (*Bitterfelder Weg*). And the films' disposition toward work is a vital signifier in applying socialist realism to fairy-tale adaptations. This chapter will show how fairy-tale films in the GDR promoted a strong work ethic and offered love rather than gold as an appropriate reward and then how the values these films promoted gradually lost their appeal and even incurred doubts.

Except for "Little Red Riding Hood," the tales analyzed in chapters 1 and 2 were not adapted in West Germany. Many tales discussed in this chapter, however, were also filmed in West Germany, including *Frau Holle* (Mother Hulda, Fritz Genschow, 1954), *Aschenputtel* (Cinderella, Fritz Genschow, 1955), *Rumpelstilzchen* (Rumpelstiltskin, Herbert B. Fredersdorf, 1955), *Dornröschen* (Sleeping Beauty, Fritz Genschow, 1955),[5] and *König Drosselbart* (King Thrushbeard, Rudolf Jugert, 1971). It stands to reason that a comparison between DEFA and West German and American/Disney versions of the tales appears in this chapter, rather than earlier. The revolutionary tales in chapter 2 appealed to DEFA, not to West German filmmakers. Famous tales that thematize hard work and love were important resources to be tapped for both German cinemas, pointing to a shared cultural legacy and social values. Both sides of the Iron Curtain were drawn to canonical tales for commercial and pedagogical reasons, but the resultant interpretations of the stories were, nevertheless, very different. In general, the West German adaptations tended to be literal, apolitical, and of low quality, with plotlines containing much singing, dancing, and farce; DEFA approached the material with more rigor and larger ambitions. If East German films were criticized for politicizing the material, West German versions could likewise be faulted for being political, with their reactionary depiction of gender and power relations.

Princesses Made to Work: *The Singing Ringing Tree* (1957) and *King Thrushbeard* (1965)

This section deals with two similar films that had drastically different receptions. One is *The Singing Ringing Tree* by the West German guest director at DEFA, Francesco Stefani. The film is based on some fragments by the Grimms.[6] The other is Walter Beck's 1965 adaptation of Grimms' "King Thrushbeard" (KHM 52). Both films are set in aristocratic circles and tell stories of "taming the shrew," in which haughty princesses are punished with work and transformed by it. *The Singing Ringing Tree* was criticized by the chief pedagogue at DEFA, Hellmuth Häntzsche, as a failed fairy-tale film for lacking socialist–realist interpretations.[7] *King Thrushbeard* was spared such a fate, however. It is clear that similar adaptations promoting work and love, when faced with changed reception circumstances, could fare quite differently, at least at the time. This section will analyze what caused the differing reception of two similar films, what role the West Germanness of Francesco Stefani played in the reception, and why *King Thrushbeard* survived the *Kahlschlag* (literally clear-cutting).

The Singing Ringing Tree was shot in *Bilderbuch* or picture book style, with the princess's kingdom on the East end and the magic realm on the West. The characters travel across the screen as if they were in a book and do not break the fourth wall by looking into the camera. When the film came out in 1957, it immediately became an audience favorite.[8] At first, the reviews were largely positive and praised the film as yet another hearty Christmas greeting to young and old alike.[9] It was shown in both Germanies and many other countries from Europe to Asia, thus contributing to DEFA's export revenue.[10] However, Charlotte Ewald wrote a scathing review in the January 1958 issue of *Deutsche Filmkunst*, faulting the film for being "filled with false monarchic romance and unable to contribute to the formation of our children's character and volition."[11] The GDR's short-lived Thaw between Stalin's death in 1953 and the suppression of the Hungarian revolt in 1956 enabled critique of the politically conformist *Little*

Tailor. However, *The Singing Ringing Tree* fell victim to the tightened cultural regimentation that emerged in 1957, which was explicitly articulated at the second film conference in July 1958 that mandated strict alignment with socialist education. DEFA was criticized at the conference for "straying into the dubious, the unclear, and the imprecise."[12] Among the films reprimanded at the conference, *The Singing Ringing Tree* was accused of "idealism" and "flight into petit-bourgeois idyll."[13] Why then did the reviewers initially embrace it and not see the film's presumed ideological failure?

In the film, the pampered, conceited, and selfish princess (Christel Bodenstein) rejects the prince's (Eckart Dux) gift of pearls and demands that he bring her the legendary singing ringing tree, which is said to banish all evil. The prince searches far and wide and finally finds it in a magic kingdom ruled by a dwarf (Richard Krüger). In the loveless eyes of the princess, however, the tree, which is indeed ordinary looking, is of little value (see Figure 3.1). As stipulated, the despondent prince returns to the magic land and a bearskin grows around him. The capricious princess orders her father to retrieve the tree. Now the plot resembles that of "Beauty and the Beast," in which the father receives the tree by promising to deliver the first thing that greets him upon his arrival home, which turns out to be his daughter instead of his dog. The king breaks his promise, which forces the bear to abduct the princess. The loss of her crown symbolizes her temporary loss of royal identity and the anticipated humbling process awaiting her.

In the magic kingdom, where "you appear as you behave," the princess's lack of inner beauty is externalized. She grows a big nose and her curly, blonde hair turns straight, green, and lifeless. The gradual recovery of her outer beauty is made possible by her improved interaction with the animals. After she learns to care for animals, she calls the bear "Dear Bear," indicating that she is on the verge of loving him. Now the dwarf tears down the shelter the bear and the princess have built and puts the blame on the bear, thus making the bear not loveworthy. The dwarf lies to her, telling her that her father is deathly ill, so she decides to go home. When she realizes the dwarf has actually deceived her and she was right to believe in the bear's kindness, the tree starts to sing and ring. She has an epiphany, realizing that the tree will be animated if she loves the prince

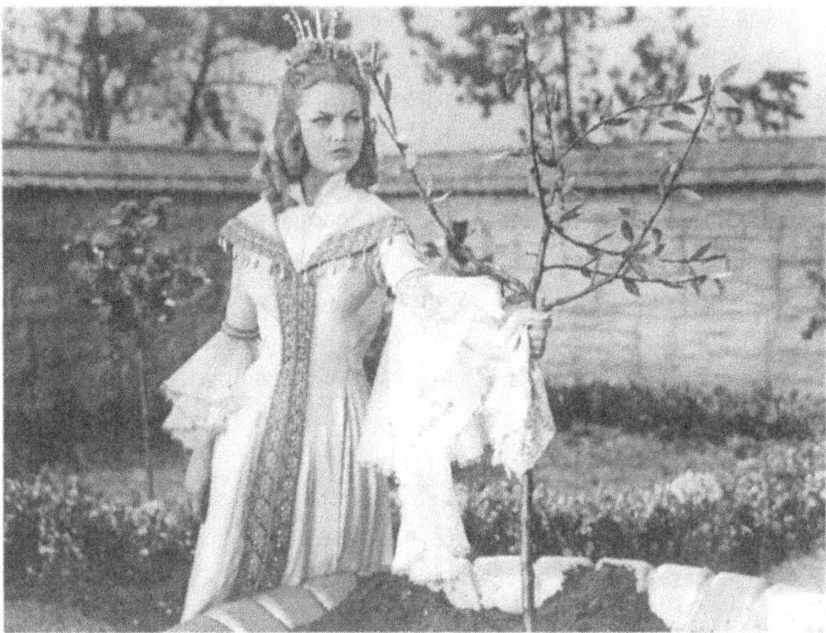

FIGURE 3.1. *Das singende, klingende Bäumchen*: Princess Tausendschön (Christel Bodenstein) with the tree in the royal garden. © DEFA-Stiftung, Kurt Schütt.

and that the bear must be the prince. Now she is determined to help the prince regain his human form. At the end of the film, the couple leaves the tree in the magic kingdom, apparently for it to assist others in finding love and conquer evil.

The reviewers initially endorsed the film apparently because it depicts the triumph of good over evil and commends virtues such as humility, kindness, and inner beauty. The dwarf represents evil and he is vanquished at the sound of the singing ringing tree, which has the magic power of dispersing evil. The bear teaches the princess that "a good deed is more powerful than evil magic."[14] The film demonstrates also the transformative and humanizing power of love. The princess's love is the prerequisite for the bear's disenchantment. Love redeems the prince as well as the princess. A symbol of love, the singing ringing tree is a variant of the rose in "Beauty and the Beast." The film is a precursor of a few more, to use Bruno Bettelheim's term, "animal groom" tales adapted by DEFA, including *Snow White and Rose Red* (1979), *The Prince behind the Seven Seas* (1982), and *The Frog King* (1988).

The harsh criticism of the film seems unjustified, because the film endorses universal values of love and work over a feudal, parasitic life. In the beginning, the princess is attached to her royal lifestyle: She wants her silver bath, golden plate, and featherbed with silken pillows and refuses to make do with the simple natural beauty around her: the lake, berries, and soft moss. She starts out hedonistic, self-indulgent, and pleasure seeking. She only wants material comfort and does not *work*. The loss of physical beauty is a wake-up call and initiates her journey toward self-awareness and emotional maturation. The process that follows of retrieving her outer beauty correlates with the process of achieving her inner beauty, during which she sheds the arrogance that causes her to see work as outrageous for a princess.

The bear gently guides her to help build their cave and carry away rocks "for a thousand times." She is subsequently seen working in three episodes: picking berries for lunch, washing a basin, and collecting moss for bedding. Each time she works, she also helps an animal. Indicatively she has converted from a person with a bourgeois, aristocratic attitude to a loving, virtuous, and working person, a desirable product of socialist education. Her transformation shows that she is reeducated in the magic realm. Had she remained in the privileged castle, this would never have occurred and she would always be spoiled, vain, and inconsiderate. In this light, the film contains desirable antifeudal and anticapitalist messages befitting GDR standards. The dialectic relation between an individual and the collective also achieves rendition here: the princess is the bourgeois outsider who needs to be reintegrated into the socialist collective. Work provides the means to reintegration. From this perspective, the film aligns with the GDR's emphasis on work and well-rounded personality, which explains why it passed censorship and was not attacked immediately upon its release.

However, measuring the film against a party-ideological yardstick, some of the film's contemporaries disagreed on whether the source material had been adapted adequately to the socialist context and whether such a literary template was fit for the new socialist context at all. In December 1957, Charlotte Czygan wrote a critique for *BZ Abend*, in which she questioned the film's dangerous equation of physical beauty with goodness and ugliness with evil; this could mislead children to draw general conclusions about appearances and could contradict pedagogical goals.[15] Charlotte Ewald expressed the same view in *Deutsche Filmkunst* in 1958: "The underlying message of the tale—that evil people are also ugly—can mislead many children to make generalizations in real life, which we by no means wish out of pedagogical reasons."[16] These reviewers seemed to have forgotten that such simplistic equations are prevalent in most fairy tales. One only needs to think about the beautiful and good stepdaughters and their ugly and malicious stepsisters. Such binary opposition was nothing special in *The Singing Ringing Tree* and continued to feature in later DEFA fairy-tale films such as *Three Hazelnuts for Cinderella* (1974) and *Rapunzel and the Magic of Tears* (1988). Moreover, Ewald was not convinced that the prince loved the coldhearted and evil princess at first sight. In her opinion, the director should have made the transformation deeper and clearer to convince children that this princess truly deserved the good prince. For Ewald, however, this constituted the entire dilemma: because such a Prince Charming was precisely the prototype of petit bourgeois ideals, he would actually be more appropriate for the "capitalist entertainment industry." She insisted that fairy-tale filmmakers should take up the task—as difficult as it was—to select fairy-tale material *from our worldviews*, instead of cultivating the old customs of "bourgeois idealistic views." The Thälmann-pioneers should "be educated as socialist citizens of the future."[17]

Referring to Ewald's review, the West German critic Steffen Wolf observed that although Stefani tried to stay close to the literary version to not repeat the same mistakes made in *Little Tailor*, Stefani's effort likewise failed because the change of a vain and arrogant princess for the better was a subject that had no place in the socialist education of youth.[18] The shift from the initially quite positive to the later negative receptions of Stefani's film shows the internal contradictions in the GDR at the time and shows that a film's evaluation was sensitized to the ideological, political, and aesthetic standards upheld at that particular historical moment. In Stefani's defense, his fairy-tale adaptation promoted the (socialist) value of work and love and deemphasized the fetishistic importance of money. The tendentious reviews ignored the film's emphasis on work and love, values that have long-lasting and universal appeal, as attested by the film's popularity abroad and after German reunification.[19]

At the time, however, the fact that Francesco Stefani was West German could have factored into the film's change of fate. DEFA had an uneasy relationship with West German artists in general. On the one hand, for various pragmatic reasons, in the first decade after the founding of DEFA in 1946, the studio relied heavily on these "bourgeois artists" who comprised a significant percentage of its workers. This personnel arrangement also agreed with the then official politics of the SED that tried to foster a *gesamtdeutsch*, or all-German, unity in those years. Through collaborations with Western filmmakers, DEFA also hoped to increase the international credibility of the newly founded studio, demonstrate its production capacity so its films could access international film festivals, and combat the domestic decrease in audience numbers.[20] On the other hand, West German filmmakers were suspected of doing a "disservice" (*Bärendienst*) to DEFA by bringing in bourgeois influences.[21] After all, "our social life must be strange to them," as was expressed at a meeting of the cultural functionaries in May 1957.[22] After 1949 in the ambience of the Cold War, West German artists were continuously employed by the DEFA studios, but they were nevertheless mistrusted due to their purported "political unreliability" and even "hostility."[23] By 1955, the percentage of West German directors, cameramen, and other specialists working for DEFA had drastically dropped as a result of the SED's deliberately targeted cultural policies. Especially from 1955 onward, "influence from the West" carried over by West German film artists was increasingly perceived as negative.[24] The SED's Thirtieth Central Committee plenum on 30 January 1957 censured "bourgeois and revisionist influence" in the arts and culture.[25] West German employees continued to be systematically reduced in 1958.[26]

It was under this general antagonism toward West German filmmakers that Stefani served as a guest director at DEFA. According to Hellmuth Häntzsche, from the very beginning his colleagues in the children's film group rejected any responsibility for this film.[27] Thus it is indeed not too farfetched to surmise that the director's West Germanness was interpreted as a threat of bourgeois revisionism on the eve of the second film conference.[28] *The Singing Ringing Tree* was attacked in the SED's attempt to discipline the "West German elements" at DEFA. This shows that the reception of DEFA (fairy-tale) films was more indicative of the historical period than the films per se. The film, however, had a successful reception abroad. In fall 1958, West Germany started to show it under a different and less poetic title—*Im Zauberreich des Berggeistes* (In the Magic Realm of the Mountain Spirit). The West German reviews were short yet consistently positive.[29] In the same year, *The Singing Ringing Tree* premiered in a film festival in Edinburgh, Great Britain. It was not until 1964—when the film was broadcast in a series called *Tales from Europe* on BBC Children's Television—that the film reached a broader spectatorship; its reruns lasted to the end of the 1970s. Since BBC did not have enough money to synchronize the film, it was not dubbed; a narrator tells the story while the original dialogues are still audible.[30] The domestic and international reception of *The Singing Ringing Tree* attested to the quality of the film, which would eventually prevail over ideologically driven criticisms.

After *The Singing Ringing Tree* was considered an ideological misfire, discussions about fundamental issues concerning the development of socialist cinema ensued in the GDR. The work group Kinder- und Jugendfilm (which lasted from 1963 to 1970) in DEFA's feature film studio[31] decided to adapt only those tales in which the essence of the stories and their typical features could be preserved and socialist morals such as good and evil and right and wrong could be captured.[32] Walter Beck's *King Thrushbeard* was this work group's first collaborative project[33] and was praised as being largely faithful to the original tale with welcoming and responsible revisions.[34] Manfred Krug's role as King Thrushbeard was a highlight of this film since by 1965 Krug had starred in numerous films, including *Fünf Patronenhülsen* (Five Cartridges, Frank Beyer, 1960) and *Auf der Sonnenseite* (On the Sunny Side, Ralf Kirsten, 1962).

After the original person cast as the protagonist, Arno Wyzniewski, became ill shortly before the shooting, Krug had the opportunity to delight the audience in his first fairy-tale performance.[35] The need for King Thrushbeard to sing as a minstrel in disguise made Krug an ideal replacement because by then Krug was a well-known jazz musician who had toured and recorded popular titles. In the same year, Krug played Balla in Frank Beyer's *Spur der Steine* (Trace of Stones, premiered in 1965, banned in 1966, and represented in 1990 at the Berlinale).[36] Karin Ugowski, who plays Princess

Roswitha, enjoyed the reputation of being the most beloved DEFA princess. After she debuted in *Mother Hulda* (1963) in the role of Goldmarie, she became the "princess on duty" (*die Prinzessin vom Dienst*) for a few years[37]; but the actress tried to free herself from the burden of always playing princesses.[38] Many reviews stressed the prominent cast in *King Thrushbeard*, pointing to the existence of a star culture in the GDR.[39] Like the publicity work for *Trace of Stones*, the advertisement for *King Thrushbeard* capitalized on the charisma of Krug. Although the Stalinist cultural functionaries preferred terms such as "popular film personalities" and "audience darlings" to "stars," Krug's popular status and the official anxiety about him attested to star discourse in the early 1960s. As reluctant as the GDR was to permit a star culture that it associated with Western cinema, it had to tolerate the emergence of its own stars, given the competition from (West German) television, Hollywood, and the drop in film attendance.[40]

King Thrushbeard's message is very similar to *The Singing Ringing Tree*'s, but *King Thrushbeard* received mostly positive reviews. A significant revision was made to portray the princess as innately good and rationalize her arrogance as arising from her contempt for the dull and suffocating courtly life. Thus she comes off as a rebel at the royal court. In the Grimms' tale, the rather sexist and patronizing King Thrushbeard aims at punishing and humiliating the beautiful but spoiled and sharp-tongued princess: "I did all that to humble your proud spirit and to punish you for the insolent way you behaved toward me." The princess then self-deprecatingly admits her little worth: "I've done a great wrong and don't deserve to be your wife" (KHM 52). It is clear that the paternalistic way of quenching female pride is justified in the Grimms' tale, which suggests that she deserves the humiliation for having been rude and haughty. In the West German *King Thrushbeard* (Rudolf Jugert, 1971), the minstrel husband does not lift a finger in the household, commands the princess to cook and take off his boots, and even threatens to hit her when she disobeys him. By contrast, the DEFA version displays a greater sensibility toward gender equality.

Contrary to the stereotypical, negative images of kings and princesses as analyzed in chapter 2, the DEFA film rewrites King Thrushbeard into a wise, patient, and loving monarch who sees the princess's good nature and lovingly turns her into a "valuable human being" so that she can lead a more fulfilling life.[41] The film gives the suitors from neighboring palaces a "cabaretistic,"[42] foppish, and preposterous portrayal, justifying the princess's mockery of them. King Thrushbeard is an exception but is not spared her biting commentary that his somewhat crooked chin resembles a thrush's beak. The princess's father (Martin Flörchinger) is irate with his daughter's hubris and promises to give her to the first beggar that comes to the palace. King Thrushbeard disguises himself as a minstrel and takes the princess to his humble hut. He patiently and quietly teaches her how to weave baskets, spin, and make earthenware and sell it on the market (see Figure 3.2). Like the bear prince in *The Singing Ringing Tree*, King Thrushbeard functions as an educator and humbles the princess, as well as himself, to resemble an ordinary citizen that GDR viewers could relate to. Work is emphasized as having transformative power that remodels the princess into a working citizen. The film gives the princess the talent of painting, a talent that she could not cultivate in the palace; now as a commoner, she can use it to embellish the earthenware. In the Grimms' tale as well as the West German adaptation, the princess is caught hiding food under her skirt and thus she is publicly humiliated as part of the process of "taming the shrew." The DEFA film, however, does not contain this episode, thereby establishing work as having the desired edifying power that guarantees change in the princess. The screenwriters Günter Kaltofen and Walter Beck intended to tell a modern love story and, in addition, they distilled a pedagogically meaningful lesson.[43] King Thrushbeard voluntarily divests himself of royal identity and becomes a down-to-earth member of the working class as though, a reviewer exclaimed, he could be "a young man of our days."[44]

Thus, although *King Thrushbeard* concerns a social class that the GDR would otherwise consider "class enemies," the king temporarily appears as a minstrel, that is, a member of the lower classes, and the princess also for some time loses her royal status, is ostracized from the palace, and has to live in a humble hut and work for a living. In addition, the revisions that the film made to the print tale were in keeping with socialist–humanist principles and left the audience with a strong impression that they were watching a modern love story unfolding between two human beings, not two royal beings. In *The Singing Ringing Tree*, both the prince and the

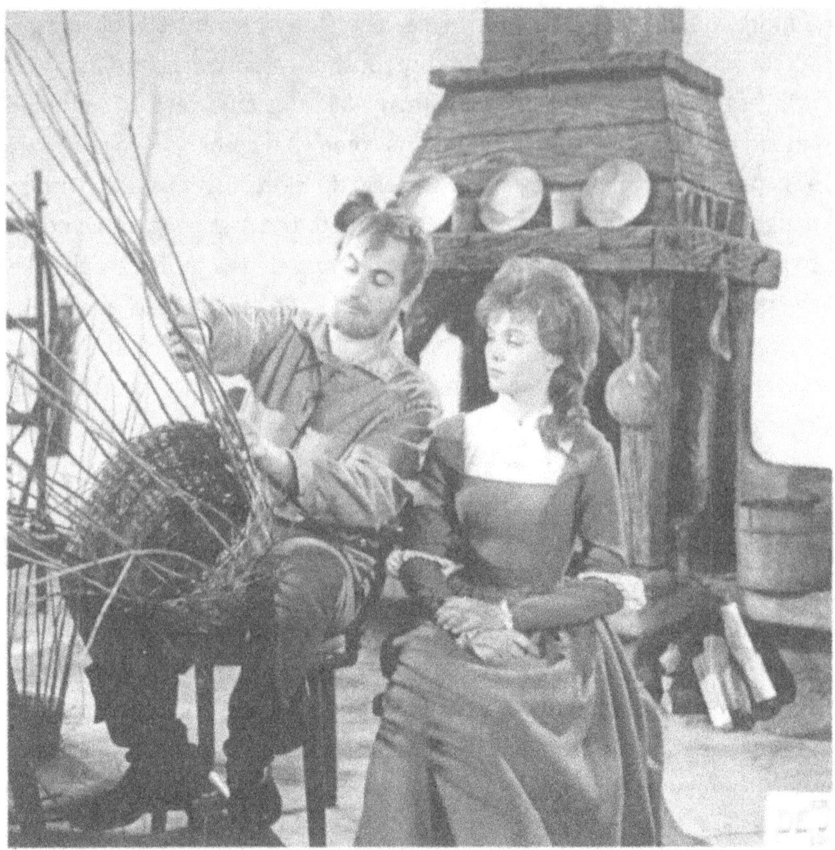

FIGURE 3.2. *König Drosselbart*: King Thrushbeard (Manfred Krug) teaches the princess (Karin Ugowski) how to weave. © DEFA-Stiftung, Max Teschner.

princess lose their royal status temporarily in the magic realm. However, the role that *work* plays in changing the princess is not as obvious as in *King Thrushbeard*. Beck gave Princess Roswitha an antibourgeois trait to explain her arrogance, whereas Princess Tausendschön in *The Singing Ringing Tree* appears simply vain, spoiled, and arrogant, and her improved behavior toward animals seems to be motivated by her desire to regain her beauty.

What further helped distinguish *King Thrushbeard* from *The Singing Ringing Tree* was the openly artificial and frontal aesthetic that Beck chose. Beck shot all the scenes on a platform in front of a bright and seemingly infinite backdrop to achieve "a bright horizon that appears unending."[45]

The minimalist production design shows the influence from the Brechtian epic theater on the film. Due to Brecht's iconic status in the GDR, his theater theory and techniques constituted an effective artistic alternative to the foreign, imposed, and inauthentic socialist–realist mode. Beck indicated that he kept the decorations to a bare minimum; only those needed to signify the locations were allowed, and they had to be subservient to the actors and be necessary to advance the story. Beck noted that this was not done because of shortage of money; in fact this was more costly than an opulent setting.[46] Whereas *The Singing Ringing Tree* conjures a romantic fairy-tale atmosphere, *King Thrushbeard* appears sobering and realistic, and indeed there is nothing supernatural in the story.

Thus when the political noose tightened, *The Singing Ringing Tree* was subject to political and ideological scrutiny in 1958, whereas *King Thrushbeard* passed muster in 1965, the year of the Eleventh Plenum, which forbade the showing of almost all the film productions of that year, often referred to as the *Kahlschlag*. Manfred Krug's other film that premiered in the same year—*Trace of Stones*—became one of the most famous forbidden films, so-called rabbit films (*Kaninchenfilme*) or shelved films (*Regalfilme*).[47] Krug's star status helped both films gain popularity; however, the potential critique of the party and the GDR's planned economy in *Trace of Stones* sealed the film's fate in the state film archives for the remainder of the GDR.

Whereas the majority of films from 1965 were censored at the Eleventh Plenum in December that year, the fairy-tale nature of *King Thrushbeard* with its ideologically successful revisions facilitated its survival. However, a review on *King Thrushbeard* published after German reunification in 1991 read a few scenes as making implicit references to the GDR: In the scene in which the suitors (Helmut Schreiber, Achim Schmidtchen, Gerd E. Schäfer, Arno Wyzniewski, Bruno Carstens, etc.) present themselves as if puppets on the checkerboard floor, their ceremonial and silly manners reminded the reviewer of a group of gray-haired potentates in the SED. In the market scene, the princess's off-putting "sales strategy," quite the opposite of the fruit merchant's (Marianne Wünscher) over-the-top touting of her wares, may appear to some degree "realistic" to GDR viewers.[48] As mentioned in the Introduction, reviews after the Berlin Wall fell often tended to pick up on critical innuendo within fairy-tale films that was either not noticed or not overtly addressed before the *Wende*. It was not uncommon for reviewers of the time to not wish to see or to remain deliberately silent about a fairy-tale film's potential critique of the state. In fact, the song that the minstrel king sings at the market implies a jibe at the economic destitution of the GDR, an embarrassing fact that the SED did not openly admit. The ballad spurns not only wealth but also poverty:

> He who is too rich loses his good sense and gives himself
> over to arrogance.
> Because he is so rich, he becomes unbearable.
> Being too rich and also too poor robs many people
> of common sense
> Because excessive wealth destroys virtue
> And poverty ruins a sound mind
> Both are rightly called bad.[49]

The Eleventh Plenum in 1965 was originally convened to discuss the economic troubles in which the state found itself. But the conversation quickly shifted to a critique of cultural productions to deflect attention from irresolvable difficulties in the economic sectors.[50] Made before the plenum, the fairy-tale camouflage allowed *King Thrushbeard* to survive censorship despite a ballad that, in a contemporary feature film, might have been unfavorably interpreted.

Reward and Punishment in Spinning Tales: *Rumpelstiltskin* (1960) and *Mother Hulda* (1963)

Industriousness is a prevalent emphasis in DEFA fairy-tale adaptations. For women, diligence is often reflected in spinning, one of the few socioeconomic possibilities for women from the medieval period to the end of the nineteenth century in Europe.[51] The Grimm scholar Ruth Bottigheimer distinguishes between the prospinning "public values" and the opposite "private preference." Society valued spinning skills as a female virtue that generated social wealth, and looked down on those who did not spin as incompetent and lazy. Tales such as "Mother Hulda" (KHM 24), "Rumpelstiltskin" (KHM 55), "The

Leftovers" (KHM 156), and "The Spindle, the Shuttle, and the Needle" (KHM 188) all show that rewards await spinning. Female spinners themselves, however, view spinning as burdensome and disfiguring and resort to trickery, deceit, or supernatural powers to avoid it; this is evident in tales such as "The Lazy Spinner" (KHM 128) and "The Three Spinners" (KHM 14).[52]

The relationship between work and money has two classic illustrations in the well-known spinning tales of "Rumpelstiltskin" and "Mother Hulda." Here, I would like to discuss the DEFA adaptations *Rumpelstiltskin* (1960) and *Mother Hulda* (1963) and how they promote work ethics and the devaluation of gold. I compare East and West German adaptations of the same tales and their specific agendas. As stated earlier, such a contrast reveals similar adaptation practices as well as different ideological subscriptions.

According to Jack Zipes, "Rumpelstiltskin" is a tale about spinning and should not belong to tale type 500—"The Name of the Helper." He examines Grimms' revision from a sociohistorical perspective by looking at the devaluation of women's spinning and male domination of mechanized linen manufacturing in the nineteenth century.[53] "Rumpelstiltskin," Maria Tatar writes, "conjoins the pro-spinning ideology of magical fairy tales with the anti–work ethic of humorous folk tales," because the miller's daughter is believed to spin her way up the social ladder, yet she manages to avoid spinning.[54] She could not spin straw into gold but her father's lie puts her in an impossible situation. Rumpelstiltskin at first appears as the magic helper, but he soon turns into a villain by demanding her first-born in return for his help. It is unclear what he intends to do with the infant. The song this "ridiculous little man who was hopping on one leg and screeching" sings not only gives away his name but also arouses the suspicion that he might be cannibalistic:

> *Today I'll brew, tomorrow I'll bake.*
> Soon I'll have the queen's namesake.
> Oh, how hard it is to play my game,
> For Rumpelstiltskin is my name! (KHM 55; [my emphasis])

Jane Yolen suggests that "Rumpelstiltskin" is an anti-Semitic story about "blood libel" and Jewish moneylending. In the annotation to her story "Granny Rumple" in *Sister Emily's Lightship and Other Stories*, Jane Yolen writes,

> So I looked more carefully at the little man, Rumpelstiltskin, himself. He has an unpronounceable name, lives apart from the kingdom, changes money, and is thought to want the child for some unspeakable blood rites. Thwack! The holy salmon of inspiration hit me in the face. Of course. Rumpelstiltskin is a medieval German story. This is an anti-Semitic tale. Little man, odd name, lives far away from the halls of power, is a moneychanger, and the old blood-rites canard.[55]

This would explain the final punishment for Rumpelstiltskin. It is to be noted that in the Ölenberg manuscript of 1807–1810, Rumpelstiltskin flies out of the window on a spoon after the queen successfully guesses his name. In the Grimms' first edition of 1812, Rumpelstiltskin furiously runs away and never returns. Not until the Grimms' second edition of 1819 does he tear himself into two pieces.[56] It is hard to know whether the 1819 version was based on a different oral version or simply came from Wilhelm Grimm. Yolen argues that this is ultimately a medieval tale. Just like her *Briar Rose* (1992), Yolen's adaptation of "Rumpelstiltskin" concerns the Holocaust. In the tale, Granny Rumple's husband is a Jewish moneychanger in a ghetto in Ukraine. He loans money to a Ukrainian girl to help her out of a dire situation: sewing beautiful dresses to marry the mayor's son. But after her marriage she denies owing him any money and calls his wife "a child stealer." The moneylender himself is later murdered. Sympathy lies with Rumpelstiltskin and his like who are punished for their initially kind deeds.

The DEFA film undertakes a radical revision by rewriting the titular hero (Siegfried Seibt) as a semisocialist worker who despises the accumulation of wealth, which is represented by the young king's and his treasurer's greed for gold (see Figure 3.3). It revises the Grimms' rather unexpected and violent ending for a once magical helper who, after all, has helped a lower-class woman become a queen. The film justifies Rumpelstiltskin's seemingly cruel insistence on the stipulated child within an anticapitalist framework: Rumpelstiltskin does not want the child to grow up among people for whom gold is the most important thing. That is also why he left mainstream society and lives in a little house off the beaten path. Rumpelstiltskin's world is

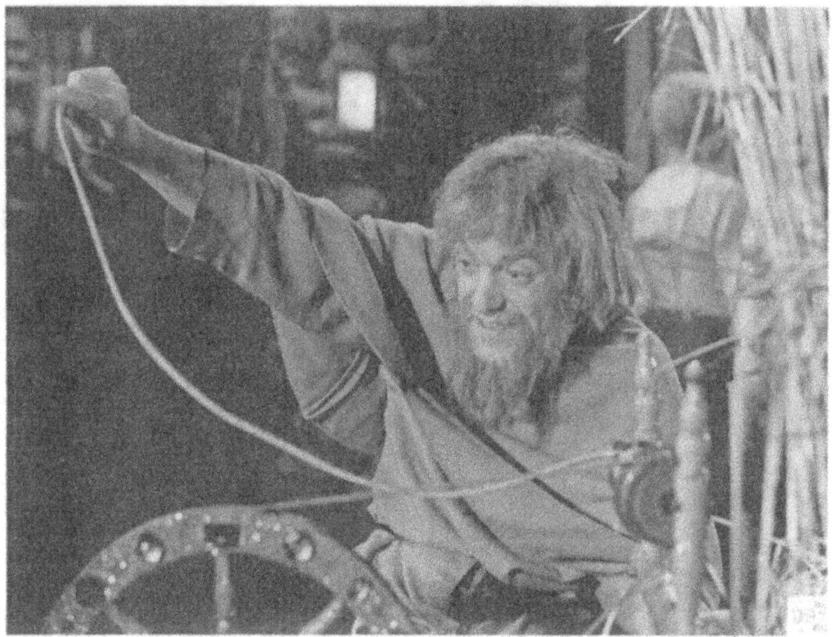

FIGURE 3.3. *Das Zaubermännchen*: Rumpelstiltskin spins straw into gold. © DEFA-Stiftung, Josef Borst.

presented as a utopian alternative to the world ruled by wealth and power, and his is presumably a better world in which to raise children. The Cold War rhetoric against capitalism obviously informs the contrasting worlds of Rumpelstiltskin and the king. Different from the negative media reaction toward changes made in *Little Tailor* (1956), reviews no longer accused such a fundamental change to the Rumpelstiltskin narrative as tendentious or disrespectful to its literary original. Instead they endorsed this revision as a very necessary change that made the message of the film clearer and more comprehensible for children.[57]

DEFA's *Rumpelstiltskin* criticizes the prioritization of money over humanity while emphasizing the virtue of hard work. The film contrasts industriousness and laziness through character types and establishes a proletarian role model in the worker. The positive characters—Rumpelstiltskin, the miller's daughter (Karin Lesch), and the lad in the mill—are diligent, and in the end their hard work pays off. The lad in the mill replaces the greedy and parasitic treasurer who is banished from the land, and the lazy, mendacious, and bragging miller is returned to work in the mill, whereas in the Grimms' story he is not punished at all. Satisfied that the young king (Nikolaus Paryla) has changed his priorities, Rumpelstiltskin returns the child to its mother and becomes a sort of uncle figure for the happy royal family. The film revises the king from the villain found in the Grimms' tale to someone merely young and inexperienced, initially seduced by the allure of gold but finally willing to give up his possessions to reward the person who can find out the dwarf's name. He is taught a lesson about greed and learns to value love and family over gold. Only after he has overcome the domination of gold is he rewarded with familial bliss. This change to a reformed young king is consistent with DEFA's common practice of portraying the new government as better, thus securing faith in a bright future. Whereas the DEFA film distills a lesson about wealth, wealth is not despised in the West German *Rumpelstiltskin* (1955), in which the king does not proclaim that he is giving away all his wealth to save his child.

Power structures in DEFA fairy-tale films stand in stark contrast to those of the West German ones; they mirror different ideological and political underpinnings. In the West German version, the greedy king of the Grimms' tale is changed to a lover of horticulture who is rather benign and kind and is only misled by his two greedy counselors. Likewise the miller is not portrayed as a detestable braggart who claims that his daughter can spin straw into gold, thus nearly causing his daughter's death. Instead Marie's father, being so proud of his daughter, seems to be speaking in a metaphorical language that only exaggerates his daughter's ability a little. Manfred Hobsch analyzes this positive depiction of paternal figures in West German fairy-tale adaptations as consistent with the conservative politics of so-called Adenauer Cinema, which features authoritarian leaders as exemplary models and emphasizes traditional values, norms, and ideals.[58]

Steffen Wolf observed that the depiction of kings and their counselors remained a major difference between fairy-tale films produced in socialist countries such as the GDR and Czechoslovakia and those made in the FRG.[59] If DEFA is guilty of tendentiously foregrounding the image of evil kings, West German fairy-tale films make even more drastic changes by turning bad kings into good ones to meet their own paternalistic agenda. In the 1955 West German adaptation—*Der Teufel mit den drei goldenen*

Haaren (The Devil's Three Golden Hairs, Hans F. Wilhelm, 1955), the evil king is changed into a respectable king to preserve amicable and benign paternal images, leaving his counselor to be the scheming evildoer.[60] Studying Nazi fairy-tale films, Ron Schlesinger points out that, even though they are unfair and contradictory figures in the original tales, kings in these pictures are markedly portrayed as the absolutely positive authority, because the king in Nazi fairy-tale films often alludes to the Führer.[61] Since the West German fairy-tale filmmakers such as Alf Zengerling, Hubert Schonger, and Fritz Genschow all continued in the same trade after the war, similarities in adaptation politics were to be expected.

The Grimms' "Mother Hulda" is a rather short and simple story about Goldmarie, the diligent stepdaughter, and her reward of a rain of gold and Pechmarie, the lazy stepsister, and her punishment with a bucket of pitch. Gold, the fairy-tale metaphor for wealth, implies that work will be rewarded with riches. Although the plot hardly offers enough substance for a feature-length film, the popularity of "Mother Hulda" and, more importantly, its emphasis on a strong work ethic factored into the decision to adapt it on both sides of the German border. The one-hour DEFA version *Mother Hulda* (1963) closely follows the Grimms' tale. It was shot in only twenty-eight days. Nonetheless, its cast, its unique and highly stylized *Bilderbuch* designs, and particularly its relevance for educational purposes contributed to good cinema attendance and positive reviews (see Figure 3.4.).

The film's reception history is worth sharing because it reveals a gap between the intentions of the filmmakers and the receipt of the intended message. A review reported on the reaction of children from a polytechnic school in Berlin-Pankow whom the National Center for Children's Film in the GDR invited to preview the film. The eight- to ten-year-olds spoke of the just reward for Goldmarie but had great sympathy for Pechmarie (Katharina Lind), with whom they could identify in many ways, because they too did not like to get up early, wash themselves, or help in the household. They felt that covering the lazy girl with tar for the rest of her life was too harsh a punishment: "She is still so young and could change later."[62] The fact that various newspapers merely reprinted

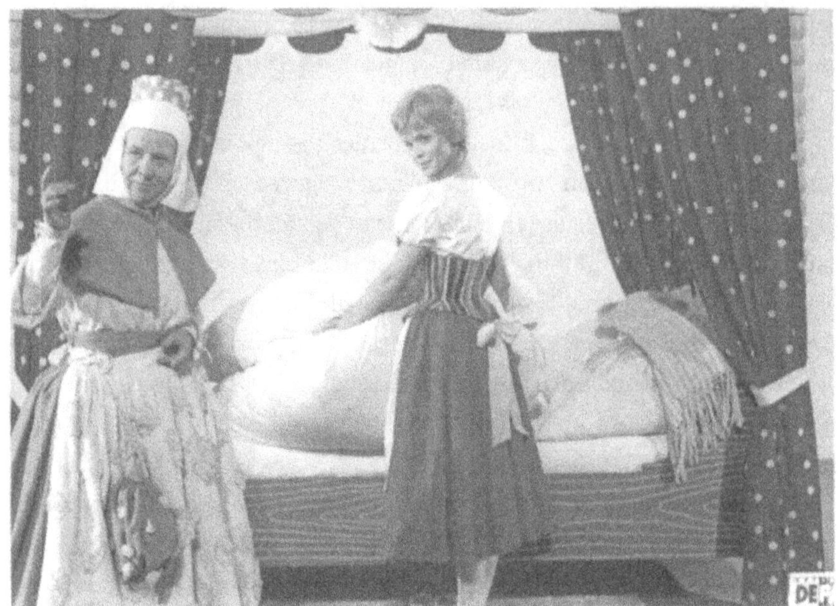

FIGURE 3.4. *Frau Holle*: Mother Hulda (Mathilde Danegger) and Goldmarie (Karin Ugowski). © DEFA-Stiftung, Horst Blümel.

this same review attests to the lack of enthusiasm for this simplistic and linear film.[63] Reviews, if different, were kept very short and uninspired. One review criticized the film's stylized, but unembellished, picture book form for having an "unpoetic, un–fairy-tale–like coolness" ("unpoetische, unmärchenhafte Kühle").[64] The film also received an extremely negative commentary in *Zwischen Marx und Muck*, expressing frustration with the one-dimensional, flat, and "intolerable" plot.[65] The film's reception makes it clear that the all too familiar message about diligence failed to arouse interest or receive its desired effect.

The importance of diligence was shared in West Germany, as evident in repeated West German adaptations of the same tale: *Frau Holle* (Mother Hulda, Fritz Genschow, 1954), *Frau Holle—Das Märchen von Goldmarie und Pechmarie* (Mother Hulda—The Tale of Golden Mary and Pitch Mary, Peter Podehl, 1961), and again *Frau Holle* (Mother Hulda, Rudolf Jugert, 1971). To take a closer look at Peter Podehl's version, his much expanded 1961 film clearly shows a touch of the *Heimat* film, at the time a popular genre in West Germany. In the story, Goldmarie is an orphan whom her aunt takes in; but her aunt and her cousin are mere substitutes for stepmother and stepsister. Typical of West German fairy-tale films, it is padded out, wordy, and slapstick. The addition of a benign elderly prince (*Fürst*) attests again to the huge difference in the views of and attitudes toward feudal rulers between West and East German fairy-tale films. In this film, the prince is looking for a spinner with the best yarn to become a tailoress at the royal court. The aunt schemes to have Goldmarie spin the yarn but let her own daughter take the credit. In the end, Goldmarie's yarn is selected as the best, but the aunt's scheme is simply not mentioned again. The ending appears cursory and inconsequential. The villains are not punished but rewarded with going to the palace with Goldmarie. Such a happy ending for all is repeated in the 1971 West German version, in which Mother Hulda reappears in the end and takes the tar off Pechmarie, believing she has learned her lesson. Considering the reaction of East German youth to the DEFA film, this appended ending would have preempted young viewers' anxiety about a lifelong punishment for Pechmarie.

Stepdaughters Rewarded: *Snow White* (1961) and *Three Hazelnuts for Cinderella* (1974)

The stories about Snow White and Cinderella belong to the most famous and most often adapted fairy tales. Both deal with the fate of a good and diligent stepdaughter at the hands of an evil stepmother who turns them into scullery maids and dispossesses them of their inheritance or even makes attempts on their lives. These industrious girls, however, are eventually rewarded with love, friendship, and royal marriage. Although and because these stories are well known, filmmakers adapt them and viewers are also curious to see their cherished stories presented on screen. DEFA likewise made recourse to these stories that contain proper lessons about work and money. Gottfried Kolditz's 1961 *Snow White* with its exquisite visuals and delightful soundtrack has become one of the most screened DEFA fairy-tale films. The Czech–DEFA coproduced *Three Hazelnuts for Cinderella* also stands out as an all-time favorite. These adaptations constituted different gender and class images than those in West Germany and the United States, which were influenced by their respective socioeconomic systems, consciously or unconsciously.

The feminist critique of Grimms' "Snow White" and of Disney's *Snow White and the Seven Dwarfs* (1937) applies somewhat to the DEFA version as well. In Kolditz's *Snow White*, Snow White (Doris Weikow) still volunteers to do housework for the dwarfs, is still so unbearably naïve that she falls for the queen's (Marianne Christina Schilling) three murder attempts, and is still saved by a prince (Wolf-Dieter Panse).[66] The feminine depiction of Snow White is attributable to the films' loyalty to the Grimms' tale. Yet DEFA's *Snow White* is less susceptible to feminist scrutiny. Although in need of a male savior, this Snow White is not as psychologically dependent on a prince's rescue as Disney's Snow White. In Disney, Snow White repeatedly sings the song "Some Day My Prince Will Come." DEFA's Snow White is portrayed as calm, controlled, and simplemindedly trustful of a good future. As if deliberately distinguishing itself from the Disney version, DEFA gives the magic mirror a female voice, thus forestalling the feminist and psychoanalytic interpretation that views Disney's male-sounding mirror as a patriarchal judgment resulting in rivalry between the queen mother and the stepdaughter.[67] It is to be noted that the mirror in the 1955 West German version of *Schneewittchen und die sieben Zwerge* (Snow White and the Seven Dwarfs, Erich Kobler) also speaks in a female voice, apparently to distinguish itself from the American version.

In addition to a slightly adjusted gender image of Snow White, the image of the queen is far less ghastly than Disney's queen, who made visual the quintessential stereotype of a brewing witch. DEFA also abandons the original ending in which the queen dances to her death in hot iron shoes. Instead it wittily creates "an eye for an eye" revenge to end the film: the prince gives the queen an apple to eat, but this time the red half goes to the queen and the white half to Snow White. Assuming the apple is poisoned, the queen flees and is banished. The more humane ending is consistent with DEFA's socialist–humanist adaptations of fairy tales. Evil stepmothers or similar evil maternal figures, Maria Tatar argues, are "almost always thinly disguised substitutes for biological mothers."[68] In the Grimms' collection, stepmothers outnumber beasts and monsters, robbers and highway men, which could not be further from reality.[69] The fathers, in contrast, are "supremely passive or positively negligent," if they have not been conveniently left out of the picture.[70] Ruth Bottigheimer criticizes the disproportionate punishment for female transgression in fairy tales.[71] In the wake of the Holocaust, the cruel penalty dealt to the queen was cited as evidence to condemn the Grimms' tales as "a manual for the torture chamber in the extermination camps."[72] The extremeness of the infliction on the queen compelled filmmakers and editors alike to revise the ending: she dies falling off a cliff in the Disney version and is killed by lightening in the West German version. In Walter Pollatschek's 1952 East German Grimm edition, the evil queen is allowed to disappear without a trace. In the East German collections edited by Anneliese Kocialek, the queen's evil heart bursts and she falls dead.[73] DEFA's *Snow White* chose to condemn the queen with isolation and loneliness, which counts as the most lenient punishment of all.

The original story of Snow White involves an abandoned princess who endears herself to seven dwarfs by being a diligent housekeeper. Snow White's diligence in the DEFA film is to be understood in the context of the GDR work culture, not as a sexist role assigned to women as in Disney. Although, especially after the 1970s, feminist-oriented discussions of housework and gender roles emerged in GDR literature and film, DEFA's *Snow White* preempts a sexist interpretation by having the dwarfs work in the household too. Once at the dwarfs' place, Snow White finds their home very clean and orderly: the beds are made, and dinner is ready on the table waiting for the hungry and tired owners. In the Disney picture, on the contrary, Snow White finds the dwarfs' home covered in dust and cobwebs and dirty dishes and clothes piled up. Thus dwarfs—being implicitly both men and children—are dirty and lazy and need a woman and a mother at home, a feminine and maternal role that Disney's Snow White plays perfectly. The Disney version condones men's bad habits when it comes to housework and suggests that these tasks are *exclusively* women's. DEFA's dwarfs, however, share household chores among themselves and Snow White's offer to take over household tasks demonstrates only her helpful nature. After Snow White's departure, they would surely resume sharing their tasks at home. Benita Blessing notes, "This behaviour was not a masculinisation of the domestic sphere; it was a clear reference to the SED's efforts in the 1960s and 1970s to teach citizens that good socialists must be 'clean and tidy, polite, kind and generally well-behaved.'"[74] How it looked in reality is a different question, but the socialist, essentially bourgeois values at the center of the GDR's self-image at least prescribed nonsexist morals about good personal hygiene.

The film announces Snow White's housekeeping ability and bond with the working class early on. As in Disney, a prince from the neighboring country appears at the start of the DEFA picture, as the queen's guest. Forbidden to attend the state banquet, Snow White goes into the kitchen to help the staff prepare another extravagant dinner for the narcissistic and self-aggrandizing queen. Thus Snow White is introduced as a well-integrated member of the working community (see Figure 3.5). While in the kitchen, Snow White solves a staffing problem by helping carry a dish to the festival, thereby catching the eyes of the prince, who then goes to the queen to ask for her hand. The royal kitchen recurs numerous times in DEFA fairy-tale films.[75] The royal kitchen serves as the threshold for a good but wronged prince/princess to be returned to his/her original identity. This is also the world of workers adjacent to that of (corrupt) royalty, allowing DEFA a class-conscious portrait that conforms to socialist ideology. These episodes allow DEFA to avow its solidarity with the workers. The cook (Fritz Schlegel), for example, complains about the queen's lavish lifestyle, which enslaves workers. A cook's assistant happily predicts that Snow White's unwanted appearance at the banquet would cause the queen to burst with rage. Later, the hunter (Harry Hindemith), a figure of resistance, openly defies the queen, praises Snow White, and calls the queen "cruel, oppressive, vain, and filled with hatred." Such direct confrontation and self-empowerment of a member of the lower class is lacking in the American and West German versions. Therefore, as apolitical as DEFA's *Snow White* seems, it received an indelible East German imprint.

The different socioeconomic systems in the two German states inform their different imagination of the dwarfs and their abodes. Although the dwarfs also dig for ore and gold in the DEFA version, there is no indication that they are wealthy. Their cottage is typical proletarian: small, plain, and humble; their clothes are patched. Obviously their productive work is not to enrich themselves. In the West German version, in contrast, the

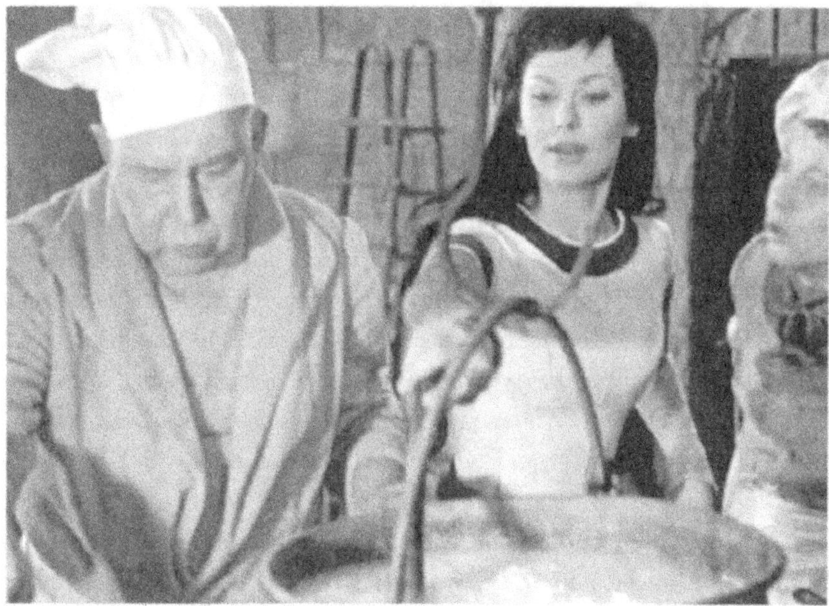

FIGURE 3.5. *Schneewittchen*: Snow White (Doris Weikow) helps in the kitchen on her birthday. © DEFA-Stiftung, Erwin Anders.

dwarfs' residence mirrors West German affluence and is well furnished with fireplace, cuckoo clock, chandelier, birdcage, musical instruments, and so on. The West German dwarfs are entitled to the dispensation of the gold and diamonds because they plan to make jewelry for Snow White. The two German socioeconomic systems have inevitably left marks on their respective fairy-tale films, consciously or unconsciously. The mining scenes in the DEFA version are redolent of the uranium mining in Wismut portrayed in Konrad Wolf's banned film *Sonnensucher* (Sun Seekers, 1958/1972).[76] However, mining in *Snow White* is cheerfully presented with theatricality, songs, and humor; even Naseweis's (Fred Delmare) accident is not deadly, resulting merely in a blister. The dwarfs all listen to their leader Rumpelbold (Arthur Reppert) and work with discipline and in good spirit. Their choreographed actions not only produce humorous theatrical effect but suggest regulated yet pleasant team work. The dwarfs seem to form a model work unit—a "brigade," to use the GDR terminology—that serves the best interests of the collective. A parallel political move can be found in the Disney version, in which, according to Jack Zipes, the happy working dwarfs represented humble American workers, who needed to keep their spirits high during the Depression of the 1930s.[77]

As mentioned in the Introduction, DEFA Außenhandel, the studio's foreign export office, purposefully did not import Disney's animated films, because it was apparently believed that only the socialist film industry could instill the right values in its children. Film reviews of DEFA fairy tales hardly mentioned Disney. In a review of *The Cold Heart*, G. H. criticized the gruesome details in the film by briefly referring to the horror in Disney's *Snow White*, which dampened one's potential pleasure in the film.[78] Due to deliberate boycotting of Disney films, they were not well known in the GDR, but familiarity with Disney's 1937 *Snow White* could of course be expected. Deliberate or not, the DEFA version contains a few intertextual references to the Disney version. For example, the scene in which the dwarfs tease one of them to wash is reminiscent of dumping Grumpy in a trough. The dwarfs are likewise named: Rumpelbold, Purzelbaum, Packe, Naseweis, Puck, Huckepack, and Pick. However, Kolditz does not use special effects to make the seven dwarfs look as small as the Little Glass Man in *The Cold Heart* or use child actors as in the 1955 West German version, in which Snow White seems like a Kindergarten teacher. The dwarfs in Kolditz's film are as big as Snow White: if they were to try their bed or the clothes hanging on the line, they would not fit in them. The size of the dwarfs, disappointing for some reviewers,[79] shows the limitations of live-action fairy-tale films that Disney's animation was able to avoid. All in all, Kolditz's *Snow White* is an entertaining film that has subtly incorporated GDR views on class, gender, wealth, and violence, which in turn distinguishes the film from adaptations by Disney and the FRG.

A similar story about the stepmother–stepdaughter relationship is depicted in another fairy-tale classic—*Three Hazelnuts for Cinderella* (1974), a coproduction of the DEFA group Berlin with the Czech film studio Barrandov in Prague. Based on the Czech revision of "Cinderella" by the woman writer Božena Němcová, Cinderella gets her three dresses from the three hazelnuts that fall into the coachman's lap, thus the title, whereas she receives the ball gowns from the hazelnut tree at her mother's grave in the Grimms' story and from a fairy godmother in Charles Perrault and in Disney's *Cinderella* (1950). What distinguishes the Czech–DEFA coproduction of *Cinderella* is the portrayal of a feisty, active, yet charming female protagonist. The image of a new woman agrees with the socialist conception of gender relations. This may be partly the reason that Hellmuth Häntzsche linked this fantastic fairy tale with socialist realism.[80] This film became an all-time favorite and enjoyed cult status partially due to its appeal to universal humanist values and a contemporary—not visibly socialist—understanding of gender relations.

As Kay Stone points out, feminists agree that earlier studies ignored the subtle inner strength of heroines such as Cinderella, who emerges as "resourceful rather than remorseful."[81] Cinderella is more of a "fetching maiden," to use a deliberately quaint term of James McGlathery, who describes young maidens such as Rapunzel, All Fur (KHM 65), and Cinderella as displaying a capacity for actively winning a young man's devotion:

> One does not usually think of Cinderella in this way; but she is portrayed in the Grimms' version (KHM 21) as not at all lacking in such skills, however indistinctively or unconsciously she may employ them. In particular, there is no reason why she rushes away from the ball each evening and hides from the prince when he tries to pursue her, other than that she wants to assure herself as to the degree of his devotion and, especially, to fan the flames of that passion to a fever pitch by appearing mysterious and unattainable. She renders herself all the more fetching to the prince, and thereby ultimately "fetches" him, by making him chase her.[82]

Despite the proactive traits Cinderella subtly or not so subtly displays, "the mass-market American 'Cinderellas,'" as Jane Yolen observes, "have presented the majority of American children with the wrong dream. They offer the passive princess, the 'insipid beauty waiting . . . for Prince Charming.'"[83] The West German *Aschenputtel* (Cinderella, Fritz Genschow, 1955) likewise lacks the kind of inspiring female protagonist found in the Czech–DEFA version. Like other West German adaptations, this one is marred with poorly synchronized singing and clichéd attempts at farce. It combines elements from the Grimms' version (e.g., the stepsisters' self-mutilation), Perrault's tale (e.g., a fairy godmother and the pumpkin-turned-chariot), and the 1950 Disney animated *Cinderella* (e.g., talking animals and musical-style singing).

The Czech–DEFA-minted Cinderella foregrounds the essence of the originally resourceful princess-in-the-making. She is an excellent horsewoman, a first-rate huntswoman, and a self-confident lover—no passive princess like Snow White and Briar Rose, who spend part of their lives asleep as if dead (see Figure 3.6). A significant change was also made in the character of the prince (Pavel Trávníček) by endowing him with an antiauthoritarian bent. Now he defies forced marriage and yearns for freedom and true love. His rebellion gains support and understanding from his mother (Karin Lesch), who appears equal, if not superior, to her spouse (Rolf Hoppe) and keeps reminding the king of his own youthful disobedience. Thus no longer a conventional rags-to-riches story, this film presents a love story in which Cinderella and the prince do not meet for the first time at the ball but much earlier in the woods. As a reviewer, Margit Voss, pointed out, this Cinderella is not at all dependent on the magic power of the hazelnuts.[84] To this end, the film downplays the importance of the dresses—they are there merely to provide her with proper clothing for the occasions, not to dazzle the prince. In fact, the prince, so bored and irritated because he is forced to pick his bride at the ball, would have stormed out of the room, passing right by the beautifully dressed Cinderella, had she not stopped him. Her dress therefore does not catch his attention a bit. Whereas in the Grimm tales usually a woman's physical beauty suffices to conquer a man's heart, the director of this film has Cinderella cover her face with a veil. She asks the prince a riddle to guess who she is. It is her abilities and wisdom that capture the prince's heart. Thus this modern love story places its focus on two human beings, not on superficial exteriors. As Margit Voss pointed out, Cinderella "marries the prince not only because he is rich but because she knows that she will enjoy going riding and hunting with him, that they enjoy teasing each other, because they will both reject conventions and refuse to be humiliated. Here the affection for a person becomes a process, is made tangible as something great, beautiful, and important."[85] For the triumphant stepdaughters such as Snow White and Cinderella, love is real wealth. Their stepmothers, driven by a hunger for domination or inheritance, are ultimately subject to ridicule and isolation.

While earlier DEFA fairy-tale films, especially those of the 1950s (*The Cold Heart*, *Little Mook*, *Little Tailor*, and *The Singing Ringing Tree*), used

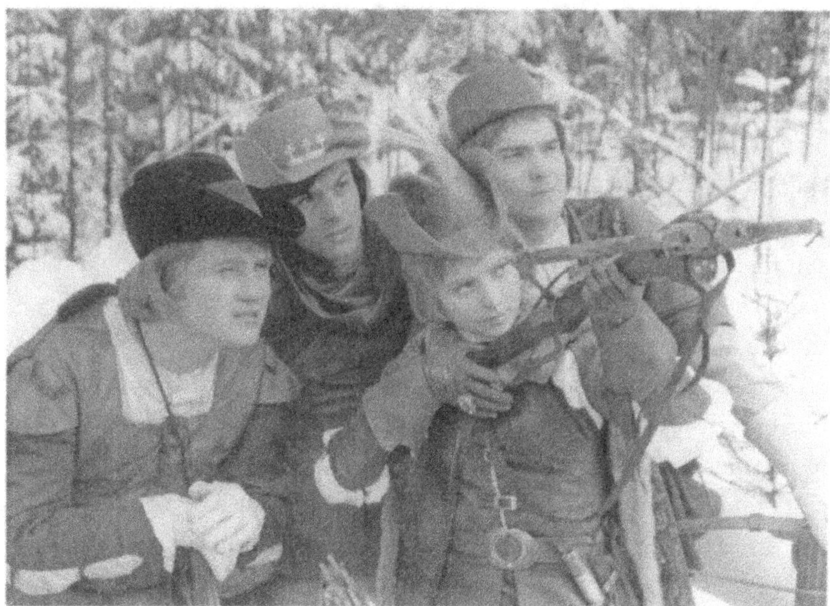

FIGURE 3.6. *Drei Haselnüsse für Aschenbrödel*: Cinderella (Libuše Šafránková) disguised as a huntsman. © DEFA-Stiftung, Jaromir Komarek.

West German directors or actors, collaboration partners shifted to other socialist countries in the Soviet bloc pretty quickly for geopolitical reasons and changes in cultural politics. During the 1970s, the relations between DEFA and Eastern European studios were well established. According to Mariana Ivanova's study on DEFA's international coproductions, these projects were not purely driven by ideology, as many would assume, but by more pragmatic considerations, such as to compete with Western cinemas, mobilize international resources, and achieve the goals of prestige, solidarity, and entertainment. DEFA's collaboration with studios and personnel in the then Czechoslovakia was one of the most productive in the 1970s. In terms of fairy-tale films, a number of them feature Czech actors or actresses as protagonists. *Three Hazelnuts for Cinderella* is the Czech–DEFA fairy-tale film that has the most Czech participation, with a Czech director, a Czech writer, many Czech actors and actresses including the two leading roles, and Czech shooting locations.

Except for a few indoor scenes at Babelsberg, the outdoor scenes at Cinderella's estate were shot at the fifteenth-century water chateau

Švihov, located in Western Bohemia. All the nature and landscape shots were also taken in Bohemia. The film is famous for its charming, snowy Bohemian forest. Director Václav Vorlíček at first conceived of a picture in which Cinderella rides across meadows and fields. The film would have been a very different one had it been shot in the spring or summer as Vorlíček originally wished. However, DEFA was too booked in spring and summer and wanted to keep its employees busy in winter. Then Vorlíček was so inspired by Pieter Brueghel's painting "Hunters in the Snow" (1565) that he finally decided to shoot the film in winter.[86] The change of plan to accommodate DEFA's staffing arrangements turned out to be a fluke. The film quickly reached a phenomenal number of viewers. In Czechoslovakia, it ran simultaneously in 400 cinemas and created a big buzz with sold-out seats everywhere.[87] The Czech involvement obviously did not give the film more socialist underpinnings, for an ideologically loaded fairy tale usually fails at the box office. On the contrary, Czech participation relieved the film from suspicion of ideological corruption and catapulted it to cult status. The fortieth anniversary of this cult film was celebrated in 2013 with three exhibits in Schloss Moritzburg near Dresden and in the Czech Republic. In Moritzburg, forty original costumes were on display in the ballroom accompanied by the film music from Karel Svoboda.[88] This film also enjoys a sustained and active fan group.[89]

In sum, work and money are writ large in DEFA fairy tales that involve stepmother–stepdaughter relationships. Similar to the princesses in *The Singing Ringing Tree* and *King Thrushbeard* discussed above, Snow White and Cinderella temporarily lose their original status and entitlements. Thus in most of these stories, the princesses lead a working life similar to their modern-day viewers so that their audience could relate to them better. On a subtle level, these stories seem a little problematic vis-à-vis GDR valuation of work, because work is at first given as punishment for these female protagonists, and since these are fairy tales, they are rewarded with true love, from a conveniently rich prince. How DEFA still appears to be promoting work is by showing Snow White and Cinderella as possessing qualities and virtues of the working class, and work is no longer beneath or foreign to members of the upper class. Precisely these innate human qualities elide class differences.

Singing Praise to Diligence: *Briar Rose* (1971)

Work and industriousness are the main themes in Walter Beck's "Sleeping Beauty" adaptation—*Briar Rose* (1971), which compellingly rewrites the bitter thirteenth fairy who is not invited to Briar Rose's birth celebration into the Fairy of Diligence (*die Fee des Fleißes*). If she had been invited, the Fairy of Diligence would have endowed the princess with the gift of diligence, which is symbolized with a spinning wheel (see Figure 3.7). The king excludes this particular fairy from the feast because diligence is a virtue befitting the poor, not a princess. The king (Helmut Schreiber), who in the Grimm tale lacks details, is now obsessed with "power and wealth," something he wishes his newborn daughter will bring him. He personifies the old, nonsocialist order, be it feudal, fascist, or capitalist. DEFA changes the originally offended and therefore vengeful fairy into an enraged wise woman with moral and judicial authority. Her initial curse that the princess (Juliane Korén) will prick her finger with a spindle apparently inspired the filmmakers to equip her with a spinning wheel as a symbol of industriousness. In the film spinning is not lamented as a deforming or resented task, as in "The Three Spinners" (KHM 14) and "The Lazy Spinner" (KHM 128).[90] The film starts and ends with a group of women spinning in good spirits, singing the praises of diligence. Their livelihood apparently depends on spinning. The feminist critique of spinning would not have served the economic needs of the GDR. Instead, Wilhelm Grimm's editorial assertion of diligence as a womanly virtue is carried on in this film.[91]

Thus the film justifies the thirteenth fairy's wrath and the subsequent fatal curse that Briar Rose will die of a spindle prick when she turns fifteen. As in the Grimms' story, the twelfth fairy mitigates that deadly spell to a century of sleep. One reviewer pointed out the self-contradiction in such a revision: "If the thirteenth fairy becomes a good fairy, why does she punish the innocent child with death, not the evil greedy father?"[92] Although DEFA promoted work and industriousness, sometimes drastic revisions created further illogic. Apparently this fairy is not entirely a fairy godmother figure who takes the princess under her wing. This particular illogic would usually go unnoticed and could be understood as a compromise the scriptwriters made with the Grimms' tale. The thirteenth fairy is

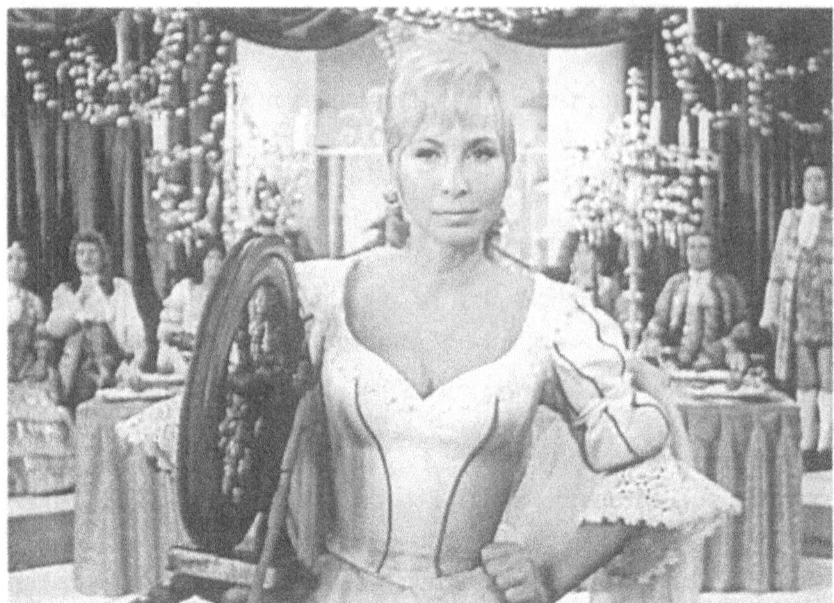

FIGURE 3.7. *Dornröschen* screenshot: The Fairy of Diligence (Vera Oelschlegel) holding a spinning wheel comes uninvited. © DEFA-Stiftung, Lothar Gerber.

not positively reimagined in the West German *Dornröschen* (Briar Rose, Fritz Genschow, 1955) or in Disney's *Sleeping Beauty* (1959). Only DEFA creates a memorable Fairy of Diligence and thereby radically changes a fairy stereotypically cast as a witch into a powerful goddess, harnessing the film to the contemporary rewriting of the witch in the GDR as well as in the Western feminist movement.[93]

The DEFA version addresses many questions the Grimm story fails to answer. For example, why is there no outrage when the king orders all the spindles to be burned and how could this selfish king continue to rule for a hundred years? In answering these questions, the DEFA adaptation revisits important socialist issues such as antifascist class struggle. The Grimms use only one sentence to cover the fact that the king decrees every spindle in the entire kingdom to be burned. Considering the importance of spinning in Europe's economy before the end of the nineteenth century, a nationwide confiscation of such a critical work tool would be devastating for the lower-class people. The film constructs, in an extended sequence, the struggle between spinning women and those responsible for executing this senseless order. As such, when the royal soldiers come to seize the spindles, spinning women courageously put up a fight. This logical expansion of the mass reaction to such a government order was positively reviewed.[94]

In a way, the spinning women have become "resistance fighters," shouting slogans as if in Soviet-style agitprop theater: "The King plunges us all into misery. He destroys people and land. The King should be cursed! . . . The King should be eliminated!"[95] Both the content and the form of this protracted episode about the burning of spindles and the subsequent resistance appear to be a direct analogy to Nazi book burning and the Communists' antifascist struggle, aligning the film with proletarian revolutionary cinema, linking, as one reviewer pointed out, "magic and reality."[96] No wonder that Hellmuth Häntzsche described this adaptation as "a socialist realist fairy-tale adaptation."[97] Interestingly though, one could also discover slave language in this scene. The king's edict that orders the burning of all spindles reads, "Whoever knows about a spindle that another has in his house or is hiding outside his house must report it immediately, otherwise he will be punished with death."[98] The peasants must inform on their neighbors' spindles, possibly alluding to the Stasi surveillance system in the GDR.[99]

The traditional motif of a sleeping beauty is maintained in the film, even true love's kiss. However, the DEFA version abides by a humanist and anticapitalist agenda. In the Grimm tale, the prince who finally kisses Briar Rose awake does not show any more qualification than his predecessors. He merely appears at the right place and at the right time. In the film, he first hears a minstrel (Martin Hellberg) singing about Briar Rose and then meets a frustrated prince (Jaecki Schwarz) returning without success, *but alive.*[100] The Grimms' story states, "Many princes had come and had tried to break through the Briar hedge, but they had got stuck and had died wretched deaths" (KHM 50). The film avoids these countless violent deaths and thus revises the unnecessary extremity in the Grimm tale. When the worthy prince (Burkhard Mann) goes to rescue Briar Rose, he does not see just a hedge, as in the Grimm story, but an impenetrable mountain. He has to climb a treacherous cliff to retrieve a spindle for the Fairy of Diligence, who then challenges him with three "screening tests"—the temptations of power, wealth, and beauty of another princess.

Implicitly none of the princes before him could resist these temptations and earn entry to the castle where Briar Rose lies. Once in the castle, he "sees" three frozen scenes, as they happened a hundred years ago; moving images are intercut with still photographs. Once Briar Rose awakens, the still images transition into motion pictures. These formal devices attest to the film's artistic deliberation, which is worth noting beyond the otherwise simple plotline.

DEFA also revises the ending of the story to align it with antifascist and anticapitalist precepts. When the Grimms' Briar Rose awakens, everything resumes as before. The film, however, questions whether it is right for such a king to continue his reign. Although the entire castle comes back alive, the king and his cohort are thereafter depicted with ashen faces. The Fairy of Diligence interrupts the king's carousing and removes his crown and scepter, thus putting an end to his despotic regime. The former aristocratic retinue flees, while the common people come to celebrate the new king's coronation and wedding. The new queen does not show any emotion for the downfall of her father and gladly accepts her role in the new society. She sits down to spin and thereby sets an example for her people, who have not been able to spin for the hundred years of her sleep. Work is not derogated as being beneath a queen. Instead it is embraced as a sign of equality and unity that blurs class boundaries. Her act reinitiates nationwide spinning, which promises economic recovery and nation building. On a symbolic level, she disavows her ties to the old power structure—represented by her father—and eagerly joins the new social order.[101]

The deposition of the old king and arrival of a new order is absent in the original tale. Yet, in 1971, such an ending appears ambiguous: On the one hand, it could distinguish the GDR government from the feudal and fascist regimes that the old king represents, and thus the film reaffirms, somewhat anachronistically, the GDR's founding myth. On the other hand, the working class still accepts a feudal government after the royalty were put to sleep for a hundred years, which then makes the ending seem quite counterrevolutionary. The film does not radically change the last prince to a commoner but presents the young monarch as good and virtuous. Thus the end of the film could constitute a more contemporaneous appeal for a popular and reformed government so that the GDR would eventually have a happy ending, despite the *Kahlschlag* plenum in 1965. In contrast to fairy-tale films from the 1950s, the 1971 *Briar Rose* no longer appeals for revolution—not another workers' revolution like the 17 June 1953 uprising or another Prague Spring—but limited reform within the current regime. Thus the film perhaps instantiates a GDR moment of demonstrating the proper citizen relationship to power around 1970.

Socialist Countertales: Refusing Unlabored Wealth in *The Goose Girl at the Spring* (1979) and *Bearskin* (1986)

This section analyzes two DEFA fairy tales that represent socialist revisions of traditional fairy tales but include radical new endings. At the end of *The Goose Girl at the Spring* (1979), the princess/goose girl no longer lives in a stately palace, as in the Grimms' original, but leads a plain life with Hans. In *Bearskin* (1986), the soldier no longer keeps the Devil's green jacket—a wellspring of gold coins—which he is entitled to according to his pact with the Devil, as in the Grimms' version. Both films make recourse to the hackneyed rhetoric of "love supersedes wealth," rendering them *socialist countertales*, and anachronistic at that. In the last decade of the GDR, such trite and overfamiliar messages lacked appeal to the public, as shown below.

Like *The Tinderbox* (1959), *The Goose Girl at the Spring* ends with a member of the lower class marrying a princess, but this time, DEFA had to first change the protagonist from Grimms' young count to a blacksmith named Hans (David Schneider). The version in the much criticized 1952 GDR Grimm edition by Walther Pollatschek still has a young count, so the change apparently is only undertaken in the film script. The reviews of *The Goose Girl at the Spring* did not criticize such a significant change to the Grimms' canon, so the film was not accused of "vulgarizing Marxism" as happened to *Little Tailor* in 1956.

Being just one more mouth to feed at home, the young blacksmith Hans goes out into the wide world to seek his fortune. He meets an elderly woman (Christine Schorn) who takes him in for one night to reward him for his help with carrying a heavy basket. At the elderly woman's cottage, he meets a goose girl (Jaroslava Schallerová), who is in fact an ostracized princess. Therefore this Grimm story contains another demoted princess, whose fate conveniently offers an antifeudal reading of the old regime. In the original tale, the elderly woman gives the young count an emerald box that contains pearls as a departing gift. When he arrives at the palace and presents the box to the king and the queen, he learns that these pearls are formed from the tears of their disowned daughter. The film, however, segments the goose girl's story into Hans's three dreams that the elderly woman induces with her witchcraft. Unlike the majority of DEFA fairy-tale films that follow a linear, single-stranded narration, this 1979 film uses extended flashbacks to fuse the present and the past and equates dreams with actual events. The dreams tell episodically why Princess Marie became a goose girl. In Hans's third dream, the king (Günter Naumann) commands his daughters to express their love for him in front of guests. Unlike her older sisters, who compare their love to sugar and pretty dresses, Marie, now fifteen, compares hers to salt because the best meal would not taste good without salt. Infuriated at such a plain answer, the king orders Marie to leave the castle with a sack full of salt. According to M. R. Cox's analysis, "The Goose Girl at the Spring" includes a "King Lear judgment": a father demands from his three daughters a declaration of love; he deems the youngest daughter's answer insufficient and banishes her.[102] Whereas Cordelia dies in Shakespeare's tragedy *King Lear*, the fairy-tale heroine becomes a Cinderella figure and only temporarily loses her royal status, as befitting the fairy-tale convention.

The class portrayal in this 1979 film does not transcend DEFA's earlier models. Not only is the protagonist now from the working class but Princess Marie shows proletarian characteristics. In Hans's first dream, viewers learn that Marie is troubled by the aristocratic lifestyle. She sneaks away from the royal company to play with the servants' children. She prefers simple gifts to what the prince from the neighboring kingdom gives her. Marie's down-to-earth longing for a normal childhood, nonexistent in the Grimms' version, counteracts many fairy tales that make little girls want to be princesses. But the king orders the "beggar gifts" to be taken away and forbids her further contact with the servants' children. Marie cries. Then a fairy—beautiful, regal, recognizably the same person as the elderly woman in the cottage—shows up and wishes that when Marie is sad, every drop of her tears would turn into a pearl. Such a rendition of a fairy godmother is not too far from the Grimms' story in which the narrator suggests at the end, "The old woman was not a witch, as people believed, but a wise woman who meant well. It was probably she who was at the birth of the princess and gave her the gift of weeping pearls instead of tears" (KHM 179). Similar to DEFA's feministic re-creation of the Fairy of Diligence, this film portrays the woman who is believed to be a witch as a well-meaning wise woman. She is also the only one who dares criticize the king: "You are arrogant and heartless, King Albrecht. But the day will come when you will curse all your power and wealth."

The count in the Grimms' story has undesirable traits (KHM 179). He is ill-disposed toward the women and thinks they are witches. Thus in the Grimms' tale, the elderly woman does not seem to have chosen a virtuous man for the disinherited princess. She chooses the young count more for his social status than his own worth. In the DEFA version, the elderly woman transcends class differences, and in the process, she not only chooses a good-natured man for her protégé but also teaches him a lesson. Hans's initial dreams of achieving "power, fame, and wealth" are revealed to be misguided. DEFA creates episodes that ridicule the greed of members of the upper class, their depreciation of the lower classes, and their greed-driven proclivity toward violence. Instead of worldly possessions, Hans realizes that love has the real power and is the true treasure. He no longer wants power and wealth from the king but asks for Marie alone: "She means to me more than all the treasures of the earth." Hans's personal and ideological transformation is complete, whereas the young count in the Grimms' version does not undergo such a renunciation of wealth and power.

For similar reasons, DEFA drastically changed the ending of the film. In the Grimms' story, the elderly fairy rewards the goose girl by transforming the cottage into a palace, but this does not occur in the DEFA version. Here the princess will marry a blacksmith and celebrate her eighteenth birthday with the servants' children, now also grown up. Since DEFA portrays life as a princess as undesirable, there is no need to turn the cottage into a palace. Hans also rejects the king's invitation to bring Marie back to the palace. This new ending indicates that the couple makes a conscious decision to live like common people, making the film a typical socialist countertale. Marie's happiness indicates that there will be no more pearls formed from tears of sadness. The revisions DEFA made clearly underplay the allure of power and wealth and demonstrate that it seeks solidarity with the *Volk*. Whereas once the paternalistic feudal rulers loathed the lower classes, the DEFA films turn the hierarchical structure on its head and suggest that the life of a commoner is more appealing and happier than that of royalty. In the late 1970s, however, this revision evoked a working-class protagonist's disillusioned search for power and wealth, thus putting an ironic spin on the GDR's foundational narratives and anticapitalist Cold War rhetoric.

In his 1986 *Bearskin*, Walter Beck gave the Grimms' "Bearskin" (KHM 101) an interestingly anticapitalistic ending. The film concerns an unpaid and homeless soldier named Christoffel (Jens-Uwe Bogadtke) who strikes a deal with the Devil: in exchange for perpetual wealth, he cannot wash, comb, or shave for seven years and he can sleep only on a bearskin. If he violates any of the preconditions, he will belong to the one with a cloven foot. His stench alienates himself from his surroundings, rich or poor; even a dog does not want to take food from him. His lack of personal hygiene drives him to utter isolation and despair. He wants to hang himself but decides to bribe prison guards for shelter. He ransoms an unfortunate goldsmith out of prison, which wins him the love of the goldsmith's youngest daughter, Katarina (Janina Hartwig). It is love that enables him to persevere through the rest of the seven-year covenant. In the end, the power dynamics reverse between the Devil and the soldier because the Devil has to wash and shave Christoffel personally when Christoffel wins the bet. At the end of the Grimms' version, Bearskin keeps the Devil's green jacket and goes to his bride as a stately prince. But in the DEFA version, the soldier nobly *returns the source of wealth* to the Devil and joins his lover as a clean, plain, but happy man.

The film obviously suggests that love renders everything else insignificant. However, the radical change of the story's ending poses a conundrum that the film fails to resolve satisfactorily: What was the real point of the seven years of filth? Is Katarina's love a just and sufficient reward for the excruciating pain and humiliation he suffered for seven years? The new, impractical ending thus troubled reviewers. Margitta Fahr wrote in *Film und Fernsehen*: "The obviously sociocritical plot of the tale cannot be reduced to a basic message: 'Money brings no good to the poor.'" Fahr continued, "The only thing left is Katarina. Nice, but is it really a shame to have money and be able to provide the girl with an existence? He has, after all, earned it after seven years of disreputable existence."[103] Another reviewer was like-minded: "In addition, the older viewers may be asking the question whether, in the world in which our fairy tale takes place, inner greatness renders mundane wealth superfluous."[104] Despite largely positive reviews, these voices disapproving Christoffel's final abandonment of wealth indicate their disagreement with the moral the film attempted to preach in the mid-1980s, thus questioning DEFA's long-held anticapitalistic precept that love alone is real wealth.

The Marxist appropriation of a suitable folktale was the time-tested principle for DEFA fairy tales. Similarly, this film exposed the social injustice members of the lower class like Christoffel suffered. Unlike the exploited soldiers in *The Tinderbox* and *The Blue Light*, Christoffel does not seek justice with magical help. Instead he braves the perverse, almost impossible challenges to acquire unlimited wealth. The Devil does not unconditionally, altruistically, or benevolently lift the lower class out of poverty, as magical helpers often do for little favor from the protagonist. The Devil appears, rather, as a member of the upper class who sets the bar high for lower class access to wealth and status by subjecting Christoffel to a prolonged unsanitary, abject existence outside of civilized society. Only ostensibly is his class status changed to the richest man on earth, but as a matter of fact he is the poorest of the poor who has not really transcended social division.

Members of elite society (with Heidemarie Wenzel playing a baroness) fake friendship and play cards with him, tolerating his stench only for the sake of his mysterious wealth. "With money I can conquer the world," claims one aristocrat. Lower-class people abhor him. He is a stinky animal (*Vieh*) that is shunned, mocked, and driven away. Farmers literally chase after him as "a wild animal" and can only be stopped by gold coins. Nearly everyone is bribable vis-à-vis the allure of gold. Bearskin's animal-like appearance becomes a challenge but also a test for love. The first townswoman feigns love for the sake of his money but turns her back on him after feeling his empty pocket: "No money, no love." The second, a peasant girl, spurns his gold due to his filth. The film was not criticized as hostile toward the people in the way *How to Marry a King* was back in 1968 (see chapter 4). Artists apparently were no longer obligated to give peasants an absolutely positive portrayal. It is obvious that the politically dogmatic scrutiny of films along the socialist–realist line waned in the 1980s. After he has Katarina's love, Christopher learns the lesson about what wealth truly means.

In the Grimms' "Bearskin," the two older sisters humiliate Bearskin when he looks inhuman and reeks. But when Bearskin returns rich and good-looking, one drowns herself and the other hangs herself—another example of disproportionate punishment for women in fairy tales. In the film, these suicides do not occur because suicide was also a taboo topic in the GDR, let alone in a film meant for children. In the final scene, Christoffel and Katarina dance away in celebration of their wedding—probably the only DEFA fairy-tale film that does not have a crowd scene at such an occasion.

The ending in which Christoffel no longer claims to own the green jacket was problematic for the reviewers. The rejection of wealth seems to follow a realistic principle for a reason similar to what a reviewer posited for *Little Mook* (1953): one should not expect production quotas to be fulfilled miraculously.[105] Whereas the Grimm tale keeps to the bourgeois dream of a member of the lower class finally ending up rich, the DEFA version idealistically preaches love as a sufficient outcome of seven years of trials and tribulations. Back in 1953, reviewers unanimously welcomed Little Mook's objection to unlabored wealth, but in the case of *Bearskin* thirty years later, some reviewers doubted whether such a humanistic yet tendentious and anachronous revision was not problematic or too idealistic. The critique did not focus on the fact that Beck made a radical change to the Grimm canon but was troubled by why the protagonist could not be rich at the end.

In many ways, *Bearskin* is comparable to the very first DEFA fairy-tale film *The Cold Heart*. Like Peter, Christoffel receives from the Devil magical pockets that can replenish themselves. In both stories, the protagonists are compromised in pursuit of wealth: Christoffel is unkempt, stinky, and animalistic and loses his humanity on the outside, while Peter becomes a monster on the inside. Their newfound wealth is not concomitant with happiness. But unlike Peter, Christoffel does not change his solidarity with the poor and his wealth is not accompanied by moral corruption. Like Peter, however, Christoffel rejects affluence stemming from black magic in the end. Both tales are concerned with one's soul and ultimate salvation. In the Grimms' "Bearskin," one of the stipulations is that the soldier not pray, but he gives money to the poor so that they pray for him. In the end Bearskin gives thanks to the Lord: "Through the grace of God I've regained my human form and have become clean again" (KHM 101). Explicit Christian references are superficially done away with in the films and reviewers routinely acquiesced about such changes. While the original stories emphasize religious salvation, the films enhance the power of love as a secular substitute. The stark resemblance between *The Cold Heart* and *Bearskin*, thirty-six years apart, suggests the anachronism of the latter film, which also partly explains low attendance in cinemas as well as apathetic audiences.[106]

On an aesthetic level, the film creatively employed highly stylized set designs similar to those of theater productions, a hallmark of Beck's directorial style.[107] All the scenes were shot inside a studio. A huge white cloth covering frameworks suggests mountains. This same setting recurs in the film but with varied modifications to suggest the passing of time. On the narrative level, however, the film created some additional scenes short of logic and gave the impression that Christoffel passed his ordeal by sheer luck.[108] In the post-GDR era when anachronism no longer matters, this film, overall well made, conveys the universal values of perseverance, compassion, love, and friendship.

Conclusion

DEFA fairy tales in all decades consistently reiterate work ethic and precedence of love over money. The socialist appropriations of old tales surrounding aristocracy and the bourgeoisie propagate this ideology of love and work with an obvious anticapitalist spin, reflecting the GDR's position in the Cold War as well as toward its own populace. Stories that involve a change in class status, upward or downward, were DEFA's favorite raw material. DEFA justified adaptations of these aristocratic and bourgeois tales by extracting socialist–humanistic values from the stories and portraying the princes and princesses as human beings who had much to learn from the working class. The image of the princes and princesses was appropriated, modernized, and made more realistic and relatable for viewers in the GDR. And the films' treatment of work made them "realistic" for the GDR audience. Whereas the lower classes often emulated the upper class in nineteenth-century tales, DEFA exalted the workers and obliged members of the upper class to acquire qualities of the working class. Hard work was promoted as instrumental in the formation of a socialist consciousness, especially given the low work morale in reality.

However, the GDR economic reality made it ironic to propagate a work ethic, because it was not that the workers were not willing to work hard but that the state had to a great extent failed them, which led to the 1953 uprising in the first place. The GDR's planned economy was notorious for its mismanagement and shortages of materials, thus the propaganda about hard work was not supported by an economic structure that would actually facilitate it. The contemporary films, especially the banned "rabbit films," problematized the workplace and the ethos of hard work, such as *Trace of Stones* (1965/1990) and *Berlin around the Corner* (1965/1990).[109] Thus fairy-tale mores appear to be a "politically correct," oversimplified compromise with DEFA's official obligation.

The East German attitude toward wealth—the disdain for gold (the fairy-tale term for money)—recurs in almost all the DEFA fairy-tale films. These films offered an alternative solution to avarice and monetary wealth, that is, through work, through good and virtuous deeds, one could find love and familial bliss. Hence, the goals in many of the original fairy tales—wealth and power—were no longer endorsed as desirable but were aligned with West German capitalistic pursuits and decried as being of a bourgeois mentality. In so doing, these socialist countertales defended East German perspectives and echoed Cold War rhetoric. They suggestively associated the capitalist West with wealth and power, represented by the aristocracy, and the socialist East with virtues like diligence, love, and humanity, exemplified by the working class.

In reality, however, money and a good standard of living were still higher priorities to the country's citizens than ethics and class consciousness, as the countless incidences of so-called *Republikflucht* before and after the erection of the Berlin Wall showed. The rejection of wealth was, however, hypocritical, since the GDR had to compete with West Germany for regime legitimacy to enhance the social welfare of its people and to convince the world of the sustainability of socialism. To that end, gold was as important to the GDR as it was to any other society. After all, the GDR's emphasis on work ultimately aimed at producing wealth for the country. Only in the absence of wealth, that is, when the GDR was not yet rich, were avarice and greed to be spurned. The rhetorical contempt for gold smacked of moralism and appeared to be a self-deceptive excuse for the GDR's sluggish economy. Love as true wealth seemed to be a useful myth aimed at mollifying the poor GDR citizens, reducing their jealousy of their rich West German neighbors and keeping them content within the GDR's borders. As Wolfgang Staudte once did with *Little Mook*, Beck may have made the change in *Bearskin* because he considered wealth from the Devil unearned and fantastic, but by the mid-1980s, reviewers apparently had had enough of the anticapitalist rhetoric and the poverty of the GDR. The reviewers' thought-provoking critique of *Bearskin*'s new ending revealed a change in the East German public discourse so it refocused on, or affirmed, consumerism and materialism. These reviewers followed a different realist paradigm, one that saw the pursuit of wealth as decent and human.

4

AMBIGUITY BETWEEN CONFORMISM AND RESISTANCE

Slave Language and Political Satires

In its founding years, the GDR felt it necessary to justify communist rule and defend its regime against its rivals in West Germany. Thus from early on, cultural officials insisted that DEFA films apply socialist realism as their chief aesthetic means of addressing and promoting the new political reality. Films lacking socialist–realist benchmarks were often criticized as bourgeois, revisionist, and not contributing to the socialist education of future generations. Like other films of their time, DEFA fairy tales in the 1950s and 1960s (see chapters 1–3) often adopted the normative aesthetic and master narratives of the GDR. One might see the power shift from a feudal king to a worker-cum-king, a common trope of these films, as symbolic of the political events of that era. But the need for self-justification gradually diminished after the GDR built the Berlin Wall in 1961. No longer having to prove itself to its own workers, the GDR reallocated its resources and energy to other matters. Starting in the late 1960s, a series of political events including the Prague Spring, the Western student revolts of 1968, and Honecker's much cited no taboo speech in 1971 prompted filmmakers to engage with contemporary society. With regard to fairy-tale films, two contrasting types of discursive practice existed and sometimes coincided in the same film: party-line conformism and subversive criticism.

This chapter turns to fairy-tale films that show this ambiguity, or hybridity, between conformism and subversion, notably Konrad Petzold's *The Robe* (1961/1991), Rainer Simon's *How to Marry a King* (1969) and *How Six Made Their Way in the World* (1972), and Egon Schlegel's *The Devil's Three Golden Hairs* (1977). It emphasizes the films' potential to be critical of the GDR government without negating other socialist propositions they might make. On the one hand, these films reiterate class struggles, themes that overlap with chapter 2. *The Robe*, for example, shows the hilarious deception of the naked emperor by two workers. *How to Marry a King* contains a peasant girl's elevation in social status via her own intelligence. *How Six Made Their Way in the World* traces how an exploited soldier settles his account with the king. *The Devil's Three Golden Hairs* tells the story of a young smith's daredevil trip to the underworld and his earthly battle with the king. All these films show solidarity with the members of the lower class in their challenging of royal, aristocratic power. Like the other fairy tales made in the 1970s—*Briar Rose* (1971), *Little Claus and Big Claus* (1971), *The Black Mill* (1975), *Die Regentrude* (*The Rain Maiden*, Ursula Schmenger, 1976), *The Rabbit Catcher* (1977), and *The Goose Girl at the Spring* (1979)—they carried on the politics of adaptation and class-conscious topoi that conformed to official imperatives. On the other hand, however, these films are not analyzed in chapter 2 but in chapter 4 because the kings in these films could no longer be easily identified as an embodiment of corrupt, old regimes that the GDR claimed to supersede, but they in fact included the GDR state itself. Although the films make no explicit references to the GDR and appear to attack abuses of power generally, the GDR simply could not extricate itself from their allusions and sarcasm.

In this way, criticism implicit in the DEFA fairy tales of the 1970s and 1980s changed from the earlier films' narrow focus against the West to broader criticisms, including internal critique. The banning of *The Robe* and the Eleventh Plenum of 1965 in particular made it very clear that direct criticism of the party and state was not tolerated. Even during Honecker's reign, as historian Dagmar Schittly notes, the seemingly propitious cultural liberalization soon turned out to be short lived. The government eventually retracted its promises and reemphasized the prerequisite of a socialist position in alignment with that of the ruling party. After the Biermann Affair, the SED reinforced its dogmatic cultural policies and repeatedly warned its writers and artists not to criticize existing circumstances but instead to praise the GDR's achievements. Critical artists experienced disruption of their projects, professional sidelining, or worse.[1]

The overall repressive cultural policies compelled writers and filmmakers to find ways to evade censorship by camouflaging criticism under the veneer of history or fairy tales. Kristin Wardetzky observes, "Starting in the 1960s, especially after the Eleventh Plenum of the Central Committee, fairy-tale adaptations increasingly became cover for political and moral problems in society. Through the symbols and ciphers of fairy tales, sociopolitical conflicts could be made public in a safer way than in a film set in contemporary times."[2] Jack Zipes observes the use of slave language (*Sklavensprache*) in the fairy-tale films of Central and Eastern Europe and argues that DEFA directors were interested in using the fairy tale as a forum to comment on the GDR's politics and society.[3] Sibylle Schönemann confirms this: "Fairy-tale films are also popular because socially critical aspects can be woven in a cryptic way, and only educated viewers are able to decipher them later."[4] Discussing literary tales in the GDR from 1976 through 1985, Gert Reifarth contends that the fairy tale is a genre that enables veiled social and political critiques. He categorizes the fairy tale as "coded literature" (*Verschlüsselungsliteratur*), because the censors failed to detect criticism in the artfully dissimulated "allegories" or were unable to identify with confidence the camouflaged critique.

Zipes's usage of slave language proves a useful concept for discussing DEFA fairy tales. Although the relative well-being of the GDR citizen cannot be compared to conditions of slavery, the word "slave" is a general term that stands for all the oppressed who resort to cryptic communication and whose shared experience enables them to understand the masked agenda. According to Lenin, the disenfranchised and downtrodden used the "Aesopian language" to communicate among themselves, but all this became unnecessary in the Soviet Union. Hence it is ironic—although understandable—that slave language thrived again in the Soviet Union as well as the Eastern bloc.[5] The East German author Christoph Hein gave an apt definition of slave language: "The term 'slave language' belongs to the political vocabulary: It identifies the social status of the speaker as that of someone who is powerless, oppressed, and enslaved. It refers to a code, with which the similarly disenfranchised communicate with each other and the decoding of which requires similar social experience."[6]

According to Wardetzky, not only those oppressed and subaltern but even those at whom the criticism is directed understand the message. Nevertheless, those criticized do not have a direct pretext to punish those who encode the messages for fear of implicating themselves, since the critique is invariably opaque and cannot be penalized with certainty.[7] Dagmar Schittly offers a slightly different opinion: the censors often did not recognize communication between the lines and the images because they were out of touch and thus too removed from the original content.[8] The safe haven created by slave language helped writers, filmmakers, and artists get away with their social criticism unscathed. This tactic was not limited to fairy-tale films but was used in films pertaining to the past in general. In analyzing heritage films, Daniela Berghahn also speaks of DEFA's "dual strategy" of supporting the GDR's cultural legitimization and utilizing costume drama to camouflage critical subtexts about contemporary society.[9]

This chapter examines how these films could be read as targeting the GDR regime. That some of these films ran into serious difficulties with censorship only confirms why such interpretations remain important. Petzold and Günther's *The Robe* will be analyzed at great length because this was the only fairy-tale film banned outright in DEFA history. Simon's debut film *How to Marry a King* was criticized for being too formalist and hostile toward the people. To Simon's astonishment, his portrayal of the king was suspected to be a parody of Walter Ulbricht.[10] The film was almost banned, as *The Robe* was. In 1968, DEFA was still plagued by a sense of insecurity in the wake of the 1965 plenum, and this anxiety intensified after the Prague Spring and its suppression by the Soviets with the help of the East German army.[11] The analogy of the oppressive kingdom in Simon's *How Six Made Their Way in the World* with the GDR appears wittier and less innocent, given the hardship Simon had with his debut. Egon Schlegel's *The Devil's Three Golden Hairs* juxtaposes a hypocritical, murderous government with the humorous and humane world of the

Devil, implicitly castigating the unpopularity of the regime that is suggestively located under the earth's surface in the film. Except for *The Robe*, these fairy-tale films passed censorship due to a lack of obvious parallels between their plotlines and common critiques of the state.

Reviews or scholarly analyses published since the fall of the Wall were quick to point out veiled, critical references to the GDR, whereas reviewers of the time either did not see or kept presciently quiet about such possibilities. Bettina Hindemith suggests that film criticism in the GDR "avoids controversial subjects and stays silent. This implies that if one wants to write about film critique in the GDR, one must read between the lines at all cost to infer what was never written."[12] This exhortation to recover, belatedly but exhaustively, what was left unsaid suggests, on the one hand, that film reviews in the GDR understated or elided levels of meaning antithetical to the official judgment of a film. On the other hand, Hindemith posits that slave language latent in many DEFA films still waits to be decrypted. Now that the GDR itself has become history, movie critics have more latitude to speculate about—or rather, assert the presence of—encoded messages against the GDR. Ralf Schenk, for example, viewed the deserted throne and scattering crowd in *The Robe* as foreshadowing the collapse of the GDR.[13] After the Wall fell, scholars pointed out the obvious parallel between the kingdom of Malabunt in Simon's *How Six Made Their Way in the World* and the "trapped" GDR.[14] A 1991 review of *King Thrushbeard* read a few scenes as making implicit references to the GDR (see chapter 3).[15] In the same vein, Jack Zipes reads *Iron Hans* (1988) as "a strange forewarning" of the GDR's collapse because, in the picture, the old corrupt rulers—one barbaric, the other infantile—continue to rule forlorn kingdoms and the next generation of rulers is not depicted as promising (see chapter 5).[16]

A Banned Brechtian Satire: *The Robe* (1961/1991)

In the list of DEFA fairy-tale films that brought the studio much fame and revenue, one film was painfully missing: *The Robe*, adapted from Hans Christian Andersen's "The Emperor's New Clothes." It was directed in 1961 by Konrad Petzold with a script from Egon Günther, but the film was banned in the same year, becoming thereby the only banned DEFA fairy-tale film.

At the same time, an adaptation of Andersen's tale by the famous Soviet playwright Eugene Schwartz—*Golyi korol'* (The Naked King, 1934)—was staged in Moscow. The Soviet play was at first banned but eventually made it through censorship. Petzold's *The Robe* was not so fortunate.

In Andersen, two swindlers claim they are weavers and the cloth they weave is invisible to anyone who is unfit for the position they are holding or unforgivably stupid. Of course, then, everyone including the emperor himself pretends they can see the new clothes. The narcissistic emperor ends up heading a parade stark naked, and all the townsfolk praise his magnificent robe until a child cries, "But he doesn't have anything on." In Andersen's tale, the ruler becomes a laughingstock when the naked truth of his incompetence is revealed. The fact that no one, except a small child, perceives his nakedness and thus exposes the ruse serves as an unsettling portrayal of a dictatorship, in which no opposition exists to point out the absurd notions of the ruling party. Whereas such a subversive idea is only implied in Andersen's tale, the film comedy develops the tale's potential for political satire.

In the film, two weavers, Hans (Horst Drinda) and Kumpan (Werner Lierck), come to a kingdom surrounded by a well-guarded and seemingly impenetrable wall. By an odd alignment of fiction and reality, the film was screened for the censors as part of the approval procedure in November after the Berlin Wall went up on 13 August 1961 (see below). Hence, a walled-in city in which "the Great Dictator" rules conjured up numerous unwanted associations with the geopolitical situation in East Germany. In addition, the mustache-wearing guard was believed to resemble Stalin and the animated sequences of a cloud that puffs up its cheeks to blow wind was believed to mock the Soviet leader Khrushchev.[17] Whether or not Petzold intended the resemblance can only be hypothesized. The sentry tells the weavers, "This is the wall that runs straight through. Behind it lies the city and happiness."[18] The choice of words "Das ist die Mauer, die quer durchgeht" is indeed peculiar and suggests that the wall cuts right through the land. Censors also took this line to be pure provocation.[19] In addition to the unfortunate timing of the film's production, the guard's claim of an affluent and happy city mocked the reality of poverty, popular unrest, and mass exodus, which prompted the building of the Berlin Wall.

In an interview with Ralf Schenk from 2000, the film's screenwriter Egon Günther said that the wall in the film was a pure coincidence, but he hoped with good intentions that the GDR would take some constructive criticism from the film:

> There is a huge wall in the film. We built it on the DEFA studio premises, seven meters high. Insane! . . . Fourteen days later the Berlin Wall was built. I could not have known that. Neither can I claim that I ingeniously foresaw it. And it was the death knell for the film. It coincided with criticism of oppression, of which I probably thought then that it does not have to be the case, and that one can change it. Perhaps, if one tells the rulers or if one holds the mirror up to them.[20]

The wall in the film was likely a coincidence, but it is worth noting that, just two months earlier in June 1961, Walter Ulbricht said during a press conference: "Nobody has the intention of building a wall."[21] This denial ironically acknowledged that East Germany might indeed construct a wall. The film then kept the wall, despite the construction of the Berlin Wall and the taboo of filming it. Egon Günther, later a director himself, was known for using double entendre in his films.[22] Günther's film—*Wenn du groß bist, lieber Adam* (When You Grow Up, Dear Adam, 1965/1990)—was banned by the Eleventh Plenum.[23] His other films constantly irked cultural functionaries, including *Abschied* (Farewell, 1968), *Der Dritte* (Her Third, 1971), *Die Schlüssel* (The Keys, 1973), *Lotte in Weimar* (1975), and *Die Leiden des jungen Werthers* (The Sorrows of Young Werther, 1976). He joined in the protest against Biermann's expatriation in 1976[24] and left the GDR in 1978 but returned to make his final DEFA film—*Stein* (1991). In any case, the film was suspected of being an allusion to the East German state as an insulated dictatorship and was certainly interpreted as such.

The wall is only in the film, not in Andersen's tale. In addition, the filmmakers consciously made significant changes to the portrayal of the emperor and the people. They also included numerous references to the 17 June 1953 workers' uprising and its brutal suppression by Soviet tanks and GDR police. Thus, in retrospect, it is not surprising that the film was deemed "objectively hostile to the party" and thought of as depicting "counterrevolutionary traits."[25] Heinz Kersten was mistaken when he argued that "unlike those productions that were shelved in 1965/1966, their predecessor [i.e., *The Robe*] did not critically illuminate the East German present, but actually only wanted to tell a fairy tale."[26]

By stowing away under a cart, the weavers slip through the security check at the city gate. With the help of a kitchen maid named Katrin (Eva-Maria Hagen) and a butcher (Günther Simon) the two weavers are smuggled into the palace. Upon spotting the "intruders," the emperor and his cohort, paranoid about safety, embarrass themselves by cowardly hiding away from the supposed "assassins, spies, agents, murderers." The scene calls to mind the 1953 workers' uprising and the government's reaction. Like the emperor, the SED interpreted the uprising as the work of fascist agents provocateurs. Like the emperor and the ministers who hide themselves away, Walter Ulbricht and other top leaders of the GDR sought refuge in the Soviet military headquarters during the night of 17 to 18 June.[27] Suggesting a metaphorically paralyzed judicial system, the crippled minister of justice (Gerry Wolff) comes forward in a wheelchair to pronounce the death sentence for the weavers. The East German judicial system was criticized again in the banned 1965 film—*Das Kaninchen bin ich* (The Rabbit Is Me, Kurt Maetzig, 1965/1990). Upon learning that the condemned are weavers, the emperor, in a manner that suggests a deranged tyrant, orders them to make an amazing outfit that exalts him:

> I would like a coat at the sight of which every creature falls to his knees. A coat at the sight of which lips tremble and eyebrows twitch. A coat that makes you hear trumpets blaring and you are at once ready to betray father and mother—and you don't know yourself anymore. You want to beg me to forgive you for being still alive at all. Whoever sees me in this coat can hardly hold himself back from screaming: He is it, the invincible one.[28]

The emperor is so obsessed with new clothes that he appointed a clothing minister (*Bekleidungsministerin*) in his cabinet and refused to see his people for a long time due to a "lack" of presentable clothes. The two weavers rack their brains to take on this challenge, from an emperor who it turns out has just thrown out all the clothes that the clothing minister had designed for him. It would be hard to imagine that Andersen's emperor, who simply wants to add the "invisible" clothes to his collection, would empty his closet. But the emperor in the film scorns his previous outfits and expects the new robe to replace them all. These megalomaniacal goals that the emperor has for his clothing are a significant change the film makes from the original tale. In Andersen's tale, it is simply the emperor's pomposity and pretention that causes him to fall into the weavers' trap. The film, however, makes it clear that it is the emperor's hunger for power and authority that has blinded him. His excessive expectations for the new clothes provoke a likewise extreme reaction from the weavers. They come up with an ingenious plan to claim that the robe they are making is invisible to those who are stupid or unqualified. In the film, the idea of deceiving the emperor is therefore a reaction to the emperor's impossible demands and not a plan for an ingenious con, as in Andersen's original tale. The film focuses its sarcasm on the emperor, twice referred to as the "Great Terrorist" (*der große Terrorist*), a scathing term applied to the embodiment of political power. The emperor is entranced by the idea of having magical clothing that asserts his intelligence and competence, while putting others to shame. Confident that he alone is fit for his position and his men are not, he basks in the sadistic pleasure of seeing his ministers exposed: "I already see fear in the pathetic faces. None of you will see the fabric. Tomorrow it will be clear who the loser is."[29] When the next morning comes, he again gleefully torments his ministers: "It is an unusual day. You can count on that. . . . I do not want to be in your shoes."[30] Ironically, in the end, his mockery of the ministers backfires.

Both the foreign minister and the clothing minister quickly realize that the so-called invisible fabric is a hoax, but they decide to lie to the emperor as a form of revenge for his lack of trust in them in the first place. News reporters who visited the set witnessed the exact scene in which the foreign minister (Gerd E. Schäfer) and the clothing minister (Lore Frisch) decide not to alert the emperor of the scheme:

> **Lore Frisch:** They have no fabric at all; these are swindlers. Have you seen how the servants smirked? We must immediately report to the emperor!
>
> **Gerd E. Schäfer:** What for? Do you love the emperor that much? Think about last night and the bursting balloons, [each representing a minister]. And now we should keep Max from bursting?[31]

The ministers can save the emperor from imminent disgrace, but no one within the emperor's inner circle is willing to put a stop to the folly surrounding the clothes. The film provides a fable that displays the impossibility of solidarity and collaboration within a totalitarian government. When the emperor arrives to inspect the clothes in person, his subordinates all collude in deceiving him. Nothing will keep the emperor from parading naked.

The parade climaxes when two kitchen boys (Ernst-Georg Schwill and Gerhard Rachold) decide to imitate the emperor. They present themselves stripped naked in front of the crowd and tell the hapless emperor that they are dressed as splendidly as the emperor himself with clothes made from the leftovers of the emperor's new robe. The crowd scatters in laughter and the procession ends abruptly. This sequence constitutes an instance of open revolt. The camera scans over the items strewn on the road and then rests on the abandoned royal chariot, seen by Ralf Schenk as foreshadowing the events in 1989, when only relics were to remain of the former government.[32]

The real subversive potential of the film lies in its interpretation of the power of the people. In Andersen's tale, it is not until the end that the people show themselves capable of correcting their mistake and perceiving the truth by stating, "He has nothing on!" The emperor, however, proves himself to be arrogant and hopelessly stubborn: despite some inkling that the people may be right, he continues to strut through the city "even more proudly" in his "new clothes." The two pitiful servants keep carrying the invisible train to play out the charade. The film makes a stronger distinction between the emperor and his people. It does not depict the people as equally gullible as the emperor. In the film, a rumor quickly spreads through the city that the weavers have woven nothing at all.[33] Although the servants catch on to the plan, they all participate in deceiving the emperor. The fact that they choose to take the side of the weavers shows that the working class has a shared interest in subverting the government (see Figure 4.1). When the weavers tell two businessmen, Skinny and Fatty (*der Dünne* and *der Dicke*), that the clothing is invisible to the stupid, Fatty (Hannes Fischer) immediately predicts that the emperor is going to head the parade naked. During the procession, Fatty laughs uncontrollably at the emperor's nudity. Skinny (Harry Riebauer), his business rival, reports him to the secret police—alluding to the Stasi—who then arrest Fatty. Two plainclothes secret policemen appear out of nowhere, indicating the omnipresence of the Stasi. Some onlookers ignore the ceremony and play cards instead. When a secret policeman confiscates their cards, they take out a new set of cards and keep playing. This is the umpteenth time that the emperor flaunts his clothes in such a parade, and people have grown weary of it. Whereas nobody laughs in Andersen's tale, in the film, at the two naked kitchen boys' prompt, the crowd dares to laugh openly at the emperor, no longer fearing reprisals. In this East German adaptation, the people have matured and become antiauthoritarian. This change to the emplotment encapsulates a key aspect of DEFA's reworking of the tale: the *Volk* are not dumb, rather they *pretend* to be dumb to subvert and attack the system. In retrospect, the alliance of the people in both secret and open defiance of the emperor can be interpreted as alluding to the workers' revolt in 1953 and as potentially threatening to the regime.

In the end, the despotic ruler is the one who suffers deep humiliation. The clothes achieve a result exactly opposite to what he has intended. Instead of bringing everyone to their knees, he has made everyone turn against him. At the closing of the film, the emperor is irritated by the tight-fitting crown. The foreign minister suggests in a sarcastic tone: "Maybe you need a bigger size?"[34] Obviously the problem is not that the crown does not fit the emperor but that the emperor no longer deserves the crown. The sarcasm invigorates the film's antigovernment stance. In this manner, the DEFA film sharpens the political meaning of Andersen's story and sends an implicit message that rulers who are blind to the reality of their subjects are doomed to fail.

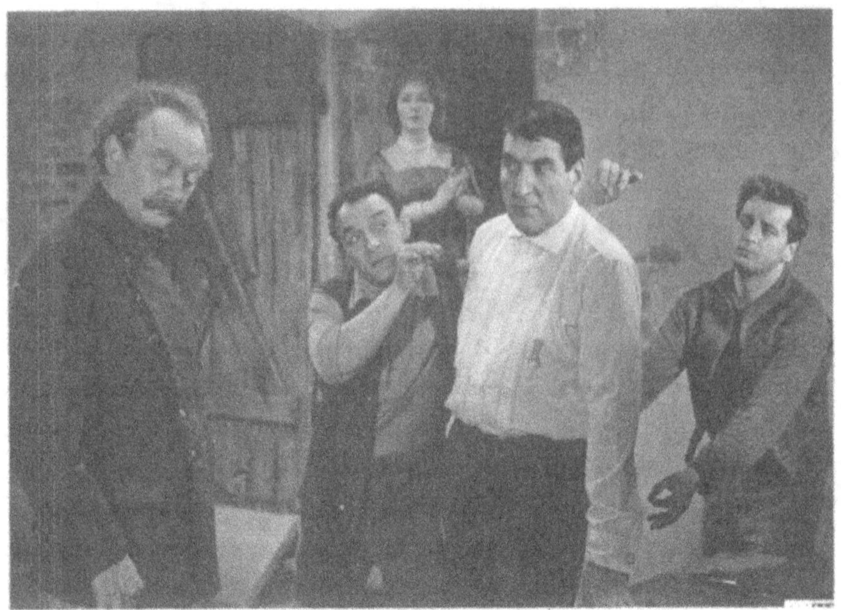

FIGURE 4.1. *Das Kleid*: The king's subordinates collude to deceive the king (Wolf Kaiser). © DEFA-Stiftung, Eberhard Daßdorf.

The emperor in Andersen's tale continues the parade even after the child's revelation of his nudity, which suggests his inability to reform. The emperor in the film is openly vindictive. He asks the foreign minister how many people have laughed and then orders 80 percent of the populace to be banished.[35] The minister recommends that the emperor simply choose "a different people," in an obvious allusion to Bertolt Brecht's poem "Die Lösung" (The Solution). The poem ends with these two lines: "Would it not be easier/In that case for the government/To dissolve the people/And elect another?"[36] Brecht wrote this sarcastic poem in the wake of the 1953 workers' uprising. In the poem, he puts an ironic twist on the official call for people to work harder to regain the trust of the government. However, the poem was published posthumously in 1959, indicating how careful Brecht was when dealing with the GDR government. Playing on the name "Stalin," which means iron in Russian, "Eisen" (Iron), another poem from *Buckower Elegien* (Buckow Elegies), criticizes the rigid Stalinist policies that the SED implemented.[37] Brecht was "a Marxist playwright" and also "a Marxist heretic."[38] His critique of Stalinism followed his teacher Karl

Korsch's early critique of Leninism and then Stalinism, for which Korsch was expelled from the communist movement in 1926.[39] The fact that the film quotes from "The Solution" suggests that its subversion was very much intentional. The censors obviously also saw it as such and therefore banned the film for the duration of the GDR's existence.

There are other examples of implicit criticism of the East German government in this Brechtian film. The two weavers wish to honestly earn their bread by making clothes for the emperor. However, it is the emperor's ridiculous expectations that make the task impossible for the weavers, much like the unrealistic work norms that the East German government imposed on its workers. The June 1953 uprising took place in the same year as the initiation of the so-called New Course in 1953 and the death of Stalin. It had multiple causes, including increased production quotas, lack of raw materials, shortage of food and other consumption goods, collectivization, increase in taxation, and so on. The failure of the uprising resulted in the strengthening of the GDR's Stalinist regime and the consolidation of Ulbricht's autocracy. And in spite of all the deficiencies and of the mass exodus of East Germans to West Germany, the Ulbricht government continued to propagate the belief that East Germany could overtake the West German population's per capita consumption level within a few years.[40] The preposterousness of the emperor's expectations mirrored the absurdity of the GDR's economic plans. The lack of support for the emperor also alluded to Ulbricht's unpopular status with both the state and common citizens.

In addition to "The Solution," the film shows prominent influences from Brechtian epic theater. In the interview mentioned above, Günther shared that he deliberately relied on Brechtian dramaturgy, because he felt that nothing new, not even stylistically, was taking place at DEFA, and everything was old UFA films in form and content; he always had the desire to look for ways to make films different from UFA dramaturgy.[41] To that end, Günther resorted to techniques used in epic theater: he inserted projection titles, cartoon episodes, and experimental visuals. When the two weavers reach the city wall of the kingdom, having not eaten in three days, the Brechtian theme song—"Das Lied von den Neigungen des Menschen" (The Song of People's Inclinations)—voices the commoners' simple desire for a better life. The song ends with accusatory questions as to who is to blame for his life, alluding to Brecht's 1935 poem "Fragen eines lesenden Arbeiters" (Questions from a Worker Who Reads).

Once inside the city, the weavers search for a place to stay with no luck. When even the poor families ignore them, a Brechtian intertitle appears boldfaced on the screen: "The poor of the city appeared hardened."[42] While the two weavers sleep in the marketplace under a table, an animated scene is inserted in which a female cat flirts with a tom cat at night, representing the emperor and his clothing minister. The weavers' honest hope to work for the emperor nearly costs them their lives. Again one of the many Brechtian intertitles appears on screen, foreshadowing the danger awaiting the weavers: "Whoever fights for the piece of bread that is withheld from him reckons with cruel enemies and almost hopeless situations!"[43] The weavers must use their creativity and cunning to find a way to save themselves from the tyrannical and murderous emperor. Anticipating the day of the parade, another intertitle summarizes the revolutionary potential of the proletariat: "On this ordinary day, two have-nots shake the platform of a state. It is known how far something like this can go in the long run."[44]

Twice in the film, instead of crosscutting, two picture frames appear side by side so that parallel events are shown at the same time, a modernist editing technique. The episode in which the emperor comes to inspect the new robe contains a special effect by Ernst Kunstmann: geometric figures stream out of the emperor's eyes, illustrating the act of seeing, or not seeing. All the modernist experimental visuals reflect a Brechtian emphasis on "interruption" and "discontinuity" to pull the audience out of a "passive consumer" state of mind.[45] This film clearly demonstrates that, while socialist realism still had strong sway over filmmakers in the early decades of the GDR, some filmmakers, including Gerhard Klein and Egon Günther, moved on to experiment with modernist techniques from Brechtian epic theater in fairy-tale films.

In addition, theatrical acting style and minimalist settings are characteristic of Brecht's epic theater. The masked soldiers walking on stilts represent the ostentatiously imposing (East German) military. The masks, for example, are reminiscent of the 1954 production of Brecht's *Der kaukasische Kreidekreis* (The Caucasian Chalk Circle, 1944), in which "the rigid expressions of the masks of Brecht's ironshirts showed the rigidity of people who have become unquestioning instruments of the powerful."[46] The film's use of Brechtian style had a lot to do with the crew's connection with the Berliner Ensemble. Günther assisted Erich Engel at the Berliner Ensemble.[47] Ruth Berghaus, later director of the Berliner Ensemble, was the choreographer of the film.[48] Many of the actors and actresses came from there, including Wolf Kaiser, who plays the emperor, and Eva-Maria Hagen, who plays the kitchen maid.

The creation of characters such as the kitchen maid and the clothing minister enhances the complexity of gender roles and the overall "sex appeal" of the film. Hagen had become one of the most famous and popular actresses by the time she was cast in *The Robe*. She began studying acting in East Berlin in 1952. Merely a year later, she became a member of the Berliner Ensemble, working with Brecht. In 1954, she married writer Hans-Oliva Hagen and had a daughter, Nina Hagen, who would become a famous singer. Her breakthrough role came in Kurt Maetzig's *Vergesst mir meine Traudel nicht* (Don't Forget My Little Traudel, 1957), and she became the "sex symbol of GDR cinema." In 1965, she got to know Wolf Biermann and became his life companion. After that, her career in East Germany suffered, as the state pressured her to either break up with Biermann or face unemployment. In 1977, after Biermann's expatriation, she left for West Germany with Nina.[49] In *The Robe*, she likewise plays the role of "the beautiful, erotic, and seductive."[50] The butcher played by Günther Simon makes repeated marriage proposals to her, but in vain (see Figure 4.2). Her love interest lies with the two weavers. When they are detained by the emperor, she brings them wine and food (see the book cover). The weavers, despite their attraction to her, decide to end the romance (*Schluss mit der Romantik*) and continue their journey at the end of the film, per comedic convention.

The production and postproduction history of the film were both quite dramatic. The film was shot in the summer of 1961 without much difficulty. Since East German newspapers often reported on upcoming DEFA films before their premiere, there were also a few rare press reports on *The Robe*.[51] These articles were related to each other, with some pas-

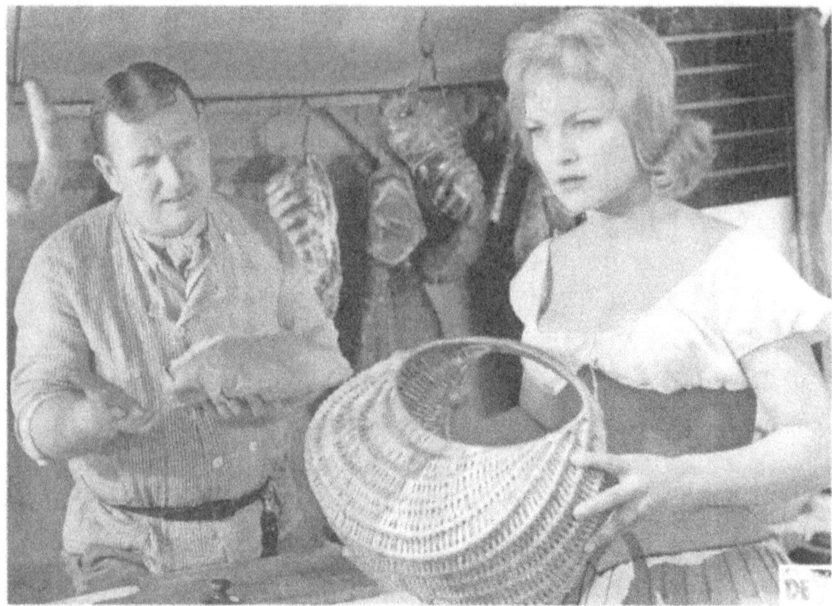

FIGURE 4.2. *Das Kleid*: The kitchen maid Katrin (Eva-Maria Hagen) and the butcher (Günther Simon) whose marriage proposals to Katrin add to the comic effect of the film. © DEFA-Stiftung, Eberhard Daßdorf

sages worded the same. They pointed out that this new DEFA film took aim at "all dictators" and "all oppressors of the people":

> They took from the Danish writer in fact only the sketch, a motif, in order to tell "a modern story." This story, which is reminiscent of Chaplin's brilliant *The Great Dictator*, should show how ridiculous all dictators essentially are in their brutality and lust for power. Yet tyrants are not only absurd, they also fear the laughter and jokes that people play on them. This new DEFA film aims, above all, at this Achilles' heel of all oppressors of the people.[52]

They wished DEFA much success with the comedy and the audience a fun movie night soon. Alas, the waiting turned out to be thirty years.

From the very beginning, the dramaturges as well as the studio management gave the film its strong support, which could be seen from the protocols in the Federal Film Archive in Berlin.[53] After the film was completed in October 1961,[54] DEFA studio director Jochen Mückenberger made a request for the film's certification to the State Film Approval Board in the Ministry of Culture (Staatliche Abnahmekommission des Ministeriums für Kultur) on 7 November 1961. The approval procedure was to take place on 15 November 1961. The following people involved in making the film were invited: studio director Jochen Mückenberger, the technical director Albert Wilkening, chief dramaturge Klaus Wischnewski, scriptwriter Egon Günther, director of the film Konrad Petzold, dramaturges Manfred Fritzsche and Dieter Scharfenberg, production manager Annie v. Zieten, and composer Günter Hauk. A confidential file from the Ministry of Culture–Sector Film Approval and Control (Ministerium für Kultur: Sektor Filmabnahme u.–kontrolle) revealed the decision made on 8 March 1962 (Protokoll Nr. 86/62) that "the film is *not* approved for public release." Another confidential document remarked that, due to strong concerns with the film, it would be screened for the minister of culture, Hans Bentzien, for a final decision. The enclosed assessment of the film read, "The fundamental concept of this film is objectively hostile to the party at its core and also contains counterrevolutionary traits. In addition, with respect to the *contemporary actualization of a fairy tale*, there is a break in style from the standpoint of socialist aesthetic. The film is created in such a way that its word and image are open to antagonistic interpretations."[55] Despite such harsh remarks on the film, on 1 March 1963 the film was submitted for the last time for approval to take place on 27 March. On the same day, however, according to another HV document dated 22 April 1963, Mückenberger indicated withdrawal of the application. On 4 May 1963, Mückenberger confirmed in writing the film's withdrawal to Genosse Pägelow at HV-Film.[56]

The Robe has a celebrity cast. But none of their social capital as artists could prevent fate from turning for the worst after the Berlin Wall was built. As is known, established actors or directors were never enough to save a DEFA film from the censors' scissors. This was the case with the first banned feature, *Das Beil von Wandsbek* (The Axe of Wandsbek, Falk Harnack, 1951), with Erwin Geschonneck playing the sympathetic butcher of resistance fighters, and then again with forbidden films in 1965.

Having made *The Robe* for an adult audience, director Petzold rejected the offer to shorten the film to make it a children's film. Thus in 1963, all 135 cases of negatives were secretly sent to the state film archives. As Erika Richter notes, "Due to this fairy-tale film's criticism of arbitrariness, need for luxury, and inanity of the ruler, although without specific reference to current circumstances, its impact appeared so incalculable that the officials did not want to take any risk and eliminated the film."[57] When the Wall came down in 1989, Petzold wanted to check up on *The Robe* and asked for permission from the Commission of the Association of GDR Film and Television, which was dealing with the rehabilitation of banned films. He found out that the film negatives were preserved but not the sound. He decided to dub the film with the original team, and he found replacements for the voices of actors who were deceased. Due to this lengthy restoration process, *The Robe* was the last of the banned films to premiere in the Babylon Theater in April 1991.[58]

In hindsight, the fate the film met is not surprising, considering the GDR's adherence to Stalinist politics despite Khrushchev's denunciation of Stalin in February 1956. The GDR's short-lived Thaw period after Stalin's death in 1953 ended with the suppression of the Hungarian revolt in 1956 because the East German leadership feared "revisionism" in the GDR, as it appeared to be spreading in Hungary and Poland. Ralf Schenk asked Günther this question: "[*The Robe*] was banned. Was it too bold for the authorities?"[59] Günther answered:

> It was not only bold, it was probably reckless, frivolous. Klaus Wischnewski as head dramaturge was very close to the project, and when he read it, he was shocked to death, because one simply tells the rulers: You are absolute oppressors, not capable of anything, and your time has basically run out. . . . Reality has caught up with the tale. You are naked; no one dares to say it. . . . The film was very close to reality. They had to ban it. Otherwise they would have been the first dictatorship, the first socialist–communist dictatorship, to tolerate something like that.[60]

Since the film's censorship, as Dieter Wiedemann points out, "it took some time for fairy-tale films to make direct, even though not so clear, reference to current problems of GDR society."[61]

During the forty years of the GDR, twenty-seven feature films were banned. The banning was never reported in the East German media, except for the films banned during the 1965 plenum. These films, including *The Rabbit Is Me* (1965/1990) and *Denk bloß nicht, ich heule* (Just Don't Think I Will Cry, Frank Vogel, 1965/1990), were publicly denounced. After the *Wende* the confiscated films were finally released or rereleased and gained belated publicity in the East and the West at festivals and on television programs. For Petzold and Günther's *The Robe*, it was the first time that the public could watch this long forgotten film in its entirety. Especially for people who once worked on this film, it was a very touching event.[62] *The Robe* was praised as Petzold's "best work"[63] and "a real gem."[64] When it reached the screen thirty years after its making, however, it had unfortunately missed the right audience and political context.[65] Not so coincidentally, Petzold ended his career with another fairy-tale adaptation—*The Story of the Goose Princess and Her Loyal Horse Falada* (1989), which was adapted from the Grimms' "The Goose Girl" (KHM 89). Harmless on the surface, this last film allowed Petzold to address late-GDR themes. At a time when the GDR government was oblivious to truth and had lost the people's trust, the film implicitly warned of the consequences of not facing truth and losing trust (see chapter 5).

So far, I have emphasized *The Robe*'s potential to be critical of the GDR's government. However, the film likewise shows ambiguity between conformism and subversion. As in earlier DEFA fairy-tale films, this banned comedy portrays class struggle by showing how two workers subvert the ruler and the state. Andersen's tale can be easily analyzed from a Marxist perspective because the two lowly commoners are able to outsmart the emperor and the entire ruling class. Yet the fact that Andersen uses the word "swindlers," or in the German translation "Betrüger," to label the two weavers, who set out to reap monetary benefits through deceit and trickery, shows his overall ambivalence toward the lower class. In comparison, Petzold's film offers a clearer analysis of class issues. The two weavers in the film are portrayed as unquestionably positive characters. The plot summary of *The Robe* that accompanied the application for HV certification also focused on the Marxist interpretation of the tale: "The DEFA adaptation of Andersen's 'The Emperor's New Clothes' is retold from *a correct class viewpoint*, and the poetic values were preserved. . . . When the emperor sees through the trick, it is too late for him. The people see him naked and recognize his weakness, his vincible power, and laugh at him."[66] In addition to the Marxist rendition of the tale, one could also find anti-fascist and anticapitalist subtext. The despotic ruler with his insatiable greed for power and consumerist obsession with clothes represented values that the GDR spurned.

However, the cultural functionaries did not want to take any chance with this provocative film. The addition of a thick, solid wall, as well as the changes the film made to the weavers, the emperor, and the people, along with the nearly direct citation of Brecht's "The Solution" opened up too many possible interpretations of this adaptation. The Brechtian aesthetic that the film explicitly employs assisted in foregrounding Marxist concerns, yet the film certification board criticized the film's aesthetic as "a break in style" in terms of its references to the present. By banning this well-intentioned film, the GDR ultimately did become like the naked emperor: whereas the emperor only suffers irreversible shame, the GDR ceased to exist after German reunification.

Unexpected Difficulties with Censorship: *How to Marry a King* (1969)

Between Walter Beck's 1965 *King Thrushbeard* and his 1971 *Briar Rose*, there was hardly any noteworthy adaptation of traditional fairy tales, except for a short TV adaptation of Andersen's "The Nightingale" into *Die Nachtigall und der Kaiser* (The Nightingale and the Emperor, Juan Corelli, 1968) and Rainer Simon's feature-length *How to Marry a King* (1969). The reason for scarce fairy-tale productions may be partly related to the departure of DEFA's special effect experts Ernst Kunstmann in 1963, after he worked on about seventy DEFA feature films. According to Ralf Schenk, when Kunstmann reached retirement age in 1963, he left the studio for good. He was known as guarding his trade skills carefully and was reluctant to let his students in on his "secrets." In addition, the film directors of cinema verité increasingly rejected artificial sets, special effects, and rear projections.[67] Therefore Kunstmann was not used as a consultant either after he left. In the second half of the 1960s, DEFA turned to what Joshua Feinstein has called "films of everyday life" (*Alltagsfilme*), 70-mm films,[68] adventure films with Manfred Krug,[69] revisitings of the Nazi past,[70] and in particular, expensive *Indianerfilme* aimed at a "big tent" demographic that included old and young, men and women.[71]

Rainer Simon debuted with *How to Marry a King*, an adaptation of the Grimms' "The Farmer's Clever Daughter" (KHM 94).[72] The same Grimms' tale also served as the basis for Carl Orff's fairy-tale opera *Die Kluge* (The Clever Girl, 1943). Another hand puppet film adaptation—*Die kluge Bauerntochter* (The Farmer's Clever Daughter, Wolfgang Bergner, 1961)—was created by DEFA's animation studio in Dresden, for which about fifteen literary versions had been studied that did not contain the marriage of the farmer's daughter to the king.[73] The painstaking effort to go beyond the Grimms' tale had as its driving force the need for class-conscious folktales that would better corroborate the GDR's antifeudal, antibourgeois ideology. In the puppet film, the farmer's daughter must come up with riddles for the king to solve, because that is his favorite pastime. The girl creates havoc in the palace, interfering in government affairs and helping farmers and fishermen.[74] She exposes the king as a stupid despot and instead marries a peasant boy named Hans.[75] The screenwriters (Günter Kaltofen and Rainer Simon) and dramaturges (Margot Beichler and Gudrun Rammler) of *How to Marry a King* obviously did not follow the Dresden studio's painstaking endeavor to search beyond the Grimms for versions in which a peasant girl rejects the king in favor of a boy of her class. If the king represented feudal, capitalist, and even fascist rule, and thus was rejected in the 1961 hand puppet version, then *How to Marry a King* in its post-1965 context used the Brothers Grimm template and refocused on political reform.

In the film, a peasant finds a golden, but lidless, casket in the piece of land he has received from the king. His daughter advises against turning it in to the king, for the king would also demand the missing casket lid. The honest but nervous father turns a deaf ear to his daughter, and the king locks him in a cage on display in the palace courtyard. To save her father, the clever girl solves the king's riddles and in the process wins his heart (see Figure 4.3). The wedding is celebrated with gusto by the common

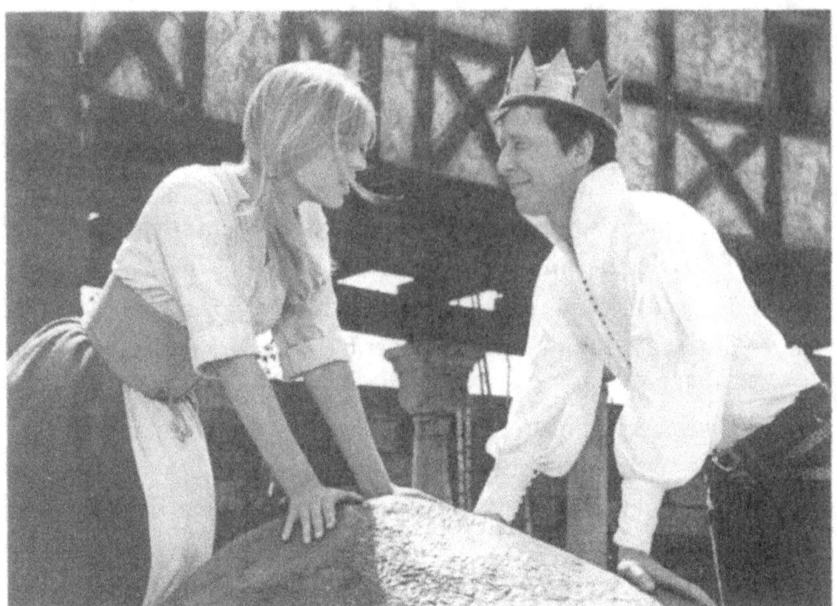

FIGURE 4.3. *Wie heiratet man einen König*: The peasant girl (Cox Habbema) cleverly guesses all the king's (Eberhard Esche) riddles. © DEFA-Stiftung, Hans Hattop; Wolfgang Reinke.

folk in the courtyard. The story does not end "happily ever after" with the wedding. Instead it continues with a marital crisis. As queen, the farmer's daughter repeatedly appears to be superior to her husband. When the king arbitrarily rules that a foal belongs to the owner of the oxen (with Winfried Glatzeder playing the *Oxenknecht*, the farmhand for the oxen owner), the queen advises the owner of the foal (Dieter Mann) to fish on dry land: if oxen can give birth to a foal, he can catch fish on dry land. As a result, the king "divorces" the impertinent queen. Allowed to take one thing endearing to her as a departing gift, she takes the king himself—sleeping after drinking drugged wine—to her peasant hut. Touched by her love, he brings her back to the palace.

Unlike the miller's daughter in *Rumpelstiltskin*, who becomes queen with magical help, the farmer's clever daughter marries the king through her wit and intelligence, which is the answer to the question posed in the film title. Some reviewers pointed out that the advice for marrying a king was anachronistic and impractical for contemporary viewers.[76] It was the case even when the tale was written. Yet it is the tale's emphasis on love and intellect that will never become obsolete.[77] The tale also embraces a more egalitarian set of gender relations and offers a refreshingly modern picture of a marriage. For Rainer Simon, the film was an examination of marital tensions relevant in the late 1960s, in that husbands were often afraid of their wives' intellectual superiority.[78] Eberhard Esche, who plays the king, also saw the story as that of "a woman's emancipation."[79] Hence, although the censors read political satire into the film, as discussed below, the director and his team seemed to understand the film initially more as social commentary on marital crisis and women's emancipation in the GDR (see chapter 5). Esche and the Dutch actress Cox Habbema were newly in love and Esche insisted that Habbema play the other main character.[80] She indeed convincingly played a beloved queen who defends justice and equality for the common people unwaveringly, and she garnered wide acclaim for her very first DEFA role.

Simon's nuanced portrayal of the king avoided a black-and-white characterization of a feudal king as in earlier DEFA fairy-tale films. In the film, the playful king shows a certain sense of justice that is nonetheless downplayed by his arbitrariness and irresponsibility toward his subjects.[81] The king justifies his autocracy by belittling the peasants for their unenlightened state: "Peasants and farmhands, what do they know about law and justice?"[82] Yet as careless and despotic as he is, the king cuts a sympathetic figure who disregards class difference and cherishes intellect. He initially decides to send the "impertinent" queen home because she appears more clever and fairer than him. But then he revises his decision and brings her back to the palace, implicitly as his equal partner and clever advisor. The king's final decision is exemplary. It is suggested that this king is capable of change. As a husband as well as a monarch, he is willing to accept an intellectually superior spouse who apparently will continue to defeat him in chess games and challenge his decisions. The ending projects a utopian democracy that the GDR would unfortunately not be able to realize.

Most of the actions in the film take place in the palace courtyard. In contrast to the enclosed and unwelcoming palace interior, the courtyard is an open space that is unpretentious and accessible to the common people. It is the threshold to the palace that connects the rulers and the ruled. In the courtyard, the king receives his people and addresses their grievances, and he gives his people seemingly unsolvable riddles and thereby obliges them to work for him. However, it is here that the clever peasant girl solves his riddles, the wedding celebration takes place, and the foal owner fishes on dry land to teach the king a lesson. The courtyard symbolizes a public space where democracy and despotism vie with each other, showing at once the king's alienation from the lower classes and his willingness to reform.

The shooting of the film wrapped in October 1968.[83] However, when the film was evaluated, it met with mixed reactions due to its alleged formalism, its enmity toward the people, and its having "unsuitable" scenes for a children's film. In an archival document dated 6 December 1968, the head of HV-Film's production department, Dr. Jahrow, recommended the film for public release. Yet in the same document, he pointed out the principal problems that this production raised: the film blurred fundamental differences "between the people and those who exploit them" (*zwischen Volk und Nutznießern der Arbeit des Volkes*). In the flight scene—in which both the courtiers and the peasants run for their life in a fast-motion sequence, taking the peasant girl for a ghost—as well as in the wedding sequence, the differences between working-class and nonworking people are almost entirely erased, resulting in "a perfect harmony between the common people and members of the royal court." According to Jahrow, the flight scene should have depicted the common people as braver, and the wedding ceremony should have portrayed them as "morally purer" (*in seinem moralischen Empfinden sauberer*).[84]

Apparently HV-Film approved the film with reservation. According to director Simon, the specter of the Eleventh Plenum rose again in 1968. Egon Günther's *Abschied* (Farewell, 1968) and Heiner Carow's *Die Russen kommen* (*The Russians Are Coming*, 1968/1987) bore the brunt of the attack this time. The then head of DEFA, Albert Wilkening, criticized some episodes in *How to Marry a King* as obscene, anarchist, and inappropriate for a children's film. Esche's style of speech was even suspected to be a parody of Ulbricht's.[85] Wilkening wanted to refuse any artistic quality rating (*Prädikatisierung*) for the film, which, as Simon feared, would have meant the end of his career as a director. But thanks to the intercession of the artistic director Wito Eichel, the film finally received the commendation of "good" after months of delay.[86]

The difficulty the film encountered with the functionaries was simply beyond Simon's expectations. But it was also known that his ambition was to make socially engaged films that critically dealt with life in the GDR.[87]

In addition to a suspected subversive parody of Ulbricht, the film review board accused the film of formalism.[88] Apparently the formalism debate of the early 1950s, which resulted in a rejection of modernist art, continued to be an assessment criterion in the late 1960s. Simon always wanted to distance himself as much as possible from the UFA aesthetic on a formal level. Alluding to films such as Walter Beck's *King Thrushbeard* (1965), Simon also rejected the then-prevalent use of stylized backdrops in fairy-tale films. Opting for a more realistic fairy-tale adaptation, Simon set the story in the Renaissance era before the Peasants' War. The authentic atmosphere created in the peasant scenes evokes the Renaissance art works of Albrecht Dürer, Hans Holbein the Younger, and Pieter Breughel (the Peasant Breughel).[89] The farmhouse, for example, directly imitated Dürer's *Weiherhäuschen* (ca. 1496/1497). For the palace, Simon reused the costly structures that resembled the decorations of the Wartburg Castle, which were built in the DEFA studio compound for Ralf Kirsten's film *Frau Venus und ihr Teufel* (Lady Venus and Her Devil, 1967).[90] Jahrow recognized this effort as inheriting the classical and humanist legacy yet argued that early bourgeois art was not absolutely identical with socialist–realist art and could not be simply imitated or uncritically adopted in the film the way it was.[91]

Like *The Robe*, *How to Marry a King* distinguished itself from other DEFA fairy-tale films with its experimental visuals. Some sequences in the film consist of still images that quickly switch from one to the next, while others deploy fast-motion cinematography. Visual experimentation was Simon's way of showing off new techniques from a younger generation of directors.[92] Both Simon and the cameraman Claus Neumann had considerable experience in documentary filmmaking. Thus Simon preferred cinema verité techniques and let his actors and actresses improvise. He selected the most suitable images of those that Neumann shot mainly with a handheld camera. Simon's directorial style also showed neorealist influence from Czech cinema. As Larson Powell in his comparative study of DEFA and Eastern European cinema says, "Characterizations of Czech 1960s film tend to centre on theatrical aspects such as acting: 'the loosely controlled acting style of professional or amateur actors, including improvised dialogue on a given topic.'"[93] The cinema verité style culminates in the wedding banquet sequence, in which peasants and courtiers celebrate with tumultuous exuberance. The long scene was shot with only one take and "only one ox roasted."[94] This extended episode quintessentially represented Simon and Neumann's documentary style because, although the original script contained merely a few lines, Simon turned it into the film's signature scene, and the film ran into trouble precisely because of the allegedly over-the-top wedding sequence (see Figure 4.4).[95]

The wedding episode met with a lot of disapproval. DEFA Außenhandel as well as delegations from Eastern European countries expressed negative views of the film, in particular the banquet scene, as drawn-out and inappropriate for children.[96] Käthe Reichel's portrayal of the hearty peasant woman Ulrike was deemed as unconventional, overly realistic, and thus "objectionable" (*anstößig*).[97] The erotic performance was viewed as rather unsavory in a children's film.[98] Simon, however, praised Reichel in 1995 as having plenty of insightful suggestions to contribute to the scenes, dialogues, and costumes. She almost always made better arguments than the director himself, just like the clever peasant girl who always outwits the king.[99] The use of great actors and actresses, ten of whom came from the Deutsche Theater and the Berliner Ensemble, enabled free-rein, improvisational acting with minimal instructions in this episode.[100]

The public release of the film finally occurred in February 1969.[101] Most print reviews were overwhelmingly positive and sang high praises of the young director's talent, the freedom he gave to actors and actresses, and the innovative style of documentary realism he chose. Horst Knietzsch, for example, wrote a largely positive review in *Neues Deutschland*, praising the film's cinematography.[102] Heinz Kersten also commented, "For a long time nothing better from the East German studio has come to its local cinemas."[103] The film was sent to film festivals and DDR-Filmwochen from India to Tanzania.[104] When the film was shown in Recklinghausen in the Ruhr region, two more screenings had to be added due to the great interest in Simon's film.[105]

The reviews, if critical, replicated the official disapproval of the film's silly, primitive, and even obscene portrayal of the peasants. Knietzsch

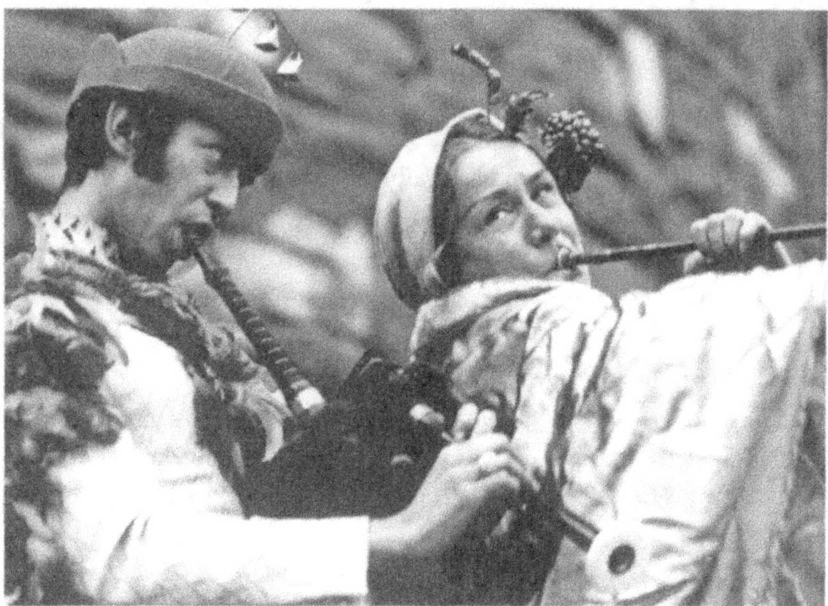

FIGURE 4.4. *Wie heiratet man einen König*: Wedding scene with Käthe Reichel playing a peasant woman and Alfredo Lugo as the court jester. © DEFA-Stiftung, Hans Hattop; Wolfgang Reinke.

critiqued the satirical portrait of peasants as misplaced.[106] Other reviews slighted the images of peasant women as "pathologically benighted" (*pathologisch unbedarft*)[107] and "hardly more sympathetic than the courtiers."[108] Interestingly, in Walter Beck's *Bearskin* (1986), both the upper and lower classes come off negatively. But *Bearskin* did not receive the same criticism of an antagonistic portrayal of the people that Simon's film did.

How to Marry a King proved to be an ambitious, well-liked project from the hands of a third-generation director. The film both inherited traditions and broke new ground. The sarcastic depiction of members of the upper class continued, yet with more nuances. The spontaneous performance simulating lower-class people incurred objection. However, reviews affirmed Simon and the cinematographer's documentary realism. Intended or not, the ultimately positive image of the king and the closeness between the government and the *Volk* could entail a petition for political reform and egalitarianism. This constitutes the slave language that the film suggests but never specifies.

Putting Talents to Use: *How Six Made Their Way in the World* (1972)

When Rainer Simon's first film was suspected of disseminating politically dubious messages and parodying Ulbricht, the experience with censorship stimulated Simon, rather than discouraged him, when the time came for his next film. His initial plan was to make a contemporary youth film titled *Liebe mit 16* (Their First Love). However, director Albert Wilkening rejected it on the grounds that "although, bad enough, sixteen-year-olds abandoned themselves to prurient sexual drives in fleeting love affairs, one does not have to show that in a DEFA film."[109] Simon saw it more as Wilkening disciplining him,[110] especially because not much later, in 1973, Herrmann Zschoche managed to make *Liebe mit 16* (1974) with Simon as one of the scriptwriters.

Simon meanwhile shot his second fairy-tale film, *How Six Made Their Way in the World* (1972), with Roland Gräf as the cinematographer.[111] In his memoire *Fernes Land* (2005), Simon explains the reason that the film title dropped the word "wide" from the Grimms' title was because an originally envisioned coproduction plan with Bulgaria or Rumania was quickly abandoned for financial reasons.[112] Then a "wide" world would no longer be appropriate because it is the kingdom of Malabunt only, a rather claustrophobic place where the king thinks three farthings are enough for traveling expenses for his discharged soldiers. It is to be noted that the Grimms' tale actually has the action set principally in only one kingdom; Simon, although not without justification, took the Grimm title literally.

The beginning sequence was shot on the island of Ralswick (Rügen), a natural border of the GDR in the north. A group of tattered and wounded soldiers who have fought a victorious war for the king are resting on the shore. The king dismisses them, however, with little pay. The rest of the story describes how one such underpaid soldier gains control of the entire state treasury by gathering five men of supernatural abilities. The famous Czech director and actor Jirí Menzel, with the synchronized voice of Eberhard Esche, plays the figure of a revolutionary leader who awakens the class consciousness in his men and unites them for a just cause. After the *Wende* in 1989, the title change led Dieter Wiedemann to argue that the film alluded to the "trapped" GDR since the building of the Wall.[113] Frank-Burkhard Habel made the same belated claim of contemporary allusion: "From today's perspective, the kingdom of Malabunt clearly reminds us of the GDR, which perhaps cannot simply be ascribed to the universality of fairy-tale–like malapropisms of any dictatorship."[114] This is a conspicuous example of critics in the postunification period drawing more analogies between fairy-tale kingdoms and the GDR. The film was shown in East and West European countries as well as in Asian countries such as Vietnam and Japan.[115] Therefore, even if the six men did not go around the wide world, the film did.

Like many earlier DEFA fairy-tale films, this film seemed to be a proletarian tale about revolution against an oppressive regime. In the end, the soldier consciously rejects the princess (Margit Bendokat) in favor of a common girl. As in the Grimms' tale, the film thematizes the collective power of the lower class: when the ill-treated commoners unite their talents, they incapacitate the ruling class. For Zipes, the ending of the Grimms' tale, in which the six men go home with the entire treasure of the king, appears anticlimactic since the heroes are "pacified with money" and "the social relations are not changed."[116] The deplorable lack of radical sociopolitical changes in the Grimms' tale rests on the curbed desire of the lower class. Yet the DEFA adaptation leaves a strong impression that, yes, the current regime continues to possess political power, but it has been shaken to the core.

A significant change the film makes is in its portrayal of the five talented teammates. They initially do not perceive their supernatural abilities as a blessing but rather as a curse and thus do not put their talents to good use. Simon changed the blower in the Grimms' text to a fiddler partly out of technical reasons regarding special effects.[117] The motif of a magic violin exists in the Grimm fairy tales, such as "Sweetheart Roland" (KHM 56) and "The Jew in the Thornbush" (KHM 110). For some reviewers, the seemingly indiscriminate debilitating effect the magic melody had on working people as well as on the king's regiment did not make the violinist a positive hero.[118] Such fastidious critique missed the film's portrayal of the compulsive dance: the friends dance gracefully and do not show signs of torture. One peasant woman humorously says that she has lost twenty pounds after the dance.[119] But only for the foes, the music becomes a weapon and defeats the entire king's regiment, just as the violinist says, "My fiddle is mightier than the king"[120] (see Figure 4.5).

The subversive music invokes an immediate association with Wolf Biermann, one of the most prominent dissidents, a singer, songwriter, and guitarist. He was one of the artists vehemently attacked in 1965 and was subsequently banned from the stage for eleven years (1965–1976).[121] In 1972 when Simon's film was made, Biermann was under this professional ban. The melancholic song the fiddler sings in the film strikes a tone similar to Biermann's, although Simon was able to defend his innocence because the text and music stem from Walther von der Vogelweide: "How is the order in our country/What a shame that even mosquitoes are governed/Woe to the world, how terribly you stand!"[122] Some reviewers were critical of the sad and serious depiction of the five.[123] One might have assumed that the solemn mood reflected the depressing situation, in which the GDR stifled its own talents as it did Biermann. One reviewer viewed the fiddler as appearing "all too real and cryptic," but Biermann's name was never mentioned.[124] The suppression of talents is thematized, for example, in Peter Kahane's *Die Architekten* (The Architects, 1990). Like the soldier, the chief architect Daniel Brenner collects his team of talented architects to design a shopping and cultural center on the outskirts of Berlin. However his team disbands, as their visionary challenge to the status quo is crushed and Daniel himself is destroyed by bureaucracy and top-down arbitrariness. Thus a fairy-tale team of six that can eventually avenge the king's exploitative treatment of soldiers remains a fairy tale after all.

Besides the potential association to Biermann and other wasted talents in the GDR, Simon's cast of Jirí Menzel in the lead role, in Simon's own words, "was tantamount to a political provocation."[125] Menzel was banned from his profession in his own country, Czechoslovakia, in the wake of the Prague Spring because he made a critical film about the Stalin era—*Skřivánci na niti* (Larks on a String, 1969/1990).[126] Thus it was surprising to Simon that the Czech government still granted a permit to cast Menzel at the last minute and the GDR officials did not raise any objections either.[127] This fortunate turnout might be owing to the fact that Menzel won an Oscar for Best Foreign Language Film for his *Ostře sledované*

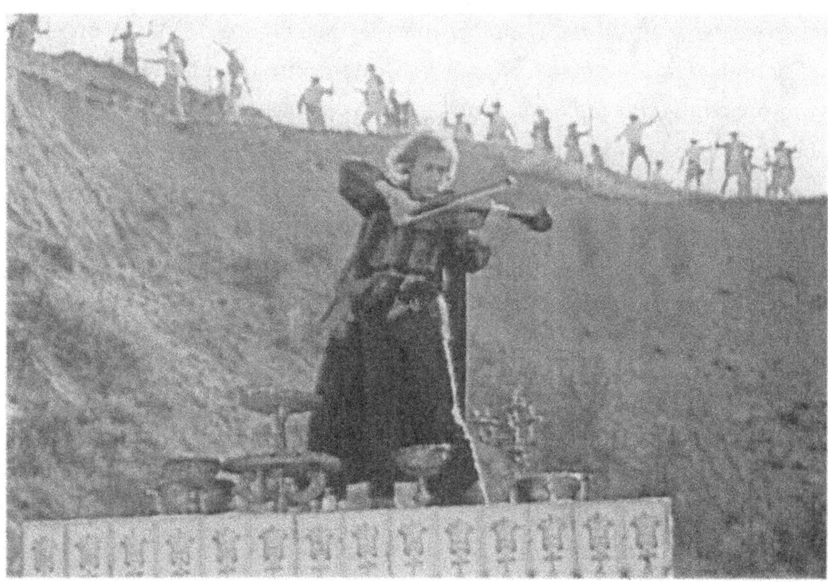

FIGURE 4.5. *Sechse kommen durch die Welt* screenshot: Music sends the royal regiment dancing till out of sight. © DEFA-Stiftung, Roland Gräf

vlaky (Closely Watched Trains, 1966), a film that parallels the protagonist's sexual quest for masculinity to the national resistance against the Nazis in the German-occupied Czechoslovakia during World War II. After Simon managed to procure Menzel an exit permit, Menzel had yet to carry with him for all his trips home an official letter from DEFA that explained his long hairstyle as necessary for his film role; otherwise a haircut could be forced on him at the border.[128]

Between *How to Marry a King* and *How Six Made Their Way in the World*, the GDR underwent a power shift from Ulbricht to Honecker in 1971. The choice of Jürgen Holtz to play the fatuous and cruel king might not be incidental, because the actor had some interesting physical resemblance to Ulbricht. Holtz himself, according to Simon, "came up with a highly political conception of his role and that of the princess." He highlighted the king's farcical stupidity in decorating the vassals, actually only three wood-carved puppets, with medals, a fact that undoubtedly mocked the king's absolute power and the lack of real advisors in his government. As Simon admitted, such a portrayal of the king "now indeed offered associations to the real existing Ulbricht and his court"[129] (see Figure 4.6). In a contemporary review in *Filmspiegel*, Margit Voss mentioned the film's "reference to the present" (*aktuelle Bezüglichkeit*),[130] but critics of the time rarely went beyond such general and nebulous claims. In a review published in 1991, however, Andre Simonovieso saw the king's wooden marshals as "allusion to real geriatric cabinets" (*Anspielung auf reale Greisenkabinette*). Historian Hans Baer has also reported a view widespread among GDR citizens that Honecker's "advisors were stupid and incompetent."[131]

In the end, the six men have humiliated the upper class and left them penniless. They do not divide the wealth among themselves as in the Grimms' version but give it away to farmers and workers standing on the roadside. They no longer egotistically enrich themselves but instead become heroes of the people. The film thereby prompts the state to think about the consequences of mishandling its citizens. The 1976 expatriation of Biermann while he was giving a concert in West Germany shows, however, that the messages of the 1972 film had fallen on deaf ears. Among those who expatriated themselves afterward were many talented actors and actresses, including the popular DEFA star Manfred Krug, who played King Thrushbeard; Katharina Thalbach, who played the thumb-sucking princess in *The Blue Light*; and Eva-Maria Hagen, who played the kitchen maid in *The Robe* (see the book cover).[132] After their departure, their films and Krug's music were banned.[133] Massive exile following the Biermann Affair left the GDR drained of much of its talent, a condition from which it never recovered.

Worldly Woes and Hellish Fun: *The Devil's Three Golden Hairs* (1977)

On the surface, Egon Schlegel's *The Devil's Three Golden Hairs* is a revolutionary tale about a simpleton's fairy-tale marriage with a princess. Yet it could be read as a very subversive film because of the embedded slave language. A curious fact in this film is that the palace is unprecedentedly subterranean. In contrast to the open and welcoming palatial courtyard in Simon's *How to Marry a King*, which gave expression to a desire for political transparency and democracy, the palace in Schlegel's 1977 film reflects the

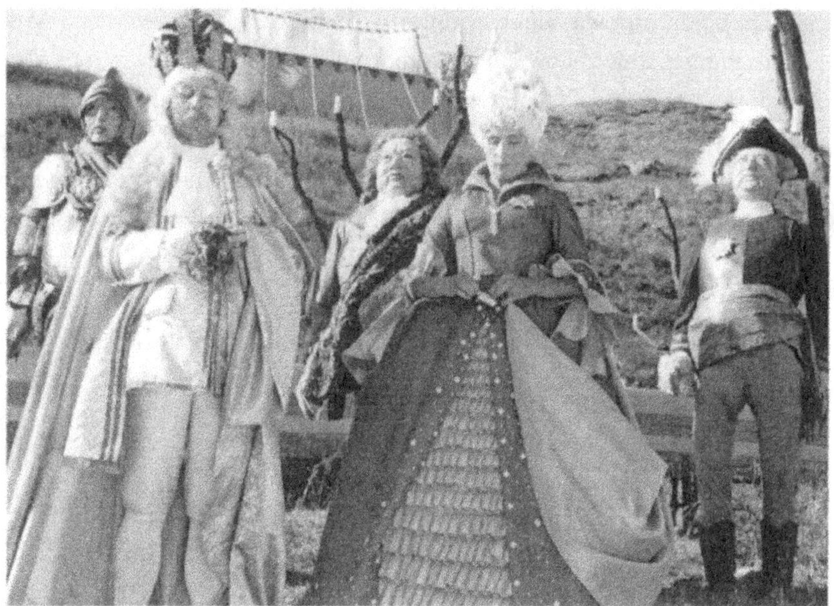

FIGURE 4.6. *Sechse kommen durch die Welt*: The king (Jürgen Holtz), the princess (Margit Bendokat), and three wooden marshals. © DEFA-Stiftung, Waltraud Pathenheimer. (Filmmuseum Potsdam)

alienation of the government from its people. The film captured an overt disillusionment with governments, the East German one not excluded.

With a script from Manfred Freitag and Joachim Nestler, the film took great liberty in adapting the Grimms' "The Devil with the Three Golden Hairs" (KHM 29). In the Grimms' original tale, a prophecy foretells that the lower-class hero will marry the princess, and the king's attempt on the hero's life is intended to rid his daughter of an undesirable suitor. The film transforms the king from only the protagonist's antagonist to that of the entire people. In the Grimms' version, the robbers appear briefly as the hero's helpers by changing the letter from the king. In the film, there are originally no robbers in the country, yet the king (Rolf Ludwig) imposes a robber tax on the impoverished people: "The king has decided that there are robbers, therefore there are robbers." This aggravating taxation turns a few incensed blacksmiths (Hans-Peter Reinecke and Peter Dommisch among others) into "robbers" to "justify" the robber tax: "Since we have to pay the robber tax, we might just as well make sure there are robbers around." Hence the unjust king himself has caused lower-class rebellions. When the king visits the town, these "robbers" throw bouquets at him with hidden horseshoes. The townspeople immediately follow suit in attacking the king and his retinue. The ceremony to welcome the king soon turns into a riot. It is immediately obvious that the current regime is unpopular among the people. Yet the king insists on the fake notion that "we are a happy government" (*Wir sind ein heiteres Regiment*) and comforts himself compulsively with sips of wine. The king's addiction to alcohol embodies the regime's self-delusion and its inability to admit to political and social reality.

A series of coincidences at the beginning of the film turns the clumsy and timid Jacob (Hans-Joachim Frank), a blacksmith's apprentice, into an unlikely hero. The elder smiths see him as good-for-nothing and often chide him with "Go to hell!"[134] The king's fear of the people ironically brands the timorous Jacob as a "robber" and "arsonist." Thus the king's letter is no longer simply to get rid of an undesirable son-in-law from the lower class but rather to do away with "the No.1 enemy of the state" (*Staatsfeind Nummer eins*). Jacob sets out on his journey to the palace, unaware that the letter orders the palace marshal to immediately execute him. As in the Grimms' tale, the "robbers" switch the letter so that now Jacob is to marry the princess without delay. The original death warrant is turned into a marriage proclamation.

A prisoner of her father's "hell," the beautiful and kind princess Rosalinde (Katrin Martin) yearns for the outside world where the sun shines and flowers bloom. The chaplain (Hans Klering) weds the couple as the king orders—or so it is believed. Upon his return, the furious king demands that the protagonist pluck three golden hairs from the Devil to validate his marriage to the princess. Along his journey to hell, Jacob comes across a dying village, a waterless mill, and a ferryboat with chained rowers—in fact the "robbers" who are being punished after their failed rebellion. He gathers three questions, to which only the Devil knows the answers. In the Grimms' story, the questions seem tedious and "depthless," to use Max Lüthi's term. The questions in the film concern the people's dire existential situations. Once in hell, there is no Devil's grandmother who would turn the fortune's favorite into an ant and pluck three golden hairs for him (see Figure 4.7). The film is a countertale of the Grimms' "A Tale about the Boy Who Went Forth to Learn What Fear Was" (KHM 4), because, as the film title goes, Jacob

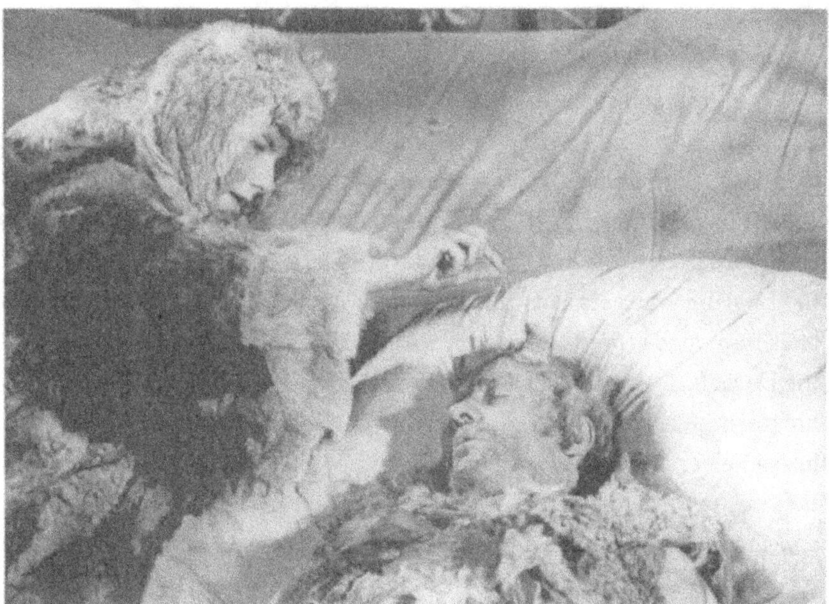

FIGURE 4.7 *Wer reißt denn gleich vor'm Teufel aus*: The protagonist plucks three golden hairs from the Devil (Dieter Franke). © DEFA-Stiftung, Hein Wenzel. (Filmmuseum Potsdam)

has to grow out of his fear and does not just run away from the Devil. Love is the catalyst for Jacob's maturation to manhood. Director Schlegel intended to depict a protagonist who, unlike in the nineteenth-century tale, is not born courageous but has to acquire bravery: "We want to show how the boy, almost a coward, comes to terms with fear: because whoever learns to deal with evil, he will also be able to cope with surprising situations in life."[135]

In contrast to the subterraneous palace, the Devil's house apparently lies *above ground* and is more easily accessible than the king's palace. The Devil (Dieter Franke) is a sympathetic and adorable character. The richly colored wooden puppets shown during the opening credits now turn out to be paraphernalia in hell. They become animated as the Devil plays his "grand piano." Indeed, the film presents hell as colorful, modern, even high tech. It is a jovial world with music and dance, which stands in stark contrast to the desolate, bleak world under the king's rule. Hell is filled with vibrancy, and the tail-wagging Devil is full of humanity, generosity, and humor. A West German review in *Tagesspiegel* also praised the comic and creative spectacle in hell that "can undoubtedly compete with the newest inventions of Hollywood's fantasy-wave."[136]

The protagonist experiences "a hell of fun" (*einen Höllenspaß*) in a literal sense. Since the Devil is shortsighted without his glasses, Jacob impersonates the Devil's wife, cooks his soup with gasoline, and plucks his three golden hairs. Instead of the random misfortunes of the original tale, the Devil reveals that the king caused all the miseries. Jacob fools around with the Devil but still gets away unscathed. As Werner Röcke summarizes, fairy tales have made three changes to the medieval and early modern image of the Devil: (1) a significant familiarization of the Devil, which takes after the nineteenth-century bourgeois family model; (2) the stylization of the Devil into a helper of the weak and disenfranchised; and (3) an increasing reduction of the Devil's power.[137] The image of the Devil in DEFA fairy-tale films appears mixed. Amicable devils, as in this film, are still rare. Mostly a devil is what a devil is believed to be, such as in *The Cold Heart* (1950), *The Devil of Mill Mountain* (1955), and *Hans Röckle und der Teufel* (Hans Röckle and the Devil, Hans Kratzert, 1974), *Godfather Death* (1980), and *Bearskin* (1986).

When back at the king's palace, Jacob would have been killed, were it not for the magical objects the village people made for him. Schlegel changed the presents Jacob receives from four donkeys laden with gold to a magic donkey and a set of connected flutes/shawms (*Schalmei*) that can function as a powerful cannon when he is in danger. A villager tells Jacob, "You can only play it when you are in great danger. It makes a hell of music." Like the fiddle-turned-weapon in *How Six Made Their Way in the World* that tortures the king's regiment with dance, the connected shawms can also fire at enemies. It is a common metaphor that a writer uses his pen as a weapon, an artist his brush, and a musician his instrument. Schlegel might have had Biermann in mind when he and his team added a musical instrument that could transform into a firing cannon. Made in the year of the Biermann Affair and premiered one year after, the film stealthily created a mirror image of the GDR in 1976–1977.

Whereas in the Grimms the king becomes the eternal ferryman because of his greed for gold, in the film it is his desire for powerful weapons. The king is not as obsessed with wealth as in earlier anticapitalist fairy-tale films, rather he is afraid of people abandoning him and revolting against him. Thus his palace is underground and accessible only with whistle blows, underground passages, secret doors, elevators, iron gates, and drawbridges. All of these actions are taken as security measures against "saboteurs, marauders, robbers," which further points to the king's paranoia. Jacob's transformation from a naïve, unwitting boy to a conscious and determined rebel is also of the king's making. He becomes the new king and celebrates the wedding with the people on a platform *in the open*, no longer a secret wedding in the depths of the earth. The wedding is interrupted by a surprise guest, the hilariously entertaining Devil. The film ends with Jacob and the Devil giving each other a wink. The rapport between the people and the Devil seems to suggest that the people have formed a "diabolical" alliance in resisting the villainous regime.

The suggestion that the worldly government, as an underworld, is (worse than) hell is a caustic critique of any oppressive regime, the SED included. Schlegel set out to make a modern fairy-tale film. The props are contemporary: the elevator that leads to the subterranean palace, the Devil's electric piano, and gasoline as an ingredient for the Devil's soup. The alcoholic Rolf Ludwig as the inebriate king also brings reality into the film given the actor's alcoholism.[138] Not unlike the government in the film, the SED has turned its people against itself. The meaningful change from the unpretentious and easily accessible courtyard in Simon's film to the impenetrable fortress in Schlegel's film reflects the alienation of the GDR government from its people in the course of the 1970s. In a 1981 interview, Schlegel implied his conscious departure from the Cold War rhetoric of the good East Germany and the bad West Germany: "With *The Devil's Three Golden Hairs*, we wanted to break away from the fairy-tale principle of *good here* and *evil over there*."[139] This implied that the filmmakers intended to give a more complex allegorical representation of the German division and did not shy away from the "bad" side of East Germany. Reviewers and censors did not read the film as infused with poignant political subtext, except one reviewer who was somewhat evasive about what he meant: "The DEFA fairy tale with its cheerful and sometimes cryptic reference to the present is not solely geared toward children."[140] Apparently most viewers watched the film simply as an innocent fairy-tale film, another Christmas present from DEFA. In the early 1980s, the film was frequently shown in West Germany.[141] Together with *Little Mook* (1953), *The Singing Ringing Tree* (1957), and *The Golden Goose* (1964), *The Devil's Three Golden Hairs* was one of the first to have an English version.

Conclusion

Due to censorship, a fairy-tale film's ability to conceal criticism had the advantage of being able to adapt specific tales to insinuate current circumstances in the GDR. Internal critique masqueraded in magic, often among general critical commentary. For these films the between-the-lines interpretation, although based on textual and visual analysis, was and is inevitably subjective and speculative. This was the dilemma with slave language and with art in an oppressive regime. Narratives using slave language resembled "history from below" or "everyday history" (*Alltagsgeschichte*) that attempted to recount historical events from the perspective of those on the margins of society.[142] The decoding of embedded slave language could not be publicized when the repressive regime was still in power and its denizens still had to resort to survival techniques using an Aesopian language.

To read the GDR into DEFA fairy-tale films was actually a rather common and officially desired practice in the production and reception of these films. GDR cultural policies mandated that artists address their social reality. But it became a problem when the films showed a kind of reality that the functionaries did not wish to be shown. A telling example is Iris Gusner's Grimm adaptation *The Blue Light* (1976), which was considered the Moscow-trained director's debut film, because her actual first feature *Die Taube auf dem Dach* (The Dove on the Roof, 1973/2010) was banned. *The Blue Light* tells the story of a wounded soldier (Viktor Semjonow, voice by Jaecki Schwarz) who is discharged without pay and acquires a magic blue light from a voluptuous witch (Marylu Poolman). With the help of a dwarf (Fred Delmare) who appears whenever the soldier lights his pipe on the blue light, he gets his revenge on the king. A significant change the film made from the Grimms' version was the ending, in which the soldier no longer becomes the king or marries the princess (Katharina Thalbach). Instead he leaves for home with his lover, an inn maid (Blanche Kommerell), an added character in the film. Made on the eve of the Biermann

Affair, hopes for regime change were nonexistent, and, likewise, no regime change takes place in this film. Moreover, *The Blue Light* is even pessimistic about the GDR's ability to reform and has the soldier predict that the king will go back to his old ways that very same day. Given director Gusner's previous controversy, critics combed *The Blue Light* for references to the GDR. A reviewer in *Filmspiegel* commented, "The film establishes references to our realistic present and touches on the problem of man exploiting man."[143] Another commentator wrote, "[Gusner's] love for small digs at GDR everyday life is perceptible. Here she acquires profundity and a lot of humor for the film."[144] Frank-Burkhard Habel also pointed out the "small insinuations about the GDR."[145] Eberhard Berger and Joachim Giera described the film dialogues as "enigmatic, with double entendre."[146]

It should be reiterated that criticism did not necessarily contradict the filmmakers' loyalty to the regime or to the socialist idea. In fact, well-meaning critiques could precisely come from the idealist desire for the regime to change for the better. For instance, Egon Günther remarked on his intention to portray an oppressive dictatorship in *The Robe* so that the East German state would not become one. The filmmakers discussed in this chapter—Konrad Petzold, Egon Günther, Rainer Simon, and Egon Schlegel—all had long careers at DEFA. But they also had their run-ins with censorship. Egon Schlegel, for example, was not able to complete his originally planned graduation film, *Ritter des Regens* (Rainbow Knights, Egon Schlegel and Dieter Roth, 1965) due to the Eleventh Plenum. Many scholars, including Dolores Augustine, Jeannette Madarász, and Eli Rubin, have pointed out that East Germans could be subversive and conformist at the same time. They have urged scholars of GDR studies to go beyond the either/or choice between a totalitarianism theory and an autonomous model of GDR history to develop more nuanced conceptions of power in GDR society. Recent research, as Augustine points out, has shown that many East Germans supported the quest for a socialist modernity but at the same time intentionally undermined aspects of the SED's agenda.[147] Madarász likewise cautions against reducing GDR history to the last two years of events. She argues that the GDR was functioning and relatively stable until 1987. The analysis of four groups—young people, women, writers, and Christians—supports her argument that large parts of GDR society enjoyed some autonomy; they cooperated with the socialist dictatorship and resisted it at the same time. Mutual compromises and constant negotiations characterized life in the GDR and made this state viable for four decades. From the unique vantage point of the production and consumption of plastic, Rubin explores the role of the quotidian to understand the nature of power in the GDR. His analysis strikes a balance between totalitarian theory and the Fulbrookian claim that the state as ruled by the SED was only a limited dictatorship. In light of these insights by historians, one should not make black-and-white judgments about DEFA films as absolutely conformist or subversive. This chapter has pointed out how fairy-tale films contained Marxist themes and at the same time could be latently subversive. The fairy-tale films incorporated socialist views, yet socialism could not contain fairy tales entirely. The edge that fairy tales had over socialism enabled these films to both support and contravene state socialism.

5

A SIGN OF THE TIMES

Tales of Civil Rights, Peace, and Ecology

In the 1980s, the final decade of the GDR, a mixture of familiar and new topics emerged that made it a period of uneasy normalization ridden with stagnation and anachronism. Yet artists could also occasionally break political and cultural taboos. The same themes such as emancipation and freedom, when repeated in the 1980s, appear somewhat stale and obsolete. Some of these films are grouped in chapters 2 and 3 because they share the same antifeudal, antibourgeois mantra or the same preference of love over wealth. However, precisely in the 1970s and 1980s, liberation from tyrants such as the power-driven king in *The Mirror of the Great Magus* (1981) and Cinnabar in *Magic around Cinnabar* (1983) seemed to assume subversive connotations. Whereas chapter 4 is devoted to critical satires primarily from the 1970s, this chapter focuses on films from the 1980s that addressed a wide array of new topics, including women's emancipation, teenage sexuality, Romanticism, peace, and ecology.

According to DEFA scholars, films of this decade were torn between conformism and protest as a result of the regime's repeated efforts to stifle criticism and—at the same time—pretended to exhibit tolerance and open communication.[1] The 1980s started off on a negative note for

DEFA with a so-called *Vater-Brief*: a scathing editorial in *Neues Deutschland* on 17 November 1981 composed by a certain Hubert Vater, suspected to be actually Erich Honecker or an editor of the state organ. In the name of an anonymous but concerned viewer from the masses, the letter titled "Erwartungen eines Lesers an DEFA und Fernsehen—was ich mir von unseren Filmemachern wünsche" (A Reader's Expectations from DEFA and Television—What I Wish Our Filmmakers Would Do) articulated his expectations for film and television to present more achievements of socialism by exemplary workers.[2] The letter apparently tried to set back the clock on film aesthetics to the zenith of socialist realism under Stalin. As a result of administrative decisions in the wake of the letter and general funding troubles, the last decade in the GDR became very demoralizing and grueling for the fourth and youngest generation of East German directors. Although they showed great ambition and potential to restore faith in DEFA, they were deprived of opportunities to realize that potential: they had tremendous difficulty in being able to shoot their own films; even if they could, they experienced frustrating delays and project failures.[3]

With regard to fairy-tale films, it was not the young generation but the seasoned children's film director Walter Beck who was able to make three Grimm adaptations in the 1980s: *The Prince behind the Seven Seas* (1982), *Bearskin* (1986), and *The Frog King* (1988). Dieter Scharfenberg, a dramaturge in his fifties, directed his first and only two films—*The Mirror of the Great Magus* (1981) and *The Swapped Queen* (1984), each of which received a lukewarm reception. These films failed to address East German reality and appeared anachronistic to viewers of the time. DEFA's unadventurous, risk-averse choice of senior directors to make these children's films was not the way to revive audience interest in DEFA, and questioning from film critics was inevitable. The fairy-tale films of the 1980s were generally poorly attended. For example, a reviewer of Beck's *Bearskin* wrote, "An exciting, well-made film and an empty movie theater. What a strange contradiction!"[4] As it turned out, DEFA faced enormous competition in the 1980s from East and West German television and, according to Rosemary Stott's study of the Western feature film import in East Germany, the dramatic increase in GDR imports of Hollywood movies.

This chapter, however, focuses on the 1980s DEFA fairy tales that frequently employed slave language to refer to contemporary issues such as women's rights, the threat of nuclear war, and environmental issues. As an established tradition within the DEFA studio, fairy-tale films were ready-made venues for channeling filmmakers' political awareness. Because projects tackling controversial topics head on rarely made it through censorship, many turned to the past to indirectly address sensitive sociopolitical issues.[5] Yet such dramatic subterfuge inevitably eroded the political edge that direct confrontation might otherwise have had. The fact that these films did not raise censors' eyebrows indicates that their political innuendos, if any, might have likewise gone unnoticed. But disguised references to the present appeared to be the only way for these filmmakers to mediate their oft-thwarted ambitions and simply continue practicing their trade.

This chapter discusses, among others, three fairy-tale films that capitalized on Romanticism's revitalization, which occurred despite—or even at the behest of—the socialist state in the 1970s. At the same time, these films problematized the state philosophy that instrumentalized Enlightenment thinking. Wolfgang Hübner's *Godfather Death* (1980) first establishes the protagonist, a male doctor, as a man of reason but then discredits him as a charlatan. The film also implicitly supports the antinuclear cause, since the concept of nuclear annihilation itself contradicts the otherwise natural processes of death. Celino Bleiweiß's television fairy tale *Magic around Cinnabar* (1983) was adapted from E. T. A. Hoffmann's anti-Enlightenment tale *Klein Zaches genannt Zinnober* (Little Zachary a.k.a. Cinnabar, 1819). Jürgen Brauer's *Gritta von Rattenzuhausbeiuns* (Gritta von Ratsinourhouse, 1985) was based on the nineteenth-century Romantic fairy-tale novel *Das Leben der Hochgräfin Gritta von Rattenzuhausbeiuns* (The Life of High Countess Gritta von Ratsinourhouse, 1925), which was coauthored by Bettina von Arnim and her daughter, Gisela.

These films tapped into the new trend of reinstated Romanticism. Before the 1970s, the GDR selectively endorsed progressive, rationalist, and realist traditions, and viewed the Reformation, the Peasants' War, Enlightenment, Classicism, *Vormärz*, and bourgeois realism as predecessors of socialist realism. In the 1950s, cultural authorities including Georg

Lukács, Heinrich Mann, Alfred Kurella, Friedrich Wolf, and Alexander Abusch all rejected Romanticism as a nationalist, mystic, reactionary, and irrational movement that ultimately served the interests of fascism.[6] They saw works of the classics, Goethe in particular, as models that could help cleanse postfascist Germany. It was Georg Lukács who, even after his fall in 1956, exerted pivotal influence on GDR cultural politics by way of his Enlightenment-centric view of the Marxist tradition. The alienation of the individual from society portrayed by Romantic writers simply did not fit the self-understanding of the socialist GDR. During the early Honecker era (1971–1976), however, when a relatively liberal cultural policy relaxed governmental control of literature and art, a new round of discussions concerning heritage and tradition (*Erbediskussion*) reevaluated and integrated Romanticism and modernism into the humanist heritage. GDR writers increasingly criticized the state appropriation of Enlightenment as instrumental thinking. Writing about Romantic writers allowed GDR authors to express their own alienation from their state.[7]

The depiction of strong women was a salient feature of DEFA fairy-tale films in contrast to the Disney pictures. The official socialist advocacy for women contributed to more self-assertive female images in DEFA. Traditional tales, as Karen Rowe maintains, assert the patriarchal status quo by making female subjugation seem romantically desirable and inevitable: "These tales which glorify passivity, dependency, and self-sacrifice as a heroine's cardinal virtues suggest that culture's very survival depends upon a woman's acceptance of roles which relegate her to motherhood and domesticity."[8] In "Some Day My Prince Will Come," Marcia Lieberman points to the exclusiveness of power and humanity when it comes to women: "Women who are powerful and good are never human; those women who are human, and who have power or seek it, are nearly always portrayed as repulsive."[9]

Different from the obedient and submissive damsels in distress in traditional tales who wait for a man to save them, DEFA fairy-tale films often presented strong, intelligent, and confident female protagonists that mirrored modern-day depictions of women. The female protagonists in *The Prince behind the Seven Seas* (1982), *Gritta von Ratsinourhouse* (1985), *Iron Hans* (1988), *The Frog King* (1988), and *Rapunzel and the Magic of Tears*

(1988) differed from the conventional image of passive heroines in fairy tales. The DEFA heroines' independence and activism was informed by contemporary gender relations in the GDR rather than those prevailing during the Grimms' time. The images of women resembled those established in their contemporary counterparts: the so-called *Frauenfilme* of the 1980s, such as *Solo Sunny* (Konrad Wolf, 1980), *Alle meine Mädchen* (All My Girls, Iris Gusner, 1980), *Wäre die Erde nicht rund* (Were the Earth Not Round, Iris Gusner, 1981), *Das Fahrrad* (The Bicycle, Evelyn Schmidt, 1982), *Bürgschaft für ein Jahr* (On Probation, Herrmann Zschoche, 1981), and *Die Beunruhigung* (Apprehension, Lothar Warneke, 1982).[10]

One cannot, however, make a sweeping statement about women's depiction in DEFA fairy tales. Snow White still is so naïve as to fall three times for the simple tricks of the queen stepmother, who is barely disguised in the DEFA version compared to Disney's; Briar Rose is still kissed awake; many other DEFA heroines await a man to save them, as in *The Tinderbox* (1959), *Rumpelstiltskin* (1960), *The Golden Goose* (1964), *The Devil's Three Golden Hairs* (1977), *The Goose Girl at the Spring* (1979), and *Jorinda and Joringel* (1986). The image of women mixed modern and conventional codes of representation, which resulted from gender relations as depicted in the original print versions and was affected by the GDR's socialist patriarchy as well as ideas of women's emancipation. The Marxist solution to realize women's equality by improving their economic status often created a double bind: work and family. One of the central complaints heard in the works by GDR women writers was precisely about this double burden. The realization that this existed, Lorna Martens argues, was crucial for GDR feminism: "One group of cultural studies scholars, led by Irene Dölling, consistently met from 1979 to 1989 to study Western feminist texts. In the GDR, the breakthrough feminist idea, which was confined to intellectual circles, was that socialism had not, as it declared in 1971, 'solved' the woman question, nor was it in fact capable of doing so, but that women constitute an independent interest group."[11]

In addition to women's rights and Romanticism, peace and ecological initiatives found staunch support in these films. The imminent nuclear crisis of the 1980s due to the escalating arms race between the United States and the Soviet Union, both of which targeted Europe as their battlefield, unnerved the Germans, East and West. The nuclear catastrophe at Chernobyl in April 1986 raised deep concerns over atomic power.[12] It is ironic that Wolfgang Staudte once created a well-liked pacifist episode in *Little Mook* (1953) in which the people's voice helps stop an impending war but that the peace movement had to go underground later in the officially still pacific and anti-imperialist GDR. The SED's position toward peace could be described as schizophrenic and disingenuous. On the one hand, it had its own peace policies (*Friedenspolitik*) and urged its artists to support peace and disarmament against NATO.[13] On the other hand, it drove underground grassroots peace initiatives that opposed the Soviet Union's involvement in the armament race and the GDR's own militarization. According to Karl Cordell, the GDR government introduced defense studies (*Wehrkunde*) as a compulsory subject for fifteen- and sixteen-year-olds in 1978, which included both theory and military-style training. The Protestant Church immediately protested. But the state's refusal to make any changes to *Wehrkunde* "acted as a catalyst for the creation of a GDR peace movement which exists on the fringes of legality and coexists uneasily alongside the official peace movement."[14]

Like the women's rights groups, these dissident movements found protection from the Protestant Church thanks to the modus vivendi worked out between the church and the state, in which the church enjoyed certain autonomy in exchange for regime loyalty. Under the aegis of the church, the group Women for Peace was founded in 1982, followed in 1986 by the Initiative for Peace and Human Rights along with other autonomous peace groups.[15] In terms of environmental issues, air pollution—caused, for example, by brown coal, the GDR's primary energy source—was severe and pervasive. Although the GDR government had official structures in place to address these concerns, such as the Ministry for Environmental Protection and Water Management and the Society for Nature and Environment, it consistently blocked pertinent, vital information about environmental effects from leaking to the public. Unofficial environmental groups secretly collected and then published relevant data.[16] These opposition movements left an imprint on DEFA fairy tales. *Godfather Death* (1980) and *Jorinda and Joringel* (1986) were tied to the peace movement. Karl Heinz Lotz chose to adapt the Grimms' "Iron Hans" (KHM 136) in advocacy of the peace and ecological movements. DEFA's last fairy-tale film *The Story of the Goose Princess and Her Loyal Horse Falada* (1989) also weaves in messages about peace and political democracy.

Enlightenment Problematized: *Godfather Death* (1980) and *Magic around Cinnabar* (1983)

The 1980s began with a rather unusual fairy-tale film, Wolfgang Hübner's *Godfather Death*, based on the Grimms' tale of the same name (KHM 44) with a script by Wera und Claus Küchenmeister. In an indirect way, the film was connected with the antinuclear movement. The allegorical figure of Death, played by Dieter Franke, states in the film that he is merciless yet fair: "I don't like to come too early, have learned to wait. . . . When it is over, it is over." Nuclear destruction, however, would cause untimely death and thus contradicted the conception of death as a natural phenomenon. The film reflects on death because, as Eberhard Berger and Joachim Giera point out, not only atomic warfare but also the question of euthanasia was discussed worldwide at the time. Against such a geopolitical backdrop, the film was intended to stimulate thought about life and death in children and adults alike through the wisdom of the old fairy tale.[17]

Godfather Death was geared toward the entire family and was intended to perform a didactic function for youth. The younger audience, as Hübner claimed, was expected to form their own attitude toward death: "Because people come in contact with death on a daily basis through news on the radio, on the television, in the newspapers, and through personal experiences with traffic accidents and serious illnesses, children should also deal with this problem in some way."[18] Thematizing death as the ultimate reality of all lives broke earlier taboos, as Egon Günther's controversial film *Die Schlüssel* (The Keys, 1973) did seven years before.[19] The fact that *Godfather Death* is an adaptation of a Grimms' tale apparently facilitated greater tolerance toward this taboo. Despite its challenging topic, the film was named the best children's film in 1980 and received the Golden Sparrow (Goldener Spatz) at the second national children's film festival in 1981 in Gera, Thuringia.

Godfather Death at first presents the protagonist as the embodiment of reason and progress, but later he is attributed with negative traits, such as the pursuit for wealth and fame and selfish cruelty toward other human life, making the film an untypical fairy tale because there is no happy ending for the protagonist. At the beginning of the film, a poor farmer (Hans-Peter Reinecke) looks for a godfather for his thirteenth child, Jörg. He renounces God due to the world's unfair wealth distribution and turns away the infamous Devil (Klaus Piontek) as well. Then he sees Death, who appears as a peasant sitting on an ox serenely pacing down the road. He accepts Death as his son's godfather because Death does not show favoritism and treats everyone, rich and poor, equally. The unlikely choice of Death as godfather is counterintuitive because one usually would look to an angelic figure to be a guardian.

In the Grimms' tale, the doctor is a charlatan with no real skills. But in the film Jörg (Jan Spitzer) acquires advanced medicine in Perugia und Casablanca, pointing to the rise of early modern medicine. Back in town, he rescues a boy dying of asphyxia through bloodletting. At the market square, he saves a Polish boy from an angry mob after his parents die of the plague. When the city council starts to burn "witches" to stem the plague, Jörg advises the mayor not to burn "witches" as scapegoats but to quarantine and sanitize: "It is not people that should be burnt, but the dead and their belongings." Thus the film at first presents Jörg as the voice of reason who single-handedly attempts to dispel superstition and fight witch burning.

Jörg is not the only change made in *Godfather Death*. The adaptation rehistoricizes a seemingly ageless tale and sets the story at the time of the plague in the early sixteenth century in Görlitz. According to Berger and Giera, the beginning of the sixteenth century was the time of the Peasant War and of the physician Paracelsus, a pioneer in modern medicine. But it was also an era beset by plague in Europe. Life at the time seemed intimately linked to death. The German Renaissance city of Görlitz was one of the powerful free cities that represented progress. Against this specific time and place, the film also changes the king and the princess to a mayor (Hannes Fischer) and his daughter Barbara (Janina Hartwig).[20] Similar to the Grimms' tale, Jörg "resurrects" the mayor and Barbara by tricking Death. In the film, but not in the Grimms, Jörg is seen in his alchemical laboratory frantically searching for the philosopher's stone to distill gold (and perhaps he has a secret desire for immortality). In subscribing to the clichéd East

German derogation of wealth and fame, the film certainly problematizes the ideals Jörg at first represents.

Despite the allegorical personification of Death, the film aims at continuing "the realistic line of tale-telling."[21] It makes philosophical inquiry into death, happiness, and the meaning of human existence. Godfather Death is not the scary or gruesome Grim Reaper with hourglass and scythe but fatherly, peaceful, amicable, down-to-earth, and trustworthy.[22] The film's primary message is that he, Death, is part of nature: "Like the wind and sound and the smoke that rises up, there is me."[23] No one can escape him: "Minerals weather, grasses wither, blossoms fall, animals decay. Why do you people want to be exceptions?"[24] Yet although it conveys the message that no one can escape death, the film did not appear pessimistic, fatalistic, or alarmist; instead it urged people to live meaningful lives. Death tells Barbara at the end of the film, "Make use of your life—Live and live well!"[25]

According to the dramaturgical notes, the film interprets the tale from a Marxist perspective as well, in that the interpretation of Death is also "a class question."[26] At the story's beginning, Death is favored over God because God is perceived as being allied with the upper class. An antireligious stance shows through Death's words that he is "eternal," whereas God and the Devil "only live in you." The film conceptually construes Death as in solidarity with the lower class, "folksy, antifeudal."[27] The city patricians dislike him "as if he would incite turmoil" like the weavers' rebellion that was suppressed merely three years ago. Hence Death represents an egalitarian philosophy associated with not only Enlightenment thinking but also Marxist philosophy. The Enlightenment rhetoric is invoked but at the same time criticized through Jörg's "Faustian" yet egotistical pursuits of wealth and fame.[28] In problematizing the actions of a man who initially subscribes to reason and progress, the film subtly makes a jab at the GDR's state philosophy.

The GDR reception of the Romantic writer E. T. A. Hoffmann proved complex. East German critics spurned "the mystical, reactionary, and otherworldly elements in his work" but endorsed "the element of social criticism and class resentment embodied in his satirical humor."[29] Thus as early as 1955, DEFA coproduced an adaptation of Hoffmann's 1819 novella *Das Fräulein von Scudéri* (Mademoiselle de Scudéri), which was directed by Eugen York.[30] Celino Bleiweiß's television film *Magic around Cinnabar* (1983) was freely adapted from E. T. A. Hoffmann's anti-Enlightenment tale *Little Zachary a.k.a. Cinnabar* (1819). It could not have been made in earlier decades, because the lower-class protagonist, Little Zachary, is a good-for-nothing and a mischievous changeling. In earlier DEFA films, working-class characters always had to be positive role models. *Magic around Cinnabar* was made possible in 1983, however, because apparently the insistence on socialist realism had irreversibly subsided, despite the government's attempt to halt the liberal tendencies in culture launched by Honecker's 1971 "no taboo" speech. Although the contrast between the Enlightenment and Romanticism is not as stark in the film as in the original tale, an adaptation of Hoffmann's satire of the Enlightenment, which was nonetheless part of the sacrosanct literary heritage, would have been out of the question without the renewed *Erbediskussion*.

The novel, as well as the film, centers on the irrational rise of Little Zachary to become the most powerful man in the state. At the beginning of the film, the former court magician Dr. Prosper (Arno Wyzniewski) seeks out the physically deformed Little Zachary (Walter Hermann) to get back at the court that banished him because he had "destroyed" (in the script "changed") the order of the state.[31] To get revenge, Prosper finds the foolish Zachary and bestows on him a strange and mysterious gift with which others' accomplishments redound to his credit and blame for his mischief is projected onto others. In Hoffmann, it is Fairy Rosabelverde who, out of pity, puts this rather absurd magic spell on Zachary, which Prosper breaks in the end.

There is no Fairy Rosabelverde in the film. Prosper is Zachary's only benefactor. He introduces the transformed Zachary into society as Cinnabar, presumably named after his cinnabar-red hair (*die zinnoberroten Haare*). Cinnabar steals the successes belonging to three other young men—Balthasar, Vincenz, and Fabian—who then recognize Cinnabar as a fraud. Similar to *Der junge Engländer* (The Young Englishman, Gottfried Kolditz, 1958, based on Wilhelm Hauff's tale of the same name) and *The Robe*, most of the populace is deluded in *Magic around Cinnabar*. They fall for a dilettante, fake, and vain pretension of success. Both Hoffmann's tale and the East German film address a state of mass hypnosis and perversion of truth. According to Hoffmann scholar James McGlathery, "The magical business in *Klein Zaches* is a vehicle for Hoffmann to indulge in humorous if also occasionally biting satire on greed, false ambition, corruptibility, and vanity in contemporary life."[32] According to the East German writer Franz Fühmann, Hoffmann got his inspiration from an autobiographical experience and wove it into a fantastic tale on his sickbed. Fühmann also offers a Marxist, anticapitalist interpretation of the tale: the magic in the tale is, in fact, money, because "all that you can't do, your money can."[33]

The tale reveals state corruption that allows for unjust reward and punishment. The staunch supporters of Enlightenment ideas (including the natural scientist Mosch Terpin played by Günter Junghans) willingly condone Cinnabar while scapegoating others for things they have not done. The state apparently welcomes charlatans over real talents. For example, Prince Paphnutius says "no problem, no problem" when Cinnabar throws food at him. The fool-made-genius plot device is a recipe for comical, ridiculous, and outrageous scenarios. In the end, Cinnabar becomes an insane dictator who orders all the fairies to be banished from the land because "they have attempted with their magic of music, colors, and poetry to confuse and bewitch the senses of the people."[34] As a result, everything in his country—from sky to clothes—turns gray. Cinnabar's banishment of art, music, and laughter results in a dull and sad life under the repressive state regimentation. This allows the filmmaker to insert a contemporary critique about the conflict between artists and politicians, as acute in Hoffmann's time as it was in the GDR. Thus this film is iconoclastic and subversive in many ways: it contradicts the precepts of socialist realism, alludes to the GDR's reception of Enlightenment at the expense of Romanticism, and criticizes the suppression of artistic freedom.

The banishment of all magic is based on the original tale. Early on in Hoffmann, Prince Paphnutius decides to evict all fairies to establish Enlightenment in his kingdom, alluding to witch hunting, which continued well into the early modern period.[35] The minister suggests to the new prince (*Fürst*) that all the fairies be evicted from the country: "Before we progress with Enlightenment . . . it is necessary that all those of dangerous dispositions, who lend no ear to reason and lead the people astray by sheer inanities, be expelled from the state." "Dangerous dispositions" refer to "those enemies of Enlightenment" who "are carrying on a dangerous trade with the miraculous and they do not shy away from spreading, *under the name of poetry*, a secret poison that makes people quite incapable of serving the Enlightenment."[36] An important agenda of Hoffmann's novel is to mock Enlightenment. In the film, Little Zachary can be seen as representing the spell of Enlightenment that befalls the (East) German state. It is in this "enlightened state" that Little Zachary, a talentless man, is taken to be the most talented poet, lover, musician, and minister, despite his apish behavior. In the 1950s, a film in which a changeling came to wield the greatest power might have easily been read as an allegory of the Nazi era. Interestingly, no review of this film harkened back to the once prevalent antifascist rhetoric, and this absence, in turn, suggests that the film's critique was seen as more general or even contemporary.

In the film, his protégé Cinnabar's rise to power takes Prosper himself by surprise, and he admits his miscalculation: "I . . . I was wrong. It failed. Why? Why? This Little Zachary is a useless object! He has no brain or character! He has abused the power I gave him! One has to work for his success."[37] Since Cinnabar attains political power that eventually goes out of Prosper's control, Prosper has to destroy his own creation. However, he himself is overpowered by Cinnabar and has to rely on the assistance of Balthasar and his friends. Per Prosper's instruction, they touch Cinnabar's vermillion hair three times to undo the magic. After that, everyone is able to see things as they are. Candida also returns to her rightful lover. The tale thus achieves a typical fairy-tale ending of happily ever after. In the end, it is not the magician but the bond of friendship and love that brings about the final victory. The film finds a more humane ending as well. In Hoffmann, Zachary drowns in his own urine, dying a humiliating death. In the film, Zachary returns to his homeland and mother. Whereas earlier portrayals of positive lower-class heroes and their social ascension proved to be a political imperative, the fact that Bleiweiß features such a misshapen and uncouth lower-class protagonist indicates at least the loosening of the socialist–realist hold on artistic expression in the fairy-tale film.

The film transforms the magician into a subversive dissident, a state enemy, whose intelligence becomes suspicious in the eyes of the state. A conversation Balthasar and Fabian have regarding the magician's falling out with the state entails a critique of the state's intolerance toward talented individuals:

> **Balthasar:** Why was he banished?
>
> **Fabian:** I don't know exactly. He probably became too clever. We should serve with all our might, but too much thinking is suspicious.
>
> **Balthasar:** How can one be clever but not show that one is clever!?
>
> **Fabian:** That is the art of diplomacy at court.

It is obvious that the magician has fallen victim to power plays in state politics, and he is banished for destroying the order of the state.

Reviewers called this film a "social parody," a "poetic parable," and a "metaphor" in a magic cloak, without spelling out what exactly was being parodied.[38] The film's dramaturge, Beate Hanspach, who also collaborated with Celino Bleiweiß on his previous TV fairy-tale films *Little Claus and Big Claus* (1971) and *The Black Mill* (1975), provided various newspapers with a similarly written account of the film. She was not specific either, but her suggestive comments invited viewers to consider how they could relate to this critical tale: "This specter, filmed by director Celino Bleiweiß almost like a nightmare—a nightmare which is not real but possible—follows Hoffmann's critical spirit. The message will be appreciated by viewers at different levels depending on their experiences."[39] Typical of DEFA's fairy-tale tradition, she added, this adaptation "unites the Romanticism of a fairy tale with the realism of historical experience."[40] Hanspach did not specify what "message" and what "historical experience" she meant. But not a single reviewer read the rise of Little Zachary as an allegory of Hitler, indicating that the film might have resonated with more contemporary issues. Cinnabar's banishment of music, poetry, and joy, for example, suggests a strong conflict between politics and art, an important theme in Hoffmann's works. In the post-Biermann era, such a new addition in the film could be alluding to the expatriation of Biermann and the subsequent departure of artists, writers, and filmmakers for the West. A uniform grayness is symbolic of a homogeneous society, reminiscent of the Nazi or Stalinist regimes. In the film, there is a commissioned painter who is ostensibly immortalizing Cinnabar with a portrait. However, he gives Cinnabar megalomaniac features, implying that artists see the truth more clearly than the authorities and society at large. As the script explains, "one can see a sparkle in the painter's eyes, as if he knew more of the model than one could see in the picture at the first glance."[41] With *Magic around Cinnabar*, Bleiweiß reveals the absurdity of state affairs, its disregard for talent, and its unfair promotion of the talentless, issues that would have been impossible for a contemporary film to raise.

Teenage Sexuality and Petition for Change: *Gritta von Ratsinourhouse* (1985)

The 1980s saw another fairy-tale film adapted from a literary tale of the Romantic era. To commemorate the 200th anniversary of Bettina von Arnim (1785–1859), Jürgen Brauer adapted her fairy-tale novel *The Life of High Countess Gritta von Ratsinourhouse* that she coauthored with her sixteen-year-old daughter, Gisela. Written in the early 1840s, the novel was originally planned for publication in 1845. However, probably due to its controversial protofeminist critique of patriarchy, the church, and monarchy, the novel instead passed into obscurity until its rediscovery in 1906. The first two editions were published by Mallon in 1925 and 1926 without an ending.[42] Not until 1986 was the ending to the novel found by the American Germanist Shawn Jarvis in Gisela's literary archives in the Hessian State Archives in Marburg, Germany.[43] Hence, Jürgen Brauer's 1985 adaptation was made before the original ending was discovered. The DEFA film listed both Bettina and Gisela von Arnim as authors, thanks to Christa Kozik, a well-known scriptwriter for East German children's films. Kozik had discovered a whole edition of Bettina von Arnim in Wiepersdorf in Jüterbog, where Bettina von Arnim lived and is now buried with her husband Achim von Arnim.[44] Kozik was fascinated by the rebellious spirit of the young countess and went on to find a single edition of the tale, published by the Kinderbuchverlag Berlin in 1968 without the original ending.[45]

This adaptation would not have been possible without an established reversal in the GDR's reception of Romanticism. In a review of *Gritta von Ratsinourhouse*, Heinz Kersten notes,

> Romanticism was very much neglected for a long time during the GDR's preservation of cultural heritage; this has changed. Christa Wolf, Günter de Bruyn, Franz Fühmann, and others have contributed a lot to the rediscovery of that literary period. East German publishers are now publishing original works by Romantic authors. Aufbau begins this year with publishing the complete works of Bettina von Arnim, because 4 April this year celebrates her 200th anniversary.[46]

The novel/film is a feminist *Bildungsroman* and a Romantic coming-of-age story about a bright, independent, and determined young countess named Gritta. Her last name "Ratsinourhouse" derives from the fact that she and her father (Hermann Beyer) live in a run-down castle infested by rats, because the count is better at inventing machines than governing. At the moment, he is working on a rescue machine for the king in exchange for money and fame. He uses Gritta and the elderly servant Müffert (Fred Delmare) as "guinea pigs." The newly arrived stepmother, Nesselkrautia, tries to impose traditional female roles on Gritta and—failing that—Gritta is sent to the convent for a "proper" education. After learning about the schemes being hatched by the greedy, scheming Pekavus, Gritta leads six girls (eleven in the novel) to escape. They then live in the forest until Prince Bonus chances on their hut. The courageous and present-minded Gritta saves the king by exposing Pekavus's evil plans for usurping the throne. In the original novel, it is not the rescue machine—which remains an unsuccessful invention—but Gritta herself who saves the king as Pekavus "[flies] up the chimney and [is] gone."[47] The film adds a parachute as the final touch to the crown-saving machine that would have worked had Pekavus not tried it before the parachute was properly installed. As a result, the villain is catapulted into the sky and presumably falls to his death.[48]

The version Kozik discovered in Wiepersdorf did not have the original ending. However, Kozik distanced herself from a possible "courtly" (*höfisch*) ending. She saw Gritta as a clever and emancipated girl who would choose a lover herself and thus deliberately left the ending open.[49] Given the unique ending, the DEFA adaptation distinguished itself from the novel, which has a contradictory and formulaic fairy-tale ending. In the novel, Gritta marries Prince Bonus, and the shepherd boy, Peter, "became—as earlier in the von Ratsinourhouse castle—a tower guard and, in addition, took over a large goose farm."[50] Inconsistent with the feminist qualities in Gritta's character, she demurely agrees to a marriage that her father and the king arrange for her: Absentminded during the wedding, she "wanted to marry to please the prince."[51] This royal marriage, however, does enable her as a woman to enter politics and prove herself to be "the model queen."[52]

The scriptwriter Kozik consciously expanded the love story between the thirteen-year-old Gritta and the goose boy Peter, a love that transcends class and champions humanity. In the film, Gritta sings Peter a love song[53] and Peter proves his love to her by passing mischievous tests. Gritta's father also open-mindedly endorses their relationship. When Peter loses his job at the miller's, the count hires him for Gritta's sake: "For you, our new trumpet blower!"[54] Only the stepmother disapproves of their frequent kissing and is relieved to have her precocious stepdaughter out of the way. The sad but romantic farewell is a vow of love:

> **Peter:** You will forget me.
>
> **Gritta:** Not in my whole life.[55]

At their reunion they kiss like two lovebirds while riding on a special bike with a sail—also one of the count's inventions. Prince Bonus develops affection for Gritta too. So at the end of the film, when both Prince Bonus and Peter want to kiss her, she cleverly dodges them so that they end up kissing each other (see Figure 5.1). According to Benita Blessing, "Although this ending was not planned, from the number of times that the image shows up on advertisements for the film, it is evident that the spontaneous ending resonated with filmgoers, young and old."[56] Based on the love that unfolds between Gritta and Peter in the film, one could assume

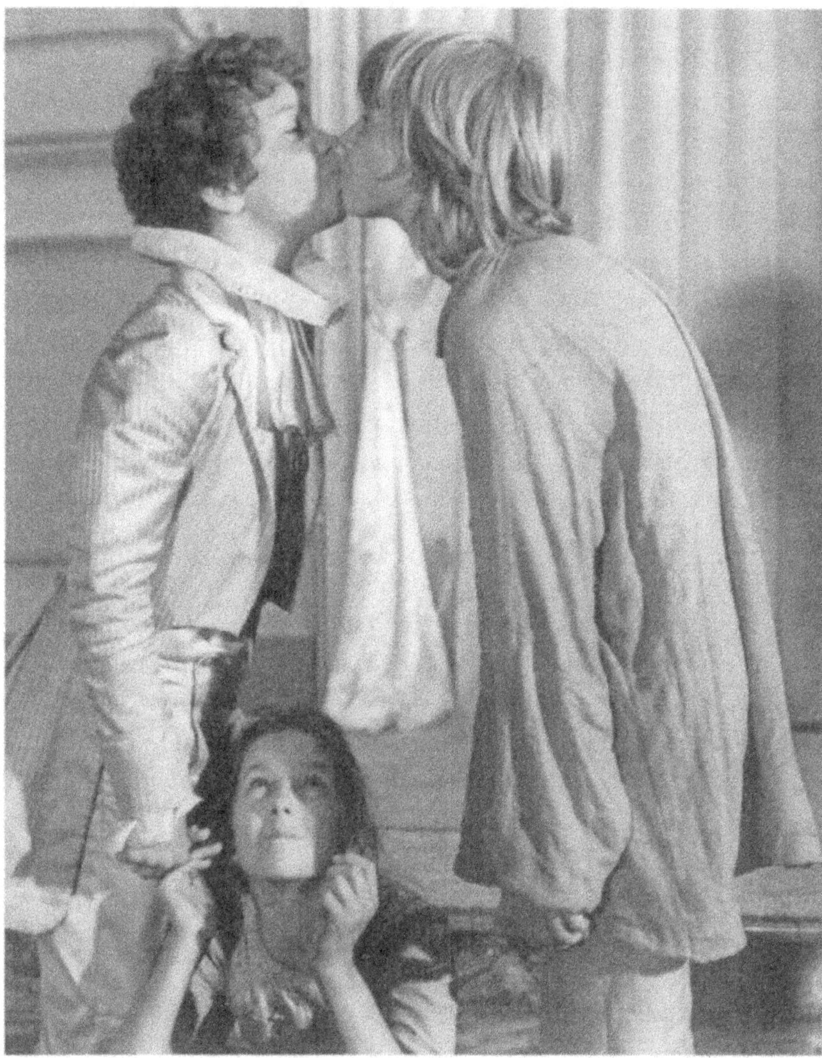

FIGURE 5.1. *Gritta von Rattenzuhausbeiuns*: Gritta (Nadja Klier) ducks and Prince Bonus and Peter end up kissing each other. © DEFA-Stiftung, Waltraud Pathenheimer. (Filmmuseum Potsdam)

that Gritta prefers the simple, earthy, and honest Peter. Yet the film leaves it open-ended, with Gritta appearing noncommittal and bathing in the admiration of both boys. After all, she is only in her teens. In a Brechtian moment of breaking the fourth wall, she naughtily winks into the camera while the narrator closes the film, as in the novel, with "Every child can learn from her example."[57]

Teenage sexuality was a taboo topic in 1972, when Rainer Simon was not allowed to make *Liebe mit 16* (Their First Love). But by 1985, Herrmann Zschoche had made a few films with this topic, including not only *Liebe mit 16* (Their First Love, 1974) but also *Sieben Sommersprossen* (Seven Freckles, 1978) and *Und nächstes Jahr am Balaton* (And Next Year at the Balaton, 1980). The fact that Christa Kozik also wrote the script for Zschoche's *Seven Freckles* may very well have influenced her adaptation of von Arnim's novel. No review ever raised any questions about teenaged Gritta being in a romantic relationship. The class-oblivious love between Gritta and Peter did not reflect nineteenth-century socialization processes but rather the GDR's humanist precepts about gender and class. A love story that favors a working-class man puts this film in line with many other DEFA love stories. Yet it is the young age of Gritta and Peter that makes this film stand out.

Besides touching on teenage sexuality, the film makes a change that is not obvious to people unfamiliar with the original novel, and this revision embodies the filmmakers' *petition for change*. In the novel, Gritta is a well-behaved, model child who never deserves a lashing. In the film, she is sharp tongued and does not hesitate to call her father all sorts of nasty names, such as "a loser, a dawdler, a flop, a drip, [and] a useless idiot,"[58] and her stepmother "a stupid cow" (*eine Zimtzicke*). Consistent with this behavior, Gritta reads many rebellious books and believes that children can change the world. The following conversation between Gritta and Peter exists only in the film:

> **Gritta:** You are like Müffert. We must be obedient—God wants it so. One cannot change the world with you either.
>
> **Peter:** Children cannot change the world. We know far too little of the world.
>
> **Gritta:** Perhaps that's exactly it. The grown-ups have already gotten used to everything, including everything bad and evil.[59]

A desire for change is seamlessly inserted into the film narrative. Considering how the young directors lacked opportunities and pushed for changes in the studio, this seemingly innocent statement appears now to have political import.

The portrayal of a progressive, open-minded monarch also carries political overtones. The name of King Anserrex, which translates to "gander" in Latin, indicates the king's naïveté, ignorance, and gullibility. This, according to Irma Zimm, alludes to King Friedrich Wilhelm IV, whom the people nicknamed "gander" because he levied a goose tax from the peasants. The king is not the villain in the story, however. Although corpulent and gluttonous, he seems benevolent and capable of reform. After Gritta locks him up in the wardrobe and reveals the truth about the evil Pekavus to him, he relieves the poor and oppressed geese farmers from the goose tax and appoints Gritta as his first female cabinet member. The fairy-tale image of a liberal monarch embodies the political aspirations Bettina von Arnim expresses in *Dies Buch gehört dem König* (This Book Belongs to the King, 1843), which, written in the same year, was an appeal to Friedrich Wilhelm IV as a potential democratic monarch despite his reactionary circles in Berlin.[60] Yet she was destined for disappointment, and her disillusionment led Jochen Wisotzki, who reviewed the DEFA adaptation for *Film und Fernsehen*, to take a swipe at the GDR:

> In the cloak of a fairy tale interwoven with autobiographical moments, one encounters Bettina von Arnim's hope for a way toward "enlightened monarchy." She searched for it but did not find it in her lifetime, "because the circumstances, they are not so." Her wish has remained a fairy tale—*one that also fits well in our time*. Its essence is realistic and is shared with the youngest audience in a gratifying way: the world is changeable without the help of magic powers when people fight like Gritta.[61]

The reviewer obviously read the film as investing hope in the young generation to bring about changes.

The film also pleased conservative and orthodox reviewers. Horst Knietzsch, the official film critic for *Neues Deutschland*, read Gritta's story as breaking out of "feudal and clerical living conditions into a humanistic way of life."[62] The dilapidated castle could signify declining aristocracy at the dawn of the industrial revolution. The film resembled other fairy-tale films in portraying excessive and lavish lifestyles at court as well as a unidimensional greedy villain. The scene in which corrupt soldiers rob geese from peasants recurs in a similar fashion in many films, but it does not happen so often that a member of the upper class would chase them away as Gritta does. Thus, although belonging to nobility, Gritta is a spokesperson for the common people. As Hans-Dieter Tok commented in *Wochenpost*, the high countess "does not take after the nobility at all."[63] The film actually presents a female protagonist, who, due to her father's mismanagement of their estate, resembles a temporarily demoted princess, lives in a rat-infested castle, and eats porridge every day. She seems an ordinary girl who has done extraordinary things—a very uplifting story for East German young viewers.

Like the novel, the film is a feminist-oriented and Romantic tale that attests to female ingenuity, strength, collaboration, and superiority over males. Advocacy of women's emancipation is consistent with the Romantic spirit of rebellion and the cultivation of the Self. The collaboration of the girls portrayed is extremely rare in fairy tales. As Michael Mendelson observes in "Forever Acting Alone," collaboration in fairy tales occurs far more often between men than between women. In stark contrast, maternal malice and sibling rivalry between stepsisters is the order of the day.[64] Although the novel/film features a problematic stepmother–stepdaughter relationship, the stepmother possesses a much more humane nature than the usual fairy-tale stepmother. The sinister elderly nun Sequestra is kept in the adaptation to indict the church establishment. Whereas culture and society represented by the patriarchal family and the church become too oppressive for women, women seek comfort in nature and establish an all-female, self-sustaining community in the forest. Gritta appears superior to Prince Bonus, a Romantic prince drawn to Gritta's world. He prefers the green grass than the golden throne but is dependent and helpless; for example, he does not know how to pack his delicate neck collars without ruining them. At the end of the film, Gritta provokes the prince to take off the stiff lace collar and his princely clothes. Not in the novel, but in the film, the removal of feudal decorum indicates the rejection of elitism and "the triumph of the ordinary," to use Joshua Feinstein's phrase.

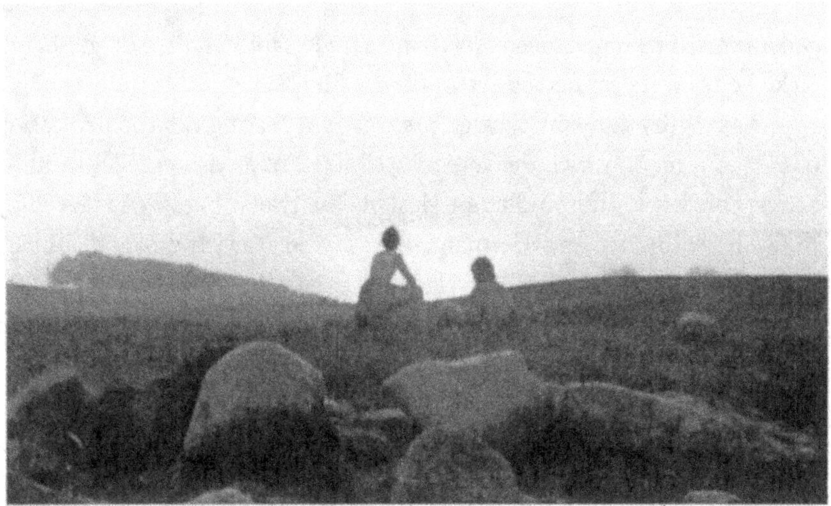

FIGURE 5.2. *Gritta von Rattenzuhausbeiuns*: Gritta and Peter discuss whether children can change the world. © DEFA-Stiftung, Jürgen Brauer.

Jürgen Brauer, the director and cameraman, brought years of experience to the project.[65] In this film, he deliberately constructed images to resemble the work of the Romantic painter Caspar David Friedrich.[66] Examples include the scene in which Gritta and Peter sit in the middle of the picture with their back facing the viewers and discuss whether children can change the world (see Figure 5.2), the scene in which they bid farewell against the backdrop of sunset, and the following sequence in which Gritta runs through the menacing, bleak forest on her way to the convent.

The initial scenes showing the rat-plagued castle and Gritta holding the rats in her nightgown might appear grotesque to viewers, because these are real rats, not animated ones as in Disney. The rats are Gritta's animal friends and magical helpers. They eventually gnaw their way through the wardrobe to release the king after the evil Pekavus snatches the key. DEFA fairy-tale films used many animals, such as lions, horses, geese, ducks, chickens, sheep, cats, and dogs, and it was not uncommon for the studio to request live animals for its films. In this case, the film team commissioned an institute in Magdeburg to crossbreed aggressive, wild gray rats with Wistar laboratory rats to create well-mannered rats. The fourth generation of the crossbreeds was considered usable, and about 300 handpicked ones were trained as extras for the film.[67]

The lengthy and complicated preparations testified to the dedication of this film team, which delivered a well-liked film with excellent music, songs, costumes, and production design. The titular heroine is played by Nadja Klier. Brauer and Hermann Beyer, who plays the count, lobbied hard to get permission to cast Nadja in the leading role, but the DEFA management rejected her at first simply because Nadja was the daughter of the civil rights activist and stage director Freya Klier, who was later arrested and then deported to West Germany in 1988.[68] Fortunately the studio board changed its mind, and reviewers unanimously praised Nadja's performance as Gritta. The film received an honorable recognition from UNICEF in 1986 and won a special prize, the Golden Sparrow, at the fifth national festival for children's films of the GDR, in Gera.[69] West German cinemas started to feature it in 1986 under a slightly different title, *Gritta vom Rattenschloß* (Gritta of Rat Castle).[70]

A Pacifist–Feminist Revision: *Jorinda and Joringel* (1986)

The year 1986 coincided with a major anniversary, that of Wilhelm Grimm's 200th birthday. In commemorating this event, Wolfgang Hübner directed a television fairy-tale adaptation of the Grimms' "Jorinda and Joringel" (KHM 69) with a script by Wera und Claus Küchenmeister. What differentiated this adaptation were the pacifist–feminist revisions made to the character of the sorceress and its historical setting of the Thirty Years' War (1618–1648), echoing again the feminist rewriting of the witch and the peace movement. The original Grimms' tale concerning Joringel's rescue of Jorinda, who is turned into a nightingale by a sorceress, is only two pages long and contains a message neither about peace nor female self-empowerment. In fact, a feminist interpretation may impugn the tale for the figure of an animal-slaying, shape-shifting sorceress who changes young girls into birds or for a helpless Jorinda, who needs a man to save her. But the DEFA film expands a terse and formulaic love story into one that extols the power of love in defeating war.

At the start of the film, a peasant couple (Hans-Peter Reinecke and Walfriede Schmitt) adopts an orphan from the pillaged countryside during their flight from the savageries of the Thirty Years' War. They name him Joringel because their daughter's name is Jorinda. Jorinda (Susanne Lüning) and Joringel (Thomas Stecher) grow up as siblings behind a bog in a humble cabin their parents have built. When they feel love's first stir, three marauders, allegorical figures of war, close in on them. A sorceress (Jutta Wachowiak), omnipresent as an owl or sometimes a juniper tree, turns Jorinda into a nightingale, as she has done many other girls to protect them from the raging wars. Joringel desperately searches for his lover and finally identifies the right cage by singing the melancholic love song Jorinda sings at the beginning of the film. But the lovers' reunion is not the happy end of the film. The marauders attack the family and are about to rape Jorinda—unprecedented sexual violence in a DEFA fairy-tale film—when Joringel manages to kill the intruders. With that, the war is over and the rest of the girls are returned to human shape.

As in his earlier television fairy tales—*The Master Thief* (1978) and *Godfather Death* (1980), Hübner and his team conceived of *Jorinda and Joringel* in realist–humanist terms. Accordingly, the actual threat to love arises from the human, not the magical, world.[71] Nor is there any magic flower of disenchantment that can counteract the sorceress's evil magic and pave the way for Joringel to save Jorinda as in the Grimms. Instead of a magic circle that delineates the territory of the witch, in the film there is an invisible glass wall in which Joringel sees his own reflection. Whoever sees his mirror image looks death in the eye, the film states. Thus only when Joringel overcomes his fear of death is he able to discover the sorceress's whereabouts.

One of the most significant changes in the film is the rewriting of an evil witch into a mythological goddess, wise woman, and suffering mother who has lost all her children to the wars. In Bruno Bettelheim's psychoanalysis, the sorceress in the Grimms' story represents none other than the mother who tries to prevent the girl from entering a sexual life too early; that is why in so many fairy tales, for example, "Jorinda and Joringel," "Rapunzel," and "The Old Woman in the Forest" (KHM 123), a sorceress or a maternal figure obstructs a young couple but goes unpunished in the end.[72] In the East German version, the sorceress wants to protect young women from wars because "war is the greatest enemy of love."[73] Director Hübner subscribes to the feminist contention that witches were pagan goddesses who were later demonized by patriarchal forces, and in his fairy-tale retelling, the witch receives a new interpretation that was more appropriate for the time. Now the sorceress embodies matriarchal ideas: her power comes from the Mothers.[74]

In protecting the girls from war, she also keeps them safe from men. In accordance with this logic, a hundred girls from Erfurt whom Hübner found through a newspaper advertisement live in a dreamlike, happy, and peaceful world of illusion that the sorceress created. Without being seen himself, Joringel watches the girls in their angelic form. The sorceress herself appears young and beautiful in her "utopian shape" (*utopischen Gestalt*).[75] When Joringel tries to grab Jorinda, everything dissolves. These scenes were filmed in the Renaissance hall of Castle Wilhelmsburg in Schmalkalden, Thuringia.[76] The second time Joringel ventures to the sorceress, he finds himself in the ruins of an old castle—shot on location at the Wanderslebener Gleiche in Thuringia—with hanging birdcages. Yet some critics questioned the validity of the sorceress's protective measure: "But what good does such magic do to real life? How could Jorinda be happy without Joringel? And the flight into an imaginary world (*Scheinwelt*) of peace does not give the world peace."[77] Likewise Gerhard Neumann commented in *Freiheit*, "But a life beyond the real world is simply no life."[78]

DEFA's reinterpretation of the sorceress as a guardian of peace and protector of women from wars was motivated by a pacifist–feminist agenda in the atomic age: "The century-old wish for peace, more urgent today than ever before, should be the concern of a story that touches young and old spectators."[79] The film's importance for current affairs was pointed out in many reviews.[80] In an interview, Hübner remarked, "We believe that fairy tales contain philosophy, social reality, and always certain ethics. We continue to tell the stories freely from our subjective and current positions, nonetheless with the greatest respect for fairy tales."[81] As a result, the short Grimm tale was expanded and reinterpreted into an allegory against war and for peace, in the past as well as in the present. Joringel's endeavor to redeem Jorinda is transformed into his triumphant fight against the war. In the end, he himself, not magic, has to defeat the murderers to reclaim happiness.

"For Me *Iron Hans* Was Such A Necessary Film": *Iron Hans* (1988) and Ecological Activism

Iron Hans is the fourth film that the forty-two-year-old Karl Heinz Lotz directed. In an interview, Lotz, with some cynicism, alluded to the late opportunities he had to direct his own films: "In this country, the forty-year-olds are now making their second, third, fourth films. They are our debutants, the directors in training. But we must soon set our own boundaries and explore them. In the meantime we have a right to make necessary films. What I do has to be necessary for cinema as such; otherwise I don't need to do it. For me *Iron Hans* was such a necessary film."[82] The necessity for making this film was tied in with urgent ecological problems facing the GDR and the world at large. Although environmental groups were illegal in the GDR, the Grimms' fairy tale (KHM 136) somehow provided a shield for bringing up the same petition. Reviewers of *Iron Hans* did not hesitate to point to ecological problems in the GDR, sometimes under the pretense that they were only addressing a global issue.[83] *Iron Hans* touched a sensitive nerve in East Germany. A contemporary film likewise on the destruction of the environment such as Rolf Losansky's *Abschiedsdisco* (Farewell Disco, 1990) was rejected earlier. The script for *Farewell Disco* about a village in Lausitz, which must evacuate for brown coal mining, was ready in 1979, but the project was canceled after long wrangling. It did not see the light of day until 1990, when there was little interest left in such films. Jörg Foth's *Biologie!* (Biology! 1990) about the protection of nature and the environment went through a similar ordeal.[84]

The beginning sequence in *Iron Hans* shows a group of hunters riding past a lush green tree with a black eagle standing at the center of the image. The voice-over nostalgically comments, "Once upon a time people lived in harmony and peace with nature. Once upon a time." The tree has by this point dried out and turned leafless, symbolizing the destruction of nature. This sequence is repeated at the end, indicating the difficulty of recovering from environmental degradation.

As the director pointed out, the perception and the function of the forest have changed from the time of the Grimm brothers to the present: "When this fairy tale was written, as it originated, the forest was something threatening, something evil, because it was dark and people could not live in it. Only rebels lived there. Today the forest is something that people must preserve and protect. The meaning has completely changed in our consciousness."[85] This change inspired the revisions undertaken in the film. Although flawed and painfully drawn-out, the film was an ambitious and responsible attempt to make a fairy-tale adaptation that would not be just another fairy-tale film. To its credit, the film addressed imminent issues that only socially aware and courageous artists would take on. Lotz was very conscious of his ambition with this film: "Because I know that this will be a very different fairy-tale film than what DEFA has made so far."[86] The main difference lay in the unambiguous contemporaneity of its topic—the alarming ecological problems that environmental activists, writers, and artists had been addressing for years.

In the Grimms' tale, the king's huntsmen mysteriously disappear in the forest so that no one dares venture into it until another huntsman captures the bogeyman—Iron Hans—at the bottom of a deep pool. The young prince frees Iron Hans only to retrieve his golden ball. In return, Iron Hans helps the prince defeat armies and win a princess. The story has a big surprise in store for the reader, revealing in the end that Iron Hans is a mighty king transformed into a wild man by a magic spell. This ending renders his murder of the huntsmen merely a savage's terror and his help for the prince ultimately self-serving. Hence, the Grimms' version concerns individual disenchantment and the pursuit of happiness. Jack Zipes reads the tale as bearing similarity to an initiation process that a young aristocrat was expected to undergo in the European Middle Ages to become a warrior and a king. He finds the reason for Wilhelm Grimm to turn the demonic wild man into a nobler savage in Wilhelm's disposition and his own psychological need for a father figure, a mentor, which is the role Iron Hans plays for the prince.[87]

In Lotz's 1988 film, however, Iron Hans becomes a guardian of the forest and a protector of wildlife. There are clues in the Grimms' tale that make this interpretation plausible. In Iron Hans's forest, the prince has to pass a test by guarding a spring: "Do you see this golden spring? It's bright and crystal clear. I want you to sit there and make sure that nothing falls in; otherwise, it will *become polluted*" (KHM 136; [my emphasis]). The boy fails the test because he accidentally let his finger, then a strand of his hair, and for the third time his entire head go in the spring. The scenarist Katrin Lange and director Lotz apparently saw the potential of Iron Hans to represent nature and the environment.

As the guardian of nature, Iron Hans stands in the way of the voracious "wild king" and his men, who hunt and have an insatiable greed for game meat, so the Black Hunter captures him to have unhindered access to natural resources. Prince Joachim (Asad Schwarz), disgusted at his father's decadent way of life, steals the key and releases Iron Hans. He is no longer the naïve boy in the Grimms' story but a rebellious and environmentally conscious future king. As the narrator foreshadows, "The kings' children are supposed to become like their fathers but we have hopes for Princess Ulrike and Prince Joachim." Ulrike (Gundula Köster), the daughter of the senile, hedonist, and incompetent mild king in another kingdom, likewise despises her father's voluptuous and materialistic lifestyle, symbolized by the upper class' predilection for sweets. The film presents a clear generational conflict and puts hope with the next generation to improve the relationship between society and nature. The director states, "I believe that one must give children hope and must not spare adults the skeptical look into the future."[88] Generational conflicts are prevalent in DEFA fairy-tale films. However, whereas the generational conflict in the films of the 1950s and the 1960s anticipated a proletarian rule, the films of the 1970s and the 1980s seemed to signal more of a utopian hope for the future. *Gritta von Ratsinourhouse* (1985) expresses the same belief in the young generation to change the world. Heinz Kersten makes a similar observation about *Iron Hans*: "The future belongs to the youth. At least in fairy tales, their environmentally friendly reason and intelligence triumph over the destruction of nature, militarism, authoritarianism, and consumer fetishism of the old generation. If you will, you can detect in the two kingdoms quite exaggeratedly caricatured features of the two German states."[89] Jack Zipes also sees a heavy dose of slave language in the making of *Iron Hans* because "it is an unusual anticipation of the collapse of the totalitarian regime in East Germany and was filled with all sorts of contradictions."[90] In the film, the old kings continue to rule forlorn kingdoms and their successors are not convincingly promising.

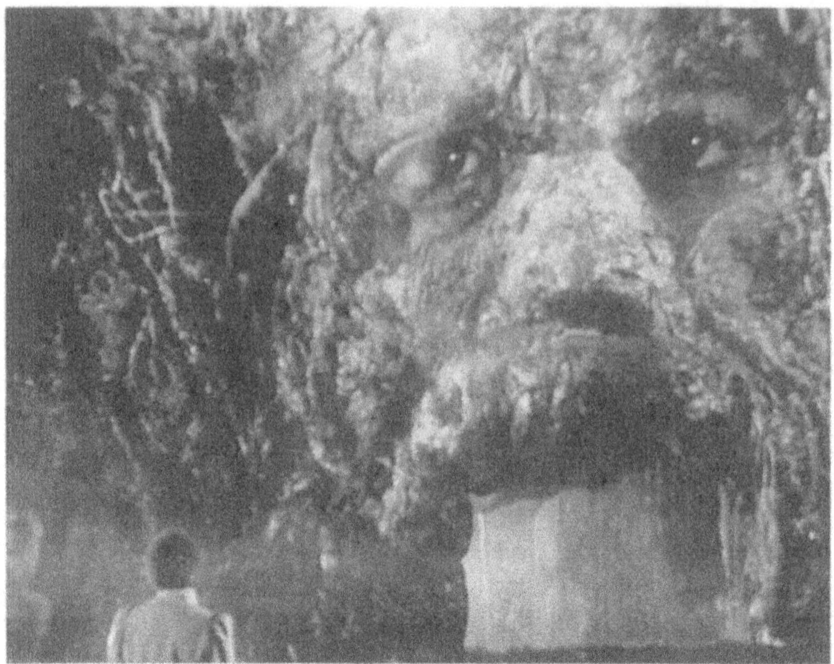

FIGURE 5.3. *Der Eisenhans*: The anthropomorphized Iron Hans, representing nature. © DEFA-Stiftung, Michael Göthe.

Since Iron Hans embodies the abstract concepts of nature and peace, the way to capture him is not, as in the Grimms' version, to bind the wild man with rope and lead him away to the castle but to pollute the water and set fire to the forest.[91] The destruction of nature achieves the simultaneous effect of imprisoning Iron Hans. Iron Hans's vulnerability suggests the limits of nature and warns of the consequences of its destruction. Although he is also locked in a cage as in the Grimms' original tale, only his voice can be heard. After his release, he is shown as a gigantic, awe-inspiring, sad, stern, android face, which is superimposed onto a mountain (see Figure 5.3). The film anthropomorphizes rocks, hills, and animals, with which people can interact and which humankind should love and respect. As Lotz explained in an interview: "To make it easier for children to understand, we decided to show [Iron Hans] in the cave through his face, the faces of rocks. This befits children's experiences and, at the same time, the symbolic idea that nature has a human face."[92]

Similar to the Grimms' tale, Prince Joachim becomes a kitchen helper at the mild king's castle. With magical help from Iron Hans, he helps win a war and marries Princess Ulrike. Thus the film loses its focus on its initial promise as a "green film." As a reviewer rightly said in his review titled "Grüner Anfang—graues Ende," the film "starts out green, but ends gray," leaving the path that it sets out on, namely, that of a film concerning the environment.[93] Instead, the film uses many genre conventions. Typical of DEFA's portrayal of classes, for example, the film creates a story of friendship between Joachim and a lower-class family, in particular, Jacob (Dirk Schoedon who also plays Iron Hans). Echoing earlier films in which work is instrumental in reeducating a member of the upper class, the film collapses class boundaries and identities through the princely kitchen helper. Reviewers did not fail to spell out the ideological and didactical significance of this episode. Norbert Tolsdorf wrote in *Filmspiegel*, "Since Engels, at the latest, we know just how much work contributes to this process [of a prince becoming a human being, *Prozess der Menschwerdung eines Prinzen*]. Princes are no exceptions. Prince Joachim has to work, gets to know people and circumstances. He has to earn a living."[94]

Due to dramaturgical and stylistic inadequacies, this ambitious film was badly received among its target audience.[95] Yet, for its thematic daringness with the ecological and feminist–pacifist agenda, *Iron Hans* duly deserved the Golden Sparrow it received in Gera in 1989 at the sixth national festival for GDR children's films.

Truth Be Revealed: *The Story of the Goose Princess and Her Loyal Horse Falada* (1989)

Konrad Petzold's banned fairy-tale comedy *The Robe* (1961/1991), intentionally or not, became in the eyes of the censors a parable about the East German state as the walled-in dictatorial country (see chapter 4). For his last film, Petzold directed another fairy-tale film, *The Story of the Goose Princess*, based on the Grimms' "The Goose Girl" (KHM 89). This film appeared to be politically unambitious and, according to *Kino DDR*, "exaggerated interpretations and contemporization have been avoided at all costs."[96] However, in an interview, the director pointed out that although he and the scriptwriter did not try to "update the tale superficially" (*vordergründig zu aktualisieren*), they surely added their own viewpoints.[97] Petzold was not specific about what viewpoints regarding the present had been covertly worked into the tale, but his remark opened up room for interpretation.

Upon closer examination, the film demonstrates a desire for peace throughout its beginning sequences. But more importantly, it presents a wise king and his dedication to getting to the truth, something the GDR party elites should have emulated. In an interesting way, this film contains a similar petition as that of *The Robe*, namely, denial or acceptance of truth will have different consequences for the government. In *The Robe*, everyone, possibly even the emperor, knows the truth, but no one is willing to tell the dictator about it, and the dictator himself lives in denial of it. That film served, according to Egon Günther, as a forewarning against a totalitarian government in the GDR. Now thirty years later, Petzold's last film again revolves around finding truth. Yet in contrast to *The Robe*, a good king is determined to bring truth to light. The just and popular regime in the film could not be further from the GDR reality in January 1989, when the film premiered.

Through the changes the film made to the original tale, it is obvious that war and peace is one issue that concerned both the director and his team. The film adds at the beginning a war sequence and changes the maid in the Grimms' version into a foster sister named Liesa, the daughter of an enemy king who invades Aurinia's country. After the war, the orphaned Liesa (Michaela Kuklová) is adopted and grows up alongside Aurinia (Dana Morávková), but the two show distinct differences in character. Aurinia is gentle, kind, and confident, whereas Liesa is strong, jealous, competitive, and cruel. The contrast foreshadows Liesa's later betrayal and usurpation of identity. In adding the war sequence and changing the maid into the belligerent Liesa, the film allegorizes the two female protagonists as the antagonistic pair of war and peace. The addition of a soldier character (Gerry Wolff) also enables Petzold to connect the film with the nation's desire for peace. Through the soldier as his mouthpiece, the director complains in the film: "War is the worst enemy of our lives."[98]

The film turns the original tale into a great love story between Princess/Goose Girl Aurinia and Prince Ivo (Alexander Höchst). From the very moment of their arrival at King Ewald's palace, Aurinia and Liesa act drastically differently. Ivo is drawn to the beautiful, humble, and saddened

Aurinia, whose princess identity is stolen by Liesa. Aurinia also possesses a special gift: she can command wind with her long golden hair. Her magic power and good nature wins her a friend in the goose boy, Little Kurt. In the Grimms' version, it is the old king who has told his son that he has the wrong bride, but in the film, Ivo has fallen in love with Aurinia and is even willing to give up his claim to the throne for the goose girl. The preference of true love to social status is a lesson found in many DEFA fairy tales. In this film, too, upper- and lower-class identities are collapsed through Aurinia and Ivo. No human difference justifies class stratification, which echoes humanistic and democratic ideas.

Interestingly, a 1962 discussion about animated films deemed the Grimms' "The Goose Girl" ineligible for adaptation because the goose girl quietly suffers injustice until the wise king rights the wrong: "It is definitely about [feudal] apologetics when resignation or forbearance of the protagonists is glorified. The fairy tale 'The Goose Girl' was named as an example. Such fairy tales are excluded in selections from the very beginning. They have no part to play in [our] artistic experience."[99] However, ideological vetting of a wise king no longer seemed problematic in late 1980s. King Ewald is neither an obtuse king typical of the 1950s films nor the sadistic, despotic emperor from *The Robe*; instead he is democratic, friendly, and just, and only such a king could discover the truth and help Aurinia to her rightful place (see Figure 5.4). One might say that the political reality at King Ewald's court was Petzold's utopian wish for the GDR. In the same interview mentioned above, Petzold stated: "We know that previous regimes had their progressive and reactionary phases. Our king [i.e., King Ewald] lives precisely in an era *in which he governs in a close relationship with the people and knows that he can do nothing without his people*. The stupid and addlebrained king of many fairy tales, under whose rule everything turns out well by pure chance, seemed too simple to us."[100] The Grimms' tale does not spell out such a democratic idea. It was rather Petzold's political stance that distilled this observation about King Ewald's rule. Petzold's remark also implied a differentiation from or even a critique of DEFA's many tendentious fairy-tale films that ridicule the feudal rulers to comply with the antifeudal and anticapitalist ideology.

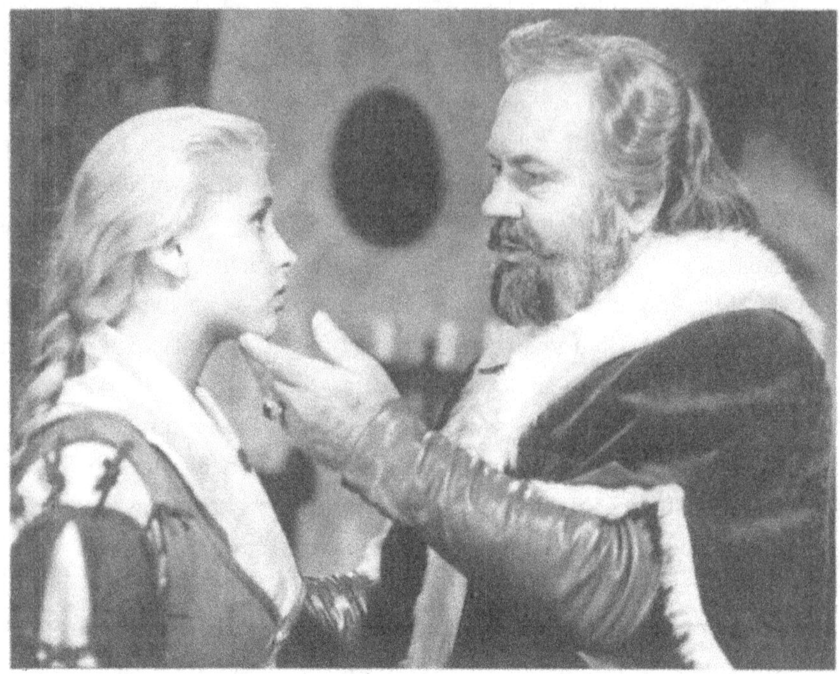

FIGURE 5.4. *Die Geschichte von der Gänseprinzessin und ihrem treuen Pferd Falada*: King Ewald (Eberhard Mellies) and the goose princess (Dana Morávková). © DEFA-Stiftung, Hans-Joachim Zillmer.

Indeed, in *The Robe*, he and the scriptwriter Egon Günther could have depicted a dim-witted emperor who would even parade naked. But they opted instead for a rather shrewd, autocratic, and sadistic emperor who is abandoned by everyone; even his closest circle wants to put him to shame. The veteran director Petzold had a problematic relationship with GDR censorship and criticism in his long film career. Before *The Robe*, two of his children's films were criticized at the second film conference in 1958: *Die Fahrt nach Bamsdorf* (The Journey to Bamsdorf, 1956) and *Abenteuer in Bamsdorf* (Adventure in Bamsdorf, 1958). He ended his career with the tale of the goose princess, which allowed him to portray a utopian reign with popular support at a time when the GDR government had lost it. It also thematized the importance of trust when King Ewald asks the false bride how to punish a crime that is neither murder nor robbery but the theft of love and trust. Trust was not something that the GDR government enjoyed either. Premiering in 1989, the film did not receive the attention it deserved because East Germans were concerned with more precarious and touchy issues. However, it enjoyed an afterlife like many DEFA fairy-tale films that were screened after the demise of the GDR.

Conclusion

Given fairy tales' ability to clad politically sensitive topics in innocent children's films, this chapter concentrates on fairy-tale films from the final decade of the GDR that reconnected to the Romantic legacy and addressed gender equality, peace, and ecology—issues of contemporary importance. To that end, the 1980s adaptations were often announced as "freely adapted." The original tale often provided only a basic plot. The changes were not at all perceived as being disrespectful of the cultural heritage. Thus very short tales such as "Godfather Death" and "Jorinda and Joringel" could be adapted without problem. Credit must be given to scriptwriters and filmmakers for creatively interweaving traditional tales with contemporary causes such as peace, the environmental movement, and democracy. Readers who are familiar with the Grimms' "Godfather Death" would not automatically associate the tale with critiquing instrumental thinking or the nuclear threat; reading the Grimms' "Jorinda and Joringel" would not immediately invoke pacifist–feminist sentiments; Grimms' "Iron Hans" does not contain an obvious connection to environmental advocacy. Yet the meaningful revisions undertaken in these films give the impression that these associations were quite organically and convincingly culled out of or added to the tales. It was also the specific East German context that endowed these films with special meanings. The authoritative position the Enlightenment tradition held in GDR culture, history, and politics inspired the transformation of "Godfather Death" into an implicitly anti-Enlightenment tale. It was the environmental devastations in the GDR that urged Lotz to turn Iron Hans the bogeyman into Iron Hans the environment protector. It was the lack of democracy and the perennial ridicule of old kings in the GDR that enabled Petzold to adapt "The Goose Girl" to promote democracy and wise governance.

In harnessing these films to political movements, DEFA fairy tales distinguished themselves from West German and Disney pictures in their ambition to incorporate serious and larger topics. Entertainment remained only one of the filmmakers' main goals; it was not DEFA's top priority. Some adaptations were intertwined with German history, such as the Thirty Years' War. And the majority of the 1980s adaptations were based on German sources, with the exception of *The Swapped Queen* (1984), which was based on a Russian literary tale. Hence this decade was not so much a stagnant era in terms of cultural production as it was a fecund period of subtle experimentation. The filmmakers produced a variety of (fairy-tale) films that were critical of past DEFA aesthetics and narratives and at the same time quite distinct from each other, mirroring a pluralistic tendency. Yet the overall political ossification and popular disillusionment with the regime took a toll on these films, so they suffered low attendance and often uninspired, mediocre reviews. Perhaps it was a sign of the times.

CONCLUSION

(Socialist) Countertales: Disenchantment and (Re)enchantment in DEFA Fairy Tales

In this book, I have focused on DEFA adaptations of classic fairy tales, many of which have not received much critical attention until now. My goal has been to narrate a cultural history of DEFA fairy-tale films, a task requiring a comparison of the films with their literary precedents. In the process, I discovered interesting revisions that led me to call these films "countertales." I deliberately avoided using "antitale" (*Antimärchen*) because of the unwanted associations that the term brings. André Jolles first used it in *Einfache Formen* (1929). The antitale revisits traditional fairy tales but subverts, inverts, or deconstructs them to present alternative versions that constitute their reinterpretation. Scholars have highlighted the postmodern or avant-garde "antiness" of select tales, notably those by Angela Carter. Characteristics that David Calvin assigns to the antitale include pessimism, subversive content, real-world context, adult themes, cynicism, moral gray areas, and even amorality.[1] DEFA fairy-tale films are, to be sure, *anything but antitales*. This is because DEFA set out to both preserve the fairy-tale quality and re-create a fairy-tale atmosphere on the silver screen. DEFA tales always end with "happily ever after," although not necessarily with the same happy ending as in the print tales due to the redefinition of "happiness" itself in the GDR. DEFA fairy-tale adaptations often employed conventional narratives. Their purpose was to maintain the German cultural heritage, as opposed to a typical antitale's purpose of creating a "rupture with literature of the past."[2] It is worth noting that many DEFA fairy tales predated the postmodern antitales. Thus "countertales" is a more appropriate word for describing DEFA's modest attempts at a socialist aesthetic that exposed the contradictions in nineteenth-century bourgeois tales and its effort to tailor existing tales to accommodate contemporary needs, be they ideological, sociopolitical, moral, educational, or recreational. DEFA products were modern adaptations of fairy tales that reversed certain known conventions.

Max Weber's idea of the disenchantment of the modern world, finding expression in cultural rationalization and the decrease of mysticism, can be borrowed in an analysis of these films. After all, the state's ideological interpretation of Enlightenment rationalism significantly guided DEFA adaptations, which adhered to a profound realist paradigm, socialist or not. Protagonists shed passivity or dependence on magic common in fairy tales, having to instead work for a better future. We see this, for example, in the male protagonist of *The Golden Goose* solving all the bride-winning tasks himself, whereas it is a magic dwarf who does his bidding in the Grimms' tale. Likewise, the hero in *The Devil's Three Golden Hairs* manages to get the hairs from the Devil himself, instead of being changed into an ant and leaving the task to the Devil's grandmother as in the story. To similar effect, magic is absent in many DEFA films that foreground the cunning of the protagonist.

In *Little Tailor*, *Poor Hassan*, *The Wooden Calf*, *The Robe*, *Little Claus and Big Claus*, and *The Master Thief*, for example, all the male protagonists rely only on their intelligence, resourcefulness, and courage to trump their often dim-witted adversaries. The happy ending for the protagonists celebrates their folk wisdom, human integrity, and revolutionary spirit. As Katie Trumpener observes, magic in DEFA fairy-tale films is instrumentalized and presented "less as dazzling special effects than as an expression of social relations."[3] In *The Blue Light*, the magic dwarf's power can go as far as the protagonist trusts himself.[4] Magic is didactically replaced by protagonists' self-confidence and self-agency. With or without supernatural phenomena, the films made a genuine attempt at *socialist disenchantment* and adhered to a profound *realist* paradigm grounded in sociohistorical reality. The elevation of the human dimension at the expense of the magical is a general tendency in these film narratives, in sync with the state's Enlightenment and socialist–humanist discourses. DEFA fairy tales did not get rid of enchantment entirely but reduced the characters' overall reliance on magic. The films *reenchanted* the stories by nevertheless making fairy tales "come true."

DEFA fairy tales deliberately disenchanted the allure of gold. Although both the Grimms' and DEFA tales despise greed, they significantly differ in their valuation of monetary reward. Pursuit of wealth, the goal of many protagonists in traditional tales, becomes what the GDR would see as false consciousness and having the wrong life priorities. While attainment of riches often equals a happy ending in old tales, it is now rendered bourgeois, capitalist, and thus despicable. In *Little Mook*, *The Goose Girl at the Spring*, and *Bearskin*, the protagonists start out seeking fortune (*Glück*), of which materialistic possession comprises an indispensable part. When near the original goal, however, they have inevitably learned a better lesson. They arrive at an interpretation of success and prosperity very different from that of the original templates. The refusal of fantastic wealth subverts the power of magic. In disenchanting the power of gold, DEFA substituted it or *reenchanted* it with love as the true wealth, which then became the new magic formula. However, one observes an interesting arc in reaction to such a tendentious abandonment of affluence. Whereas rejection of magical items in Staudte's *Little Mook* still garnered praise, the same renunciation of unlabored wealth in Beck's *Bearskin* raised doubts in reviewers, who preferred to see the desire to be rich as a basic human attribute. Reviewers in the mid-1980s showed less hostility toward capitalism, mirroring the changed ideological, political, and economic circumstances in the GDR.

In another move toward disenchantment, it often happened that DEFA heroes did not hesitate to reject a princess and marrying an ordinary girl instead. Routinely in traditional tales, the princess is endeared and beloved, and her flaws, if any, are benevolently forgiven. But in DEFA films, there are as many bad princesses as good ones. A princess is not entitled to feudal privileges or adoration by default. Rather, she is a member of nobility, and if she does not act differently from her "class mates," she deserves to be criticized like her kin. This conception of the princess comprises another countertale element. The desirability of a princess is contingent on her personality rather than her royalty. If the rejection of the princess is a disenchantment of familiar tales, DEFA reenchanted them with its own socialist happy ending: the common girl from the working class was a better choice for true happiness.

With such adaptive logic, *Little Tailor* addressed the contradiction in the old tale and at the same time modernized it for the ideological prerequisites of the GDR. However, (re)viewers at the time appeared not particularly interested in this kind of socialist countertale. They preferred a more conservative adaptation practice that preserved the tale's original outcome. The film was accused of promoting a kind of vulgar Marxism. Nonetheless, despite the initial taboo against radical revisions out of respect for cultural heritage, scriptwriters and filmmakers continued to expand and substantiate old tales in ways that reflected the GDR's new understanding of realism. Iris Gusner's *The Blue Light* and Ursula Schmenger's *The Rabbit Catcher* likewise changed the bride from the princess to a peasant girl. And interestingly, in the mid-1970s, reviewers no longer took issue with such changes, indicating that Marxist appropriations had become part of the norm.

Differences from nineteenth-century, National Socialist, West German, and Disney pictures also abound in the films' transformed images of women (including princesses, witches, mothers, and stepmothers) to better accommodate the GDR's position on gender and power. In addition to the "antiprincess" discussed above, the "good witch" in DEFA also reversed the traditional stereotype. The stepmother-cum-witch in Disney's *Snow White* typifies the conventional fantasy of a witch as an evil, ugly, and elderly woman possessing black magic. Feminist scholars complain about the prevalence of powerful but evil women in traditional tales, especially in the Grimms' collection. DEFA notably did not adapt "Hansel and Gretel" (KHM 15), "The Juniper Tree" (KHM 47), "Foundling" (KHM 51), and "Sweetheart Roland" (KHM 56), all of which contain a murderous maternal figure. Although evil stepmothers and witches do appear in DEFA's *Little Mook, The Tinderbox, Snow White, Three Hazelnuts for Cinderella*, and *The Blue Light*, they are outnumbered by strong and wise women. DEFA transformed the image of evil witches most notably in *Briar Rose, Jorinda and Joringel*, and *Rapunzel and the Magic of Tears*. Wise women can be found in *Mother Hulda, The Rain Maiden*, and *The Goose Girl at the Spring*. Another conspicuous example, *The Black Mill*, adapted from a Sorbian folktale, celebrates maternal power: if a mother comes to the evil Black Miller to claim her enslaved son, the miller cannot but hand him over. If she holds a burning candle, she can overcome the miller's evil magic. Such welcome revisions in women's image befit the perception of gender relations in the second half of the twentieth century.

Although commonplace in traditional tales, violence is anathema to DEFA fairy tales and is consistently edited out of the stories, a fact necessitated by not only recent German history but also the educational missions these films were intended to accomplish. Hence DEFA adaptations often end differently by changing violent punishment originally doled out to villains to more humane endings. These examples illustrate this: In the Grimms' "Snow White," the prince orders the queen to dance in hot iron shoes to her death. In DEFA's *Snow White*, the prince gives the queen the red half of an apple to eat. Assuming the apple is poisoned like the one she gave to Snow White, the queen flees. The wolf in DEFA's *Little Red Riding Hood* does not die; his stomach is stitched back together and he is carried away so that he can no longer cause harm. The Czech–DEFA coproduction *Three Hazelnuts for Cinderella* contains neither the notorious scenes of the stepsisters' self-mutilations nor those of the birds pecking out their eyes. Instead, the stepmother and her biological daughter fall into icy but shallow water as punishment. Whereas in E. T. A. Hoffmann's *Little Zachary, a.k.a. Cinnabar*, Zachary dies in public humiliation, in DEFA's *Magic around Cinnabar*, he simply returns to his humble origins. In the Grimms' "Bearskin," two older sisters who earlier mocked Bearskin's appearance and stench kill themselves when Bearskin returns rich and good-looking; in DEFA's *Bearskin*, such extreme and unnecessary suicides are omitted. In the Grimms' "The Goose Girl," the maid is stripped naked and put in a barrel studded with pointed nails inside, and two white horses are to drag her until she is dead; in DEFA's *The Goose Princess*, she simply flees on a horse.

Ever since *The Cold Heart* had been criticized for its gruesome imagery, insistence on purging violence from fairy-tale adaptations appeared to be a widespread obsession, as attested by reviews and letters from viewers. Any alleged residual violence in the films was inevitably criticized, for example, in *The Cold Heart*, *Little Red Riding Hood*, and *Jorinda and Joringel*. In the wake of the Nazi era, the omission of brutality and violence was an obvious attempt to further the "humanist, antifascist, and democratic" goals of (re)education in the GDR.[5] In modern-day antitales by Roald Dahl, for example, violence is actually reincorporated into the tales. Dahl did this to recover the original flavor of fairy tales.[6] In his "Little Red Riding Hood and the Wolf," the little girl shoots the wolf dead with a pistol.[7] This would never have been possible in a DEFA fairy tale, in which the wolf does not even die. The anti-Grimm ending in DEFA makes up another countertale element. Whereas at the end of Charles Perrault's version of Little Red Riding Hood the wolf gobbles up the little girl and does not die either, evil has absolutely no chance of winning in DEFA films. Overall, DEFA fairy-tale films were visually sanitized and critics found fault with scenes that did not seem to be appropriate for young people.

Besides the many traits that characterize DEFA fairy-tale films, the chapters of this book also have pointed out many tensions and contradictions associated with these adaptations. Chapter 1 suggested that the GDR carried on not only the humanist tradition but also the very bourgeois elements that the state intended to repudiate. Chapter 2 showed that despite the socialist bent of films such as *The Devil of Mill Mountain*, *Little Tailor*, *Poor Hassan*, and *The Wooden Calf*, these "politically partisan" films were actually controversial in the GDR. It argued that the symbolic worker-cum-king ending did not really reflect the GDR's political reality, because East Germany was not in fact ruled by the working class but by a Stalinist party that took violent measures against its workers. Chapter 3 probed the hypocrisy of the GDR's rejection of wealth as thematized in many films. The political and economic structures in the GDR did not facilitate good work ethics as promoted in the films. Chapter 4 examined tensions between conformism and subversion in films that showed evidence of slave language as well as contradictions between the filmmakers' intention and the censors' overreaction. Chapter 5 explored the tension between Enlightenment and Romanticism as reflected in the films, varied depictions of female characters, contradictions in the GDR's peace policies that necessitated an underground peace movement, and tensions between ambitions expressed in the film and a political reality that rendered suggestions for reform obsolete.

These films not only departed from classic and Western tales but also stood in uneasy relationship to socialist realism, a benchmark for the cultural officials to judge these films. At first glance, magical tales and socialist realism appear unlikely bedfellows. However, following the Soviet lead, fairy-tale fantasy was intertwined with elements of socialist realism to form a unique generic mix, which distinguished these films both artistically and ideologically from their counterparts in the West. As laid out in the Introduction, fairy tales show great potential for adaptations in the socialist–realist style. Tales of nineteenth-century poor folk aspiring to social mobility through magic transformation tended to coincide with socialist realism's moral alliance with the working class. Romantic heroism and the optimism of fairy-tale protagonists are conducive to conveying revolutionary romanticism, a component of socialist realism. Yet the fairy-tale genre also enabled filmmakers to take a genuine aesthetic break from the otherwise binding limitations of socialist realism in other film genres. It is obvious that, despite constraints, filmmakers always maintained a desire to apply modernist techniques to fairy tales. This indicates that the pedagogical and entertainment value of the fairy-tale films outweighed their formal divergence from the state-sanctioned aesthetic. Socialist realism controlled the films more in content than in form. Starting in the late 1960s, more critical tales emerged that rendered the authority of socialist realism more nominal than substantial.

In retrospect, DEFA *Märchenfilme* have sufficiently transcended and survived the country that produced them. They not only occupy a distinct niche in the history of East German film culture but also were and are able to traverse borders in ways that other DEFA films could not. They remain not easily identifiable as East German or socialist. Their appeal to shared cultural traditions "normalizes" those films that espouse the comparably bourgeois values of industry, order, modesty, and obedience as well as universal concepts of love, friendship, family, and community. The continuity of humanist and bourgeois aspirations spoke—and continue to speak—to audiences beyond the GDR, making these films internationally marketable. In a way, the popularity of the GDR fairy-tale cinema made the country less "the Other" than it otherwise appeared to be.

Despite the domestic and international reputation of these DEFA fairy-tale films, however, they have been generally ignored in scholarship. The fact that they have dealt with the same types of serious issues that contemporary films have is often not taken into account. Thus DEFA fairy-tale films seem to fall through the cracks: they are too serious to rival Disney's films in terms of mass entertainment, yet they are not serious enough—an erroneous impression that children's fairy tales give—to merit the full-blown scholarship that often attends contemporary feature films. The 1958 fairy-tale film *The Young Englishman* addresses rock 'n' roll, but it is nowhere mentioned in works related to GDR popular culture. The 1980 *Godfather Death* directly thematizes death, but it is not noticed in DEFA scholarship dealing with works that break the taboo of discussing death. Although *Iron Hans* obviously concerns environmental issues, in her excellent chapter on 1980s films, Elke Schieber maintains that Jörg Foth's *Biology!* (1990) is "the only environmental film of DEFA."[8] Likewise the fairy-tale adaptations of Theodor Storm, E. T. A. Hoffmann, Bettina von Arnim, and Hans Fallada are not discussed in studies of DEFA's literary adaptations.[9] This book addresses this blind spot in general film scholarship.

This much neglected fairy-tale film history evolved over four decades. The approximately chronological organization of this book demonstrates that, over the course of those forty years, the films gradually waned in ideological fervor and increased their veiled critiques and suggestive overtones. If earlier fairy-tale films allegorized communist struggles and starkly contrasted socialist virtues with capitalist greed, films of the 1970s and 1980s provided more subterfuge for political parodies and social satires of the existing socialist state. My findings concur with and build on many arguments that have been made about DEFA. DEFA films did not function just as a propagandistic mouthpiece but, rather, show us today the diverse ways film in the GDR fulfilled entertainment, pedagogical, political, moral, and critical functions, not dissimilar to other national cinemas. Although their quality may vary, DEFA fairy-tale films remain worthy of our attention and critical engagement.

APPENDIX

List of DEFA Fairy-Tale Adaptations of Classic Tales

	PREMIERE	GERMAN TITLE	ENGLISH TITLE	DIRECTOR	ORIGINAL VERSION
1	1950	*Das kalte Herz*	*The Cold Heart*	Paul Verhoeven	Wilhelm Hauff, "Das kalte Herz"
2	1953	*Die Geschichte vom kleinen Muck*	*The Story of Little Mook*	Wolfgang Staudte	Wilhelm Hauff, "Die Geschichte vom kleinen Muck"
3	1955	*Der Teufel vom Mühlenberg*	*The Devil of Mill Mountain*	Herbert Ballmann	A legend from the Harz mountain
4	1956	*Das tapfere Schneiderlein*	*The Brave Little Tailor*	Helmut Spieß	KHM 20 "Das tapfere Schneiderlein"
5	1957	*Das singende, klingende Bäumchen*	*The Singing Ringing Tree*	Francesco Stefani	Fragments in KHM
6	1958	*Die Geschichte vom armen Hassan*	*The Story of Poor Hassan*	Gerhard Klein	A Uighur folktale
7	1958	*Der junge Engländer*	*The Young Englishman*	Gottfried Kolditz	Wilhelm Hauff, "Der Affenmensch"

8	1959	*Das Feuerzeug*	*The Tinderbox*	Siegfried Hartmann	Hans Christian Andersen, "The Tinderbox"
9	1960	*Das Zaubermännchen*	*Rumpelstiltskin*	Christoph Engel and Erwin Anders	KHM 55 "Rumpelstilzchen"
10	1959/May 1961	*Das hölzerne Kälbchen*	*The Wooden Calf*	Bernhard Thieme	KHM 61 "Das Bürle"
11	1961	*Die goldene Jurte*	*The Golden Yurt*	Gottfried Kolditz and Rabschaa Dordschpalam	A Mongolian tale
12	1961/1991	*Das Kleid*	*The Robe*	Konrad Petzold	Hans Christian Andersen, "The Emperor's New Clothes"
13	Oct. 1961	*Schneewittchen*	*Snow White*	Gottfried Kolditz	KHM 53 "Sneewittchen"
14	1962	*Rotkäppchen*	*Little Red Riding Hood*	Götz Friedrich	KHM 26 "Rotkäppchen"
15	1963	*Frau Holle*	*Mother Hulda*	Gottfried Kolditz	KHM 24 "Frau Holle"
16	1964	*Die goldene Gans*	*The Golden Goose*	Siegfried Hartmann	KHM 64 "Die goldene Gans"
17	1965	*König Drosselbart*	*King Thrushbeard*	Walter Beck	KHM 52 "König Drosselbart"
18	1968	*Die Nachtigall und der Kaiser*	*The Nightingale and the Emperor*	Juan Corelli	Hans Christian Andersen, "The Nightingale"
19	1969	*Wie heiratet man einen König*	*How to Marry a King*	Rainer Simon	KHM 94 "Die kluge Bauerntochter"
20	1971	*Dornröschen*	*Briar Rose*	Walter Beck	KHM 50 "Dornröschen"
21	1971, TV	*Der kleine und der große Klaus*	*Little Claus and Big Claus*	Celino Bleiweiß	Hans Christian Andersen, "Little Claus and Big Claus"
22	1972	*Sechse kommen durch die Welt*	*How Six Made Their Way in the World*	Rainer Simon	KHM 71 "Sechse kommen durch die ganze Welt"
23	1974	*Drei Haselnüsse für Aschenbrödel*	*Three Hazelnuts for Cinderella*	Václav Vorlíček	A version by Božena Němcová

24	1975, TV	*Die schwarze Mühle*	*The Black Mill*	Celino Bleiweiß	A Sorbian folktale
25	1976, TV	*Die Regentrude*	*The Rain Maiden*	Ursula Schmenger	Theodor Storm, "Die Regentrude"
26	1976	*Das blaue Licht*	*The Blue Light*	Iris Gusner	KHM 116 "Das blaue Licht"
27	1977	*Wer reißt denn gleich vor'm Teufel aus*	*The Devil's Three Golden Hairs*	Egon Schlegel	KHM 29 "Der Teufel mit den drei goldenen Haaren"
28	1977, TV	*Der Hasenhüter*	*The Rabbit Catcher*	Ursula Schmenger	Ludwig Bechstein, "Der Hasenhüter und die Königstochter"
29	1977	*Die zertanzten Schuhe*	*The Worn-Out Dancing Shoes*	Ursula Schmenger	KHM 133 "Die zertanzten Schuhe"
30	1978 TV, 1979	*Der Meisterdieb*	*The Master Thief*	Wolfgang Hübner	KHM 192 "Der Meisterdieb"
31	1979	*Schneeweißchen und Rosenrot*	*Snow White and Rose Red*	Siegfried Hartmann	KHM 161 "Schneeweißchen und Rosenrot"
32	1979 TV, 1981	*Die Gänsehirtin am Brunnen*	*The Goose Girl at the Spring*	Ursula Schmenger	KHM 179 "Die Gänsehirtin am Brunnen"
33	1980 TV, 1981	*Gevatter Tod*	*Godfather Death*	Wolfgang Hübner	KHM 44 "Der Gevatter Tod"
34	1981	*Der Spiegel des großen Magus*	*The Mirror of the Great Magus*	Dieter Scharfenberg	Different fairy-tale motifs
35	1982	*Der Prinz hinter den sieben Meeren*	*The Prince behind the Seven Seas*	Walter Beck	KHM 88 "Das singende springende Löweneckerchen"
36	1983, TV	*Zauber um Zinnober*	*Magic around Cinnabar*	Celino Bleiweiß	E. T. A. Hoffmann, *Klein Zaches, genannt Zinnober* (1819)
37	1984	*Die vertauschte Königin*	*The Swapped Queen*	Dieter Scharfenberg	A Russian literary tale by Andrej Platonow, "Die Schustersfrau als Zarin"

38	1985	*Gritta von Rattenzuhausbeiuns*	*Gritta von Ratsinourhouse*	Jürgen Brauer	Bettina und Gisela von Arnims, *Das Leben der Hochgräfin Gritta von Rattenzuhausbeiuns*
39	1986, TV	*Jorinde und Joringel*	*Jorinda and Joringel*	Wolfgang Hübner	KHM 69 "Jorinde und Joringel"
40	1986	*Der Bärenhäuter*	*Bearskin*	Walter Beck	KHM 101 "Der Bärenhäuter"
41	1988	*Froschkönig*	*The Frog King*	Walter Beck	KHM 1 "Der Froschkönig oder der eiserne Heinrich"
42	1988	*Der Eisenhans*	*Iron Hans*	Karl Heinz Lotz	KHM 136 "Der Eisenhans"
43	1988, TV	*Rapunzel oder der Zauber der Tränen*	*Rapunzel or the Magic of Tears*	Ursula Schmenger	KHM 12 "Rapunzel" and KHM 198 "Jungfrau Maleen"
44	29 Jan. 1989	*Die Geschichte von der Gänseprinzessin und ihrem treuen Pferd Falada*	*The Story of the Goose Princess and Her Loyal Horse Falada*	Konrad Petzold	KHM 89 "Die Gänsemagd"

NOTES

Introduction

1. M. H., "Die Kluge kommt aus Holland: 'Morgen'-Gespräch mit Rainer Simon und Cox Habbema zu dem Märchenfilm 'Wie heiratet man einen König,'" *Der Morgen* 22 Dec. 1968.
2. Such films include *Das kalte Herz* (1950), *Die Geschichte vom kleinen Muck* (1953), *Das singende, klingende Bäumchen* (1957), *Wie heiratet man einen König* (1969), *Wer reißt denn gleich vor'm Teufel aus* (1977), *Der Meisterdieb* (1978), and *Rapunzel oder der Zauber der Tränen* (1989).
3. The original German title is given whenever a film is mentioned for the first time. Subsequently only the English title is used. The English translation of the fairy-tale titles and texts is primarily from Jack Zipes's translation of the Grimms' fairy tales. Where English titles are not available, the translation is my own.
4. "Rapunzel traumhaft verfilmt," *NDR Magazin* 19 Dec. 1990. The original German quotes from secondary sources, including newspapers and archival materials, are not reprinted here. All translations of these quotes are mine unless otherwise noted.
5. Doris Blum, "Der aufhaltsame Abstieg des Kinderfilms," *Frankfurter Allgemeine Zeitung* 4 June 1975; Greune et al. 40; see also Felsmann and Sahling 49–51.
6. There are different fairy-tale traditions and often many versions of a single tale. This book usually refers to the German tradition—the Grimms, in particular. After all, there are twenty-three feature-length fairy-tale adaptations of the Grimm tales. Thus out of the 200 DEFA children's films, more than 10 percent are Grimm adaptations. The primary source for this count is Habel's *Das große Lexikon der DEFA-Spielfilme* and archives in Berlin and Potsdam.
7. Giera, "Vom Kohlenmunk-Peter" 300. The controversial *Simsala Grimm* that Joachim Giera mentions is an animated series of Grimm fairy-tale adaptations produced by Greenlight Media AG. It is the most successful television series in postwar German television, but it also provoked heated debates. The two animal characters (Yoyo the

fox and Dr. Crock the alligator) act as interlocutors of the isolated fairy-tale heroes and heroines. Their intervention in the original tales was heavily criticized because the central figures of the Grimms' fairy tales lost importance as a result (see Franz and Kahn).

8. Jack Zipes points out the similarities and differences between the precapitalist folktales and the nineteenth-century literary fairy tales: "The folk tale is part of a pre-capitalist people's oral tradition which expresses their wishes to attain better living conditions through a depiction of their struggles and contradictions. The term fairy tale is of aristocratic and bourgeois coinage and indicates the advent of a new literary form which appropriates elements of folklore to address and criticize the aspirations and needs of an emerging middle class audience" (*Breaking the Magic Spell* 32). For the sake of simplicity, this book uses the term fairy tale indiscriminately.
9. Wischnewski 223.
10. Heiduschke 32, 42, 53.
11. Byg, "Introduction" 6–8.
12. Inside Kino. *The Story of Little Mook* (13.0 million, shown in the FRG in 1955), *The Cold Heart* (9.8 million, FRG 1955), *Snow White* (7.6 million), *The Singing Ringing Tree* (5.9 million, FRG 1958), *Little Red Riding Hood* (5.8 million), *Tinderbox* (5.4 million, FRG 1961), *Briar Rose* (4.6 million), *Rumpelstiltskin* (4.5 million), *The Devil of Mill Mountain* (4.3 million, FRG 1955), and *Snow White and Rose Red* (3.2 million).
13. Wiedemann, "Reise ins DEFA-Märchenland" 11; K.-D. Felsmann 191; "und ein Blick auf die Abschlüsse des DEFA-Außenhandels zeigt, daß zahlreiche andere Kinderfilme aus den Studios der DDR sich in aller Welt der gleichen Beliebtheit erfreuen. Die USA und Kanada, Frankreich und Westdeutschland sind unter den Käufern" in O. B. "'Fuchs und Ingel' in der Kindervorstellung," *National-Zeitung* 27 Jan. 1959.
14. B. Felsmann 73.
15. B. Felsmann 73; Hake 98.
16. Inside Kino.
17. Felsmann and Sahling 13-63.
18. Felsmann and Sahling 20–63.
19. Felsmann and Sahling 40–51.
20. Thomas Thiel qtd. in K.-D. Felsmann 193. See also Felsmann and Sahling 17.
21. Reinhold Elschot, *Frankfurter Rundschau* 1 Sep. 1983; Habel 463.
22. Oinas, "Political Uses" 77.
23. Oinas, "Political Uses" 78.
24. Heimann 17.
25. H. Günther 103.
26. Oinas, "Political Uses" 80.
27. H. Günther 104–6.
28. H. Günther 106.
29. H. Günther 106.
30. Wardetzky, "Der Märchenstreit" 79.
31. Wardetzky, "Der Märchenstreit" 80.
32. Wardetzky, "Der Märchenstreit" 82.
33. Bastian 187; see Steinlein 104.
34. Steinlein 93.
35. Wardetzky, "Der Märchenstreit" 82.

36. Wardetzky, "Grimms Märchen" 190.
37. Richter-de Vroe 19; Silberman, "First DEFA Fairy Tales" 109.
38. According to Dau, Haase, and Kliche, the cultural heritage includes not only the works of the great classical writers and artists but also the classics of Marxism–Leninism, the cultural traditions of the revolutionary workers' movement, the legacy of Soviet art and culture, the traditions of the antifascist struggle, international cultures of the socialist brother countries, and eventually also the GDR's own cultural achievements (1414)
39. Qtd. in Feinstein 24.
40. See, e.g., Hohendahl; Herminghouse.
41. Herminghouse 4.
42. Bathrick, *Powers of Speech* 168.
43. Bathrick, *Powers of Speech* 168.
44. Wardetzky, "Der Märchenstreit" 87.
45. Wardetzky, "Der Märchenstreit" 87.
46. Wardetzky, "Der Märchenstreit" 87.
47. Steinlein 93.
48. Throughout this volume, years separated by a slash indicate the year a film was produced and the year it was released or rereleased.
49. Berger and Giera 139.
50. W. J., "'Das kalte Herz': Der erste große Farbfilm der Defa," *Freies Volk*, Düsseldorf 7 Jan. 1951.
51. Also spelled "Yevgeny Shvarts" or "Evgeny Shvarts"; the German is "Jewgeni Schwarz."
52. Hanspach 48.
53. E.g., watching a fairy-tale film is a stronger collective experience than hearing it read to a child; the unexpected technical possibilities that a film offers shows fantastic occurrences to a child's eyes and thus stimulates the imagination. See Hortzschansky 17.
54. Hortzschansky 19.
55. Wiedemann, "Erkundungen" 11.
56. In post-1930s Soviet Union, Russian folkloristics went through the political mill under Stalin and again during Zhdanovism, which pursued stricter governmental control of art. The fraught history of fairy-tale reception in the Soviet Union contributed to reservations about fairy tales in 1946–1949 in the Soviet Occupation Zone. See Oinas's two essays: "Folklore and Politics" and "Political Uses."
57. Wiedemann, "Erkundungen" 10.
58. Klaus Schulze, "Unsere Kinder erleben Märchenfilme: Eine Anregung für die DEFA," *Die Neue Filmwelt* 5, 1951.
59. Schenk, *Eine kleine Geschichte* 20.
60. Byg, "Introduction" 6–7.
61. Zipes, *Enchanted Screen* 346.
62. Häntzsche and Stock, *Kinder- und Jugendfilme* 8-124.
63. Heller 688–91.
64. Deltl 137.
65. Abusch 261–70.
66. Kersten, "Junge Pioniere" 120–21; Wiedemann, "DEFA-Kinderfilm" 22; Häntzsche, *Spiel- und Trickfilm* 18; Wolf 159.
67. Beck, "Geschichte" 187; Heimann 212.

68. Jungnickel 84; see also Wolf 156.
69. Allan, "DEFA: An Historical Overview" 10; Wolf 163.
70. Höfig 259.
71. Wolf 160; cf. Beck "Geschichte" 193, 197.
72. Petersdorf, "'König Drosselbart': Ein Kinderfilm der DEFA mit Manfred Krug," *Freiheit*, Halle 29 July 1965.
73. Wiedemann, "DEFA-Kinderfilm" 24.
74. Blessing, "Happily Socialist Ever After?" 240.
75. Bathrick, *Powers of Speech* 37; Heiduschke 27.
76. Jungnickel 86.
77. Hanspach 49.
78. Egon Schlegel qtd. in Hanspach 50.
79. Simon 92.
80. Beck, "Geschichte" 197; Hanspach 49.
81. Christoph Funke, "Hassan befreit sich," *Der Morgen*, Berlin 26 Nov. 1958.
82. Wolf 163; Heiduschke 17–18, 22.
83. Filmmakers including Gottfried Kolditz, Siegfried Hartmann, Walter Beck, Wolfgang Hübner, Ursula Schmenger, Celino Bleiweiß, and Dieter Scharfenberg; script writers including Kurt Bortfeldt, Günter Kaltofen, Anneliese Kocialek, Manfred Freitag, Joachim Nestler, and Wera and Claus Küchenmeister; cinematographers including Bruno Mondi for *The Cold Heart*, Roland Gräf for *The Devil's Three Golden Hairs*, and Jürgen Brauer for *Gritta von Ratsinourhouse*; special effect experts Ernst Kunstmann and his daughter Vera Kunstmann; architect Alfred Hirschmeier, etc. There is useful biographical information on many of the DEFA filmmakers, scriptwriters, dramaturges, cinematographers, and architects in Berger and Giera 371–410.
84. Kersten, *So viele Träume* 28–29.
85. Heimann 138, 221, 266.
86. Wolf 163; see also Simon 90.
87. "Neue Kinderfilme: 'Wer reißt denn gleich vorm Teufel aus,'" *Kino DDR* 12, 1977.
88. Gö. "Das Märchen vom Rumpelstilzchen," *Bauernecho* 13 Aug. 1960.
89. Hanspach 44.
90. Beck, "Geschichte" 191.
91. H. H., "Ein Märchen in realer Welt: 'Dornröschen'-Film aus dem DEFA-Studio/Neu erzählt," *Brandenburgische Neueste Nachrichten*, Potsdam 14 Apr. 1971.
92. Sybill Mehnert, "Schneewittchen und die 7 Zwerge: Soll ein Märchenfilm nur Illustration eines Märchenbuches sein?" *Junge Welt* 28 Oct. 1961.
93. Hindemith 28.
94. Hindemith 28.
95. Schittly 315.
96. Wiedemann, "Erkundungen" 14; Habel 531.
97. Schenk, "Das Kleid."
98. Zipes, *Enchanted Screen* 347.
99. Byg, "Generational Conflict."
100. Wiedemann, "Erkundungen" 10.
101. Wiedemann and Lohmann 38–51.

102. Eugen York's 1955 *Das Fräulein von Scudéri* (Mademoiselle de Scudéri), an East German/Swedish coproduction based on Hoffmann's 1819 novella. Hake 98; Ivanova, "DEFA and Eastern European Cinemas."
103. Schittly 164–273.
104. Schenk, "Ein Meister" 14.
105. "Gespräch mit Regisseur Walter Beck," *Kino DDR* 7, 1988.
106. It is to be noted that Ursula Schmenger made five feature-length fairy-tale films, all commissioned by *DDR Fernsehen*; see Appendix.
107. Berger and Giera 100.
108. Hanspach 51.
109. Blessing, "Happily Socialist Ever After?"
110. Paramonowa 142.
111. See Schlesinger (9–10) for information on where one can watch these films.
112. Endler 219–20.
113. Endler 216–17.
114. Schlesinger, *Rotkäppchen* 11–12.
115. Schlesinger, *Rotkäppchen* 22.
116. Schlesinger, "NS-Propaganda."
117. Schlesinger, *Rotkäppchen* 27.
118. Schlesinger, *Rotkäppchen* 91.
119. Schlesinger, *Rotkäppchen* 37 and "NS-Propaganda."
120. Schlesinger, *Rotkäppchen* 100–104.
121. Schlesinger, *Rotkäppchen* 28–34.
122. Schlesinger, *Rotkäppchen* 34. Such contemporization might have been a forced compromise with the ruling Nazis, because Genschow was a member of the KPD, which caused him to suffer professionally. He was tolerated by the Nazis only because of his professional skills. See Endler 361.
123. Endler 362.
124. Wolf 62.
125. Wolf 73–74.
126. Rheinpfalz qtd. in Schneider 30.
127. Walter Scherf qtd. in Wolf 73.
128. Steffen Wolf quoted from the "Protokoll der Arbeitstagung über Kinderfilm und Fernsehsendung für Kinder," Hamburg 1959 (2).
129. Wolf 45; Hobsch 5; Ried 9.
130. Wolf 48; Zipes, *Enchanted Screen* 424.
131. Wolf 65.
132. Brandt 14.
133. Wolf 49; Hobsch 6.
134. Trumpener, *Divided Screen*.
135. E.g., *Schneewittchen und die sieben Zwerge* (Erich Kobler, FRG, 1955), *Frau Holle—Das Märchen von Goldmarie und Pechmarie* (Peter Podehl, FRG, 1961).
136. Wolf 53; Hobsch 4.
137. Hobsch 9.
138. Wolf 66; also qtd. in Hobsch 5–6 and Brandt 14.
139. Hobsch 9; Felsmann and Sahling 15–16.

140. Hobsch 16.
141. Berghahn, *Hollywood behind the Wall* 34.
142. Schneider 32.
143. Hobsch 13; Wolf 68.
144. Zipes, *Enchanted Screen* 322.
145. See Stott, *Crossing the Wall.*
146. Based on my email communication with Rosemary Stott on 30 Jan. 2014. Cf. Schenk, "Vor vierzig Jahren" 323. Disney's *Snow White* is not mentioned specifically in the article, but it might well be one of the 2,500 titles screened by CAMERA.
147. Here is the list of Disney features and nature films that were shown on East German Television (in order of broadcast date): 7.4.1986 *Die Wüste lebt* (The Living Desert, James Algar, 1953); 24.12.1986 *Wunder der Prärie* (The Vanishing Prairie, James Algar, 1954); 14.2.1988 *Wunder der Prärie*; 5.8.1989 *Die Million-Dollar-Ente* (Filmkomödie, The Million Dollar Duck, Vincent McEveety, 1971); 8.10.1989 *Der einsame Puma* (Charlie, The Lonesome Cougar, Rex Allen and Winston Hibler, 1968); 14.1.1990 *Lefty, der Luchs* (Lefty, The Dingaling Lynx, Winston Hibler, 1971); 24.2.1990 *Sein Freund Jello* (Old Yeller, Robert Stevenson, 1957); 18.3.1990 *Die Spur der Antilope* (The Track of the African Bongo, Frank Zuniga, 1977); 15.4.1990 *Die Reise von Natty Gann* (The Journey of Natty Gann, Jeremy Kagan, 1985); 13.5.1990 *Zwei Cowboys* (Trail of Danger, Andrew V. McLaglen, 1977); 26.5.1990 *Flucht des Pumas* (Run, Cougar, Run, Jerome Courtland, 1972); 3.6.1990 *Insel am Ende der Welt* (The Island at the Top of the World, Robert Stevenson, 1974); 18.8.1990 *Wenn die Wölfe heulen* (Never Cry Wolf, Carroll Ballard, 1983); 14.10.1990 *Die Reise von Natty Gann*; 23.12.1990 *Zwei in der Arktis* (Two Against the Arctic, Bernard McEveety, 1974); 13.1.1991 *Paka, die Polarbärin* (Snow Bear, Gunter von Fritsch, 1970); 3.3.1991 *Die Schatzinsel* (Treasure Planet, Byron Haskin, 1950); 9.3.1991 *Der einsame Puma*; 4.5.1991 *Lefty, der Luchs*. I thank Dr. Jörg-Uwe Fischer at Deutsches Rundfunkarchiv in Potsdam-Babelsberg for the valuable information.
148. Smith and Clark 49.
149. G. H., "Heiße Köpfe um das 'kalte Herz': Der erste Märchenfilm der DEFA im Kreuzfeuer der Diskussion des Berliner Publikums," *National-Zeitung* 16 Jan. 1951.
150. Wasko 111–113.
151. Zipes, "Breaking the Disney Spell" 344.
152. Zipes, "Breaking the Disney Spell" 344.
153. Zipes, "Breaking the Disney Spell" 351.
154. Wasko 16–18.
155. Blessing, "DEFA Children's Films" 244.
156. Zipes, "Breaking the Disney Spell" 352.
157. Gabler 221.
158. These films follow the Proppian structure based on the function of the dramatis personae; they possess the typical characteristics of a fairy tale that Lüthi mentions, such as one dimensionality, depthlessness, and abstract style. Propp; Lüthi.
159. Blessing, "Happily Socialist Ever After?", "DEFA Children's Films", "'Films to Give Kids Courage!'"
160. Fritzsche, "'Keep the Home Fires Burning.'"
161. Berghahn, "Ein Kultfulm zum Gruseln" 405–20.

162. Ecke; University of Massachusetts at Amherst et al. Similar guides exist for *Rumpelstiltskin* and *The Singing Ringing Tree*.
163. Powell 224, 242.
164. "Wie heiratet man einen König," BArch DR 1-Z/280.
165. "Wie heiratet man einen König," BArch DR 1-Z/280.
166. Byg, "Introduction" 6.
167. Heiduschke 33–35.

Chapter 1

1. Hinz. Maureen Thum also wrote, "But, while puzzling over his popularity, academic critics have for the most part rejected [his tales] as the flawed reflection of Hauff's petty bourgeois and philistine spirit" (n. pag.). Jack Zipes noted in this regard, "[Hauff's tales] have generally been associated with the Biedermeier period, and Hauff has never been considered a progressive writer but more a writer for the morally upright, and some critics have even argued that his ideological perspective is that of a philistine" (*Enchanted Screen* 344).
2. Heimann 104, 114, 138, 189.
3. Schlesinger, *Rotkäppchen* 7.
4. Rentschler 196.
5. Schlesinger, *Rotkäppchen* 111–18.
6. Feinstein 30.
7. Before DEFA, there were two silent film adaptations of "The Cold Heart," both in 1923, one directed by Fred Sauer and the other by Adolf Wenter; a silent film, *Der kleine Muck* (Wilhelm Prager, 1921); and another feature film, *Der kleine Muck* (Franz Fiedler, 1944) See Giera, "Wilhelm Hauff."
8. Inside Kino; cf. eleven million in Münz (25–26).
9. Zipes, "Struggle" 167.
10. Ilse Galfert, "Das kalte Herz: Erster DEFA-Farbfilm hatte Uraufführung im Babylon," *BZ am Abend* 12 Dec. 1950.
11. Zapf 31.
12. Beck, "Geschichte" 186.
13. Leopold Magon qtd. in Beck, "Geschichte" 186.
14. Heimann 64, 94.
15. Heimann 65.
16. János Veiczi, "'Das kalte Herz': Ein farbiger Märchenfilm der DEFA, der uns enttäuscht," *Junge Welt* 96, 15 Dec. 1950.
17. Ilse Galfert, "Das kalte Herz," *BZ am Abend* 12 Dec. 1950.
18. Silberman, "First DEFA Fairy Tales" 109.
19. "Kinderfilme—Die Steinerne Blume," *Kino DDR* 2, 1990.
20. Hortzschansky 175.
21. Oinas, "Folklore and Politics."
22. Balina 114.
23. Zipes, *Enchanted Screen* 324.
24. Zipes, *Enchanted Screen* 324.
25. H. Günther 105.
26. H. Günther 104.

27. H. Günther 96, 105.
28. Heimann 92–95; Schenk, *Eine kleine Geschichte* 56; Feinstein 25.
29. The majority of Bazhov's tales are based on the plot of testing. See Lipovetsky 269.
30. Lipovetsky 265–66.
31. Lipovetsky 274.
32. Lipovetsky 269; Fritzsche 56–58
33. Fritzsche 61.
34. Zipes, *Enchanted Screen* 324.
35. Zipes, *Brothers Grimm* 97.
36. Jenkins, "Disenchantment, Enchantment and Re-Enchantment"; Weber, "Science as a Vocation."
37. König 78. Leni Riefenstahl's *Das blaue Licht* (The Blue Light, 1932) at the end of the silent era was not adapted from the Grimms' tale of the same name. See Rentschler's discussion of Riefenstahl's *The Blue Light*, 27–51.
38. Giera, "Vom Kohlenmunk-Peter" 296–97.
39. Schenk, *Eine kleine Geschichte* 43.
40. Habel 306; Schenk, *Das zweite Leben* 56.
41. Protokoll der Sitzung der "DEFA-Kommission" 14 Mar. 1950; Heimann 121.
42. Hinz 118.
43. "Den braven Mann aber, der ihnen abgeraten, verkaufte der Holländer Michel an einen Seelenverkäufer, und man hat nichts mehr von ihm gehört" (Hauff, *Märchen* 277).
44. Hauff, "The Cold Heart" 210.
45. Hauff, "The Cold Heart" 211.
46. Thum, "Wilhelm Hauff"; Zipes, *Enchanted Screen* 344–45.
47. The film, as in the original version, has a specific reference to the Holy Scripture. When Dutch Michael throws a stick at Peter, the stick turns into a snake (Hauff, "The Cold Heart," 126). This refers to the snake in the Garden of Eden tempting Adam as well as in Exodus, where the staff of Moses transformed into a snake and then back into a staff (Exodus 4:2–4).
48. Hauff, "The Cold Heart" 127.
49. Hauff, "The Cold Heart" 203.
50. Qtd. from Silberman, "First DEFA Fairy Tales" 113.
51. Feinstein 69.
52. Heimann 98.
53. Hauff, "The Cold Heart" 201.
54. János Veiczi, "'Das kalte Herz,'" *Junge Welt* 96, 15 Dec. 1950.
55. Habel 306. For more on special effects, see Fleischer and Trimpert.
56. Herman Müller, "'Das kalte Herz' / Ein farbiger Märchenfilm der DEFA," *Neues Deutschland* 12 Dec. 1950.
57. "Das kalte Herz," *Mitteldeutscher Rundfunk* 4 June 1995.
58. Leonie Weymann and Ewald Thoms, "Jugendliche schreiben an die DEFA," *Junge Welt* 96, 15 Dec. 1950.
59. Wolf 149.
60. H. Günther 104.
61. Heimann 96.
62. "Das kalte Herz," *Mitteldeutscher Rundfunk* 4 June 1995.

63. G. H., "Heiße Köpfe um das 'kalte Herz,'" *National-Zeitung* 16 Jan. 1951.
64. G. H., "Heiße Köpfe um das 'kalte Herz.'"
65. Herman Müller, "'Das kalte Herz,'" *Neues Deutschland* 12 Dec. 1950.
66. Bosley Crowther, "La Belle et la Bete (1946): The Screen in Review," *New York Times* 24 Dec. 1947.
67. G. H., "Heiße Köpfe um das 'kalte Herz,'" *National-Zeitung* 16 Jan. 1951. According to Joachim Giera, however, the film was not cut ("Vom Kohlenmunk-Peter" 295–96).
68. Silberman, "First DEFA Fairy Tales" 111–12; König 78–79; Fritzsche.
69. G. H., "Heiße Köpfe um das 'kalte Herz,'" *National-Zeitung* 16 Jan. 1951.
70. G. H., "Heiße Köpfe um das 'kalte Herz.'" See also Herman Müller, "'Das kalte Herz,'" *Neues Deutschland* 12 Dec. 1950.
71. János Veiczi, "'Das kalte Herz,'" *Junge Welt* 96, 15 Dec. 1950.
72. "Das kalte Herz," *Mitteldeutscher Rundfunk* 4 June 1995.
73. Silberman, "First DEFA Fairy Tales" 109.
74. Trumpener, *Divided Screen.*
75. Hecht; Teschner 14–15; Gersch; Schenk, "Lastern der Welt"; Mueller; Joachim Giera, "Das Märchen ihres Lebens," *Neues Deutschland* 23 Dec. 2003; Knut Elstermann, "Da lacht der Teppichknüpfer: Der Defa-Film 'Die Geschichte vom kleinen Muck' wird 50 Jahre alt," *Berliner Zeitung* 20/21 Dec. 2003.
76. Giera, "Das Märchen ihres Lebens," *Neues Deutschland* 23 Dec. 2003.
77. Giera, "Das Märchen ihres Lebens." According to Münz (25), *Little Mook* has been distributed in over sixty countries; see also Hanspach 45; Habel 205.
78. Felsmann and Sahling 20–63.
79. Elstermann, "Da lacht der Teppichknüpfer," *Berliner Zeitung* 20/21 Dec. 2003; B. Felsmann 73.
80. Qtd. in Giera, "Das Märchen ihres Lebens," *Neues Deutschland* 23 Dec. 2003.
81. Giera, "Das Märchen ihres Lebens."
82. Feinstein 38.
83. Hauff, "The Tale of Little Mook" 52.
84. Qtd. in König 85.
85. Sieg, *Ethnic Drag.*
86. Torner, "The Race-Time Continuum" 121–22; Piesche.
87. Based on my email communication with Evan Torner on 17 Apr. 2014.
88. Siegfried Schröder, *Junge Welt* 1 Jan. 1954; see König 85.
89. Giera, "Das Märchen ihres Lebens," *Neues Deutschland* 23 Dec. 2003; Schenk, *Das zweite Leben* 83.
90. Wiedemann, "Erkundungen" 11.
91. Zipes, *Enchanted Screen* 346.
92. Hauff, "The Tale of Little Mook" 35.
93. Giera, "Das Märchen ihres Lebens," *Neues Deutschland* 23 Dec. 2003; Susanne König, "Die Geschichte vom kleinen Muck," *Neues Deutschland* 30 Dec. 1953.
94. Giera, "Das Märchen ihres Lebens"; Susanne König, "Die Geschichte vom kleinen Muck."
95. Heimann 65.
96. Mückenberger 27; Schenk, *Eine kleine Geschichte* 39.
97. Susanne König, "Die Geschichte vom kleinen Muck," *Neues Deutschland* 30 Dec. 1953.

98. H. U. E., "DEFA-Weihnachtsgeschenk 'Die Geschichte vom kleinen Muck,'" *Berliner Zeitung* 24 Dec. 1953. See also Habel 205; König 85.
99. Giera, "Vom Kohlenmunk-Peter" 296; Kümpel 46.
100. C. Z. L., "Das große Abenteuer im Märchenland: 'Die Geschichte vom kleinen Muck', ein Wolfgang-Staudte-Farbfilm der DEFA," *Tribüne* 31 Dec. 1953.
101. Wilhelm Hauff took *The Arabian Nights* as his role model. See Hinz 111, 119.
102. Davies 59.
103. Allan, "Ruptures and Continuities" 42.
104. Schenk, *Das zweite Leben* 56.
105. Giera, "Vom Kohlenmunk-Peter" 296; Kümpel 46.
106. Wolf 148.
107. Heimann 134.
108. Wolf 161.
109. Anton Ackermann qtd. in Wolf 161.
110. Giera, "Vom Kohlenmunk-Peter" 297.
111. *Sächsisches Tageblatt*, Dresden, 29 Dec. 1953; see König 85.
112. Qtd. in Giera, "Das Märchen ihres Lebens," *Neues Deutschland* 23 Dec. 2003.

Chapter 2

1. Ernst Bloch, qtd. in Zipes, *Breaking the Magic Spell* 150–51.
2. Zipes, *Breaking the Magic Spell* 175.
3. Wolf 158.
4. Kersten, "Junge Pioniere" 120–21; Wiedemann, "DEFA-Kinderfilm" 22; Heimann 183, 212; Häntzsche, *Spiel- und Trickfilm* 18–52.
5. Hortzschansky 18.
6. Hortzschansky 18.
7. Wolf 68. Häntzsche, however, disagrees with this conclusion Wolf made in 1969. According to Häntzsche, the controversy surrounding *The Brave Little Tailor* showed that the socialist position on fairy-tale adaptation distanced itself from such tendentious depictions of kings. See Häntzsche, *Spiel- und Trickfilm* 54.
8. Wardetzky, "Der Märchenstreit" 84.
9. See, e.g., Behrends, Lindenberger, and Poutrus.
10. Henryk Keisch, "Rotkäppchen: Deutsche Erstaufführung im 'Theater der Freundschaft,' Berlin," *Neues Deutschland* 6 Jan. 1952.
11. Abusch 261–70.
12. Wolf 194; Heimann 246.
13. Münz 33. See Bortfeldt and Probst.
14. Ewald, "Weshalb wurde 'Der Teufel vom Mühlenberg' kein Kinderfilm?"
15. Frank Sandau, "Der Teufel vom Mühlenberg," *Neues Deutschland* 14 Apr. 1955.
16. Giera, "Vom Kohlenmunk-Peter" 296.
17. Walter Schmitt qtd. in Wolf 182.
18. Sandau, "Der Teufel vom Mühlenberg," *Neues Deutschland* 14 Apr. 1955.
19. Münz 33.
20. Inside Kino.
21. König 90.

22. Schenk, *Das zweite Leben* 126; König 91.
23. Heimann 272–75.
24. Heimann 275; Schenk, *Eine kleine Geschichte* 108.
25. Heimann 353.
26. Heimann 336.
27. "Helmut Spieß"; "Wolfgang Schleif."
28. Elstermann, "Da lacht der Teppichknüpfer," *Berliner Zeitung* 20/21 Dec. 2003; B. Felsmann 73.
29. Feinstein 199.
30. Münz 39.
31. Zipes, *Breaking the Magic Spell* 155.
32. "'Das tapfere Schneiderlein' im DEFA-Kostüm," *National-Zeitung*, Berlin 28 Sept. 1956.
33. Kurt Bortfeldt, "Zu meinem Drehbuch: Das tapfere Schneiderlein," *Filmspiegel* 6, 1956.
34. Horst Knietzsch, "Die seltsame Mär vom Schneiderlein: Zu einem neuen Farbfilm für unsere Kinder," *Neues Deutschland* 3 Oct. 1956.
35. Knietzsch, "Die seltsame Mär"; Christoph Funke, "Das tapfere Schneiderlein—leicht frisiert: Ein DEFA-Märchenfilm unter der Regie von Helmut Spieß," *Der Morgen* 2 Oct. 1956.
36. Knietzsch, "Die seltsame Mär."
37. Knietzsch, "Die seltsame Mär."
38. Knietzsch, "Die seltsame Mär."
39. Günter Stahnke, "Das aktuelle Schneiderlein: Offene Worte zu einem neuen DEFA-Märchenfarbfilm," *Junge Welt* 5 Oct. 1956.
40. Häntzsche and Stock 26; Häntzsche, *Spiel- und Trickfilm* 53.
41. Münz 39.
42. Häntzsche, *Sozialistischer Kinderfilm* 216.
43. Beck, "Geschichte" 188.
44. Zipes, "Struggle" 167–206.
45. Kurt Bortfeldt, "Zu meinem Drehbuch," *Filmspiegel* 6, 1956.
46. See, e.g., "Das tapfere Schneiderlein," *Berliner Zeitung* 30 Sept. 1956.
47. Heimann 258.
48. Schenk, *Das zweite Leben* 133.
49. Schenk, *Eine kleine Geschichte* 116.
50. Allan, "DEFA: An Historical Overview" 10; Wiedemann, "DEFA-Kinderfilm" 23.
51. The German translation of "Der arme Hassan und Bey Machmud" is printed in Kabirow and Schachmatow 50–56. See Jelenski.
52. Dau, Haase, and Kliche 1414.
53. Shen, "Deconstructing Orientalism."
54. Berger and Giera 41; König 111; Shen, "DEFA *Märchenfilme*."
55. Feinstein 56.
56. Hohendahl 15.
57. Lunn 14.
58. Lunn 14–15.
59. Silberman, "Postmodernized Brecht?" 4.
60. Brooker 214.
61. Reinhold Grimm suggests that "epic" is more or less synonymous with the adjective "narrative," not "heroic" (40).

62. The parrot comes closest to resembling a magical helper that functions as "a comrade" with higher consciousness. The choice of a parrot, an animal that can imitate human speech, is interesting because the humanization of the bird is contrasted with Hassan's animalization.
63. Brechtian *Gestus* (translated as "gist," "gesture," or "attitude") is demonstrated in performance or in gestic acting, which evokes V-effects. "[Epic actors] would therefore demonstrate the social gest implicit in an action or event in such a way that its contradictory emotions and motives were situated or 'historicised.'" *Gestus* has social content attached to it and "allows conclusions to be drawn about the social circumstances" (Brooker 219–21). To see how Brechtian *Verfremdung* and *Gestus* are created, see Steinweg, especially 36–40.
64. See, e.g., Stephan Suschke's "Geniales Kind im Mörderhaus," which was written on the occasion of Ekkehard Schall's seventieth birthday.
65. Geschonneck, especially 181–86.
66. Silberman, "Brecht and Film" 213.
67. Byg, "Brecht" 222.
68. Uscha Geisler, *Forum*, Berlin, 11 Dec. 1958; see König 112.
69. Lunn 15.
70. Eddershaw 279.
71. Qtd. in Feinstein 71.
72. Christoph Funke, "Hassan befreit sich," *Der Morgen*, Berlin 26 Nov. 1958.
73. Rosemarie Rehan, *Wochenpost*, Berlin 50, 1958; see König 112.
74. Wolf 183.
75. Häntzsche, *Spiel- und Trickfilm* 56.
76. Wiedemann, "Erkundungen" 13.
77. "Dieses Neo-Biedermeier hat in unseren Filmen nichts zu suchen" (qtd. in Wolf 190).
78. König 118; Wolf 190.
79. Abusch 261–70.
80. "Links, rechts, die Geduld geht mir nun aus./Steig nur herab vom goldenen Thron./'Hol dir vom Teufel deinen Lohn.'/Sieh zu, sieh zu."
81. "The Tinderbox" in Andersen, *Complete Fairy Tales* 1-7, here 4.
82. König 117.
83. M. H., "Besuch im Film-Märchenland: Die DEFA dreht in Neu-Fahrland 'Das Feuerzeug,'" *Neues Deutschland* 21 Sept. 1958.
84. Helmut [sic] Häntzsche, *Deutsche Filmkunst* Berlin 7, 1959; see König 118.
85. Habel 169; Inside Kino.
86. Münz 112–15.
87. Morton, "The Golden Goose."
88. Beuchler; Münz, 114–15.
89. "Lach nicht, wenn du kannst: Von der ganz ersten Prinzessin in der 'Goldenen Gans,'" *Morgen* 31 May 1964.
90. Czygan, ". . . wie für Erwachsene, nur besser!"
91. Hake 92.
92. Simons 45–47; also see Münz 71–72.
93. Goeckel 211.
94. Czygan, ". . . wie für Erwachsene, nur besser!"
95. Feinstein 32.

96. Simons 45.
97. "Der kleine und der große Klaus."
98. C. M., "Kinderfilm," *Frankfurter Allgemeine* 14 Apr. 1972.
99. See "Little Red Riding Hood" in Bettelheim 66–181; Dundes; Zipes, "'Little Red Riding Hood.'"
100. Schlesinger, *Rotkäppchen* 7–8 and 28–34, "Farbdramaturgie," and "NS-Propaganda."
101. Friedrich, "Rotkäppchen auf der Leinwand" 346.
102. Häntzsche, *Spiel- und Trickfilm* 54.
103. Schwartz 3.
104. Schwartz 15.
105. Schwartz 52.
106. Schwartz 52.
107. Schwartz 45.
108. Heimann 25–26.
109. Wardetzky, "Grimms Märchen" 191.
110. "Perceptive Audience," *New York Herald Tribune* 12 Feb. 1952, qtd. in Wardetzky, "Grimms Märchen" 192.
111. Heimann 131.
112. See Friedrich, "Rotkäppchen auf der Leinwand"; Häntzsche, "Das Für und Wider."
113. Schwartz 29.
114. Schwartz 43.
115. A. K., "Rotkäppchen," *Sächsische Neueste Nachrichten*, Dresden 29 July 1962.
116. Häntzsche, *Sozialistischer Kinderfilm* 147–48.
117. Häntzsche, *Sozialistischer Kinderfilm* 1-26; Berger and Giera 50.
118. Häntzsche, *Sozialistischer Kinderfilm* 6.
119. Häntzsche, *Sozialistischer Kinderfilm* 6.
120. Häntzsche, *Sozialistischer Kinderfilm* 3.
121. Häntzsche, *Sozialistischer Kinderfilm* 4.
122. Friedrich, "Rotkäppchen auf der Leinwand" 346.
123. König 132.
124. Friedrich, "Rotkäppchen auf der Leinwand" 346.
125. Friedrich, "Rotkäppchen auf der Leinwand" 346.
126. Berger and Giera 381.
127. Baer, *Crumbling Walls and Tarnished Ideals*; Gaddis, *The Cold War: A New History*.
128. Heimann 9–11.

Chapter 3

1. Steinlein 98.
2. Gaddis 112–15.
3. Rubin 5; see also Nye.
4. Beck, "Geschichte" 201.
5. "Sleeping Beauty—Fritz Genschow."
6. However, according to Rosemary Creeser, "A careful search of the *Grimms' Tales* fails to reveal any story of the same name or with a direct connection to the film's plot. It can only be assumed that, having chosen to adopt several of the common themes and

motifs, the director Francesco Stefani and his co-writer Anne Geelhaer created a title for the film by juxtaposing fragments of the names of the *Grimms' Tales*—for example, *the Juniper Tree* and *The Singing, Soaring Lark*" (Creeser 123).

7. Häntzsche and Stock 26; Häntzsche, *Spiel- und Trickfilm* 53.
8. Münz 66.
9. Margot Schröder, "Das singende, klingende Bäumchen: Ein farbenprächtiger Märchenfilm der DEFA," *Junge Welt* 14 Dec. 1957; Tz., "Im Zaubergarten am Ende der Welt: Der DEFA-Märchenfilm 'Das singende, klingende Bäumchen,'" *Thühringer Tageblatt* 21 Dec. 1957; H. B., "Das singende, klingende Bäumchen: Ein Weihnachtsgeschenk für unsere Kleinen—ein neuer Märchenfilm der DEFA," *Bauern-Echo* 20 Dec. 1957; Wb., "Ein schönes Weihnachtsgeschenk auf der Leinwand: Der DEFA-Märchenfilm 'Das singende, klingende Bäumchen' läuft an," *Liberal-Demokratische Zeitung, Halle* 16 Dec. 1957; "Architekt Erich Zander zaubert: Phantastische Dekorationen für einen neuen Märchenfilm," *Der Morgen, Berlin* 5 July 1957.
10. O. B., "'Fuchs und Ingel' in der Kindervorstellung," *National-Zeitung* 27 Jan. 1959.
11. Ewald, "Zwei neue Kinderfilme der DEFA."
12. Schenk, "Jugendfilm in der DDR" 24.
13. König 109; Habel 553; Wiedemann, "Erkundungen" 12. Films criticized at the second film conference in July 1958 included Konrad Petzold's *Die Fahrt nach Bamsdorf* (1956), *Abenteuer in Bamsdorf* (1958), and Siegfried Hartmann's *Fiete im Netz* (1958).
14. "Eine gute Tat ist immer mächtiger als böser Zauber."
15. Charlotte Czygan, "Das singende klingende Bäumchen," *BZ am Abend* 17 Dec. 1957.
16. Ewald, "Zwei neue Kinderfilme der DEFA."
17. Czygan, "Das singende klingende Bäumchen."
18. Wolf 182.
19. Birgit Galle, "Und der Mond hängt da: DEFA-Erbe wieder im Kino: 'Das singende, klingende Bäumchen,'" *Berliner Zeitung* 25 Nov. 2000.
20. Ivanova, "DEFA and Eastern European Cinemas."
21. Heimann 313.
22. Heimann 302.
23. Heimann 141.
24. Heimann 233.
25. Heimann 301.
26. Heimann 310.
27. Häntzsche, *Spiel- und Trickfilm* 54.
28. Heimann 314.
29. K. B., "Unter Prinzen: 'Im Zauberreich des Berggeistes' im Capitol," *Telegraf*, Berlin, Westsektor 23 Sept. 1958; F. M., "Klingendes Bäumchen," *Der Tag*, Berlin, Westsektor 3 Oct. 1958; A. B., "Berggeist: 'Im Zauberreich des Berggeistes,'" *Berliner Morgenpost* 26 Sept. 1958; Sp., "Märchenstunde," *Der Abend*, Berlin, Westsektor 22 Sept. 1958; Ha., "Im Zauberreich des Berggeistes," *Der Tagesspiegel* 24 Sept. 1958; ra., "Im Zauberreich des Berggeistes," *Der Kurier*, Berlin, Westsektor 22 Sept. 1958.
30. Berghahn, "Ein Kultfilm zum Gruseln."
31. Wolf 160; cf. Beck, "Geschichte" 193, 197.
32. Gerda Kohlmey, *Deutsche Filmkunst*, Berlin 1, 1960; see König 109.

33. Petersdorf, "'König Drosselbart': Ein Kinderfilm der DEFA mit Manfred Krug," *Freiheit*, Halle 29 July 1965.
34. Holger Jancke, "König Drosselbart," *Die Tageszeitung* 30 Aug. 1991.
35. Habel 331.
36. Soldovieri, "Managing Stars."
37. Habel 180.
38. Münz 115.
39. M. Heide, "König Krug," *Neue Berliner Illustrierte* 4 Mar. 1965; G. S., "Die Prinzessin als Spielmannsfrau: DEFA-Märchenfilm 'König Drosselbart' in prominenter Besetzung," *Neue Zeit* 30 July 1965; Petersdorf, "'König Drosselbart'"; H. R., "Manfred Krug als 'König Drosselbart.'" *Bauernecho: Organ der demokratischen Bauernpartei Deutschlands* 18 Aug. 1965.
40. Soldovieri, "Managing Stars" and "The Politics of the Popular"; Heiduschke 4, 27–30.
41. G. S., "Die Prinzessin als Spielmannsfrau," *Neue Zeit* 30 July 1965.
42. Kai, "'Manne' als Spielmann: Krug im Kinderfilm 'König Drosselbart,'" *Mitteldeutsche Neueste Nachrichten*, Halle 28 Aug. 1965.
43. G. S., "Die gebändigte Prinzessin," *Neue Zeit* 20 Dec. 1964.
44. M. H., "König Drosselbart," *Berliner Zeitung* 29 July 1965.
45. Qtd. in "'König Drosselbart' erlebt," *Märkische Volksstimme*, Potsdam 28 May 1965; G. S., "Die gebändigte Prinzessin," *Neue Zeit* 20 Dec. 1964; Münz 121; Berger and Giera 58–59.
46. Beck, "Geschichte" 195.
47. Feinstein 176–93.
48. Rust, *Film-Dienst* 18 (1991).
49. "Wer überreich wird ohne Sinn/Und gibt dem Hochmut dann sich hin/Weil er so reich, der wird auch unerträglich/Zu reich und auch zu arm betören täglich bei vielen Menschen den Verstand/Weil großer Reichtum Zucht verschlingt/Und Armut um Besinnung bringt/Wird beides rechtens schlecht genannt."
50. Agde, "Zur Anatomie eines Testes."
51. Zipes, "Fate of Spinning" 584 and "Rumpelstiltskin" especially 61–66.
52. Bottigheimer, "Spinning and Discontent," in *Grimms' Bad Girls & Bold Boys* 112–22.
53. Zipes, "Rumpelstiltskin."
54. Tatar, *Hard Facts* 123.
55. Yolen, "Granny Rumple."
56. See Professor D. L. Ashliman's website.
57. This live action film was DEFA's first attempt at adapting a theater piece, in this case a children's play performed by the same ensemble at the Hans-Otto Theater in Potsdam. Because of its origin as a stage performance, the film's style was not consistent and reminded viewers of dialogues and decorations in the play. Reviews also observed that DEFA had produced a silhouette film of *Rumpelstiltskin* in which the dwarf tears himself into two halves. See Gö., "Das Märchen vom Rumpelstilzchen," *Bauernecho* 13 Aug. 1960; Os., "Perlen, Gold und bunte Steine: Zwei neue Kinderfilmprogramme in unseren Lichtspieltheatern," *Der Morgen*, Potsdam 20 Aug. 1960; "'Das Zaubermännchen,'" *BZ am Abend*, 12 Aug. 1960;; Czygan, "Realität und Märchen"; Habel 704; Münz 78; Wolf 184.
58. Hobsch 5.
59. Wolf 68.

60. Hobsch 13; Wolf 68.
61. Schlesinger, "NS-Propaganda."
62. "Zuviel Pech für die Marie? Kinder diskutierten über DEFA-Film 'Frau Holle,'" *Der Morgen* 12 Jan. 1964.
63. The same article was printed in "Zuviel Pech für die Marie?"; "Kinder testen 'ihre' Filme: Eine begrüßenswerte Einrichtung des Nationalen Zentrums für Kinderfilme," *Märkische Union*, Potsdam 28 Jan. 1964; "Kinder urteilen über Kinderfilme," *Der Demokrat*, Schwerin 20 Jan. 1964; "Erwachsene durften nur zuhören: Kinder diskutierten über DEFA-Kinderfilm," *Thüringer Tageblatt*, Weimar 16 Jan. 1964; "Kinderfilm-Diskussion: Das Nationale Zentrum für Kinderfilm der DDR hat immer Gäste," *Lausitzer Rundschau*, Cottbus 14 Jan. 1964.
64. "Frau Holle," *Der Morgen*, Berlin 20 Oct. 1963.
65. König 142.
66. For early feminist criticism of Disney's *Snow White and the Seven Dwarfs* as asserting traditional gender roles and sexist labor division, see Zipes's "Breaking the Disney Spell"; also see Stone, "Things Walt Disney Never Told Us"; Liebermann.
67. Zipes, *Enchanted Screen* 115–33; Gilbert and Gubar.
68. Tatar, *Hard Facts* 144.
69. Tatar, *Hard Facts* 139–40.
70. Tatar, *Hard Facts* 148.
71. Bottigheimer, "Prohibitions, Transgressions, and Punishments," in *Grimms' Bad Girls & Bold Boys* 81–94.
72. Bastian 186f. Bastian quotes from an article in *Tagesspiegel* 7 Feb. 1947 (qtd. in Steinlein 104, note 1).
73. Steinlein 97.
74. Richthofen qtd. in Blessing, "Happily Socialist Ever After?" 240.
75. E.g., in *King Thrushbeard, Briar Rose, The Swapped Queen, The Frog King, Iron Hans, Rapunzel and the Magic of Tears*, and *The Story of the Goose Princess and Her Loyal Horse Falada*.
76. Hake 95.
77. Zipes, *Fairy Tale as Myth* 90.
78. G. H., "Heiße Köpfe um das 'kalte Herz,'" *National-Zeitung* 16 Jan. 1951.
79. "Das Märchen von Schneewittchen," *Berliner Zeitung* 12 Oct. 1961.
80. Häntzsche and Stock 115.
81. Stone, "Feminist Approaches to Interpretation" 231.
82. McGlathery, "Fetching Maidens and True Brides" 137–38.
83. Yolen, "America's Cinderella" 303.
84. Margit Voss, "Ein Märchen als poetische Liebesgeschichte," *Filmspiegel*, Berlin 8 May 1974.
85. Voss, "Ein Märchen als poetische Liebesgeschichte."
86. Münz 148–51.
87. König 191.
88. Schiller, "DEFA-Stiftung *Newsletter*."
89. Heiduschke 38–39. See the fan site: "Drei Haselnüsse für Aschenbrödel."
90. Bottigheimer 112–22; Tatar, *Hard Facts* 106–33.
91. Wilhelm Grimm moved the adjective "nasty" from describing spinning to describing women who do not like to spin. See Bottigheimer 116.
92. H. H., "Ein Märchen in realer Welt," *Brandenburgische Neueste Nachrichten* 14 Apr. 1971.

93. Shen, "From Jacob Grimm to GDR 'Witches.'"
94. H. H., "Ein Märchen in realer Welt."
95. "Der König stürzt uns alle ins Elend. Er verdirbt Leute und Land. Der König soll verflucht sein. . . . Der König soll vertilgt werden."
96. H. H., "Ein Märchen in realer Welt."
97. Häntzsche and Stock 105.
98. "Wer von einer Spindel weiß, die ein anderer in seinem Hause hat oder außerhalb seines Hauses versteckt, muss das so gleich anzeigen oder auch er ist des Todes."
99. I thank one of the peer reviewers for pointing this out.
100. Despite his small role, Schwarz—whose debut film *Ich war neunzehn* (I Was Nineteen, Konrad Wolf, 1968) made him famous—warrants mentioning in the title of a review: "Jaecki Schwarz im 'Dornröschen'-Film" (*Junge Welt* 6 Aug. 1970) alluding again to the star culture in the GDR. Schwarz starred in other fairy-tale films, such as *The Blue Light* (1976), *Die klugen Dinge* (The Clever Things, Rainer Hausdorf, 1973), and *Die zertanzten Schuhe* (The Worn-Out Dancing Shoes, Ursula Schmenger, 1977).
101. H. H., "Ein Märchen in realer Welt," *Brandenburgische Neueste Nachrichten* 14 Apr. 1971.
102. Bettelheim 245. Whereas Cordelia dies in Shakespeare's tragedy *King Lear*, the fairy-tale heroine becomes a Cinderella figure and only temporarily loses her royal status, as befitting the fairy-tale convention.
103. Margitta Fahr, "Ein merkwürdiger Teufelspakt," *Film und Fernsehen* Nov. 1986.
104. Tom, "Der Bärenhäuter," *Sächsische Neueste Nachrichten*, Dresden 25 Jan. 1986.
105. *Land und Forst* 10 Jan. 1954 qtd. in König 85.
106. Fahr, "Ein merkwürdiger Teufelspakt"; Alex Geiß, "Christoffels Wette mit dem Teufel: Zum DEFA-Film 'Der Bärenhäuter' nach den Grimms von Walter Beck," *Brandenburgische Neueste Nachrichten* 12 Mar. 1986.
107. Birgit Höppner, "Der Bärenhäuter," *Sächsische Zeitung* 31 Jan. 1986.
108. He once would have slept in bed all night and would have violated his covenant with the devil had he not been rolled out of bed onto his bearskin by someone trying to steal his money. Then he would have bathed himself in prison had not the goldsmith been thrown into prison at the right moment.
109. Kramer, in Allan and Sandford 131–45.

Chapter 4

1. Schittly 164–273.
2. Wardetzky, "Grimms Märchen" 193.
3. Zipes, *Enchanted Screen* 321–48.
4. Schönemann 80.
5. Wardetzky, "Sklavensprache" 184.
6. Christoph Hein qtd. in Wardetzky, "Sklavensprache" 179–80.
7. Wardetzky, "Sklavensprache" 191–92.
8. Schittly 315.
9. Berghahn, *Hollywood behind the Wall* 98–133.
10. Simon 98; König 167; Habel 692–93; Andre Simonovieso, "Kein Kindermärchen: Im Märchenfilm 'Sechse kommen durch die Welt' versteckte der nicht linientreue Regisseur Rainer Simon Kritik an der Gesellschaft," *TIP* 26, 1991.

11. König 167; Habel 692–93.
12. Hindemith 28.
13. Schenk, "Das Kleid."
14. Wiedemann, "Erkundungen" 14; Habel 531.
15. Rust, *Film-Dienst* 18 (1991).
16. Zipes, *Enchanted Screen* 347.
17. Schenk, "Das Kleid"; Heinz Kersten, "Märchen von der ummauerten Stadt: Konrad Petzolds DEFA-Film 'Das Kleid' nach dreißigjährigem Verbot uraufgeführt," *Tagesspiegel* 19 May 1991.
18. "Das ist die Mauer, die quer durchgeht. Dahinter liegt die Stadt und das Glück."
19. Schenk, "Das Kleid."
20. Günther and Schenk 54.
21. Gaddis 137.
22. Wardetzky, "Sklavensprache" 180.
23. Richter 205.
24. Schittly 209.
25. "Das Kleid," BArch DR 1-Z/549; Ralf Schenk, "Feuer im Bierbauch," *Berliner Zeitung* 3 Nov. 2005.
26. Kersten, "Märchen von der ummauerten Stadt," *Tagesspiegel* 19 May 1991.
27. Dennis 65–72; Feinstein 34.
28. "Ein Kleid möcht' ich, vor dessen Anblick jede Kreatur in die Knie geht. Ein Kleid bei dessen Anblick Lippen zittern und Augenbrauen zucken. Ein Kleid, daß du Posaunen schmettern hörst und auf Anhieb bereit bist, Vater und Mutter zu verraten—dich selbst nicht mehr kennst. Du möchtest mich um Verzeihung bitten, daß du überhaupt noch lebst. Wer mich sieht in diesem Kleid, kann sich nur mit Gewalt zurückhalten vor dem Schrei: Er ist's, der Unüberwindliche!" This passage also appears in E. Kiessling, "Das Kleid," *Leipziger Volkszeitung* 1 Oct. 1961.
29. "Ich sehe schon Angst in den armseligen Gesichtern. Keiner von euch wird den Stoff sehen. Morgen wird es sich herausstellen, wer ein Versager ist."
30. "Das ist ein ungewöhnlicher Tag. Verlasst ihr euch darauf. . . . In eurer Haut möchte ich nicht stecken."
31. Frau Frisch: "Die haben gar keinen Stoff; das sind Schwindler. Haben Sie gesehen, wie die Diener gegrient haben? Wir müssen das sofort dem Kaiser melden!" Gerd E. Schäfer: "Wozu! Lieben Sie den Kaiser so sehr? Denken Sie an gestern abend und die platzenden Ballons. Und jetzt sollen wir Max vor dem Platzen bewahren?" (noa. "Hoffentlich eine echte Filmkomödie: DEFA dreht 'Das Kleid' nach einem Motiv von Andersen," *Ostsee-Zeitung* 3 June 1961); "Filmkomödie mit Ambitionen: 'Das Kleid,'" *Berliner Zeitung* 18 June 1961.
32. Schenk, "Das Kleid."
33. "In der Stadt redet man herum, die zwei Weberburschen haben überhaupt keinen Stoff gewebt."
34. "Vielleicht bräuchten Sie eine Nummer größer?"
35. "Die Bevölkerung wird ausgewiesen."
36. Brecht, "Buckow Elegies" 440. "Wäre es da/Nicht doch einfacher, die Regierung/Löste das Volk auf und/Wählte ein anderes?" (Brecht, "Die Lösung").

37. "In a dream last night/I saw a great storm./It seized the scaffolding/It tore the cross-clasps/The iron ones, down./But what was made of wood/Swayed and remained" (Brecht, "Buckow Elegies" 442).
38. Grimm 45.
39. Grimm 45; Kellner 283.
40. Dennis 86; Hake 100.
41. Günther and Schenk 56.
42. "Die Ärmeren der Stadt zeigten sich verhärtet."
43. "Wer kämpft um das Stück Brot, das ihm vorenthalten wird, rechne mit grausamen Gegnern und fast hoffnungslosen Lagen."
44. "An diesem gewöhnlichen Tage erschüttern zwei Habenichtse die Plattform eines Staates. Es ist bekannt, wie weit so etwas mit der Zeit gehen kann."
45. Mueller 78; Brady 304; Schoeps 71; Silberman, "Brecht and Film" 202.
46. Kleber 6.
47. Kersten, "Märchen von der ummauerten Stadt," *Tagesspiegel* 19 May 1991.
48. Kersten, *So viele Träume* 349.
49. Volk, "Mit Kraft und Verve. Die Mimin hinter der Figur: Eva-Maria Hagen."
50. Volk, "Mit Kraft und Verve."
51. noa, "Hoffentlich eine echte Filmkomödie," *Ostsee-Zeitung* 3 June 1961; "Filmkomödie mit Ambitionen: 'Das Kleid,'" *Berliner Zeitung* 18 June 1961; E. Kiessling, "Das Kleid," *Leipziger Volkszeitung* 1 Oct. 1961.
52. noa, "Hoffentlich eine echte Filmkomödie."
53. "Das Kleid," BArch DR 1-Z/549.
54. E. Kiessling, "Das Kleid," *Leipziger Volkszeitung* 1 Oct. 1961.
55. "Das Kleid," BArch DR 1-Z/549; my emphasis.
56. "Das Kleid," BArch DR 1-Z/549.
57. Richter 161.
58. "In der Sklavensprache erzählt: Immer noch nicht im Kino: Der Defa-Film 'Das Kleid,'" *Neue Zeit* 3 May 1991; Kersten, *So viele Träume* 348–50.
59. Günther and Schenk 54.
60. Günther and Schenk 54.
61. Wiedemann, "Erkundungen" 13.
62. "In der Sklavensprache erzählt"; Kersten, "Märchen von der ummauerten Stadt," *Tagesspiegel* 19 May 1991.
63. Kersten, "Märchen von der ummauerten Stadt."
64. Frank-Burkhard Habel, "Das Kleid," *Filmkurier* 2, 1991.
65. Richter 161.
66. "Das Kleid," BArch DR 1-Z/549; my emphasis.
67. Schenk, "Ein Meister" 14.
68. Schenk, "Ein indisches Abenteuer."
69. E.g., *Mir nach, Canaillen!* (Ralf Kirsten, 1964) and *Hauptmann Florian von der Mühle* (Werner W. Wallroth, 1969).
70. E.g., *Abenteuer des Werner Holt* (Joachim Kunert, 1964/1965), *Ich war neunzehn* (Konrad Wolf, 1968), and *Die Fahne von Kriwoi Rog* (Kurt Maetzig, 1969).
71. Wiedemann, "Erkundungen" 14; Torner, "The Red and the Black" and "DEFA 'Indianerfilm.'"
72. "Altes Märchen modern erzählt," *Die Union*, Dresden 15 Dec. 1968.

73. Häntzsche, *Sozialistischer Kinderfilm* 207–8.
74. "Die kluge Bauerntochter."
75. Richter-de Vroe 21–22.
76. Erika Gromnica, "Ein neuer DEFA-Märchenfilm," *Berliner Zeitung* 26 Jan. 1969; Klaus Meyer, "Spielfilm," *Sonntag* 13 Apr. 1969.
77. Heinz Hofmann, "Ein Film für die ganze Familie," *Märkische Volksstimme,* Potsdam 17 Apr. 1969.
78. "Altes Märchen modern erzählt," *Die Union,* Dresden 15 Dec. 1968; "Keine Märchenehe," *Neue Berliner Illustrierte* 3 Dec. 1968.
79. "Keine Märchenehe," *Neue Berliner Illustrierte* 3 Dec. 1968.
80. Simon 95.
81. He fines his marshal (Peter Dommisch) for killing a peasant's goat but keeps half of the fine for himself. He also rules that after his tax collector (Gerd E. Schäfer) was publicly humiliated he does not have to return the eggs he stole from the peasant women.
82. "Die Bauern und Ochsenknechte, was verstehen die von Recht und Gerechtigkeit?"
83. "Märchenfilm," *Neues Deutschland* 12 Aug. 1968.
84. Jahrow, "Stellungnahme zur staatlichen Zulassung des DEFA-Spielfilmes 'Wie heiratet man einen König,'" in "Wie heiratet man einen König," BArch DR 1-Z/280.
85. Simon 98; König 167; Habel 692–93; Simonovieso, "Kein Kindermärchen," *TIP* 26, 1991.
86. Simon 97–98; Habbema qtd. in Münz 133; see also Wolf 157 about *Prädikatisierung.*
87. Simon 91.
88. Simon 98; König 167.
89. König 168; Habel 692–93.
90. Simon 93–94.
91. Jahrow, "Stellungnahme zur staatlichen Zulassung des DEFA-Spielfilmes 'Wie heiratet man einen König,'" in "Wie heiratet man einen König," BArch DR 1-Z/280.
92. "Altes Märchen modern erzählt," *Die Union,* Dresden 15 Dec. 1968.
93. Powell 225.
94. M. H., "Die Kluge kommt aus Holland," *Der Morgen* 22 Dec. 1968.
95. Simon 94.
96. "Wie heiratet man einen König," BArch DR 1-Z/280.
97. König 167.
98. "Wie heiratet man einen König," BArch DR 1-Z/280.
99. Habel 693; Simon 94.
100. Yvonne Merin, "Niederlage eines Königs: Die kluge Bäuerin," *Norddeutsche Neueste Nachrichten,* Rostock 1 Feb. 1969.
101. Erika Gromnica, "Ein neuer DEFA-Märchenfilm," *Berliner Zeitung* 26 Jan. 1969.
102. Horst Knietzsch, "Zähmung eines Königs: Premiere des DEFA-Film 'Wie heiratet man einen König?'" *Neues Deutschland* 13 Mar. 1969.
103. Simon 99.
104. Simon 99.
105. Kersten, *So viele Träume* 28–29.
106. Knietzsch, "Die seltsame Mär," *Neues Deutschland* 3 Oct. 1956.
107. Hans Lücke, "Morgen DEFA-Premiere 'Wie heiratet man einen König': Märchen aufgefrischt," *BZ am Abend* 1 Mar. 1969.

108. M. Jelensk, "Auf der Leinwand: Wie heiratet man einen König?" *Berliner Zeitung* 11 Mar. 1969.
109. Simon 111.
110. Simon 111.
111. Simonovieso, "Kein Kindermärchen," *TIP* 26, 1991.
112. Simon 123.
113. Wiedemann, "Erkundungen" 14.
114. Habel 531.
115. Münz 145.
116. Zipes, *Breaking the Magic Spell* 38.
117. "Ein neuer Märchenfilm der DEFA: 'Sechse kommen durch die ganze Welt,'" *Märkische Volksstimme*, Potsdam 7 Mar. 1972.
118. Hans-Jörg Rother, "Wider Könige und Cliquen: Die neue Lesart eines Märchens/ Zum DEFA-Film 'Sechse kommen durch die Welt,'" *Forum* Oct. 1972; K. J. Wendlandt, "Eine eigenwillige, phantasievolle Märchengroteske," *Neues Deutschland* 20 Aug. 1972.
119. "Zwanzig Pfund habe ich abgenommen."
120. "Mein Fiedel ist mächtiger als König."
121. Agde, "Zur Anatomie eines Testes."
122. "'Wie steht in unserem Land die Ordnung/Welche Schande, daß selbst die Mücke regiert wird/Oh weh, dir Welt, wie schlimm du stehst'" (Simonovieso, "Kein Kindermärchen," *TIP* 26, 1991); Simon 127–28.
123. Ehrentraut Novotny, "Der siegreichste König aller Zeiten wird besiegt: Neuer DEFA-Märchenfilm: 'Sechse kommen durch die Welt,'" *Berliner Zeitung* 24 Aug. 1972; Margit Voss, "Poesie mit Problemen: 'Sechse kommen durch die Welt,'" *Filmspiegel* 13 Sept. 1972.
124. Heinz Hofmann, "Märchen plus Satire: Eine interessanter Versuch für Jung und Alt: 'Sechse kommen durch die Welt'/Mit phantastischen Mitteln," *Thüringer Neueste Nachrichten*, Erfurt 2 Sept. 1972.
125. Simon 124.
126. Schenk, *Eine kleine Geschichte* 174.
127. Simon 123–24; Habel 532.
128. Simon 124; Habel 532; Simonovieso, "Kein Kindermärchen," *TIP* 26, 1991.
129. Simon 125–26.
130. Voss, "Poesie mit Problemen," *Filmspiegel* 13 Sept. 1972.
131. Baer 69.
132. Allan, "DEFA: An Historical Overview" 15.
133. Schittly 212.
134. "Geh zum Teufel und komm nicht unter die Augen." "Scher dich zum Teufel!"
135. Horst Knietzsch, "Keine Angst mehr vor den großen Teufeln," *Neues Deutschland* 6 Dec. 1977.
136. R. T., *Tagesspeigel* 9 Apr. 1982; see König 243.
137. Röcke 170–71.
138. Hanisch, "Clown mit Charakter."
139. "Ereignis Kino, Interview mit Egon Schlegel," *Film und Fernsehen* 2, 1981; my emphasis. Also qtd. in Hobsch 13.

140. Hermann Schirrmeister, "Zum Film-Märchen der DEFA für Kleine und Große—'Wer reißt denn gleich vorm Teufel aus': Reizvoll und abenteuerlich," *Tribüne* 8 Dec. 1977.
141. Felsmann and Sahling 20–63.
142. Eli Rubin mentions the *Alltagshistoriker* (historians of everyday life), including Alf Lüdtke, Dorothee Wierling, Alexander von Plato, and Lutz Niethammer (5).
143. Ingeborg Zimmerling, *Filmspiegel*, Berlin 3, 1976; see König 219.
144. König 218.
145. Habel 78.
146. Berger and Giera 85.
147. Augustine 633–34.

Chapter 5

1. Wiedemann and Lohmann 43; Geiss McGee, "'Ich wollte ewig einen richtigen Film machen!'" 315; Steingroever, "On Fools and Clowns," "2 February 1988."
2. McGee, "Revolution in the Studio?" 446; Schieber 266; Schittly 236.
3. Schieber; McGee, "Revolution in the Studio?" 448ff, "'Ich wollte ewig einen richtigen Film machen!'"
4. Axel Geiß, "Christoffels Wette mit dem Teufel," *Brandenburgische Neueste Nachrichten* 12 Mar. 1986.
5. Feinstein 250–52; Schittly 237.
6. Herminghouse 4.
7. See, e.g., Hohendahl; Herminghouse; Heukenkamp; Philpotts and Rolle.
8. Rowe 210.
9. Lieberman 197.
10. Schittly 257–60.
11. Martens 11.
12. Gaddis 195–236.
13. Schittly 240.
14. Cordell 52.
15. Behrend, "The Rise and Fall of the East German Civil Rights Movement."
16. DeBardeleben, "'The Future Has Already Begun': Environmental Damage and Protection in the GDR."
17. Berger and Giera 109.
18. Gudrun Skulski, "Dem Niemandsland entrückt: Nach dem Märchen der Brüder Grimm dreht Wolfgang Hübner 'Gevatter Tod,'" *Neue Zeit* 20 Nov. 1980.
19. Schittly 184–85.
20. Berger and Giera 109.
21. "Gevatter Tod."
22. G. Krug, "Der Gevatter Tod: Interessanter Fernsehfilm jetzt im Kino," *Der Morgen* 2/3 Jan. 1982; Eva Buch, "Sinnlicher Spaß—Erkenntnisgewinn: 'Gevatter Tod' im Fernsehen," *Märkische Volksstimme* 30 Dec. 1980; Skulski, "Dem Niemandsland entrückt," *Neue Zeit* 20 Nov. 1980.
23. "Keine Angst, mein Junge, wie es den Wind gibt und den Schall, und der Rauch von unten nach oben steigt, so gibt's mich."

24. "Minerale verwittern. Das Gras verdorrt, und die Blüten fallen ab. Tiere verwesen. Warum wollt ihr Menschen Ausnahmen sein?"
25. "Gebrauch dein Leben, Mädchen—Lebe! Und lebe wohl!"
26. "Gevatter Tod."
27. "Gevatter Tod."
28. G. Krug, "Der Gevatter Tod," *Der Morgen* 2/3 Jan. 1982.
29. McGlathery, *E. T. A. Hoffmann* 30–31.
30. Ivanova, "DEFA and Eastern European Cinemas."
31. "Zauber um Zinnober."
32. McGlathery, *E. T. A. Hoffmann* 123.
33. Fühmann 174. According to McGlathery (*E. T. A. Hoffmann* 170, note 13), "An analysis from the standpoint of social and political history as interpreted by Marxist theory was made by Jürgen Walter." Walter argued that the tale was "a reflection of the political powerlessness . . . experienced by a large part of the middle-class intelligentsia in Germany around 1815" (44). For an interpretation of the tale as a depiction of negative effects of the Enlightenment on man and society, see Kesselmann.
34. "Zauber um Zinnober."
35. Behringer, *Witches and Witch-Hunts*.
36. Hoffmann, *Little Zaches, Great Zinnober* 12–13.
37. "Zauber um Zinnober."
38. Gisela Hoyer, "Ein Märchen voller Magie und Dialektik: Phantastischer 'Zauber um Zinnober' auf dem Bildschirm," *Der Morgen* 27 Dec. 1983; Heinz Hofmann, "Schöne Lebenslust: Vergnügliche Nachdenklichkeit im Kinderfernsehen," *National-Zeitung*, Berlin 30 Dec. 1983.
39. Hanspach, "Vorzug und Wagnis einer Literaturadaption: Der lebendige Klein Zaches," *Deutsche Lehrerzeitung* 2 Dec. 1983.
40. Hanspach, "Vorzug und Wagnis."
41. "Zauber um Zinnober" 66.
42. Ohm, "Introduction."
43. Ohm xv.
44. Heinz Kersten, "Bettina von Arnims Märchenroman: . . . wiederentdeckt für einen DEFA-Jugendfilm: 'Gritta vom Rattenschloß,'" *Frankfurter Rundschau* 12 Sept. 1986.
45. Based on a letter to me from the author dated 26 Nov. 2013. The single edition she mentioned is von Arnim, *Gritta von Rattenzuhausbeiuns: ein Märchenroman*. Berlin: Kinderbuchverlag, 1968.
46. Heinz Kersten, "Wiederentdeckte Romantik: Eine Bettina-von-Arnim-Verfilmung aus Babelsberg," *Der Tagesspiegel* 31 Mar. 1985.
47. Arnim, *Life of High Countess* 136.
48. Restricted by the length limit, the film omits numerous episodes from the long novel, such as the tale of the Amazon-like ancestor—Lady Orsina Sylvia—the story of the abused Harmony whom Gritta rescues, the entire episode about the abduction of the girls by a ship captain engaging in human trafficking, the fantastic stories of the Butterfly People and the isle of shadows that a sailor tells the girls, and the girls' own cloister in the forest. The film traces Gritta from her home to the convent and then to the forest and on to the palace. Except for the rat king, which wears a diamond earring and can speak, the film adheres to realistic

storytelling and leaves out numerous supernatural occurrences contained in the original novel.

49. Based on a letter to me from the author dated 26 Nov. 2013.
50. Arnim, *Life of High Countess* 152.
51. Arnim, *Life of High Countess* 145.
52. Arnim, *Life of High Countess* 152.
53. "Ach, ist es nötig dann, dass ich dich lassen kann/Habe dich von Herzen lieb/das glaube mir/du hast das Herzelein so ganz genommen, nein/dass ich keinen anderen lieb als dich allein."
54. "Für dich, unser neuer Turmbläser."
55. Peter: "Du wirst mich vergessen."
    Gritta: "Im ganzen Leben nicht."
56. Blessing, "Happily Socialist Ever After?" 244.
57. Arnim, *Life of High Countess* 152.
58. "eine Niete, ein Trödelfritze, ein Versager, eine trübe Tasse, ein Pflaumenaugust."
59. Gritta: "Du bist wie Müffert. Wir müssen gehorsam sein. Gott will es so. Mit dir kann man die Welt auch nicht verändern."
    Peter: "Kinder können die Welt nicht verändern. Wir wissen viel zu wenig von der Welt."
    Gritta: "Vielleicht gerade deshalb. Die Erwachsen haben schon an alles gewöhnt. Und auch alles Böse und Schlechte."
60. Kersten, "Bettina von Arnims Märchenroman," *Frankfurter Rundschau* 12 Sept. 1986.
61. Jochen Wisotzki, "Gritta von Rattenzuhausbeiuns: Märchen ohne Feenzauber," *Film und Fernsehen* June 1985; my emphasis.
62. Horst Knietzsch, "Realistische Sicht in einem phantastischen Gewand," *Neues Deutschland* 19 Mar. 1985.
63. Hans-Dieter Tok, "Anmutig und keß," *Wochenpost* 29 Mar. 1985.
64. Mendelson, "Forever Acting Alone."
65. He was the cinematographer for *Die Legende von Paul und Paula* (Heiner Carow, 1973) and *Die Verlobte* (The Fiancée, Günther Rücker and Günter Reisch, 1979/1980). His debut film was *Pugowitza* (1980). After the slated director of *Gritta* dropped the project. Brauer insisted on continuing with it and he took on the task as the director for *Gritta* (see Berger and Giera 374).
66. Hans-Dieter Tok, "Anmutig und keß," *Wochenpost* 29 Mar. 1985; Stefan Senefeld, "Gritta von Rattenzuhausbeiuns: Romantischer Märchenfilm der DEFA von Jürgen Brauer," *Sonntag* 7 Apr. 1985.
67. Münz 216–17.
68. Habel 220; Schittly 221; McGee, "Revolution in the Studio?" 448.
69. Irma Zimm, "Die kleine Gräfin mit der großen Courage: 'Gritta von Rattenzuhausbeiuns' (DEFA)," *BZ am Abend* 15 Mar. 1985.
70. Kersten, "Bettina von Arnims Märchenroman," *Frankfurter Rundschau* 12 Sept. 1986.
71. Hübner, "Wechselspiegel"; Jochen Wisotzki, "Jorinde und Joringel: Fernsehfilm von Wolfgang Hübner und Wera und Claus Küchenmeister," *Sonntag* 30 Mar. 1986.
72. Bettelheim 284.
73. "Jorinde und Joringel."
74. Hübner, "Wechselspiegel"; Jochen Wisotzki, "Jorinde und Joringel," *Sonntag* 30 Mar. 1986.
75. "Jorinde und Joringel."

76. J. Rommel, "Mit Jorinde und Joringel barfuß durchs Gras: Drehstab des DDR-Fernsehens zu Aufnahmen in den Thühringer Bergen—100 Erfurter Mädchen vor der Kamera," *Thüringische Landeszeitung* 11 Sept. 1985; E. S., "Jorinde und Joringel," *Filmspiegel* 25, 1985, 8–9.
77. Beate Hanspach, "*Jorinde und Joringel*: Ein neuer Märchenfilm nach den Gebrüdern Grimm," *Deutsche Lehrerzeitung* 21 Feb. 1986; "Jorinde und Joringel."
78. Gerhard Neumann, "Ein neuer Fernseh-Märchenfilm für Kinder und für Erwachsene: 'Jorinde und Joringel' zum 200. Geburtstag von W. Grimm," *Freiheit,* Halle 28 Feb. 1988.
79. "Jorinde und Joringel."
80. "Neu verfilmt," *FF-Dabei* 20, 1986: 43; Renate Hassmann, "Jorinde und Joringel," *Lausitzer Rundschau* 28 Feb. 1986.
81. E. Schmidt, "Das Märchen und die vier Ebenen: 'Jorinde und Joringel' im Fernsehen," *Berliner Zeitung* 22–23 Feb. 1986.
82. Beatrix Langner, "Neue Kinderfilme: Eisenhans," *Kino DDR* 9, 1988.
83. Beatrix Langner, "Zucker und Schwert—ein Märchen zum Wecken: 'Der Eisenhans,'" *Film und Fernsehen* Nov. 1988.
84. Schieber 320; Schittly 312.
85. Norbert Tolsdorf, "Der unfaßbare 'Eisenhans,'" *Filmspiegel* 1, 1988.
86. Langner, "Neue Kinderfilme: Eisenhans," *Kino DDR* 9, 1988.
87. Zipes, *Fairy Tale as Myth* 109.
88. Langner, "Neue Kinderfilme: Eisenhans," *Kino DDR* 9, 1988.
89. Heinz Kersten, "Deutschland, ein Grimm-Märchen? Die DEFA-Märchenverfilmung 'Der Eisenhans' von Karl Heinz Lotz," *Tagesspiegel* 27 Nov. 1988.
90. Zipes, *Enchanted Screen* 347.
91. "Schmutz in die klaren Quellen und Feuer in die Wälder."
92. Langner, "Neue Kinderfilme: Eisenhans," *Kino DDR* 9, 1988.
93. Günther Eiben, "Grüner Anfang—graues Ende: 'Eisenhans,'" *Filmspiegel* 22, 1988.
94. Tolsdorf, "Der unfaßbare 'Eisenhans,'" *Filmspiegel* 1, 1988.
95. König 191.
96. "Neue Kinderfilme: 'Die Geschichte von der Gänseprinzessin und ihrem treuen Pferd Falada,'" *Kino DDR* 2, 1989.
97. "Neue Kinderfilme: Die Geschichte von der Gänseprinzessin," *Kino DDR* 2, 1989.
98. "Der Krieg ist unseres Lebens ärgster Feind."
99. Häntzsche, *Sozialistischer Kinderfilm* 216–17.
100. "Neue Kinderfilme: Die Geschichte von der Gänseprinzessin," *Kino DDR* 2, 1989.; my emphasis.

Conclusion

1. McAra and Calvin 3.
2. McAra and Calvin 13.
3. Trumpener, *Divided Screen.*
4. The dwarf says to the soldier, "Der Mensch kann nur das, was er sich selber zutraut."
5. Bathrick, "From UFA to DEFA" 170.
6. Murdoch 164–72.

7. Dahl, in Tatar 21–22.
8. Schieber 320.
9. This book does not discuss Bodo Fürneisen's *Die Geschichte vom goldenen Taler* (1985), which is based on a novella by Hans Fallada, because it focusses on adaptations of classic tales.

FILMOGRAPHY

Note: The DEFA fairy-tale films listed in the Appendix are not included in this Filmography.

Algar, James. Dir. *Die Wüste lebt* [The Living Desert]. 1953. Walt Disney film.

———. Dir. *Wunder der Prärie* [The Vanishing Prairie]. 1954. Walt Disney film.

Allen, Rex, and Winston Hibler. Dir. *Der einsame Puma* [Charlie, the Lonesome Cougar]. 1968. Walt Disney film.

Báky, Josef von. Dir. *Münchhausen*. 1943.

Ballard, Carroll. Dir. *Wenn die Wölfe heulen* [Never Cry Wolf]. 1983. Walt Disney film.

Ballmann, Herbert. Dir. *Das geheimnisvolle Wrack* [The Mysterious Wreck]. 1954.

———. *Das Traumschiff* [The Dream Ship]. 1956.

———. *Tinko*. 1957.

Bergner, Wolfgang. Dir. *Die kluge Bauerntochter* [The Farmer's Clever Daughter]. 1961. Animated film.

Beyer, Frank. Dir. *Fünf Patronenhülsen* [Five Cartridges]. 1960.

———. *Spur der Steine* [Trace of Stones]. 1965.

Blatchford, Gary, Chris Doyle, Gerhard Hahn, and David Incorvala. Dirs. *Simsala Grimm*. Germany. Original Airing 1999. Television Series.

Brauer, Jürgen. Dir. *Pugowitza*. 1980.

Carow, Heiner. Dir. *Die Legende von Paul und Paula* [The Legend of Paul and Paula]. 1973.

———. *Die Russen kommen* [The Russians Are Coming]. 1968.

Cocteau, Jean. Dir. *La Belle et la Bête* [Beauty and the Beast]. 1946.

Courtland, Jerome. Dir. *Flucht des Pumas* [Run, Cougar, Run]. 1972. Walt Disney film.

Deppe, Hans. Dir. *Die Kuckucks* [The Cuckoos]. 1949.

———. *Schwarzwaldmädel* [The Black Forest Girl]. 1950.

Disney, Walt. "Puss in Boots." 1922 . Silent animated film.

Felsenstein, Walter. Dir. *Das schlaue Füchslein* [The Cunning Little Fox]. 1956. Musical.

Ferguson, Norm, Wilfred Jackson, et al. Dirs. *Dumbo the Flying Elephant*. 1941. Walt Disney animated film.

Fiedler, Franz. Dir. *Der kleine Muck: Ein Märchen für große und kleine Leute* [Little Mook: A Fairy Tale for Big and Small People]. 1944.

Foth, Jörg. Dir. *Biologie!* [Biology!]. 1990.

Fredersdorf, Herbert B. Dir. *Rumpelstilzchen* [Rumpelstiltskin]. 1955.

Fritsch, Gunter von. Dir. *Paka, die Polarbärin* [Snow Bear]. 1970. Walt Disney film.

Fürneisen, Bodo. Dir. *Die Geschichte vom goldenen Taler* [The Story of the Golden Coin]. 1985.

Ganiyev, Nabi. Dir. *The Adventures of Nasreddin*. 1947. USSR.

Genschow, Fritz. Dir. *Aschenputtel* [Cinderella]. 1955.

———. *Dornröschen* [Briar Rose]. 1955.

———. *Frau Holle* [Mother Hulda]. 1954.

Genschow, Fritz, and Renée Stobrawa. Dirs. *Rotkäppchen und der Wolf* [Little Red Riding Hood and the Wolf]. 1937.

Geronimi, Clyde, Hamilton Luske, and Wilfred Jackson. Dirs. *Cinderella*. 1950. Walt Disney animated film.

Geronimi, Clyde, Les Clark, Eric Larson, and Wolfgang Reitherman. Dirs. *Sleeping Beauty*. 1959. Walt Disney animated film.

Geronimi, Clyde, Wilfred Jackson, and Hamilton Luske. Dirs. *Alice in Wonderland*. 1951. Walt Disney animated film.

Günther, Egon. Dir. *Abschied* [Farewell]. 1968.

———. *Der Dritte* [Her Third]. 1971.

———. *Die Leiden des jungen Werthers* [The Sorrows of Young Werther]. 1976.

———. *Die Schlüssel* [The Keys]. 1973.

———. *Lotte in Weimar*. 1975.

———. *Stein*. 1991.

———. *Wenn du groß bist, lieber Adam* [When You Grow Up, Dear Adam]. 1965.

Gusner, Iris. Dir. *Alle meine Mädchen* [All My Girls]. 1980.

———. *Die Taube auf dem Dach* [The Dove on the Roof]. 1973.

———. *Wäre die Erde nicht rund* [Were the Earth Not Round]. 1981.

Hand, David, William Cottrell, Wilfred Jackson, Larry Morey, Perce Pearce, and Ben Sharpsteen. Dirs. *Snow White and the Seven Dwarfs*. 1937. Walt Disney animated film.

Harlan, Veit. Dir. *Jud Süß* [Jew Süss]. 1940.

Harnack, Falk. Dir. *Das Beil von Wandsbek* [The Axe of Wandsbek]. 1951.

Hartmann, Siegfried. Dir. *Fiete im Netz* [Fiete in a Net]. 1957.

———. Dir. *Hatifa*. 1960.

Haskin, Byron. Dir. *Die Schatzinsel* [Treasure Planet]. 1950. Walt Disney film.

Hausdorf, Rainer. Dir. *Die klugen Dinge* [The Clever Things]. 1973.

Heinrich, Hans. Dir. *Meine Frau macht Musik* [My Wife Makes Music]. 1958.

Hibler, Winston. Dir. *Lefty, der Luchs* [Lefty, the Dingaling Lynx]. 1971. Walt Disney film.

Janssen, Walter. Dir. *Rotkäppchen* [Little Red Riding Hood]. 1954.

Jugert, Rudolf. Dir. *König Drosselbart* [King Thrushbeard]. 1971.

Kagan, Jeremy. Dir. *Die Reise von Natty Gann* [The Journey of Natty Gann]. 1985. Walt Disney film.

Kahane, Peter. Dir. *Die Architekten* [The Architects]. 1990.
Kirsten, Ralf. Dir. *Auf der Sonnenseite* [On the Sunny Side]. 1962.
———. *Frau Venus und ihr Teufel* [Lady Venus and Her Devil]. 1967.
———. *Mir nach, Canaillen!* 1964.
Klein, Gerhard. Dir. *Berlin—Ecke Schönhauser* [Berlin—Schönhauser Corner]. 1957.
———. *Berlin um die Ecke* [Berlin around the Corner]. 1965.
Kobler, Erich. Dir. *Schneewittchen und die sieben Zwerge* [Snow White and the Seven Dwarfs]. 1955.
Kratzert, Hans. Dir. *Hans Röckle und der Teufel* [Hans Röckle and the Devil]. 1974.
Kunert, Joachim. Dir. *Abenteuer des Werner Holt* [The Adventures of Werner Holt]. 1964/1965.
Lamprecht, Gerhard. Dir. *Irgendwo in Berlin* [Somewhere in Berlin]. 1946.
Lang, Fritz. *Metropolis.* 1927.
Losansky, Rolf. Dir. *Abschiedsdisco* [Farewell Disco]. 1990.
———. *Ein Schneemann für Afrika* [A Snowman for Africa]. 1977.
Mach, Josef. Dir. *Die Söhne der großen Bärin* [The Sons of Great Bear]. 1966.
Maetzig, Kurt. Dir. *Die Fahne von Kriwoi Rog* [The Banner of Krivoy Rog]. 1969.
———. *Das Kaninchen bin ich* [The Rabbit Is Me]. 1965.
———. *Vergesst mir meine Traudel nicht* [Don't Forget My Little Traudel]. 1957.
Mailland, Jean Michaud. Dir. *Hamida.* 1966.
McEveety, Bernard. Dir. *Zwei in der Arktis* [Two Against the Arctic]. 1974. Walt Disney film.
McEveety, Vincent. Dir. *Die Million-Dollar-Ente* [The Million Dollar Duck]. 1971. Walt Disney film.
McLaglen, Andrew V. Dir. *Zwei Cowboys* [Trail of Danger]. 1977. Walt Disney film.
Menzel, Jirí. Dir. *Ostře sledované vlaky* [Closely Watched Trains]. 1966. Czechoslovakia.
———. *Skřivánci na niti* [Larks on a String]. 1969. Czechoslovakia.
Milestone, Lewis. Dir. *All Quiet on the Western Front.* 1930.
Orff, Carl. Dir. *Die Kluge* [The Clever Girl]. 1943. Opera.
Petzold, Konrad. Dir. *Abenteuer in Bamsdorf* [Adventure in Bamsdorf]. 1958.
———. *Die Fahrt nach Bamsdorf* [The Journey to Bamsdorf]. 1956.
Podehl, Peter. Dir. *Frau Holle—Das Märchen von Goldmarie und Pechmarie* [Mother Hulda—The Tale of Golden Mary and Pitch Mary]. 1961.
Pohl, Arthur. Dir. *Spielbank-Affäre* [Murder in the Casino]. 1957
Powell, Michael, and Emeric Pressburger. Dirs. *The Red Shoes.* 1948. Great Britain.
Prager, Wilhelm. Dir. *Der kleine Muck* [Little Mook]. 1921. Silent film.
Ptushko, Alexander. Dir. *Kamenny zwetok* [Die steinerne Blume/The Stone Flower]. 1946. USSR.
Remani, Ernesto. Dir. *Die Schönste* [The Most Beautiful]. 1957/2002.
Riefenstahl, Leni. Dir. *Das blaue Licht* [The Blue Light]. 1932.
Rou, Alexander. Dir. *Po shchuchemu veleniyu* [Der Zauberfisch/Wish upon a Pike]. 1938. USSR.
———. *Vasilisa prekrasnaya* [Die schöne Wassilissa/Vasilisa the Beautiful]. 1939. USSR.
Rücker, Günther, and Günter Reisch. Dirs. *Die Verlobte* [The Fiancée]. 1979/1980.
Ruttmann, Walter. Dir. *Berlin: Die Sinfonie der Großstadt* [Berlin: Symphony of a Metropolis]. 1927.
Sauer, Fred. Dir. *Das kalte Herz* [The Cold Heart]. 1923. Silent film.

Schlegel, Egon, and Dieter Roth. Dirs. *Ritter des Regens* [Rainbow Knights]. 1965. Incomplete film.

Schmidt, Evelyn. Dir. *Das Fahrrad* [The Bicycle]. 1982.

Schonger, Hubert. Dir. *Der standhafte Zinnsoldat* [The Steadfast Tin Soldier]. 1940.

Spieß, Helmut. Dir. *Hexen* [Witches]. 1954.

Staudte, Wolfgang. Dir. *Die Mörder sind unter uns* [The Murderers Are among Us]. 1946.

———. *Rotation*. 1949.

———. *Der Untertan* [The Kaiser's Lackey]. 1951.

Stevenson, Robert. Dir. *Insel am Ende der Welt* [The Island at the Top of the World]. 1974. Walt Disney film.

———. Dir. *Sein Freund Jello* [Old Yeller]. 1957. Walt Disney film.

Stöger, Alfred. Dir. *Tischlein deck dich, Esel streck dich, Knüppel aus dem Sack!* [The Magic Table, the Golden Donkey, and the Club in the Sack!]. 1938.

Stranka, Erwin. Dir. *Susanne und der Zauberring* [Susanne and the Magic Ring]. 1973.

Trousdale, Gary, and Kirk Wise. Dirs. *Beauty and the Beast*. 1991. Walt Disney animated film.

Verhoeven, Paul. Dir. *Das kleine Hofkonzert* [The Little Court Concert]. 1945.

Vogel, Frank. Dir. *Denk bloß nicht, ich heule* [Just Don't Think I Will Cry]. 1965.

Wallroth, Werner W. *Hauptmann Florian von der Mühle*. 1969.

Warneke, Lothar. Dir. *Die Beunruhigung* [Apprehension]. 1982.

Weiler, Kurt. Dir. *Das tapfere Schneiderlein* [The Brave Little Tailor]. 1964. Animated film.

Wenter, Adolf. Dir. *Das kalte Herz* [The Cold Heart]. 1923. Silent film.

Wilhelm, Hans F. Dir. *Der Teufel mit den drei goldenen Haaren* [The Devil's Three Golden Hairs]. 1955.

Wolf, Konrad. Dir. *Ich war neunzehn* [I Was Nineteen]. 1968.

———. *Solo Sunny*. 1980.

———. *Sonnensucher* [Sun Seekers]. 1958.

Wolff, Carl Heinz. Dir. *Schneewittchen und die sieben Zwerge* [Snow White and the Seven Dwarfs]. 1939.

York, Eugen. Dir. *Das Fräulein von Scudéri* [Mademoiselle de Scudéri]. 1955. East German and Swedish coproduction.

Zengerling, Alf. Dir. *Dornröschen* [Briar Rose]. 1936.

———. *Der Froschkönig* [The Frog King]. 1940.

———. *Der gestiefelte Kater* [Puss in Boots]. 1935.

———. *Der Hase und der Igel* [The Hare and the Hedgehog]. 1940.

———. *Rumpelstilzchen* [Rumpelstiltskin]. 1940.

Zschoche, Herrmann. Dir. *Bürgschaft für ein Jahr* [On Probation]. 1981.

———. *Liebe mit 16* [Their First Love]. 1974.

———. *Philipp, der Kleine* [Phillip the Small]. 1975.

———. *Sieben Sommersprossen* [Seven Freckles]. 1978.

———. *Und nächstes Jahr am Balaton* [And Next Year at the Balaton]. 1980.

Zuniga, Frank. Dir. *Die Spur der Antilope* [The Track of the African Bongo]. 1977. Walt Disney film.

WORKS CITED (SELECTED LIST)

Abusch, Alexander. "Aktuelle Probleme und Aufgaben unserer sozialistischen Filmkunst." *Deutsche Filmkunst* 9 (1958): 261–70.

Agde, Günter. "Zur Anatomie eines Testes: Das Gespräch Walter Ulbrichts mit Schriftstellern und Künstlern am 25. November 1965 im Staatsrat der DDR." *Kahlschlag: Das 11. Plenum des ZK der SED 1965: Studien und Dokumente.* By Agde. Berlin: Aufbau, 1991. 128–47.

Allan, Seán. "DEFA: An Historical Overview." *DEFA: East German Cinema.* Allan and Sandford 1–21.

———. "Ruptures and Continuities: DEFA, History and the Rise and Fall of the GDR." *Moving Images of East Germany.* Bgy and Betheny 35–55.

Allan, Seán, and Sebastian Heiduschke, eds. *Re-imagining DEFA. East German Cinema in Its National and Transnational Context.* New York: Berghahn. Forthcoming.

Allan, Seán, and John Sandford, eds. *DEFA: East German Cinema, 1946–1992.* New York: Berghahn, 1999.

Andersen, Hans Christian. *The Complete Fairy Tales and Stories.* Trans. Erik Christian Haugaard. Foreword by Virginia Haviland. Garden City, NY: Doubleday, 1974.

———. "Nightingale." *The Complete Andersen: All of the 168 Stories by Hans Christian Andersen.* Trans. and introd. Jean Hersholt. New York: Heritage, 1942. 167–77.

Arnim, Bettine von, and Gisela von Arnim Grimm. *Gritta von Rattenzuhausbeiuns: ein Märchenroman.* Berlin: Kinderbuchverlag, 1968.

———. *The Life of High Countess Gritta von Ratsinourhouse.* Trans. and introd. Lisa Ohm. Lincoln: U Nebraska P, 1999.

Ashliman, D. L. "Rumpelstilzchen von den Brüdern Grimm: Ein Vergleich der Fassungen von 1810, 1812 und 1819: zusammengestellt von D. L. Ashliman." 27 Dec. 1997. www.pitt.edu/~dash/rumpelstilzchen.html.

Augustine, Dolores L. "The Power Question in GDR History." *German Studies Review* 34.3 (2011): 633–52.

Baer, Hans A. *Crumbling Walls and Tarnished Ideals: An Ethnography of East Germany before and after Unification*. Lanham, MD: UP of America, 1998.

Balina, Marina. "Introduction (for Part II: Fairy Tales of Socialist Realism)." *Politicizing Magic: An Anthology of Russian and Soviet Fairy Tales*. Ed. Marina Balina, Helena Goscilo, and M. N. Lipovetsky. Evanston, IL: Northwestern UP, 2005. 105–21.

Bastian, Ulrike. *Die "Kinder- und Hausmärchen" der Brüder Grimm in der literaturpädagogischen Diskussion des 19. und 20. Jahrhunderts*. Frankfurt a. M., Germany: Haag + Herchen, 1981.

Bathrick, David. "From UFA to DEFA: Past as Present in Early GDR Films." *Contentious Memories: Looking Back at the GDR*. Ed. Jost Hermand and Marc Silberman. New York: Peter Lang, 1998. 169–85.

———. *The Powers of Speech: The Politics of Culture in the GDR*. Lincoln: U Nebraska P, 1995.

Bazhov, Pavel. *The Malachite Casket: Tales from the Urals*. Trans. Alan Moray Williams. London: Hutchinson, 1944.

Bechstein, Ludwig. "Der Hasenhüter und die Königstochter." *Sämtliche Märchen*. Munich, Germany: Winkler, 1968. 148–52.

———. "The Rabbit Catcher." *The Rabbit Catcher and Other Fairy Tales of Ludwig Bechstein*. Translated and Introduced by Randall Jarrell. New York: The MacMillan Company, 1962. 2–12.

Beck, Walter. "Märchenfilme und ihre Zeit." *Märchenspiegel* 1 (Nov. 2002): 23–25; 2 (Feb. 2003): 12–15; 3 (May 2003): 10–13.

———. "Zur Geschichte des DEFA-Märchenspielfilms für Kinder." *Hören, Lesen, Sehen, Spüren: Märchenrezeptionen im europäischen Vergleich*. Ed. Regina Bendix und Ulrich Marzolph. Baltmannsweiler, Germany: Schneider Verlag Hohengehren, 2008. 184–208.

Behrend, Hanna. "The Rise and Fall of the East German Civil Rights Movement." *New Politics* 6.3 (1997): n. pag. nova.wpunj.edu/newpolitics/issue23/behren23.htm.

Behrends, Jan C., Thomas Lindenberger, and Patrice G. Poutrus. *Fremde und Fremd-Sein in der DDR: Zu historischen Ursachen der Fremdenfeindlichkeit in Ostdeutschland*. Berlin: Metropol, 2003.

Behringer, Wolfgang. *Witches and Witch-Hunts: A Global History*. Cambridge, UK: Polity, 2004.

Berger, Eberhard, and Joachim Giera, eds. *77 Märchenfilme: Ein Filmführer für Jung und Alt*. Berlin: Henschel, 1990.

Berghahn, Daniela. "Ein Kultfilm zum Gruseln. Zur Rezeption von *Das singende, klingende Bäumchen* in Großbritannien." Wedel et al. 405–20.

———. *Hollywood behind the Wall: The Cinema of East Germany*. Manchester, UK: Manchester UP, 2005.

Bettelheim, Bruno. *The Uses of Enchantment: The Meaning and Importance of Fairy Tales*. New York: Knopf, 1976.

Beuchler, Bärbel. "Super Illu Interviews—Kaspar Eichel und Karin Ugowski." 26 Sept. 2007. maerchenfilm.pytalhost.com/superillu-interviews-kaspareichelkarinugowski.html.

Blessing, Benita. "DEFA Children's Films: Not Just for Children." Silberman and Wrage 243–62.

———. "'Films to Give Kids Courage!': Children's Films in the German Democratic Republic." *Family Films in Global Cinema: The World beyond Disney*. Ed. Noel Brown and Bruce Babington. London: I. B. Tauris, 2015. 155–70.

———. "Happily Socialist Ever After? East German Children's Films and the Education of a Fairy Tale Land." *Oxford Review of Education* 36.2 (2010): 233–48.

Blunk, Harry, and Dirk Jungnickel, eds. *Filmland DDR. Ein Reader zur Geschichte, Funktion und Wirkung der DEFA*. Cologne, Germany: Wissenschaft und Politik, 1990.

Bortfeldt, Kurt, and Anneliese Probst. *Der steinerne Mühlmann*. Berlin: Henschelverlag, 1954.

Bottigheimer, Ruth B. *Grimms' Bad Girls & Bold Boys: The Moral & Social Vision of the Tales*. New Haven, CT: Yale UP, 1987.

Brady, Martin. "Brecht and Film." *The Cambridge Companion to Brecht*. Ed. Peter Thomson and Glendyr Sacks. Cambridge, UK: Cambridge UP, 2006. 297–317.

Brandt, Gabi. "Ein Genre gerät in Verruf." Brandt and Ried 11–16.

Brandt, Gabi, and Elke Ried, eds. *Vom Zauberwald zur Traumfabrik. Fachtagung des Kinder- und Jugendfilmzentrums in der Bundesrepublik Deutschland zum Thema "Märchen und Film" vom 1. bis 5. Dezember 1986 in Remscheid*. Munich, Germany: Kinder-und Jugendfilmzentrums in der Bundesrepublik Deutschland und Kinderkino München, 1987.

Brecht, Bertolt. "Buckow Elegies." *Poems: 1913–1956*. Ed. John Willett and Ralph Manheim, with the co-operation of Erich Fried. New York: Methuen, 1979. 439–46.

———. *Buckower Elegien*. Brecht, *Gesammelte Werke* 10: 1009.

———. *Der kaukasische Kreidekreis*. Brecht, *Gesammelte Werke* 5: 1999–2105.

———. *Die Ausnahme und die Regel*. Brecht, *Gesammelte Werke* 2: 791–822.

———. "Die Lösung." *Die Welt*. 1959. en.wikipedia.org/wiki/Die_Lösung.

———. "Fragen eines lesenden Arbeiters." Brecht, *Gesammelte Werke* 9: 656.

———. *Gesammelte Werke*. Frankfurt a. M.: Suhrkamp, [ca. 1967] 1975.

Brooker, Peter. "Key Words in Brecht's Theory and Practice of Theatre." *The Cambridge Companion to Brecht*. Cambridge, UK: Cambridge UP, 2006. 209–24.

Byg, Barton. "Brecht, New Waves, and Political Modernism in Cinema." Mews 220–37.

———. "Generational Conflict and Historical Continuity in GDR Film." *Framing the Past: The Historiography of German Cinema and Television*. Ed. Bruce A. Murray and Christopher J. Wickham. Carbondale: Southern Illinois UP, 1992. 197–219.

———. "Introduction: Reassessing DEFA Today." Byg and Moore 1–23.

Byg, Barton, and Betheny Moore, eds. *Moving Images of East Germany: Past and Future of DEFA Film*. Washington, DC: American Institute for Contemporary German Studies, 2002.

Cordell, Karl. "The Role of the Evangelical Church in the GDR." *Government and Opposition* 25.1 (1990): 48–59.

Crafton, Donald. *Before Mickey: The Animated Film 1898–1928*. Cambridge: Massachusetts Institute of Technology Press, 1982.

Creeser, Rosemary. "Cocteau for Kids: Rediscovering *The Singing Ringing Tree*." *Cinema and the Realms of Enchantment: Lectures, Seminars and Essays*. Ed. Marina Warner and Duncan Petrie. London: British Film Institute, 1993. 111–24.

Czygan, Charlotte. "Realität und Märchen: 'Hatifa' und 'Das Zaubermännchen.'" *Deutsche Filmkunst* 9, 1960.

———. ". . . wie für Erwachsene, nur besser!" *Deutsche Filmkunst* 9, 1961.

Dahl, Roald. "Little Red Riding Hood and the Wolf." Tatar, *The Classic Fairy Tales* 21–22.

"Das Kleid." BArch DR 1-Z/549.

Dau, Rudolf, Horst Haase, and K. Kliche. "Zur Aneignung des kulturellen Erbes in der DDR." *Weimarer Beiträge* 30.9 (1984): 1413–22.

Davies, Tony. *Humanism*. Florence, KY: Routledge, 1996.

DeBardeleben, Joan. "'The Future Has Already Begun': Environmental Damage and Protection in the GDR." *International Journal of Sociology* 18.4. (1988/1989): 144–64.

Deltl, Sylvia. "Vorwärts und nicht vergessen . . .—Zur Propaganda in DEFA-Filmen." *Der geteilte Himmel: Höhepunkte des DEFA-Kinos 1946–1992. Band 2. Essays zur Geschichte der DEFA und Filmografien von 61 DEFA-RegisseurInnen*. Ed. Raimund Fritz. Vienna, Austria: Filmarchiv, 2001. 133–48.

Dennis, Mike. *The Rise and Fall of the German Democratic Republic 1945–1990*. Harlow, UK: Longman, 2000.

"Der kleine und der große Klaus." Deutsches Rundfunkarchiv, Babelsberg, Schriftgutbestand Fernsehen. Sg. 043.

"Die kluge Bauerntochter." DEFA-Stiftung. www.defa.de/cms/DesktopDefault.aspx?TabID=412&FilmID=Q6UJ9A002NFR.

"Drei Haselnüsse für Aschenbrödel." 3hfa.jimdo.com.

Dundes, Alan. "Interpreting 'Little Red Riding Hood' Psychoanalytically." *Little Red Riding Hood: A Casebook*. By Dundes. Madison: U Wisconsin P, 1989. 192–236.

Ecke, Peter. "DEFA-Märchenfilme zur Vermittlung von Deutsch als Fremdsprache." *Die Unterrichtspraxis/Teaching German* 37.1 (2004): 43–52.

Eddershaw, Margaret. "Actors on Brecht." *The Cambridge Companion to Brecht*. Ed. Peter Thomson and Glendyr Sacks. Cambridge, UK: Cambridge UP, 2006. 278–96.

Endler, Cornelia A. *Es war einmal . . . im Dritten Reich: Die Märchenfilmproduktion für den nationalsozialistischen Unterricht*. Frankfurt a. M., Germany: Peter Lang, 2006.

Ewald, Charlotte. "Weshalb wurde 'Der Teufel vom Mühlenberg' kein Kinderfilm?" *Deutsche Filmkunst* 3 (1955): 111–13.

———. "Zwei neue Kinderfilme der DEFA." *Deutsche Filmkunst* 1, 1958.

Feinstein, Joshua. *The Triumph of the Ordinary: Depictions of Daily Life in the East German Cinema. 1949–1989*. Chapel Hill: U North Carolina P, 2002.

Felsmann, Barbara. "Vor der Kamera wurde das Spiel für mich Wirklichkeit: Kinderdarsteller der DEFA erinnern sich." *apropos: Film 2004. Das 5. Jahrbuch der DEFA-Stiftung*. Ed. Ralf Schenk, Erika Richter, and Claus Löser. Berlin: Bertz & Fischer, 2004. 70–86.

Felsmann, Klaus-Dieter. "Eine feste Bank. DEFA-Kinderfilme in 25 Berlinale-Jahren." *apropos: Film 2002*. Ed. Ralf Schenk and Erika Richter. Berlin: Bertz, 2002. 190–99.

Felsmann, Klaus-Dieter, and Bernd Sahling. *Deutsche Kinderfilme aus Babelsberg: Werkstattgespräche – Rezeptionsräume*. Berlin: DEFA-Stiftung, 2010.

Fleischer, Uwe, and Helge Trimpert. "'Kunstmännchen macht das . . .' Ernst Kunstmann—Trickkameramann, Spezialist für Spiegel-und Modelltrick." *Wie haben Sie's gemacht? Babelsberger Kameramänner öffnen ihre Trickkiste*. By Fleischer and Trimpert. Marburg, Germany: Schüren, 2005. 67–91.

Fox, Thomas C. *Stated Memory: East Germany and the Holocaust*. Rochester, NY: Camden House, 1999.

Franz, Kurt, and Walter Kahn, eds. *Märchen—Kinder-Medien. Beiträge zur medialen Adaption von Märchen und zum didaktischen Umgang*. Hohengehren, Germany: Schneider, 2000. www.uni-due.de/imperia/md/content/perspicuitas/sullivan.pdf.

Friedrich, Götz. "Rotkäppchen auf der Leinwand." *Deutsche Filmkunst* 9 (1962): 346–47.

Fritzsche, Sonja. "'Keep the Home Fires Burning': Fairy Tale Heroes and Heroines in an East German Heimat." *German Politics and Society* 30.4 (2012): 45–72.

Fühmann, Franz. "'Klein Zaches genannt Zinnober.'" *Klein Zaches genannt Zinnober: Ein Märchen*. By E. T. A. Hoffmann. Munich, Germany: C. H. Beck, 1990. 155–73.

Gabler, Neal. *Walt Disney: The Triumph of the American Imagination*. New York: Knopf, 2006.

Gaddis, John Lewis. *The Cold War: A New History*. New York: Penguin, 2005.

Geiß, Axel. *Repression und Freiheit: DEFA-Regisseure zwischen Fremd- und Selbstbestimmung*. Potsdam, Germany: Brandenburgische Landeszentrale für politische Bildung, 1997.

Gersch, Wolfgang. *Film bei Brecht: Bertolt Brechts praktische und theoretische Auseinandersetzung mit dem Film*. Munich, Germany: Hanser, 1975.

Geschonneck, Erwin. *Meine unruhigen Jahre*. Ed. Günter Agde. Berlin: Dietz, 1984.

"Gevatter Tod." Deutsches Rundfunkarchiv, Babelsberg, Schriftgutbestand Fernsehen. Sg. 030.

Giera, Joachim. "Vom Kohlenmunk-Peter, dem kleinen Muck und seinen Leuten . . . Märchenfilme aus den DEFA-Filmstudios." *Die Kunst des Erzählens. Festschrift für Walter Scherf*. Ed. Helge Gerndt and Kristin Wardetzky. Potsdam, Germany: Berlin-Brandenburg, 2002. 293–300.

———. "Wilhelm Hauff: 'Das kurze Leben und der lange Ruhm.'" *Kinder- & Jugendfilmkorrespondenz* 90.2 (2002). www.kjkmuenchen.de/archiv/index.php?id=1289.

Gilbert, Sandra M., and Susan Gubar. "The Queen's Looking Glass." Zipes, *Don't Bet on the Prince* 201–8.

Goeckel, Robert F. "Church and Society in the GDR: Historical Legacies and 'Mature Socialism.'" *International Journal of Sociology* 18.4 (1988–1989): 210–27.

Greune, Rotraut, et al. *10 Jahre Internationales Kinderfilmfestival in Frankfurt am Main*. Frankfurt a. M., Germany: Remscheid, 1985.

Grimm, Jacob, and Wilhem Grimm. *Kinder- und Hausmärchen*. Ed. Walther Pollatschek and Hans Siebert. Berlin: Kinderbuch, 1952.

———. *Die Kinder- und Hausmärchen*. Ed. Anneliese Kocialek. Berlin: Kinderbuch, 1956.

Grimm, Reinhold. "Alienation in Context: On the Theory and Practice of Brechtian Theater." Mews 35–46.

Günther, Egon, and Ralf Schenk. "Die verzauberte Welt. Nachdenken über Film und Politik." *apropos: Film 2000. Das Jahrbuch der DEFA-Stiftung*. Ed. Ralf Schenk and Erika Richter. Berlin: Das Neue Berlin. 50–75.

Günther, Hans. "Soviet Literary Criticism and the Formulation of the Aesthetics of Socialist Realism, 1932–1940." *A History of Russian Literary Theory and Criticism: The Soviet Age and Beyond*. Ed. Evgeny Dobrenko and Galin Tihanov. Pittsburgh: U Pittsburgh P, 2011. 90–108.

Haase, Donald, ed. *The Greenwood Encyclopedia of Folktales and Fairy Tales*. Westport, CT: Greenwood, 2007.

Habel, Frank-Burkhard. *Das große Lexikon der DEFA-Spielfilme. Die vollständige Dokumentation aller DEFA-Spielfilme von 1946 bis 1993*. Berlin: Schwarzkopf & Schwarzkopf, 2000.

Hake, Sabine. *German National Cinema*. London: Routledge, 2002.

Hanisch, Michael. "Clown mit Charakter: Der Schauspieler Rolf Ludwig." *Film-Dienst* 15, 2005. www.defa.de/15/2005.

Hanspach, Beate. "Märchen—Man weiss sie und liebt sie." Brandt and Ried 44–52.

Häntzsche, Hellmuth. "Das Für und Wider der kleinen Leute (Testmaterial zu dem Märchenfilm 'Rotkäppchen')." *Sozialistischer Kinderfilm, sozialistische Filmerziehung*. Berlin: Der Deutsche Zentralstelle für Filmforschung, Sektion Jugend und Film, 1962. 154–75.

———. *Der Spiel- und Trickfilm für Kinder in der DDR*. Berlin: Kinderbuchverlag, 1980.

———. *Sozialistischer Kinderfilm—Sozialistische Filmerziehung. Film: Filmwissenschaftliche Mitteilungen*. Berlin: Die Deutsche Zentralstelle für Filmforschung, Sektion Jugend und Film, 1962.

Häntzsche, Hellmuth, and Hans-Jürgen Stock. *Kinder- und Jugendfilme. VEB DEFA-Studio für Spielfilme. Fernsehspiele für Kinder. Fernsehen der DDR*. Potsdam: Hochschule für Film und Fernsehen der DDR, 1976.

Hauff, Wilhelm. "The Cold Heart." *Tales by Wilhelm Hauff*. Trans. S. Mendel. London: George Bell and Sons, 1890. 111–38, 194–219.

———. *Jud Süß: Novelle*. 1827. Ed. Lars-Thade Ulrichs. Göttingen, Germany: Peust & Gutschmidt, 2010.

———. *Märchen*. Nach den Ausgaben der Märchenalmanache 1826 bis 1828, textkritisch revidiert. Ed. Hans-Jörg Uther. Kreuzlingen/Munich, Germany: Heinrich Hugendubel Verlag, 1999.

———. "The Tale of Little Mook." *Tales by Wilhelm Hauff*. Trans. S. Mendel. London: George Bell and Sons, 1890. 33–52.

———. "The Young Englishman." *Tales by Wilhelm Hauff*. Trans. S. Mendel. London: George Bell and Sons, 1890. 151–69.

Hecht, Werner. "Staudte verfilmt Brecht: Die abgebrochene *Mutter Courage* und die durchgefallene *Dreigroschenoper*." *apropos: Film 2003. Das 4. Jahrbuch der DEFA-Stiftung*. Ed. Ralf Schenk and Erika Richter. Berlin: Bertz, 2003. 8–23.

Heiduschke, Sebastian. *East German Cinema: DEFA and Film History*. New York: Palgrave Macmillan, 2013.

Heimann, Thomas. *DEFA, Künstler und SED-Kulturpolitik: Zum Verhältnis von Kulturpolitik und Filmproduktion in der SBZ/DDR 1945 bis 1959*. Berlin: Vistas, 1994.

Heller, Leonid. "A World of Prettiness: Socialist Realism and Its Aesthetic Categories." *Socialist Realism without Shores*. Trans. John Hendriksen. Ed. Thomas Lahusen and Evgeny Dobrenko. Durham, NC: Duke UP, 1995. 687–714.

"Helmut Spieß." de.wikipedia.org/wiki/Helmut_Spieß_(Regisseur).

Herminghouse, Patricia. "The Rediscovery of Romanticism: Revisions and Reevaluations." *Studies in GDR Culture and Society* 2 (1982): 1–17.

Heukenkamp, Ursula. "Diskurse über den Irrationalismus in der SBZ/DDR zwischen 1945 und 1960." *Neue Ansichten: The Reception of Romanticism in the Literature of the GDR*. Ed. Howard Gaskill, Karin McPherson, and Andrew Barker. Amsterdam: Rodopi, 1990. 98–113.

Hindemith, Bettina. "Der DEFA-Spielfilm und seine Kritik: Probleme und Tendenzen." Blunk and Jungnickel 27–46.

Hinz, Ottmar. *Wilhelm Hauff: Mit Selbstzeugnissen und Bilddokumenten*. Reinbek bei Hamburg, Germany: Rowohlt Taschenbuch, 1989.

Hobsch, Manfred. "Deutsche Märchenfilme für das Kino." *Lexikon des Kinder- und Jugendfilms im Kino, im Fernsehen und auf Video*. Ed. Horst Schäfer, Christel Strobel, and Hans Strobel. Meitingen, Germany: Corian-Verlag, 2001. 2–22.

Hoffmann, E. T. A. *Das Fräulein von Scudéri*. 1819. Stuttgart, Germany: Klett, 1972.

———. *Little Zaches, Great Zinnober. A Fairy Tale*. Trans. Michael Haldane. 2005. www.michaelhaldane.com/kleinzaches.pdf.

Höfig, Willi. "DEFA Fairy Tale Films." Haase 259–61.

Hohendahl, Peter. "Theorie und Praxis des Erbens: Untersuchungen zum Problem der literarischen Tradition in der DDR." *Literatur der DDR in den siebziger Jahren*. Frankfurt a. M., Germany: Suhrkamp, 1983. 13–52.

Hortzschansky, Werner. "Das Märchen im Film." *Beilage zu Deutsche Filmkunst (Berlin/DDR)* 4 (1955): 175–77; 5 (1955): 17–20.

Hübner, Wolfgang. "Wechselspiegel von historischer Konkretheit und märchenhafter Überhöhung—Eine Verlockung für die Regie." Brandt and Ried 53–57.

Inside Kino. "Die erfolgreichsten DDR-Filme in der DDR." www.insidekino.de/DJahr/DDRAlltimeDeutsch.htm.

Ivanova, Mariana. "DEFA and Eastern European Cinemas: Co-Productions, Transnational Exchange, and Artistic Collaborations." Diss. U of Texas, 2011.

Jelenski, Manfred. "Ein zwiespältiges Experiment 'Die Geschichte vom armen Hassan.'" *Deutsche Filmkunst* 2 (1959): 40–41.

Jenkins, Richard. "Disenchantment, Enchantment and Re-Enchantment: Max Weber at the Millennium." *Max Weber Studies* 1.1 (2000): 11–32.

Jolles, André. *Einfache Formen*. 1929. Tübingen, Germany: Niemeyer, 1968.

"Jorinde und Joringel." Deutsches Rundfunkarchiv, Babelsberg, Schriftgutbestand Fernsehen. A047–04–011 0003. Titel-Sfg: 041.

Jungnickel, Dirk. "Aspekte des DEFA-Kinderfilmschaffens." Blunk and Jungnickel 83–94.

Kabirow, M. N., and B. F. Schachmatow, eds. "Der arme Hassan und Bey Machmud." *Die Stadt der tauben Ohren und andere uigurische Volksmärchen*. By Kabirow and Schachmatow. Berlin, Germany: Alfred Holz Verlag, 1957. 50–56.

Kellner, Douglas. "Brecht's Marxist Aesthetic." Mews 281–95.

Kersten, Heinz. "Junge Pioniere, Tagträumer und Indianer: Die Kinder- und Jugendfilme der DEFA." *Der geteilte Himmel: Höhepunkte des DEFA-Kinos 1946–1992. Band 2. Essays zur Geschichte der DEFA und Filmografien von 61 DEFA-RegisseurInnen*. Ed. Raimund Fritz. Vienna, Austria: Filmarchiv, 2001. 119–32.

———. *So viele Träume: DEFA-Film-Kritiken aus drei Jahrzehnten*. Ed. Christel Drawer. Berlin: Vistas, 1996.

Kesselmann, Heidemarie. "E. T. A. Hoffmanns 'Klein Zaches': Das phantastische Märchen als Möglichkeit der Wiedergewinnung einer geschichtlichen Erkenntnisdimension." *Literatur für Leser* 2 (1978): 114–29.

Kleber, Pia. "Introduction." *Re-interpreting Brecht: His Influence on Contemporary Drama and Film*. Ed. Pia Kleber and Colin Visser. Cambridge, UK: Cambridge UP, 1990. 1–18.

König, Ingelore, Dieter Wiedemann, and Lothar Wolf, eds. *Zwischen Marx und Muck: DEFA-Filme für Kinder*. Berlin: Henschel, 1996.

Kramer, Karen Ruoff. "Representations of Work in the Forbidden DEFA Films of 1965." *DEFA: East German Cinema, 1946–1992*. Allan and Sandford 131–45.

Kümpel, Patricia. *Zur Stilistik der DEFA-Märchen: Exemplarische Analysen zur filmischen und narrativen Gestaltung von Märchenverfilmungen aus der ehemaligen DDR*. Saarbrücken, Germany: VDM Verlag Dr. Müller Aktiengesellschaft & C. KG, 2009.

Lieberman, Marcia K. "'Some Day My Prince Will Come': Female Acculturation through the Fairy Tale." Zipes, *Don't Bet on the Prince* 185–200.

Lipovetsky, Mark. "Pavel Bazhov's *Skazy*: Discovering the Soviet Uncanny." *Russian Children's Literature and Culture*. Ed. Marina Balina and Larissa Rudova. New York: Routledge, 2008. 263–83.

Lunn, Eugene. "Marxism and Art in the Era of Stalin and Hitler: A Comparison of Brecht and Lukács." *New German Critique* 3 (autumn 1974): 12–44.

Lüthi, Max. *The European Folktale: Form and Nature*. Philadelphia: Institute for the Study of Human Issues, 1982.

Madarász, Jeannette Z. *Conflict and Compromise in East Germany, 1971–1989: A Precarious Stability*. New York: Palgrave Macmillan, 2003.

Martens, Lorna. *The Promised Land?: Feminist Writing in the German Democratic Republic*. Albany: State U of New York P, 2001.

McAra, Catriona, and David Calvin, eds. *Anti-Tales: The Uses of Disenchantment*. Newcastle upon Tyne, UK: Cambridge Scholars, 2011.

McGee, Laura Green. "'Ich wollte ewig einen richtigen Film machen! Und als es soweit war, konnte ich's nicht!' The End Phase of the GDR in Films by DEFA *Nachwuchsregisseure*." *German Studies Review* 26.2 (2003): 315–32.

———. "Revolution in the Studio? The DEFA's Fourth Generation of Film Directors and Their Reform Efforts in the Last Decade of the GDR." *Film History* 15.4 (2003): 444–64.

McGlathery, James. *E. T. A. Hoffmann*. New York: Twayne, 1997.

———. "Fetching Maidens and True Brides." *Fairy Tale Romance: the Grimms, Basile, and Perrault*. By McGlathery. Urbana: U of Illinois P, 1991. 135–54.

Mendelson, Michael. "Forever Acting Alone: The Absence of Female Collaboration in *Grimms' Fairy Tales*." *Children's Literature in Education* 28.3 (1997): 111–25.

Mews, Siegfried, ed. *A Bertolt Brecht Reference Companion*. Westport, CT: Greenwood, 1997.

Morton, Jim. "The Golden Goose." eastgermancinema.com/2011/12/23/the-golden-goose.

Mückenberger, Christiane. "DEFA's First Postwar Films in the Soviet Zone and the GDR." Byg and Moore 24–34.

Mueller, Roswitha. *Bertolt Brecht and the Theory of Media*. Lincoln: U of Nebraska P, 1989.

Münz, Franziska, ed. *Die DEFA Märchenfilme*. Berlin: DEFA-Stiftung und Zweitausendeins, 2010.

Murdoch, Christina. "The Phoney and the Real: Roald Dahl's *Revolting Rhymes* as Anti-Tales." McAra and Calvin 164–72.

Nye, Joseph S. Jr. "Public Diplomacy and Soft Power." *The Annals of American Academy of Political and Social Science* 616 (March 2008): 94–109.

Ohm, Lisa. "Introduction: The Fairy Tale of Women's *Bildung* in the Nineteenth Century." In Arnim, *The Life of High Countess Gritta von Ratsinourhouse*. xi–xxxv.

Oinas, Felix J. "Folklore and Politics in the Soviet Union." *Slavic Review* 32.1 (1973): 45–58.

———. "The Political Uses and Themes of Folklore in the Soviet Union." *Folklore, Nationalism and Politics*. Ed. Felix Oinas. Columbus, OH: Slavica, 1978. 77–97.

Paramonowa, Kira K. "Wie schön sind die Märchen!" Trans. Renate Georgi. Berger and Giera 139–47.

Perrault, Charles. "Cinderella, or the Little Glass Slipper." *The Great Fairy Tale Tradition: From Straparola and Basile to the Brothers Grimm: Texts, Criticism*. Ed. Zipes. New York: Norton, 2001. 449–55.

———. "Little Red Riding Hood." Tatar, *The Classic Fairy Tales* 11–13.

Philpotts, Matthew, and Sabine Rolle, eds. *Contested Legacies: Constructions of Cultural Heritage in the GDR*. Rochester, NY: Camden House, 2009.

Piesche, Peggy. "Irgendwo ist immer Afrika . . . 'Blackface' in DEFA-Filmen." 30 Jul. 2004. www.bpb.de/gesellschaft/migration/afrikanische-diaspora/59339/blackface-in-defa-filmen?p=all.

Pinkert, Anke. *Memory and Film in East Germany*. Bloomington: Indiana UP, 2008.

Pohlmann, Carola, and Berthold Friemel, eds. *Rotkäppchen kommt aus Berlin: 200 Jahre Kinder- und Hausmärchen in Berlin*. Berlin: Staatsbibliothek zu Berlin-Preußischer Kulturbesitz, 2012.

Powell, Larson. "'Wind from the East': DEFA and Eastern European Cinema." Silberman and Wrage 224–42.

Probst, Anneliese, ed. *Sagen und Märchen aus dem Harz*. Berlin: Altberliner, 1954.

Propp, Vladimir. *Morphology of the Folktale*. Austin: U of Texas P, 1968.

Reifarth, Gert. *Die Macht der Märchen: Zur Darstellung von Repression und Unterwerfung in der DDR in märchenhafter Prosa (1976–1985)*. Würzburg, Germany: Königshausen & Neumann, 2003.

Rentschler, Eric. *The Ministry of Illusion: Nazi Cinema and Its Afterlife*. Cambridge, MA: Harvard UP, 1996.

Richter, Dieter, and Johannes Merkel. *Märchen, Phantasie und soziales Lernen*. Berlin: Basis, 1974.

Richter, Erika. "Zwischen Mauerbau und Kahlschlag 1961 bis 1965." Schenk 159–211.

Richter-de Vroe, Klaus. "Zwischen Wirklichkeit und Ideal." Berger and Giera 15–23.

Ried, Elke. "Umstritten und Verdrängt: Der Märchenfilm." Brandt and Ried 9–10.

Röcke, Werner. "Mit dem Teufel auf Du und Du. Die Entdämonisierung des Bösen in den Märchen der Brüder Grimm: Mit einem Nachtrag zum Berliner Puppentheater 'Hans Wurst Nachfahren.'" Pohlmann and Friemel 169–77.

Rowe, Karen E. "Feminism and Fairy Tales." Zipes, *Don't Bet on the Prince* 209–26.

Rubin, Eli. *Synthetic Socialism: Plastics and Dictatorship in the German Democratic Republic*. Chapel Hill: U of North Carolina P, 2008.

Rust, Roland. *Film-Dienst* 18 (1991).

Schenk, Ralf. "Das Kleid." *Kinder-und Jugendfilmkorrespondenz*. 78.2 (1999). www.kinderfilm-online.de/film-abc/das-kleid-1961.html.

———, ed. *Das zweite Leben der Filmstadt Babelsberg: DEFA-Spielfilme 1946–1992*. Berlin: Henschel, 1994.

———. "Ein indisches Abenteuer: Die DEFA, das 70mm-Kino und Alexander der Große." Wedel et al. 233–48.

———, ed. *Eine kleine Geschichte der DEFA: Daten, Dokumente, Erinnerungen*. Berlin: DEFA-Stiftung, 2006.

———. "Ein Meister des Film-Tricks." *Film-Dienst* 48 (1995): 14.

———. "Jugendfilm in der DDR." *Zwischen Bluejeans und Blauhemden*. Ed. Ingelore König, Dieter Wiedemann, and Lothar Wolf. Berlin: Henschel, 1995. 21–30.

———. "Von den Lastern der Welt: Bertolt Brecht und die DEFA—Ein unvollendetes Kapitel." *Film-Dienst* 59 (2006): 15–17.

———. "Vor vierzig Jahren: Studio CAMERA." *apropos: Film 2003. Das Jahrbuch der DEFA-Stiftung*. Ed. Ralf Schenk, Erika Richter, and Claus Löser. Berlin: Bertz + Fischer, 2003. 323.

Schieber, Elke. "Anfang vom Ende oder Kontinuität des Argwohns: 1980 bis 1989." Schenk, *Das zweite Leben* 265–326.

Schiller, Konstanze, and Laurence Wegener, eds. "DEFA-Stiftung Newsletter" 5. Ausgabe. Dec. 2013.

Schittly, Dagmar. *Zwischen Regie und Regime: Die Filmpolitik der SED im Spiegel der DEFA-Produktionen*. Berlin: Links, 2002.

Schlesinger, Ron. "Farbdramaturgie im Filmmärchen: Rotkäppchen und der Wolf (1937)." suite101.de/article/farbdramaturgie-im-filmmaerchen-rotkaeppchen-und-der-wolf-1937-a119062#.VA132MJdUuc.

———. "NS-Propaganda: Einmarsch ins Märchenreich." www.spiegel.de/einestages/ns-propaganda-a-948787.html.

———. *Rotkäppchen im Dritten Reich: die deutsche Märchenfilmproduktion zwischen 1933 und 1945. Ein Überblick*. Berlin: DEFA-Stiftung, 2009.

Schneider, Wolfgang. "Über die unheilige Allianz zweier Medien: Vom Märchenbuch zum Märchenfilm." Brandt and Ried 27–32.

Schoeps, Karl-Heinz. "Brecht's *Lehrstücke*: A Laboratory for Epic and Dialectic Theater." Mews 70–87.

Schönemann, Sibylle. "Stoffentwicklung im DEFA-Studio für Spielfilme." Blunk and Jungnickel 71–81.

Schwartz, Eugene. *Little Red Riding Hood. A Play in One Act*. Trans. George Shail. Chicago: Dramatic Publishing, 1992.

Shakespeare, William. *King Lear*. New York: St. Martin's Press, 1992.

Shen, Qinna. "Deconstructing Orientalism: DEFA's Fictions of East Asia." Forthcoming in Allan and Heiduschke.

———. "DEFA *Märchenfilme* as Brechtian Parables: Gerhard Klein's *Die Geschichte vom armen Hassan* and Konrad Petzold's *Das Kleid*." *The Brecht Yearbook 35: Brecht, Marxism, and Ethics*. By Friedemann J. Weidauer. Madison: U of Wisconsin P, 2010. 112–31.

———. "From Jacob Grimm to GDR-'Witches': Feminist Witchcraft and Magical Realism in East German Women's Writing." Diss. Yale U, 2008.

Sieg, Katrin. *Ethnic Drag: Performing Race, Nation, Sexuality in West Germany*. Ann Arbor: U of Michigan P, 2002.

Silberman, Marc. "Brecht and Film." Mews 197–219.

———. "The First DEFA Fairy Tales: Cold War Fantasies of the 1950s." *Framing the Fifties: Cinema in a Divided Germany*. Ed. John Davidson and Sabine Hake. New York: Berghahn Books, 2007. 106–235.

———. "A Postmodernized Brecht?" *Theatre Journal* 45.1 (1993): 1–19.

Silberman, Marc, and Henning Wrage, eds. *DEFA at the Crossroads of East German and International Film Culture. A Companion*. Berlin: De Gruyter, 2014.

Simon, Rainer. *Fernes Land: Die DDR, die DEFA und der Ruf des Chimborazo*. Berlin: Aufbau Taschenbuch, 2005.

Simons, Rotraut. *Der Pfarrer bleibt vom Bild her problematisch. Ausgewählte Dokumente der Auseinandersetzung mit der Darstellung von Christen in Kinofilmen in der DDR 1956 bis 1989/90*. Berlin: Gesellschaft zur Förderung vergleichender Staat-Kirche-Forschung, 2003.

"Sleeping Beauty—Fritz Genschow." www.youtube.com/watch?v=6fWd-OcOcac.

Smith, Dave, and Steven Clark. *Disney: The First 100 Years*. New York: Hyperion, 1999.

Soldovieri, Stefan. "Managing Stars: Manfred Krug and the Politics of Entertainment in GDR Cinema." Bgy and Betheny 56–71.

———. "The Politics of the Popular: *Trace of the Stones* (1966/89) and the Discourse on Stardom in the GDR Cinema." *Light Motives: German Popular Film in Perspective*. Ed. Randall Halle and Margaret McCarthy. Detroit: Wayne State UP, 2003. 220–36.

Steingroever, Reinhild. "2 February 1988: Last Generation of DEFA Directors Calls in Vain for Reform." *A New History of German Cinema*. Ed. Jennifer M. Kapczynski and Michael D. Richardson. Rochester, NY: Camden House, 2012. 497–501.

———. "On Fools and Clowns: Farewell to the GDR in Two Final DEFA Films: Egon Günther's *Stein* and Jörg Foth's *Letztes aus der DaDaeR*." *German Quarterly* 78.4 (2005): 441–60.

Steinlein, Rüdiger. "Berliner Ausgaben der *Kinder- und Hausmärchen* nach 1945." Pohlmann and Friemel 91–105.

Steinweg, Reiner. *Lehrstück und episches Theater: Brechts Theorie und die theaterpädagogische Praxis*. Frankfurt a. M.: Brandes & Apsel, 1995.

Stone, Kay. "Feminist Approaches to the Interpretations of the Fairy Tales." *Fairy Tales and Society: Illusion, Allusion, and Paradigm*. Ed. Ruth B. Bottigheimer and Lutz Röhrich. Philadelphia: U of Pennsylvania P, 1986. 229–36.

———. "Things Walt Disney Never Told Us." *Women and Folklore*. Ed. Claire R. Farrer. Austin: U of Texas P, 1975. 42–50.

Storm, Theodor. "Die Regentrude." *Storms Werke in zwei Bänden*. Berlin: Aufbau-Verlag, 1969. 81–110.

Stott, Rosemary. *Crossing the Wall: The Western Feature Film Import in East Germany*. Oxford, UK: Peter Lang, 2012.

Suschke, Stephan. "Geniales Kind im Mörderhaus." *New Essays on Brecht. The Brecht Yearbook* 26. Ed. Maarten Van Dijk. Madison: U of Wisconsin P, 2001. 34–45.

Tatar, Maria, ed. *The Classic Fairy Tales*. New York: W.W. Norton, 1999.

———. *The Hard Facts of the Grimms' Fairy Tales*. Princeton, NJ: Princeton UP, 1987.

Teschner, Ulrich. ". . . die haben unseren Sozialismus nicht verstanden." Blunk and Jungnickel 9–25.

Thum, Maureen. "Wilhelm Hauff." *Oxford Companion to Fairy Tales*. 3 May 2014. www.answers.com/topic/wilhelm-hauff-1.

Torner, Evan. "The DEFA 'Indianerfilm': Narrating the Postcolonial through Gojko Mitic." *Re-imagining DEFA*. Allan and Heiduschke. Forthcoming.

———. "The Race-Time Continuum: Race Projection in DEFA Genre Cinema." Diss. U of Massachusetts, 2013.

———. "The Red and the Black: Race in the DEFA Film Osceola." *New German Review* 25 (2011): 61–81.

Trumpener, Katie. *Divided Screen: The Cinemas of Postwar Germany*. Princeton, NJ: Princeton UP. Forthcoming.

University of Massachusetts at Amherst, DEFA Film Library, Icestorm International, DEFA. *Snow White: A Teaching Guide for the DEFA Children's Film, Schneewittchen*. Amherst, MA: DEFA Film Library, U of Massachusetts at Amherst, 1999.

Volk, Stefan. "Mit Kraft und Verve. Die Mimin hinter der Figur: Eva-Maria Hagen." *Film-Dienst* 21, 2004. 8 Apr. 2014. www.defa.de/21/2004.

Walter, Jürgen. "E. T. A. Hoffmanns Märchen 'Klein Zaches genannt Zinnober': Versuch einer sozialgeschichtlichen Interpretation." *Mitteilungen der E. T. A. Hoffmann-Gesellschaft* 19 (1973): 27–45.

Wardetzky, Kristin. "Der Märchenstreit—Nachkriegszeit und Anfangsjahre der DDR." Pohlmann and Friemel 79–89.

———. "Grimms Märchen auf Berliner Schauspielbühnen 1844–1990: Eine Recherche." Pohlmann and Friemel 179–201.

———. "Sklavensprache: Märchen und Fabeln in repressiven Gesellschaftssystemen." *Kinder—Lesen—Literatur: Analysen—Modelle—Konzepte*. Ed. Monika Plath and Gerd Mannhaupt. Baltmannsweiler, Germany: Schneider, 2008. 179–93.

Wasko, Janet. *Understanding Disney: The Manufacture of Fantasy*. Cambridge, UK: Polity, 2001.

Weber, Max. "Science as a Vocation." *The Vocation Lectures*. Indianapolis, IN: Hackett, 2004. 1–31.

Wedel, Michael, Barton Byg, Andy Räder, Skyler Arndt-Briggs, and Evan Torner, eds. *DEFA international: Grenzüberschreitende Filmbeziehungen vor und nach dem Mauerbau (Film, Fernsehen, Medienkultur)*. Wiesbaden, Germany: Springer, 2013.

"Wie heiratet man einen König." BArch DR 1-Z/280.

Wiedemann, Dieter. "Der DEFA-Kinderfilm—zwischen pädagogischem Auftrag und künstlerischem Anliegen." König 21–31.

———. "Es war einmal . . . Erkundungen im DEFA-Märchenland." *Die DEFA Märchenfilme*. Münz 9–15.

———. "'Es war einmal . . . '—Reise ins DEFA-Märchenland." *Märchen: Arbeiten mit DEFA-Kinderfilmen*. Ed. Ingelore König, Dieter Wiedemann, and Lothar Wolf. Munich, Germany: KoPäd, 1998. 11–15.

Wiedemann, Dieter, and Hans Lohmann. "Der DEFA-Spielfilm zwischen Anpassung und Protest: Daten, Meinungen und Hypothesen zur Funktion des DEFA-Films in den achtziger Jahren." *Zeitschrift für Literaturwissenschaft und Linguistik* 82 (1991): 38–51.

Wischnewski, Klaus. "Träumer und gewöhnliche Leute 1966 bis 1979." Schenk, *Das zweite Leben* 213–63.

Wolf, Steffen. *Kinderfilm in Europa*. Munich, Germany: Dokumentation, Saur KG, 1969.

"Wolfgang Schleif." de.wikipedia.org/wiki/Wolfgang_Schleif.

Yolen, Jane. "America's Cinderella." *Cinderella: A Folklore Casebook*. Ed. Alan Dundes. New York: Garland, 1982. 294–303. Rpt. of *Children's Literature in Education* 8 (1977): 21–29.

———. *Briar Rose*. New York: Doherty, 1992.

———. "Granny Rumple." *Sister Emily's Lightship and Other Stories*. By Yolen. New York: Doherty, 2000. 44–55, 288.

Zapf, E. "Der DEFA-Farbfilm 'Die Geschichte vom kleinen Muck.'" *Deutsche Filmkunst* 2 (1954): 30–34,

"Zauber um Zinnober." Deutsches Rundfunkarchiv, Babelsberg, Schriftgutbestand Fernsehen. A047–04–011 0003. Titel-Sig: 109.

Zimm, Irma. "Die Kleine Gräfin mit der großen Courage: 'Gritta von Rattenzuhausbeiuns' (DEFA)." *BZ am Abend* 15 Mar. 1985.

Zipes, Jack. "Breaking the Disney Spell." Tatar, *The Classic Fairy Tales* 332–52.

———. *Breaking the Magic Spell: Radical Theories of Folk and Fairy Tales*. Lexington: UP Kentucky, 2002.

———. *The Brothers Grimm: From Enchanted Forests to the Modern World*. 2nd ed. New York: Palgrave Macmillan, 2002.

———. ed. *Don't Bet on the Prince: Contemporary Feminist Fairy Tales in North America and England*. New York: Methuen, 1986.

———. *The Enchanted Screen: The Unknown History of Fairy-Tale Films*. New York: Routledge, 2011.

———. *Fairy Tale as Myth/Myth as Fairy Tale*. Lexington: UP Kentucky, 1994.

———. "The Fate of Spinning." *The Great Fairy Tale Tradition: From Straparola and Basile to the Brothers Grimm: Texts, Criticism*. Ed. Zipes. New York: Norton, 2001. 584.

———. "'Little Red Riding Hood' as Male Creation and Projection." *The Brothers Grimm and Folktale*. Ed. James M. McGlathery. Urbana: U Illinois P, 1988. 121–28.

———. "Rumpelstiltskin and the Decline of Female Productivity." Zipes, *Fairy Tale as Myth* 49–71.

———. "The Struggle for the Grimms' Throne: The Legacy of the Grimms' Tales in the FRG and the GDR since 1945." *The Reception of Grimm's Fairy Tales: Responses, Reactions, Revisions*. Ed. Donald Haase. Detroit: Wayne State UP, 1993. 167–206.

INDEX

www.ingramcontent.com/pod-product-compliance
Lightning Source LLC
LaVergne TN
LVHW020431080826
844660LV00034B/1388

* 9 7 8 0 8 1 4 3 3 9 0 3 9 *